The Empire of Ice Cream

JEFFREY FORD

With an Introduction by
Jonathan Carroll

GOLDEN GRYPHON PRESS • 2006

"The Annals of Eelin-Ok," first published in *The Faery Reel: Tales from the Twilight Realm*, edited by Ellen Datlow and Terri Windling, Tor, 2004.

"The Beautiful Gelreesh," first published in *Album Zutique*, edited by Jeff VanderMeer, Ministry of Whimsy Press, 2003.

"Boatman's Holiday," first published in *Book of Voices* (a Sierra Leone PEN benefit project), edited by Mike Butscher, Flame Books UK, 2005.

"Botch Town," copyright © 2006 by Jeffrey Ford. Previously unpublished.

"Coffins on the River," first published in *Polyphony 3*, edited by Deborah Layne and Jay Lake, Wheatland Press, 2003.

"The Empire of Ice Cream," first published online on SCIFICTION, February 26, 2003.

"Giant Land," first published in *The Journal of Pulse-Pounding Narratives #2*, 2005.

"The Green Word," first published in *The Green Man: Tales from the Mythic Forest*, edited by Ellen Datlow and Terri Windling, Viking, 2002.

"Jupiter's Skull," first published in *Flights: Extreme Visions of Fantasy*, edited by Al Sarrantonio, Roc, 2004.

"A Man of Light," first published online on SCIFICTION, January 26, 2005.

"A Night in the Tropics," first published in *Argosy Magazine*, January/February 2004.

"Summer Afternoon," first published in *Say . . . is this a cat?*, edited by Christopher Rowe, The Fortress of Words, 2002.

"The Trentino Kid," first published in *The Dark: New Ghost Stories*, edited by Ellen Datlow, Tor, 2003.

"The Weight of Words," first published in *Leviathan Three*, edited by Jeff VanderMeer and Forrest Aguirre, Ministry of Whimsy Press, 2002

The Empire of Ice Cream copyright © 2006 by Jeffrey Ford

Introduction copyright © 2006 by Jonathan Carroll

Cover illustration copyright © 2006 by John Picacio

Edited by Marty Halpern

LIBRARY OF CONGRESS CATALOGUING–IN–PUBLICATION DATA

Ford, Jeffrey, 1955–
    The Empire of ice cream / by Jeffrey Ford ; with an introduction by Jonathan Carroll. — 1st ed.
        p.   cm.
    ISBN 1-930846-39-8 (hardcover : alk. paper)   I. Title.
PS3556.O6997   E47   2006
813'.54dc22   2005024035

Printed in the United States of America.

First Edition.

Contents

For Lynn
whose love has rescued me time and again
on the slippery slopes of the Empire of Ice Cream

Acknowledgements

Any writer who's had even one book published knows that it takes a group effort to get that book into the hands of the reading public. Listed below, though not in order of importance—as they were all equally and absolutely integral to the final product—are my compatriots in publishing *The Empire of Ice Cream*. I thank each and every one of them for their dedication and hard work in making this collection possible.

Gary Turner, publisher of Golden Gryphon Press, has done an amazing job of bringing readers quality books by quality writers. GGP can claim a large share of the responsibility for keeping the short story collection alive and vibrant in the realm of Fantastic Literature. First, as a reader, I want to thank Gary for doing what he does; and then I want to thank him for publishing a second collection of my work.

Marty Halpern, who also edited my collection *The Fantasy Writer's Assistant and Other Stories* for GGP, did his usual, wonderful job on this collection. His dedication to the material, his attention to detail, and his ability to see a disparate group of stories as an integrated collection, make him one of the very best editors of short story collections in the field.

Jonathan Carroll's novels and stories are perceived by many as existing in the marchland between what is called "mainstream literature" and the genre of the "dark fantastic." At first glance, this might seem true, but for those of us who have read most, if not all, of his fiction and are inspired by it, we understand that Carroll's work transcends these simplistic attempts at definition. We are aware that his fiction is its own unique country. The most effective passage of contemporary fiction I've read can be found in the closing pages of his novel, *The Wooden Sea*—a scene in which a man digs a grave. I'm grateful for his having taken the time to write the introduction for this collection.

John Picacio's incredible cover art has finally come to the attention of both major publishers and the Hugo Awards. I feel blessed to have met him at the outset of his career; otherwise, we may not have been able to engage his time and talents for this cover. His style is both easily recognizable and powerfully original. John's cover for my previous GGP title, *The Fantasy Writer's Assistant,* was easily my favorite cover of any of my books—until, of course, this one. His artistic vision continues to grow and change with each new piece, and I believe that when all is said and done, John Picacio will be considered one of the greats.

Howard Morhaim's advice, encouragement, and guidance are behind every book of mine that gets published. One couldn't ask for a better agent.

In addition to those listed above, I'd like to thank all of the editors who published the works found herein—their editorial insights and help made each of these stories stronger. Lastly, I'd be remiss if I didn't give a nod to Bill Watkins, Rick Bowes, and Mike Gallagher who read all of these stories before they were sent out and gave me valuable feedback with which to make them better.

Introduction

ONE OF THE MOST TERRIBLE LOSSES MAN ENDURES in his lifetime is not even noticed by most people, much less mourned. Which is astonishing because what we lose is in many ways one of the essential qualities that sets us apart from other creatures.

I'm talking about the loss of the sense of wonder that is such an integral part of our world when we are children. However, as we grow older, that sense of wonder shrinks from cosmic to microscopic by the time we are adults. Kids say "Wow!" all the time. Opening their mouths fully, their eyes light up with genuine awe and glee. The word emanates not so much from a voice box as from an astonished soul that has once again been shown that the world is full of amazing unexpected things.

When was the last time you let fly a loud, truly heartfelt "WOW"?

Not recently I bet. Because generally speaking wonder belongs to kids, with the rare exception of falling madly in love with another person, which invariably leads to a rebirth of wonder. As adults, we are not supposed to say or feel Wow, or wonder, or even true surprise because those things make us sound goofy, ingenuous, and childlike. How can you run the world if you are in constant awe of it?

Of course there are exceptions. One need only look at the astounding success of *Harry Potter, The Lord of the Rings, Star*

Wars, and the novels of Stephen King (the list is much longer than that), to see that people are really hungry for wonder. Still, most adults wouldn't fess up to that though because they don't want to admit how gorgeous it feels to sit transfixed in a movie theater or reading chair, thoroughly absorbed in a world ten times more interesting and diverse than their own. The human heart has a long memory though and remembers what it was like to live through days where it was constantly surprised and delighted by the world around it. Unfortunately we have been taught control, control, control all of our lives by parents, by society, by our education. If you can't control something then get rid of it or get out of it or get away from it.

Yet we know that the imagination really is most alive when it is *not* in control of things, flying through the air without a safety net below to catch it. To live surrounded by wonder means the unknown and the dangerous also surround you as well (as in a great love affair).

When I sat down to read Jeffrey Ford's *The Empire of Ice Cream*, I knew only one thing: that for the next few hundred pages my mind would be swinging on a trapeze high above the ground with no net below. No matter what, the experience would be exhilarating, dangerous, and challenging, not necessarily in that order. Because anything goes in Ford's worlds. Tiny creatures live exciting noble lives full of great love and high adventure inside those disintegrating sand castles we pass on the beach but rarely ever look at twice. When I began reading that story I was smiling already about five pages into it because I thought, Okay, that's it—I will never look at a sand castle the same way again. Then my sense of reawakened wonder rubbed its hands together and asked what else is he going to show me? A lot, in fact: Bottle glass and threads of ancient clothes that wash up from the sea carrying their own powerful, peculiar magic. Too many cups of coffee cause not only the jitters but also the kind of visions that change a life in an instant, and not always for the good.

Like any strong short story collection, you can pick this one up and read around in it, sample various stories like food at a great buffet. Or you can read the book straight through, as I did. There isn't a bad taste, a bad story here. Some are wilder than others, some are very concerned with the minutiae of our everyday. But the common thread running through all of them is Ford's delight in showing us the wonder in worlds both utterly different and very much like our own. There are fairies and giants in Ford country, yes, but there are also heartwrenching love stories, and middle-aged pals getting stoned behind the shed together while ruefully discussing what it feels like to be lost in one's own life. Because he is a very good writer, Ford never forces any of these things on us. He is the intriguing stranger at the hotel bar, just back from Madagascar and full of strange and exotic stories that keeps you riveted to your stool. You persist in asking him to tell you another; you pay for all of his drinks just to keep him there and talking. Or he is that charismatic camp councilor sitting by the bonfire telling ghost stories so real that the hair starts to stand up on your arm. You have to pee so badly that you think you're going to explode, but still you don't move because you *must* hear the end of this story.

Ford sees wonder everywhere and embraces it fully. A generous writer, he is willing to share it with us. The precision and clarity with which he gives us his vision is really the next best thing to being there. In the end, what greater compliment can you give to a writer?

Jonathan Carroll
Vienna, Austria
May 2005

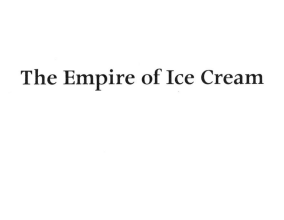

The Empire of Ice Cream

The Annals of Eelin-Ok

W HEN I WAS A CHILD SOMEONE ONCE TOLD ME
that gnats, those miniscule winged specks that swarm in
clouds about your head on summer evenings, are born, live out
their entire lives, and die all in the space of a single day. A brief existence, no doubt, but briefer still are the allotted hours of that
denizen of the faerie world, a Twilmish, for its life is dependent
upon one of the most tenuous creations of mankind, namely, the
sand castle. When a Twilmish takes up residence in one of these
fanciful structures, its span of time is determined by the durability
and duration of its chosen home.

Prior to the appearance of a sand castle on the beach, Twilmish
exist merely as a notion: an invisible potentiality of faerie presence.
In their insubstantial form, they will haunt a shoreline for centuries, biding their time, like an idea waiting to be imagined. If
you've ever been to the beach in the winter after it has snowed and
seen the glittering white powder rise up for a moment in a miniature twister, that's an indication of Twilmish presence. The
phenomenon has something to do with the power they draw from
the meeting of the earth and the sea: attraction and repulsion in a
circular fashion like a dog chasing its tail. If on a perfectly sunny
summer afternoon, you are walking along the shoreline during the
time of the outgoing tide and suddenly enter a zone of frigid cold
air no more than a few feet in breadth, again, it indicates that your

beach has a Twilmish. The drop in degree is a result of their envy of your physical form. It means one is definitely about, searching for the handy-work of industrious children.

No matter how long a Twilmish has waited for a home, no matter the degree of desire to step into the world, not just any sand castle will do. They are as shrewd and judicious in their search as your grandmother choosing a melon at the grocery, for whatever place one does decide on will, to a large extent, define its life. Once the tide has turned and the breakers roar in and destroy the castle, its inhabitant is also washed away, not returning to the form of energy to await another castle, but gone, returned physically and spiritually to Nature, as we are at the end of our long lives. So the most important prerequisite of a good castle is that it must have been created by a child or children. Too often with adults, they transfer their penchants for worry about the future and their reliance on their watches into the architecture, and the spirit of these frustrations sunders the effect of *Twilmish Time*: the phenomenon that allows those few hours between the outgoing and incoming tide to seem to this special breed of faerie folk to last as long as all our long years seem to us.

Here are a few of the other things they look for in a residence: a place wrought by children's hands and not plastic molds or metal shovels, so that there are no right angles and each inch of living space resembles the unique contours of the human imagination; a complex structure with as many rooms and tunnels, parapets, bridges, dungeons, and moats as possible; a place decorated with beautiful shells and sea glass (they prize most highly the use of blue bottle glass tumbled smooth as butter by the surf, but green is also welcome); the use of driftwood to line the roads, or a pole made from a sea horse's spike flying a seaweed flag; the absence of sand crabs, those burrowing, armored nuisances that can undermine a wall or infest a dungeon; a retaining wall of modest height, encircling the entire design, to stave off the sea's hungry high-tide advances as long as possible but not block the ocean view; and a name for the place, already bestowed and carefully written with the quill of a fallen gull feather above the main gate, something like *Heart's Desire* or *Sandland* or *Castle of Dreams*, so that precious seconds of the inhabitant's life might not be taken up with this decision.

Even many of those whose life's work it is to study the lineage and ways of the faerie folk are unfamiliar with the Twilmish, and no one is absolutely certain of their origin. I suppose they have been around at least as long as sand castles, and probably before, inhabiting the sand caves of Neanderthal children way back at the dawn of human history. Perhaps, in their spirit form, they had come into existence with the universe and had simply been waiting eons for sand castles to finally appear, or perhaps they are a later development in the evolution of the faerie phylum. Some believe them to be part of that special line of enchanted creatures that associate themselves with the creativity of humans, like the *monkey of the ink pot*, attracted to the work of writers, or the *painter's demon*, which plays in the bright mix of colors on an artist's pallet, resulting in never before seen hues.

Whichever and whatever the case may be, there is only one way to truly understand the nature of the Twilmish, and that is to meet one of them. So here, I will relate for you the biography of an individual of their kind. All of what follows will have taken place on the evening of a perfect summer day after you had left the beach, and will occupy the time between tides—from when you had sat down to dinner and five hours later when you laid your head upon the pillow to sleep. There seemed to you to be barely enough time to eat your chicken and potatoes, sneak your carrots to the dog beneath the table, clean up, watch your favorite TV show, draw a picture of a pirate with an eye patch and a parrot upon her shoulder, brush your teeth, and kiss your parents good night. To understand the Twilmish, though, is to understand that in a mere moment, all can be saved or lost, an ingenious idea can be born, a kingdom can fall, love can grow, and life can discover its meaning.

Now, if I wasn't an honest fellow, I would, at this juncture, merely make up a bunch of hogwash concerning the biography of a particular Twilmish, for it is fine to note the existence of a race, but one can never really know anything of substance about a group until one has met some of its individuals. The more one meets, the deeper the understanding. There is a problem, though, in knowing anything definitive about any particular Twilmish, and that is because they are no bigger than a human thumbnail. In addition, they move more quickly than an eye-blink in order to stretch each second into a minute, each minute into an hour.

I've never been a very good liar, and as luck and circumstance would have it, there is no need for it in this situation, for out of the surf one day in 1999, on the beach at Barnegat Light in New Jersey, a five-year-old girl, Chieko Quigley, found a conch shell at the shoreline, whose spiral form enchanted her. She took it home and used it as a decoration on the windowsill of her room. Three years later, her cat, Madelain, knocked the shell onto the floor and from within the winding labyrinth, the opening to which she would place her ear from time to time to listen to the surf, fell an exceedingly tiny book, no bigger than ten grains of sand stuck together; its cover made of sea-horse hide, its pages, dune grass. Since I am an expert on faeries and faerie lore, it was brought to me to discern whether it was a genuine artifact or a prank. The diminutive volume was subjected to electron microscopy, and was discovered to be an actual journal that had once belonged to a Twilmish named Eelin-Ok.

Eelin-Ok must have had artistic aspirations as well, for on the first page is a self-portrait, a line drawing done in squid ink. He stands, perhaps on the tallest turret of his castle, obviously in an ocean breeze that lifts the long, dark hair of his topknot and causes his full-length cape to billow out behind him. He is stocky, with broad shoulders, calf muscles and biceps as large around as his head. His face, homely handsome, with its thick brow and smudge of a nose, might win no beauty contests but could inspire comfort with its look of simple honesty. The eyes are intense and seem to be intently staring at something in the distance. I cannot help but think that this portrait represents the moment when Eelin-Ok realized that the chaotic force of the ocean would at some point consume himself and his castle, *While Away*.

The existence of the journal is a kind of miracle in its own right, and the writing within is priceless to the Twilmish historian. It seems our subject was a Twilmish of few words, for between each entry it is evident that some good portion of time has passed, but taken all together they represent, as the title page suggests: *The Annals of Eelin-Ok*. So here they are, newly translated from the Twilmish by the ingenious decoding software called *Faerie Speak* (a product of Fen & Dale Inc.), presented for the first time to the reading public.

HOW I HAPPENED

I became aware of It, a place for me to be, when I was no more than a cloud, drifting like a notion in the breaker's mist. It's a frightening thing to make the decision to be born. Very little ever is what it seems until you get up close and touch it. But this castle that the giant, laughing architects created and named "While Away" (I do not understand their language but those are the symbols the way they were carved) with a word-scratched driftwood plaque set in among the scalloped, maroon cobbles of the courtyard, was like a dream come true. The two turrets, the bridge and moat, the counting room paneled with nautilus amber, the damp dungeon and secret passage, the strong retaining wall that encircled it, every sturdy inch bejeweled by beautiful blue and green and clear glass, decorated with the most delicate white shells, seemed to have leaped right out of my imagination and onto the beach in much the same way that I leaped into my body and life as Eelin-Ok. Sometimes caution must be thrown to the wind, and in this instance it was. Those first few moments were confusing what with the new feel of being, the act of breathing, the wind in my face. Some things I was born knowing, as I was born full grown, and others I only remember that I have forgotten them. The enormous red orb, sitting atop the horizon, and the immensity of the ocean, struck me deeply; their powerful beauty causing my emotions to boil over. I staggered to the edge of the lookout post on the taller turret, leaned upon the battlement, and wept. "I've done it," I thought, and then a few moments later after I had dried my eyes, "Now what?"

PHARGO

Upon returning from a food expedition, weighed down with a bit of crabmeat dug out from a severed claw dropped by a gull and a goodly portion of jellyfish curd, I discovered a visitor in the castle. He waited for me at the front entrance, hopping around impatiently: a lively little sand flea, black as a fish eye, and hairy all over. I put down my larder and called him to me, patted his notched little head. He was full of high spirits and circled round me, barking in whispers. His antics made me smile. When I finally lifted my goods and trudged toward the entrance to the turret that held the dining hall, he followed, so I let him in and gave him a name, Phargo. He is my companion, and although he doesn't understand a word of Twilmish, I tell him everything.

FAERIE FIRE

Out of nowhere came my memory of the spell to make fire—three simple words and a snapping of the fingers. I realize I have innate powers of magic and enchantment, but they are meager, and I have decided to not rely on them too often as this is a world in which one must learn to trust mainly in muscle and brain in order to survive.

MAKING THINGS

The castle is a wondrous structure, but it is my responsibility to fill it with items both useful and decorative. There is no luckier place to be left with nothing than the seashore, for with every wave useful treasures are tossed onto the beach, and before you can collect them, another wave carries more. I made my tools from sharp shards of glass and shell, not yet worried smooth by the action of the waters. These I attached to pieces of reed and quills from bird feathers and tied tight with tough lanyards of dune grass. With these tools I made a table for the dining hall from a choice piece of driftwood, carved out a fireplace for my bedroom, created chairs and sofas from the cartilage of bluefish carcasses. I have taught Phargo the names of these tools, and the ones he can lift, he drags to me when I call for them. My bed is a mussel shell; my wash basin a metal thing discarded by the giant, laughing architects, on the back of which are the characters "Root Beer," and smaller, "twist off," along with an arrow following the circular curve of it (very curious); my weapon is an axe of reed handle and shark's tooth head. Making things is my joy.

THE FISHING EXPEDITION

Up the beach, the ocean has left a lake in its retreat, and it is swarming with silver fish as long as my leg. Phargo and I set sail in a small craft I burned out of a block of driftwood and rigged with a sail made from the fin of a dead sea-robin. I took a spear and a lantern —a chip of quartz that catches the rays of the red orb and magnifies them. The glow of the prism stone drew my prey from the depths. Good thing I tied a generous length of seaweed round the spear, for my aim needed practice. Eventually, I hit the mark, and dragged aboard fish after fish, which I then bludgeoned with my axe. The boat was loaded. As we headed back to shore, a strong gust of wind caught the sail and tipped the low-riding craft perilously to one side. I lost my grip on the tiller and fell overboard into the deep water. This is how I learned to swim. After much struggling and many deep, spluttering draughts of brine, Phargo whisper-barking frantically from on board, I made it to safety and climbed back aboard. This, though, my friend, is also how I learned to die. The feeling of the water rising around my ears, the ache in the lungs, the frantic racing of my mind, the approaching blackness, I know I will meet again on my final day.

DUNE RAT

The dunes lie due north of While Away, a range of tall hills sparsely covered with a sharp, forbidding grass I use to tie up my tools. I have been to them on expeditions to cut blades of the stuff, but never ventured into their recesses, as they are vast and their winding paths like a maze. From out of this wilderness came a shaggy behemoth with needle teeth and a tail like an eel. I heard it squeal as it tried to clear the outer wall. Grabbing my spear I ran to the front gate and out along the bridge that crosses the moat. There I was able to take the shell staircase to the top of the wall. I knew that if the rat breached the wall the castle would be destroyed. As it tried to climb over, though, its hind feet displaced the sand the battlement was made of and it kept slipping back. I charged headlong and drove the tip of my spear into its right eye. It screeched in agony and retreated, my weapon jutting from the oozing wound. There was no question that it was after me, a morsel of Twilmish meat, or that others would eventually come.

THE RED ORB HAS DROWNED

The red orb has sunk into the ocean, leaving only pink and orange streaks behind in its wake. Its drowning has been gradual and it has struggled valiantly, but now darkness reigns upon the beach. Way above there are points of light that hypnotize me when I stare too long at them and reveal themselves in patterns of—a sea gull, a wave, a crab. I must be sure to gather more driftwood in order to keep the fires going, for the temperature has also slowly dropped. Some little time ago, a huge swath of pink material washed ashore. On it was a symbol belonging, I am sure, to the giant, laughing architects: a round yellow circle made into a face with eyes and a strange, unnerving smile. From this I will cut pieces and make warmer garments. Phargo sleeps more often now, but when he is awake he still bounds about senselessly and makes me laugh often enough. We swim like fish through the dark.

IN MY BED

I lie in my bed writing. From beyond the walls of my castle I hear the waves coming and going in their steady, assuring rhythm, and the sound is lulling me toward sleep. I have been wondering what the name assigned to my home by the architects means. While Away—if only I could understand their symbols, I might understand more the point of my life. Yes, the point of life is to fish and work and make things and explore, but there are times, especially now since the red orb has been swallowed, that I suspect there is some secret reason for my being here. There are moments when I wish I knew, and others when I couldn't care less. Oh, to be like Phargo, for whom a drop of fish blood and a hopping run along the beach is all the secret necessary. Perhaps I think too much. There is the squeal of a bat, the call of a plover, the sound of the wind, and they mix with the salt air to bring me closer to sleep. When I wake, I will. . . . .

WHAT'S THIS?

Something is rising out of the ocean in the east, being born into the sky. I think it is going to be round like the red orb, but it is creamy white. Whatever it is, I welcome it, for it seems to cast light, not bright enough to banish the darkness, but an enchanted light that reflects off the water and gracefully illuminates the beach where the shadows are not too harsh. We rode atop a giant, brown armored crab with a sharp spine of a tail as it dragged itself up the beach. We dined on bass. Discovered a strange fellow on the shore of the lake; a kind of statue but not made of stone. He bobbed on the surface, composed of a slick and somewhat pliable substance. He is green from head to toe. He carries in his hands what appears to be a weapon and wears a helmet, both also green. I have dragged him back to the castle and set him up on the tall turret to act as a sentinel. Hauling him up the winding staircase put my back out. I'm not as young as I used to be. With faerie magic I will give him the power of sight and speech, so that although he does not move, he can be vigilant and call out. I wish I had the power to cast a spell that would bring him fully to life, but alas, I'm only Twilmish. I have positioned him facing the north in order to watch for rats. I call him Greenly, just to give him a name.

200 STEPS

I now record the number of steps it is at this point in time from the outer wall of the castle to where the breakers flood the beach. I was spied upon in my work, for the huge white disk on the horizon has just recently shown two eyes over the brim of the ocean. Its light is dreamlike, and it makes me wonder if I have really taken form or if I am still a spirit, dreaming I am not.

A MOMENTOUS DISCOVERY

Phargo and I discovered a corked bottle upon the beach. As has become my practice, I took out my hatchet and smashed a hole in its side near the neck. Often, I have found that these vessels are filled with an intoxicating liquor that in small doses warms the innards when the wind blows, and in large doses makes me sing and dance upon the turret. Before I could venture inside, I heard a voice call out, "Help us!" I was frozen in my tracks, thinking I had opened a ship of ghosts. Then, from out of the dark back of the bottle came a figure. Imagine my relief when I saw it was a female faerie. I am not exactly sure which branch of the folk she is from, but she is my height, dressed in a short gown woven from spider thread, and has alluring long, orange hair. She staggered forward and collapsed in my arms. Hiding behind her was a small faerie child, a boy, I think. He was frightened and sickly looking, and said nothing but followed me when I put the woman over my shoulder and carried her home. They now rest peacefully down the hall in a makeshift bed I put together from a common clamshell and a few folds of that pink material. I am filled with questions.

THE MOON

Meiwa told me the name of the white circle in the sky, which has now revealed itself completely. She said it was called the Moon, the bright specks are Stars, and the red orb was the Sun. I live in a time of darkness called the Night, and amazingly, there exists a time of brightness when the sun rules a blue sky and one can see a mile or more. All these things I think I knew at one time before I was born into this life. She knows many things including some secrets of the giant architects. The two of them, she and her son, are Willnits, seafaring people apparently who live aboard the ships of the giants. They had fallen asleep in an empty rum bottle, thinking it was safe, but when they awoke, they found the top stopped with a cork and their haven adrift upon the ocean. Sadly enough, her husband had been killed by one of the giants, called Humans, who mistook him for an insect and crushed him. I can vouch that she is expert with a fishing spear and was quite fierce in helping turn back an infestation of burrowing sand crabs in the dungeon. The boy, Magtel, is quiet but polite and seems a little worse for wear from their harrowing adventures. Only Phargo can bring a smile to him. I made him his own axe, to lift his spirits.

A SMALL NIGHT BIRD

Meiwa has enchanted a small night bird by attracting it with crumbs of a special bread she bakes from thin air and sea foam, and then using her lovely singing voice to train it. When she mounted the back of the delicate creature and called me to join her, I will admit I was skeptical. Once upon the bird, my arms around her waist, she made a kissing noise with her lips and we took off into the sky. My head swam as we went higher and higher and then swept along the shoreline in the light of the moon. She laughed wildly at my fear, and when we did not fall, I laughed too. She took me to a place where the giants live, in giant houses. Through a glass pane, we saw a giant girl drawing a colorful picture of a bird sitting upon a one-eyed woman's shoulder. Then we were off, traveling miles, soaring and diving, and eventually coming to rest on the bridge moat of While Away. The bird is not the only creature who has been enchanted by Meiwa.

150 STEPS

Magtel regularly accompanies me on the search for food now. When we came upon a blue claw in the throes of death, he stepped up next to me and put his hand in mine. We waited until the creature stopped moving, and then took our axes to the shell. Quite a harvest. It is now only 150 steps from the wall to the water.

GREENLY SPEAKS

I did not hear him at first as I was sleeping so soundly, but Meiwa, lying next to me, did and pinched my nose to wake me. We ran to the top of the turret, where Greenly was still sounding the alarm, and looked north. There three shadows moved ever closer across the sand. I went and fetched my bow and arrows, my latest weapon, devised from something Meiwa had said she'd seen the humans use. I was waiting to fire until they drew closer. Meiwa had a plan, though. She called for her night bird, and we mounted its back. We attacked from the air, and the monsters never got within 50 steps of the castle. My arrows could not kill them but effectively turned them away. I would have perished without her.

WHILE MEIWA SLEPT

While Meiwa slept, Magtel and I took torches, slings for carrying large objects upon the back, and our axes, and quietly left the castle. Phargo trailed after us, of course. There was a far place I had been to only one other time before. Heading west, I set a brisk pace and the boy kept up, sometimes running to stay next to me. Suddenly he started talking, telling me about a creature he had seen while living aboard the ship. "A whale," he called it. "Bigger than a hundred humans, with a mouth like a cavern." I laughed and asked him if he was certain of this. "I swear to you," he said. "It blows water from a hole on its back, a fountain that reaches to the sky." He told me the humans hunted them with spears from small boats, and made from their insides lamp oil and perfume. What an imagination the child has, for it did not end with the whale, but he continued to relate to me so many unbelievable wonders as we walked along I lost track of where we were and, though I watched for danger and the path through the sand ahead, it was really inward that my vision was trained, picturing his fantastic ideas. Before this he had not said but a few words to me. After turning north at the shark skeleton, we traveled awhile more and then entered the forest. Our torches pushed back the gloom, but it was mightily dark in there among the brambles and stickers. A short way in I spotted what we had come for: giant berries, like clusters of beads, indigo in color and sweating their sweetness. I hacked one off its vine and showed Magtel how to chop one down. We loaded them into our slings and then started back. There were a few tense moments before leaving the forest, for a long, yellow snake slithered by as we stood stiller than Greenly, holding our breath. I had to keep one foot lightly on Phargo's neck to keep him from barking or hopping and giving us away. On the way home, the boy asked if I had ever been married, and then a few minutes later if I had any children. We presented the berries to Meiwa upon her waking. I will never forget the taste of them.

THE BOY HAS A PLAN

Magtel joined Meiwa and me as we sat on the tall turret enjoying a sip of liquor from a bottle I had recently discovered on the beach. He said he knew how to protect the castle against the rats. This was his plan: Gather as much dried seaweed that has blown into clumps upon the beach, encircle the outer wall of the castle with it. When Greenly sounds the alarm, we will shoot flaming arrows into it, north, south, east, and west, creating a ring of fire around us that the rats cannot pass through. I thought it ingenious. Meiwa kissed him and clapped her hands. We will forthwith begin collecting the necessary seaweed. It will be a big job. My boy is gifted.

100 STEPS

I don't know why I checked how far the ocean's flood could reach. 100 is a lot of steps.

WE ARE READY

After a long span of hard work, we have completed the seaweed defense of the castle. The rats are nowhere in sight. I found a large round contrivance, one side metal, one glass, buried in the sand. It had a heartbeat that sounded like a tiny hammer tapping glass. With each beat, an arrow inside the glass moved ever so slightly in a course describing a circle. Meiwa told me it was called a Watch, and the humans use them to mark the passage of Time. Later, I returned to it and struck it with my axe until its heart stopped beating. The longer of the metal arrows I have put in my quiver.

THE TRUTH, LIKE A WAVE

Magtel has fallen ill. He is too tired to get out of bed. Meiwa told me the truth. They must leave soon and find another ship, for they cannot exist for too long away from one. She told me that she had used a spell to keep them alive for the duration they have been with me, but now the spell is weakening. I asked her why she had never told me. "Because we wanted to stay with you at While Away forever," she said. There were no more words. We held each other for a very long time, and I realized that my heart was a castle made of sand.

THEY ARE GONE

In order to get Magtel well enough to endure the flight out to sea on the night bird, I built a bed for him in the shape of a ship, and this simple ruse worked to get him back upon his feet. We made preparations for their departure, packing food and making warm blankets to wrap around them as they flew out across the ocean. "We will need some luck to find a ship," Meiwa told me. "The night bird is not the strongest of fliers and she will be carrying two. We may have to journey far before we can set down." "I will worry about your safety until the day I die," I told her. "No," she said, "when we find a home on the sea, I will have the bird return to you, and you will know we have survived the journey. Then write a note to me and tie it to the bird's leg and it will bring us word of you."

This idea lightened my heart a little. Then it was time to say good-bye. Magtel, shark's tooth axe in hand, put his arms around my neck. "Keep me in your imagination," I told him, and he said he always would. Meiwa and I kissed for the last time. They mounted the night bird. Then with that sound she made, Meiwa called the wonderful creature to action and it lit into the sky. I ran up the steps to the top of the tall turret in time to see them circle once and call back to me. I reached for them, but they were gone, out above the ocean, crossing in front of the watchful moon.

50 Steps

It has been so long, I can't remember the last time I sat down to record things. I guess I knew this book contained memories I have worked so hard to overcome. It is just Phargo and me now, fishing, gathering food, combing the shore. The moon has climbed high to its tallest turret and looks down now with a distant stare as if in judgment upon me. 50 steps remain between the outer wall and the tide. I record this number without trepidation or relief. I have grown somewhat slower, a little dimmer, I think. In my dreams, when I sleep, I am forever heading out across the ocean upon the night bird.

Greenly Speaks

I was just about to go fishing when I heard Greenly pipe up and call, "Intruders." I did not even go up to the turret to look first, but fetched my bow and arrows and an armful of driftwood sticks with which to build a fire. When I reached my lookout, I turned north, and sure enough, in the pale moonlight I saw the beach crawling with rats, more than a dozen.

I lit a fire right on the floor of the turret, armed my bow, and dipped the end of the arrow into the flames until it caught. One, two, three, four, I launched my flaming missiles at the ring of dry seaweed. The fire grew into a perfect circle, and some of the rats were caught in it. I could hear them scream from where I stood. Most of the rest turned back, but to the west, where one had fallen into the fire, it smothered the flame, and I saw another climb upon its carcass and keep coming for the castle. I left the taller turret and ran to the smaller one to get a better shot at the attacker. Once atop it, I fired arrow after arrow at the monster, which had cleared the retaining wall and was within the grounds of While Away. With shafts sticking out of it, blood dripping, it came ever forward, intent upon devouring me. Upon reaching the turret on which I stood, it reared back on its haunches and scrabbled at the side of the structure, which started to crumble. In one last attempt to fell it, I reached for the metal arrow I had taken from the watch and loaded my bow. I was sweating profusely, out of breath, but I felt more alive in that moment than I had in a long while. My aim was true; the shaft entered its bared chest, and dug into its heart. The rat toppled forward, smashed the side of the turret, and then the whole structure began to fall. My last thought was, "If the fall does not kill me, I will be buried alive." That is when I lost my footing and dropped into thin air. But I did not fall, for something caught me, like a soft hand, and eased me down to safety upon the ground. It was a miracle I suppose, or maybe a bit of Meiwa's magic, but the night bird had returned. The smaller turret was completely destroyed, part of it having fallen into the courtyard. I dug that out, but the entire structure of the place was weakened by the attack and since then pieces of wall crumble off every so often and the bridge is tenuous. It took me forever to get rid of the rat carcass. I cut it up and dragged the pieces outside what remained of the retaining wall and burned them.

A Letter

The night bird stayed with me while I repaired, as best I could, the damage to the castle, but as soon as I had the chance, I sat down and wrote a note to Meiwa and Magtel, trying desperately and, in the end, ultimately failing, to tell them how much I missed them. Standing on the turret with Phargo by my side, watching the bird take off again brought back all the old feelings even stronger, and I felt lost.

The Moon, The Sea, The Dark

The water laps only 10 steps from the outer wall of the castle. Many things have happened since I last wrote. Once, while lying in bed, I saw, through my bedroom window, two humans, a giant female and male, walk by hand in hand. They stopped at the outer wall of the castle and spoke in booming voices. From the sound of their words, I know they were admiring my home, even in its dilapidated state. I took back the enchantment from Greenly, so he would not have the burden of sight and speech any longer; his job was finished and he had done it well. I dragged him to the lake and set him in my boat and pushed it off. Oh, how my back ached after that. If the rats come now, I will not fight them. The dungeon has been overrun by sand crabs, and when I am quiet in my thoughts, I hear their constant scuttling about down below, undermining the foundation of While Away. A piece of the battlement fell away from the turret, which is not a good sign, but gives me an unobstructed view of the sea. Washed up on the beach, due east of the castle, I found the letter I had sent so long ago with the night bird. The ink had run and it was barely legible, but I knew it was the one I had written. I am tired.

THE STARS FALL

I have just come in from watching the stars fall. Dozens of them came streaking down. I smiled at the beauty of it. What does it mean?

A VISITOR

I saw the lights of a ship out on the ocean and then I saw something large and white descending out of the darkness. Phargo was barking like mad, hopping every which way. I cleared my eyes to see it was a bird, a tern, and a small figure rode upon its back. It was Magtel, but no longer a boy. He was grown. I ran down from the turret, nearly tripping as I went. He met me by the bridge of the moat and we hugged for a very long time. He is now taller than I. He could only stay a little while, as that was his ship passing out at sea. I made us clam broth and we had jellyfish curd on slices of spearing. When I asked him, "Where is Meiwa?" he shook his head. "She took ill some time ago and did not recover," he said. "But she asked me to bring this to you if I should ever get the chance." I held back my tears not to ruin the reunion with the boy. "She stole it from one of the humans aboard ship and saved it for you." Here he produced a little square of paper that he began to unfold. When it was completely undone and spread across the table, he smoothed it with his hands. "A picture of the Day," he said. There it was, the sun, bright yellow, the sky blue, a beach of pure white sand lapped by a crystal-clear turquoise ocean. When it came time for Magtel to leave, he told me he still had his axe and it had come in handy many times. He told me that there were many other Willnits aboard the big ship and it was a good community. We did not say goodbye. He patted Phargo on the head and got upon the back of the large white bird. "Thank you, Eelin-Ok," he said, and then was gone. If it wasn't for the picture of Day, I'd have thought it all a dream.

THE TIDE COMES IN

The waves have breached the outer wall and the sea floods in around the base of the castle. I have folded up the picture of Day and have it now in a pouch on a string around my neck. Phargo waits for me on the turret, from where we will watch the last seconds of While Away. Just a few more thoughts, though, before I go to join him. When first I stepped into myself as Eelin-Ok, I worried if I had chosen well my home, but I don't think there can be any question that While Away was everything I could have asked for. So too, many times I questioned my life, but now, in this final moment, memories of Phargo's whisper-bark, the thrill of battle against the rats, fishing on the lake, the face of the moon, the taste of blackberries, the wind, Greenly's earnest nature, the boy holding my hand, flying on the night bird, lying with Meiwa in the mussel-shell bed come flooding in like the rising tide. "What does it all mean?" I have always asked. "It means you've lived a life, Eelin-Ok." I hear now the walls begin to give way. I have to hurry. I don't want to miss this.

The Annals of Eelin-Ok

Story Notes

When I was a kid, the New York Daily News *ran a comic in its Sunday color funny pages called "The Teenie Weenies." This was a full or sometimes half-page comic of only one large panel. It was about a tiny race of people who lived under a rosebush. They rode on the backs of dragonflies, made feasts of acorns, battled mice, and generally lived the good, small life. I was enchanted by them, as I think most kids are by diminutive representations of things. Remembering this comic and the wonder it wrought in me was the impetus for "Eelin-Ok." As I've gotten older, I rarely feel that same enchantment, although there are other experiences equally as powerful. One place I still can sense it is at the beach where my wife and I and our two sons have been going every summer since our family started. So it was that my small hero wound up living in a sand castle at the edge of the shore.*

I dedicate this story to one cool kid, Chieko Quigley, ice skating aficionado. "Eelin-Ok" was published by Terri Windling and Ellen Datlow in the second volume of their young adult series for Viking, The Faery Reel: Tales from the Twilight Realm. *The story won the Speculative Literature Foundation's Fountain Award, an annual juried award given to a speculative short story of "exceptional literary quality."*

Jupiter's Skull

MRS. STRELLOP HAD A LITTLE SHOP CALLED Thanatos in the Bolukuchet district at the south end of a cobbled street facing the canal. On evenings in late summer, for those few breezy weeks preceding the monsoons, she would fix her door ajar with a large, dismorphic skull and sit by the entrance, inviting in passersby for a cup of foxglove tea.

She was a handsome woman of advanced years with a long braid the color of iron that she wound around her neck twice and tucked into the front of her loose blouse between her breasts. Her wrinkles—the crow's-feet at the edges of her eyes, the lines descending from the corners of her lips—belied her charm more so than her age and were in no way at odds with the youthful beauty of her elegant hands or the glint in her green eyes.

She wore loose garments—wraps and tunics and sometimes a shawl—all fixed with glitter and sequin designs. Her earrings were thin hoops of crystal that caught the light of the candles positioned about her shop and transformed it into stars on the dark draperies that covered the walls. Her only other piece of jewelry was a ring on the left middle finger that held no precious stone, but instead the polished eyetooth of a man who was said to have once betrayed her.

That tea she served, redolent of the digitalis, slowed the heart and tinged the mind with a dreamlike effect that seemed to negate the passage of time, so that, after a single cup and what seemed a brief conversation, I would look up and notice the sun rising out over the treetops of the forest beyond the waterway. The sudden realization of a new day would place me back in reality, and invariably I would turn to her and ask, "What exactly were we discussing?"

She would smile, eyes closed, and shoo me home with a weary wave of the back of her hand. "A pleasant week then, Mrs. Strellop," I'd say. She would offer me the same and, as I stepped into the street, add the rejoinder, "Good days are ahead, Jonsi." It was only later, while lying in the cot in my small room over Meager's Glass Works, listening to the morning wind and the distant tolling of the bell over in the Dunzwell district, that I would try in vain to piece together what she had told me through the night. With all my concentration I could only bring up slivers of her tales, and these I could not see but only feel the irritation of like thistle spines in my memory. The effort to do even this exhausted me beyond reason, and when I finally awoke later on, it was with an indistinct and transient belief, like a morning mist already evaporating, that my dreams had brought me closer to a recounting of her words than any conscious effort. In truth, every atom of these baroque nightmares was completely lost to me.

Like Mrs. Strellop, I had also known betrayal and was drawn to the Bolukuchet the way the others who wandered the world with a hole in the heart were, as if by a great magnet that attracted emptiness. The majority of us had a little bit of money, at least enough to live comfortably, and those who didn't worked at some lazy job from ten in the morning till three in the afternoon when the café opened and generous old Munchter served the first round for free. I had originally landed in that purgatorial quadrant of a crumbling town on the banks of the muddy Meerswal with the ridiculous idea that I might, in my middle years, revive my youthful interest in poetry. Though I jotted down some words upon waking each morning, the writing was, in all honesty, a dodge.

Mrs. Strellop owned a shop the way I wrote poetry, for although she trafficked in talk and that mischievous tea, they came free of charge. There was no product or service I could readily discern. I knew very little about her, save for the fact that she was the first one to welcome me to the district. Ever since then, I'd gone by her place from time to time for a sip of oblivion and a session of amnesia therapy. I never saw her that the sun wasn't in its descent, and I saw her most just prior to the autumn rains. It was Munchter who told me about the ring she wore. I inquired, "What sort of betrayal?" "What difference does it make?" he replied, and then with a shrug, denoting something close to sympathy, refilled my glass for free.

There were many engaging personalities I could have written about in the Bolukuchet. In fact, there were as many as there were individuals living there, for everyone had a tale they were reluctant to tell, a past heightened to mythos by the ingredients of time, distance, and the distorting forces of exquisite lassitude. We wandered the narrow alleyways, sat, smoking, in darkened doorways, leaned lazily on the rusting, floral-designed railings of second-story verandas, like spectral characters in the mind of an aged novelist impotent to envision what happens next.

It is a certainty that nothing good ever transpired in the district, for that would be a contradiction to its idiosyncratic metaphysics of gravity, but nothing terribly dreadful happened either, until, of course, this. On a windy afternoon of dust devils and darkening skies, two days before the monsoon struck, the body was discovered by Maylee, the new prostitute recently in the employ of Mother Carushe. Mrs. Strellop had hired the young woman to fetch fresh fruit and vegetables each day from the barge that docked at the canal quay three streets up. When Maylee, carrying a basket of fresh carrots and white eggplant, pushed open the door to Thanatos, she was met by a ghastly sight. Eyes popping, blackened tongue lolling, Mrs. Strellop, draped in a plum wrap decorated with quartz chips in a design of the constellation of the goat, sat slumped back in her chair, one beautiful hand holding an empty vial that it was later determined had contained a draught of cyanide and the other clutching the doorstop skull in her lap.

She was buried quickly, before the rains would have made the digging impossible, and the next day the entire district turned out at Munchter's for a sort of informal wake of testimony and tearful besotment. We shared tales and descriptions of her, and, after my third Lime Plunge, I must have told everyone of her usual parting phrase to me, "Good days are ahead, Jonsi." Mother Carushe had suggested that I compose a eulogy in the form of a poem in Mrs. Strellop's honor and though it was begun, I could never find the words to finish it. Instead, the bargeman, Bill Hokel, played a dirge on his mouth organ. When the last mournful note had wavered away, there was a moment of silence before we heard the rain begin its patter on the corrugated tin of the roof. In that brief span, I wondered if Mrs. Strellop's taking of her own life was an act of courage or cowardice.

The rain was cold and unforgiving. For the first two days of the monthlong downpour, I simply sat on the veranda of my small apartment, drinking and smoking, and watched as the large, relentless droplets decimated the last white blossoms of the trailing vine that grew like a net over the facade of the abandoned fish market across the street. Mushrooms sprouted out of stucco, and great, gray seagoing birds huddled under the overhangs, heads beneath wings as if ashamed not to be flying. At times the wind was wild, lifting pieces of roof tile off the old buildings and buffeting off course anyone unlucky enough to be out on the street. On the second morning, Munchter trudged along the street beneath me and I called to him, but it was obvious he could not hear my voice above the howl of the wind.

With the death of Mrs. Strellop, my usual feeling of blankness gave way to a kind of depressive loneliness. I knew others in the district much better, but she and her tea and our nightlong sessions had always centered me enough to keep that damnable sense of desire at bay. I wouldn't have gone so far as to call it therapy, because as I understand it the therapist does the listening. It was she who always talked, telling me those long, intricate stories I would never remember. Somehow, they worked their way into my system invisibly, without a trace, and alleviated me of any judgment concerning the state of stasis that was my life.

On the third day of the rain I was awakened by a knock upon my door. I knew it couldn't be Meager come up from the shop below to share a cup of coffee and peruse my latest fragment of verse, since he always went west for the drowned month and gave his two assistants the time off as well. I dressed and answered the door. Standing on the landing of the rickety wooden stairs that led up from the back of the Glass Works, drenched to the skin, was Maylee. Her usually wavy locks (Mother Carushe knew a thing or two about hair fashion) were slicked and stringy from the downpour, making her already large eyes more prominent. Her fair complexion had a bluish tinge and she was shivering. I stepped back and let her in.

As soon as the door was closed, I went into the back room and brought a blanket to wrap around her shoulders. She thanked me, her teeth still chattering, and I ushered her over to a chair at the small table near the veranda. Shutting the glass doors to keep the chill off her, I then sat down in the opposite seat. Before I could speak, she lifted a small leather pouch with a drawstring onto the table.

"From Mrs. Strellop," she said.

"How so?" I asked.

"She told me many times, especially in her last weeks, that if anything should happen to her, I should give this to you."

"What's in it?"

She shook her head.

I reached out and grabbed the satchel, pulling it along the table toward me. As I undid the drawstring, Maylee said to me, "Would you like me to leave?"

I laughed. "No, at least get warmed up before going back out in it."

She nodded, looking relieved.

Then I opened the pouch, and a familiar scent wafted up. I lifted the bag and held it to my nose for a moment. "Foxglove tea," I said with a smile.

"Oh, yes," said Maylee, leading me to believe that she had tasted the strange brew.

"Shall I make some now? It might warm you a little."

"Please," she said.

I went immediately over to my stove, got a fire going, and put a kettle of water on. As I filled the big copper tea ball, I noticed for the first time that the stuff was multicolored, made up of flecks of red and yellow, a pale green and some miniscule blue nuggets, suggesting that there were other ingredients in it besides the dried petals of its namesake. It struck me then that perhaps there was no foxglove in it at all, that it had just been a name the missus had assigned it.

I rejoined Maylee at the table while waiting for the water to boil. "You knew Mrs. Strellop quite well, didn't you?" I asked, lifting my cigarettes off the tabletop. I offered one to her, and she accepted. Striking a match, I lit my own and then reached across to share the flame.

She took a drag and nodded. "I saw her every day. I would bring her vegetables from the barge that comes down from the farm country. She gave me three dollars for my effort, which I had to give to Mother Carushe, but then Mrs. Strellop would also give me a cup of this tea. 'Just for you, my dear,' she'd say."

"That tea is something, isn't it?" I asked, laughing.

"I'd take the tea and sit with her for an hour. She always had some story to tell. It was so relaxing. But when it was time for me to leave, I could never remember a single word she had spoken."

"You don't have to tell me. I sat whole nights with her and can't recall a blessed thing."

"I think she was a witch," said Maylee.

I laughed, but this time she didn't. "What makes you say that?" I asked.

"When I would return home in the afternoon from taking the vegetables to Thanatos, Mother would bless me with a special holy water she kept in a bottle that had the shape of a saint before accepting the three dollars. Then she would take the bills and put them in the icebox for a day before spending them. I think she was afraid of Mrs. Strellop."

"If you don't mind my asking, how is it working for Mother Carushe?" I said, trying to hide behind my cigarette. I thought for a moment I had offended Maylee, but then I realized she was really considering my question.

"I have been in the district for only six months, and . . . May I be frank with you, Mr. Jonsi?"

"Please," I said, "just Jonsi, no mister necessary. And there is nothing left in the world that will offend me. I'm not after the details; I just like to hear how others live. You know, sort of as a barometer for my own life."

"Well, I and the other three young women who work for Mother, we are supposed to be prostitutes—no sense in trying to dress it up. Not the life I had at one time envisioned for myself. There was a period when I had designs on being an actress and saw myself delivering great speeches from the stage. I might even have had some talent for it, but I allowed myself to be drawn away from my dream by a loathsome man who eventually left me stranded and broke."

"I can commiserate," I said.

"But that's all in the past. One needs to survive. But, sir, there is something wrong with the gentlemen of the Bolukuchet," she said.

"What do you mean?" I asked, feeling some vague offense.

"I have had only five commissions so far in the time I have been here, and every one of them . . ." Here she grinned slightly and stubbed out her cigarette. "Limp as dishrags."

I couldn't help but laugh, for a variety of reasons.

"Yes, they have money and they have an idea they would like to spend time with me, but when I get close to them, they back away. Instead of me taking them in hand, they want to hold *my* hand. And they are paying astronomical sums for this. One fellow last month had me simply sleep for an hour in the bed next to him. He never laid a finger on me. When I got up to leave, he sniffed the pillow where my head had been and started crying."

"An interesting observation," I said.

"Granted, I have only been with five of them, but I sense it, a plague of deep sorrow, shall we say?"

Luckily, the water came to a boil then and I got up and prepared us each a cup. The perfumed-forest aroma of it was comforting, and for the first time since the rains started, I felt a measure of peace. Maylee and I did not speak while taking the tea. She stared at the table, and I at the pressed tin design of the ceiling. During this long pause, the sound of the rain changed from monotonous to beautiful. Out on the street someone yelled. I closed my eyes and remembered the cool of the evening, sitting in the doorway of Thanatos, watching the patterns of fireflies at the edge of the forest across the canal. Mrs. Strellop's voice started in my memory and then spiraled down through the center of my being, leaving a sense of calm in its wake.

I rested my cup on the table, empty, just as Maylee did hers. She looked over at me, her eyes not half so big anymore, and smiled.

"And Mrs. Strellop told me that you are a poet," she said, her words having slowed to a drawl.

I laughed and shook my head. "I sniff the pillow of poetry and weep," I told her, preparing to forge forward with an honest recitation of my own days to even the account, but she abruptly cut me off.

"—Wait," she said, and held up her hand. "That is the first time I ever remembered something Mrs. Strellop had told me." She breathed deeply. "What a sense of relief."

"I can imagine, believe me," I said, and clapped for her.

"Oh, my god, there's something else . . . *something else*," she nearly yelled, squirming in her seat. "That odd skull she had. Do you remember it?"

"Of course," I said.

"She called it Jupiter."

I scanned my memory, and sure enough, yes, in that moment, I remembered her telling me the same. That crumb of information shifted like a grain in a sand pile, and with the insignificant revelation something else became clear to me. "My turn," I said. She looked on excitedly. "He was a throwback, not quite a man—"

"Or more than a man," she said quickly. "Did they not find him in a mountain valley in the range that overlooked her village?"

I pushed my chair back from the table. "The old hunter Fergus brought him back from an expedition into the clouds. From the altitude to which he climbed he could see the planets clearly, and Jupiter watched him like an eye the night he captured the strange lad in a trap that was a hole dug like a grave and covered with flimsy branches." For the last half a sentence, she recited the words with me.

We sat for a moment in stunned silence, and then she said, "I feel light headed . . . but not dizzy. Like I'm waking up."

"Every time you voice a string of Mrs. Strellop's words," I said, "the next comes into my mind."

"Yes," she said, "like a magician pulling scarves from his pocket."

"What now?" I asked.

"Fergus believed him to be more ape than human."

"He brought Jupiter back to the village and put him on display in a cage made of branches lashed with lanyards."

"Each of the townspeople paid a silver coin to see him; covered from top to toe with a reddish brown fuzz, cranium like a cathedral, thumbs on his feet, and jutting jaw," she said, staring at the wall as if the cage was there and she was seeing him. She shook her head sadly.

"For a time he was a renowned attraction and many came to view him," I added.

Maylee sighed. "And then like everything—for some, even life itself—the sense of wonder wore off."

"Fergus spent so much time with the wild boy that he came to realize the boy was more human than ape, and the lad learned to read and write and speak perfectly."

"He was no longer confined to the cage," she said, as if reading from a book, "but went about in human clothes, helping the aged hunter, now wracked with arthritis, get through his days."

"Actually," I said, as if setting her straight, "this Jupiter, this beast boy, was quite a prodigy. Fergus taught him to carve wood with a knife, and the hairy apprentice created a likeness of his master, his father, from a log of oak that stood six feet tall and perfectly mirrored the hunter."

Maylee did not immediately reply, and for a moment, I feared she had lost the thread of events, until she finally blurted out, "Then Jupiter grew, tall and strong—"

"Like this," I said, and not even knowing what I was about, stood up as if carved from words and animated only by the story. I thrust my chest out and flexed my biceps. My bottom jaw pushed forward and, furrowing my brow, I bent my knees slightly and took slow, big steps in a circle.

"That's him," she said. "But then Fergus died."

I felt the air leave me as if I'd been punched in the stomach, and, retaining my simulation of Jupiter, I hung my head and slouched forward. "And the boy was set adrift in an alien world," I said.

"Your eyes," said Maylee.

I could feel the tears on my cheeks. "Time passed," I said, and, with this, sat down and lit two cigarettes, passing one to my guest. We smoked in silence, time passing, but I felt the persistence of the tale like a slight pressure behind my eyes, in my solar plexus. The tea had me in its fog. The light from the lamps appeared unnaturally diffuse, and I heard, whisper soft, traces of a children's choir emanating from my ears. Still, one small part of me clung to reason, and in that thimble of rational self, I trembled with wonder and fear at what was happening.

Maylee stubbed out her cigarette and said, "After Jupiter buried Fergus, he set about making the bottom floor of the old man's home into a shop from which to sell his remarkable carvings."

Her words again initiated the story, which broke open inside of me like the monsoon, washing away any volition on my part. I stood and assumed my primate pose. "He created beautiful objects with his knife," I said. "Animals of the forest so lifelike, customers swore they moved, circus acrobats whose hands clasped the trapeze, monsters full of dignity and courage." My fingers wriggled with the grace of snakes as I turned and carved an invisible figurine.

"The people of the town remained wary of Jupiter, afraid of his size and skeptical of his intelligence. To them he was either a horrid freak or the result of a deal with the devil, but never human," she said, and slowly stood.

She turned her back on me and took two steps as I added, "They did not mind him so much as long as he remained in his shop, a curiosity to visit every now and then and buy a gift from for the holidays or a wedding, but they did not want him on their streets. For his part, Jupiter longed for companionship, someone with whom to discuss what he had read, the mundane events of his every day."

"He felt their distrust for him on the street, so one day he hired a young woman to bring him groceries from the market each afternoon. Her name was Zel Strellop, a kind girl, unafraid of Jupiter's demeanor and enchanted by his craft," said Maylee, dropping the gray blanket from her shoulders and spreading her arms wide as if breaking free from a cocoon.

I could almost see a young Mrs. Strellop in the features of Maylee, and I wondered if to her I appeared as Jupiter. The story possessed us yet more fully, and although we continued to tell it as we spoke, we began simulating every little action our two characters might have undertaken. I noticed that when she told the words of Zel, her voice changed, becoming higher and lighter, and that my own words, when quoting Jupiter, were far more bass than I was accustomed to. For the exposition, our voices remained our own. We moved in and around the apartment, no longer allowing the table to separate us.

There was a series of meetings between the wood carver and the young woman, and they grew increasingly interested in each other. I felt the flame of attraction spark to life in my chest, felt weak in the knees as Maylee, as Zel Strellop, approached, lightly touched my arm, whispered a secret to me, and finally kissed me for the first time, gently on the lips. I wanted it to continue, but Maylee broke it off and fled to the stove that stood in for Zel's parents' house.

"And then," said I, "Jupiter wrote her a poem to express his love for her," and I walked over and sat hunched at my writing desk. My knife hand reached for the pen. I lifted it and wrote rapidly.

> *When the sun is high*
> *I watch out the window*
> *for a cloud of dust in the distance,*
> *you on the path,*
> *bringing me oranges, melons, and plums.*
> *My impatience is sharp*
> *and carves your likeness*
> *on every moment.*

The instant I had penned the last word, Maylee swept the paper away and pressed it to her breast. I stood and turned to face her. "And they kissed more heatedly," she said, and we did.

"His apelike hands swept across the curves of her body," I said from the corner of my mouth, our lips still pressed, and my hands did.

She stepped back, and in one fluid motion lifted her damp dress off over her head. "Zel disrobed in a fit of passion," she said, breathing heavily.

When she stooped to remove her undergarments, I undid my trousers and let them drop to the floor, not forgetting to add, "He grew brave in his desire and followed her example."

Maylee left me and went back to the table. Over her shoulder she verily shouted, "There was no bed, so they made do on his workbench." With this, she bent forward and with one sweep of her arm sent the teacups and ashtray and cigarettes onto the floor.

"He approached her from behind," I said.

"His member was pulsing with all the energy he'd brought with him from the mountain," she said.

I looked down and even in my fog was surprised to see that she was right.

"She gasped as he entered her," she gasped.

I tried to say, "With slow thrusts, he vented his passion," but it sounded as a series of short grunts.

Maylee missed a line or two, herself, in which she was to have described Zel's own pleasure, I'm certain, but filled in with panting and a protracted groan.

For a span of time, I was lost to my life, my role in the story, transported beyond the Bolukuchet, flying somewhere above the rain.

As I pulled out of her, Maylee said, "Time passed," and reached down to grab the cigarettes and ashtray off the floor. We lit up and took our seats at the table, both still heaving from the encounter.

When we had managed to catch our breath, she said, "The townspeople started to become wary of the arrangement between Zel and Jupiter. She was spending far too much time out at his shop. Something about her look had changed."

"Late one afternoon," I said, "Jupiter was visited by the sheriff, a man who had been close friends with old Fergus. He warned Jupiter that people were suspicious and if he wanted the best for Zel, he should leave town immediately."

"Yes," said Maylee, "but what he did not know was that the sheriff had also, that very evening, warned Zel to stay away from Jupiter. As soon as it got dark, though, she sneaked out and made for his shop."

We both stood at this point and each walked halfway around the table to meet face to face. "She confronted him as he was clasping shut his suitcase," I said.

"Where are you going?" asked Zel.

"I must leave," said Jupiter.

"I'm coming with you," she said.

"No, you can't," he told her. "It will end in tragedy."

"*I'm coming!*" screamed Maylee, with all the pain of injustice and loss.

"He simply shook his head, tears in his eyes," I said.

"Her anger at the world turned to rage."

"She struck out at him," I said, but did not see Maylee's fist coursing through the air. Her punch landed square on the right side of my mouth. I staggered back and then fell to my knees. My lip was split and I could taste blood. I spit, and a tooth came with it out onto the wooden floor. "He betrayed her," I said, my hand covering my mouth.

Maylee bent over and lifted the tooth, her eyes widening as if it glinted like a diamond. She looked up at me. "Because he loved her," she said.

With this, the spell instantly lifted, more rapidly than a curtain closing, with the speed of falling rain, and, without conversation, we both staggered to the bed and fell into a bottomless sleep.

In the morning, I woke to find her gone, but her scent remained upon the pillow. What I remembered most clearly from the bizarre play we had enacted the previous day was that when she had struck me, in the moment or two when I thought I might pass out, I had realized I must leave the district.

That afternoon, after hurriedly packing and leaving much behind, I left the Bolukuchet and traveled for many days back to the city. At first the change was frightening, and I moved through the days like a somnambulist directed by commands that came from my dreams. Somehow I managed to make all the right moves, and it was not long before a memory of my life prior to the Bolukuchet returned to me and I began to feel at home in my new surroundings.

As soon as I had established myself, gotten a place and employment, I wrote to Maylee, care of Mother Carushe, to see if I could persuade her to join me. Oddly enough, all of my letters, more than three dozen, returned unopened with an explanation that the address could not be located. I sent another batch to Munchter's café, to Meager's, and the results were precisely the same.

In fact, no matter whom I asked or what inquiries I made at libraries or post offices, no one had ever heard of the Bolukuchet. Although my new life was fast paced and the basic excitement and wonder of mere existence had mysteriously returned to me, I missed my old friends and the tired, decrepit district. Luckily I had taken with me the pouch of foxglove tea. At first I imbibed it to try to discover how exactly Zel Strellop had come by Jupiter's skull, but that part of the story was not to be mine. I did, though, revisit my memories of nights at Munchter's, the fireflies in the forest across the canal, Meager showing me the finest prism he had ever created and the blizzard of color with which it filled the room, the soulful tunes of Bill Hokel's mouth organ, et cetera. When these visions came to me, I made them into poems. Years passed and I had enough to collect into a book, which was miraculously published. Its title—*Jupiter's Skull*.

The book won great renown, and I was asked to give readings at colleges and libraries and coffee shops. When I was interviewed, the question most often asked was, "How did you dream up a place like the Bolukuchet?" I would answer every time that I had lived there, which would cause the interviewer to smirk or smile as if we were complicit in the lie I was telling.

Many years later, on a rainy night, I gave a reading at a local bookstore. Afterward, as was my practice, I sat at a table and, one by one, people who'd purchased a copy of my book would come forward and I would sign it and chat with them briefly. At the end of a modest line, a woman stepped forward. Before I looked up to take in her face, she said to me, "I bet you could use a Lime Plunge right now."

She had my attention instantly. She was rather plain but pleasant looking in her appearance: brown hair, medium build, late middle age, dressed in a yellow raincoat. "Last week I was in Munchter's," she said.

"Finally," I said, "someone who's been to the district."

"I know," she told me, "out here it's as if it never existed."

She told me that Munchter and Meager and the rest of the old crew were still fine, and that she had read my book and I had captured them perfectly.

"Did you know a young woman, Maylee?" I asked.

"Oh, yes, not so young, really. She owned a little shop, Thanatos, over near the canal. Very long, gray hair, wrapped twice around her neck? I went there often and had tea with her. We rarely used her first name, though. She preferred Mrs. Strellop. I'm sorry to tell you that she passed away only a few days before I left."

"By her own hand?" I asked.

"Why, yes. I wasn't going to say, but I believe it was cyanide."

"And the skull?"

"A woman's skull? Zel, was the name she had for it. Apparently there was an entire story associated with the thing."

"I see," I said.

Before this woman left, she shook my hand, and when she smiled, I noticed the gap from a missing tooth. "Well," she said, "it's good to be back from the district." Then she left the store, and I watched through the window as she disappeared into the rain.

Jupiter's Skull

Story Notes

The writer and anthologist Al Sarrantonio is one of the first people I met when I entered the speculative fiction trade back in 1997. We've kept in touch and remained friends through the years. One of the first things Al told me was, "When you're a writer, your neighbors are going to think you're a weirdo. There's two ways to avoid that. Either join a local bowling league or every time you have a book come out, walk up to each of their doors, knock, and hand them a copy of the book. After a while you just become the poor schmuck who writes the books and everything will be fine." If you live in suburbia like I do, it's good advice. So, when Al was doing his anthology Flights: Extreme Visions of Fantasy, *he asked me for a story, and I was happy to comply. This piece took a long time gestating, and when it finally began to show itself, I had no idea where it was going. This was one of those stories where the drama in my mind was only ever about a sentence or two ahead of my typing fingers. I love working that way, and my own method of invention mirrored the process that the narrator and Maylee go through in creating their own story.*

A Night in the Tropics

THE FIRST BAR I EVER WENT TO WAS THE
Tropics. It was, and still is, situated between the grocery store
and the bank along Higbee Lane in West Islip. I was around five or
six, and my old man would take me with him when he went there
to watch the Giants games on Sunday afternoons. While the men
were all at the bar, drinking, talking, giving Y. A. Tittle a piece of
their minds, I'd roll the balls on the pool table or sit in one of the
booths in the back and color. The jukebox always seemed to be
playing "Beyond the Sea" by Bobby Darin, while I searched for figures, the way people do with clouds, in the swirling cigar and
cigarette smoke. I didn't go there for the hard-boiled eggs the bartender proffered after making them vanish and pulling them out of
my ear, or for the time spent sitting on my father's lap at the bar,
sipping a ginger ale with a cherry in it, although both were welcome. The glowing, bubbling beer signs were fascinating, the foul
language was its own cool music, but the thing that drew me to The
Tropics was a thirty-two-foot vision of paradise.

Along the south wall of the place, stretching from the front door
back to the entrance of the bathrooms was a continuous mural of a
tropical beach. There were palm trees with coconuts and stretches
of pale sand sloping down to a shoreline where the serene sea rolled
in lazy wavelets. The sky was robin's egg blue, the ocean, six different shades of aquamarine. All down the beach, here and there,

frozen forever in different poses, were island ladies wearing grass skirts but otherwise naked save for the flowers in their hair. Their smooth brown skin, their breasts, their smiles were ever inviting. At the center of the painting, off at a distance on the horizon, was depicted an ocean liner with a central funnel issuing a smudgy trail of smoke. Between that ship and the shore, there bobbed a little rowboat with one man at the oars.

I was entranced by that painting and could sit and look at it for long stretches at a time. I'd inspected every inch of it, noticing the bend of the palm leaves, the sweep of the women's hair, the curling edges of the grass skirts, which direction the breeze was blowing and at what rate. I could almost feel it against my face. The cool clear water, the warmth of the island light, lulled me into a trance. I noticed the tiny crabs, shells, starfish on the beach; the monkey peering out from within the fronds of a palm. The most curious item, though, back in the shadows of the bar, just before paradise came to an end by the bathroom door, was a hand, pushing aside the wide leaf of some plant as if it were *you* standing at the edge of the jungle, spying on that man in the rowboat.

Eventually, as time went on and life grew more chaotic, my father stopped going to The Tropics on Sundays. Supporting our family overtook the importance of the Giants, and until my mother passed away only a few years ago, he worked six days a week. When my own bar years began, I never went there as it was considered an old man's bar, but the memory of that mural stayed with me through the passing seasons. At different times in my life when things got hectic, its placid beauty would come back to me, and I'd contemplate living in paradise.

A couple of months ago, I was in West Islip visiting my father, who still lives, alone now, in the same house I grew up in. After dinner we sat in the living room and talked about the old times and what had changed in town since I'd been there last. Eventually, he dozed off in his recliner, and I sat across from him contemplating his life. He seemed perfectly content, but all I could think about were those many years of hard work drawing to a close in an empty house, in a neighborhood where he knew no one. I found the prospect depressing, so as a means of trying to disperse it I decided to go out for a walk. It was a quarter after ten on a weeknight, and the town was very quiet. I traveled up onto Higbee Lane and turned down toward Montauk. As I passed The Tropics, I noticed the door was open and the old beer sign in the window was bubbling. No lie, the jukebox was softly playing Bobby Darin. Through the window I could see that the year-round Christmas lights bordering the mirror behind the bar were lit. On a whim, I decided to go in and have a few, hoping that in the decades since I'd last been in there no one had painted over the mural.

There was only one patron, a guy sitting at the bar, who was so wrinkled he looked like just a bag of skin with a wig, wearing shoes, pants, and a cardigan. He had his eyes closed, but he nodded every now and then to the bartender, who towered over him, a huge, bloated hulk of a man in a T-shirt that only made it a little past the crest of his gut. The bartender was talking almost in whispers, smoking a cigarette. He looked up when I came in, waved, and asked me what I wanted. I ordered a VO and water. When he set my drink down on a coaster in front of me, he said, "Play much hoop lately?" and smirked. I'm no paragon of physical fitness, myself, these days, so I laughed. I took it as a joke on all three of us beat-up castaways in The Tropics. After paying, I chose a table where I could get a good look at the south wall without rudely turning my back on my bar mates.

To my relief, the mural was still there, almost completely intact. Its colors had faded and grown dimmer with the buildup of tobacco smoke through the years, but I beheld paradise once again. Someone had drawn a mustache on one of the hula ladies, and the sight of the indiscretion momentarily made my heart sink. Otherwise, I just sat there, reminiscing and digging the breeze in the palms, the beautiful ocean, the distant ship, that poor bastard still trying to reach the shore. It came to me then that the town should declare the mural a historic treasure or something. My reverie was interrupted when the old guy pushed back his bar stool and slouched toward the door. I watched him as he passed, his eyes glassy, his hand in the air, trembling. "Okay, Bobby," he barked, and then he was out the door.

Bobby, I said to myself, and looked over at the bartender as he started wiping down the bar. When he looked back at me, he smiled, but I turned quickly away and concentrated on the mural again. A couple of seconds later, I snuck another look at him because it was beginning to dawn on me that I knew the guy. He was definitely somebody from the old days, but time had disguised him. I went back to paradise for a few seconds, and there, in the sun and the ocean breeze, I remembered.

Bobby Lennin had been what my mother called a *hood*. He was a couple years ahead of me in school and light years ahead of me in life experience. I'm sure by the time he was in the sixth grade, he'd gotten laid, gotten drunk, and gotten arrested. By high school, he was big, and though always in sloppy shape, with a gut, his biceps were massive and the insatiable look in his eyes left no doubt that he could easily kill you with little remorse. His hair was long and stringy, never washed, and he wore, even in summer, a black leather jacket, jeans, a beer-stained white T-shirt, and thick, steel-toed black boots that could kick a hole in a car door.

I'd seen him fight guys after school by the bridge, guys who were bigger than him, cut with muscles, athletes from the football team. He wasn't even a good boxer; all his swings were these wild, round-house haymakers. He could be bleeding out of his eye and been kicked in the stomach, but he was relentlessly fierce, and wouldn't stop till his opponent was on the ground unconscious. He had a patented throat punch that put the school's quarterback in the hospital. Lennin fought someone almost every day; sometimes he'd even take a swing at a teacher or the principal.

He had a gang, three other misfits in leather jackets, nearly as mean but minus their leader's brains. Whereas Lennin had a wicked sense of humor and a kind of sly intelligence, his followers were confused lunkheads who needed his power and guidance in order to be anyone at all. His constant companion was Cho-cho, who, when a kid in Brooklyn, had been hung by a rival gang to his older brother's. His sister found him before he'd died and cut him down. Ever since, he wore the scar, a melted flesh necklace he tried to hide with the chain of a crucifix. The lack of oxygen to his brain had made him crazy, and when he spoke, in a harsh whisper, usu-ally no one understood him except Lennin.

The second accomplice was Mike Wolfe, whose favorite past time was huffing paint remover in his grandfather's shed. He actu-ally had a lupine look to his face, and with his pencil mustache and sort of pointed ears, reminded me of Oil Can Harry. Then there was Johnny Mars, a thin, wiry guy with a high-pitched, annoying laugh you could light a match on and a strong streak of paranoia. One night, because of some perceived slight by a teacher, he shot out all of the windows on one side of the high school with his old man's .22.

Lennin and his gang scared the shit out of me, but I was lucky, because he liked me. My connection to him went back to when he was younger and played little league football, before he fell totally down the chute into delinquency. He was trouble even back then, but he was a good tackle and played hard. His problem was he didn't take direction all too well and would tell the coaches to fuck off. This was back in the days when saying "fuck" meant something, and it didn't endear him to the folks in charge.

One day when Lennin was in seventh grade, he threw a rock at a passing car up on Higbee and broke the side window. The cops caught him on the side of the road. My father happened to be passing by at the time, saw what was going on, and pulled over. He knew Bobby because my father had been a ref for a lot of the games in the football league. The cops told him they were going to book Lennin, yet somehow my father worked it out with them to let him go. He paid the driver of the car to get his window fixed, and then drove Bobby home.

For whatever reason, maybe because he never knew his own father, that incident stuck with Lennin; and although he couldn't follow the advice my old man gave him that day and would continue to screw up, he took it upon himself to watch out for me as repayment for the kindness shown. The first time I had any inkling that this was the case, I was riding my bike through the grade-school grounds on my way to the basketball courts. To get there, I had to pass by a spot where the hoods played handball against the tall brick wall of the gym. I was always relieved when they weren't there, but that day they were.

Mike Wolfe, eyes red, snarling like his namesake, ran out and grabbed my bike by the handlebars. I didn't say anything; I was too scared. Joey Missoula and Stinky Steinmuller, hood hangers-on, were ambling over to join him in torturing me. Just then Lennin appeared from somewhere with a quart bottle of beer in his hand, and he bellowed, "Leave him alone!" They backed off. Then he said, "Come over here, Ford." He asked me if I wanted any beer, which I turned down, and then told me to hang out if I wanted to.

I didn't want to seem scared or ungrateful, so I stayed for a while sitting on the curb, watching them play handball, while Johnny Mars explained that if you jerked off into a syringe and then gave yourself a shot with it and then fucked your wife, your kid would come out a genius. When I finally rode away, Lennin told me to say hello to my father, and when I was well across the field, he yelled after me, "Have a fucking nice summer."

Lennin's interest in protecting me made it possible for me and my brother to pass through the school field after dark, whereas anyone else would have had their asses beaten. One night we ran into Lennin and his gang down by the woods, where Minerva Street led to the school grounds; he had a silver handgun in his belt. He told us he was waiting for a guy from Brightwaters to show up and they were going to have a duel. "For my honor," he said, and then drained his beer, smashed the bottle against the concrete opening of the sewer pipe, and belched. When a car pulled up on Minerva and blinked its lights on and off twice, he told us we better get going home. We were almost around the block to our house, when in the distance, we heard a gunshot.

Occasionally, Lennin would surface and either save me from some dire situation, like the time I almost got mixed up in a bad dope deal at a party, and he came out of the dark, smacked me in the side of the head, and told me to go home, or I'd hear about him through gossip. He and his gang were forever in trouble with the cops—knife fights, joy rides in hot-wired cars, breaking and entering. I know each of them did some time in juvenile lockup in Central Islip before I graduated. Finally, I finished high school, moved away from home to go to college, and lost track of him.

Now I was in The Tropics, just coming out of a daydream of paradise and the past, and there he was, standing at my table, holding a bottle of VO, a bucket of ice and a tumbler, looking like someone had taken him down to the gas station and put the air hose in his mouth.

"You don't remember me, do you?" he asked.

"I thought it was you," I said, and smiled. "Bobby Lennin." I stuck my hand out to shake.

He laid the bottle and bucket on the table and then reached out and shook my hand. His grip didn't have any trace of the old power.

He sat down across from me and filled my glass before pouring one for himself.

"What are you doin' here?" he asked.

"I came in to see the mural," I said.

He smiled and nodded wistfully, as if he completely understood. "You visiting your old man?" he asked.

"Yeah, just for an overnight."

"I saw him in the grocery store a couple of weeks ago," said Bobby. "I said hi but he just nodded and smiled. I don't think he remembers me."

"You never know," I said. "He does the same thing with me half the time now."

He laughed and then asked about my brother and sisters. I told him my mother had passed away, and he said his mother had also died quite a while back. He lit a cigarette and then reached over to another table to get an ashtray. "What are you up to?" he asked.

I told him I was teaching college and also that I was a writer. Then I asked if he still saw Cho-cho and the other guys. He blew out a stream of smoke and shook his head. "Nah," he said, looking kind of sad, and we sat there quietly for a time. I didn't know what to say.

"You're a writer?" he asked. "What do you write?"

"Stories and novels—you know, fiction," I said.

His eyes lit up a little and he poured another drink for each of us. "I got a story for you," he told me. "You asked about Cho-cho and the gang? I got a wild fuckin' story for you."

"Let's hear it," I said.

"This all happened a long time ago, after you left town but before Howie sold the pizza place, around the time Phil the barber's kid got knocked off at the track," he said.

"Yeah, I remember my mother telling me about that," I said.

"Well, anyway, none of us, me, Cho-cho, Wolfey, the Martian, ever graduated high school, and we were all hanging out doing the same old shit, only it was getting deeper all the time. We were all drinking and drugging and beginning to pull some serious capers, like once we broke into the grocery store and stole a couple hundred dollars worth of cigarettes, or we'd heist a car now and then and sell it to a chop shop one of Mars's relatives owned. Occasionally we'd get caught and do a little time, a couple of months here or there.

"We weren't pros by any means, and so we would have to get real jobs from time to time, and, of course, the jobs all sucked. One night I was in here having a few beers, and this guy came in who I remembered from high school. Your brother would probably remember him. Anyway, he starts talking to the bartender. Remember old man Ryan?"

"Yeah," I said. "He served me my first drink—a Shirley Temple."

Lennin laughed and went on. "Well, this guy was back in town, and he'd graduated from college with a degree in engineering, had a cushy job at Grumman, was getting married, and had just bought a big house down by the bay. I overheard this, and I thought to myself, shit, I could go for some of that. But there was no way it was going to happen. And as a matter of fact, I was looking at the mural and thinking I was like that guy in the boat in the painting there, stuck forever outside the good life. In other words I was starting to see that the outlaw scene was going to get very old very soon.

"Now, I'm not crying in my beer, but let's face it, me and the group didn't have much help in life—busted homes, alcoholic parents, head problems . . . We were pretty fucked from word *go*. It was easier for us to scare people into respecting us than it was ever going to be for them to just do it on their own. It seemed like everyone else was heading for the light and we were still down in the shadows munching crumbs. I wanted to be on the beach, so to speak. I wanted a home and a wife and kid and long quiet nights watching the tube and holidays. As for the other guys, I don't think they got it. Shit, if God would have let them, they'd still be muscling high school kids for pocket change.

"Since it was clear I wasn't going to get there by regular means, I decided what we needed was one big heist, one real job in order to get the cash necessary to live in the real world. After that, I'd part company with them and move on. So I spent a long time thinking about what kind of scam we could pull, but I was blank. We'd spent so many years nickel-and-diming, I couldn't get out of that head. Until, one night, we were sitting at that table right over there, drinking, and a ragged, hopped-up Wolfey, eyes showing almost nothing but white, mentioned something, and I thought I felt the rowboat move a few feet closer to shore.

"This old guy had just moved in on Wolfey's block. What is it, over there by Minerva, Alice Road? Anyway, this old guy, blind, in a wheelchair, moved in. Remember Willie Hart, the guy in high school with the plastic arm? Well, his younger sister Maria, who, by the way, the Wolfeman was banging every once in a while back in his grandfather's shed in between hits of Zippoway, went to work for the old guy. She cleaned his house and would take him out for walks in his wheelchair and so forth.

"Maria told Wolfey that the old fart was super strange, and although he understood English, he always spoke to himself in another language she thought was Spanish. Maria, if you remember her, was no genius, and for all she knew the guy could have been talking fucking Chinese. Anyway, she said he was kind of feeble in the head, because he had this chess set he would take out and play against himself. She asked him once if he was winning or losing, and he responded, 'Always losing. Always losing.'

"What really caught her interest, though, were the pieces. She said they were beautiful, golden monsters. The guy didn't like to be disturbed in the middle of a game, but she had to ask him if they were real gold. He told her, 'Yes, solid gold. This set is very rare, worth hundreds of thousands of dollars. Very old—goes back to the sixteenth century.' The best part of Maria's story was that he kept the set in a drawer in his hutch—no lock.

"So we had a blind guy in a wheelchair with hundreds of thousands of dollars of gold without a lock. Of course, I made a plan to swipe it. I had Wolfe get Maria to tell him what time she walked the guy—Mr. Desnia was his name—in the afternoon, so we could get a look at him. I thought about doing the job when they were out of the house, but in that neighborhood during daylight hours, I knew someone would see us. We drove by them slowly a couple of days later as she pushed him down the street.

He was bent over in the chair, his bald head like a shelled peanut, looking thin and haggard. His hands shook slightly. He wore dark glasses, no doubt to cover his fucked up eyes, and a black, tight fitting get-up like what a priest would wear but with no white collar. 'That's the guy with our gold,' I said after we drove past them. 'A blind guy in a wheelchair?' said Mars. 'Jesus, he might as well just hand it over now.' We decided not to wait but to do the job the next night.

"The cops had our prints, so we went and stole some plastic gloves from the grocery store, you know, the kind you could pick up a dime with. We told Maria we'd cut her in if she kept her mouth shut and left the back door unlocked on her way out the night of the job. She agreed, I think because she was in love with Wolfe, which shows you where her head was at. I warned the other guys, whatever they did, not to speak each other's names during the job. The plan was to get in there, cut the phone wire, put a gag over the old guy's mouth, and swipe the gold. Plain and simple, no one had to get hurt.

"The big night came and we spent the early part of it here, in The Tropics, building up our courage with shots of Jack. When it got to be about midnight, we set out in Mars's Pontiac. We parked on the next street over, snuck through the yard there, and scaled this ten-foot stockade-like fence into Desnia's backyard. We were all a little high, and climbing over was rough. I didn't bother bringing a flashlight, 'cause I figured if the guy was blind we could just turn the lights on, but I did bring a pillowcase to carry the gold in and a crowbar in case Maria was wrong about the lock.

"Maria had left the back door open as planned. We sent Cho-cho in first, as usual. Then, one at a time, we entered into the kitchen. The lights were out there and it was perfectly quiet in the house. All I remember hearing was the wall clock ticking off the seconds. A light was shining in the next room over, the living room. I peeked around the corner and saw Desnia sitting in his wheel-chair, a big blanket covering his legs and midsection, dark glasses on. If he could see, he would have been looking straight at me, which was a little nerve-wracking. To his left was the hutch.

" 'Let's go,' I whispered.

"The second I spoke, he called out, 'Who's there? Maria?'

"Cho-cho moved around behind Desnia with a piece of duct tape for his mouth. Mars said to him, 'Take it easy and you won't get hurt.' Wolfe stood there looking confused, as if he had just come off his high. I got down on my haunches and had to open two draw-ers of the hutch before I found the board and pieces. It struck me as odd that he didn't keep them in a box or a bag or something, but the entire board was set up inside the drawer. It took only a second to swipe every one of them up and toss them in the pillowcase. I didn't bother with the board.

"I was just going to tell the others, 'Let's get out of here,' when Desnia reached up and pulled the tape off his mouth. Cho-cho tried to lean over and stop him, but the old man drove his fist straight up, connected with Cho-cho under the chin, and sent him sprawling backward into the corner of the room where he knocked over a lamp and fell on his back.

"With his other hand, the old man flung something at Wolfe that moved through the air so fast I could hardly see it. A split second later, Mike had his hand to the side of his head and there was a sharp piece of metal sticking out of it, blood running down across his face. He went over like a ton of shit. Me and Mars were in shock, neither of us moving, when Desnia flung off the blanket and pulled out this big fucking sword. I'm not shitting you, this sword was like something out of a movie. Then he leaped out of the chair. That's when Johnny decided it was time to book. Too late, though; the old guy jumped forward into a crouch, swung that sword around, and took a slice out of Mars's leg like you wouldn't believe. I mean the blood just sort of fell out all over the place and from the lower thigh down was hanging on by a piece of gristle. He hit the deck and started howling like a banshee.

"Desnia wasn't done yet, though. Following the slash on Johnny, he twirled around toward me like a goddamn dancer, and swung the sword again. Luckily, I had the crowbar and held it up in front of me at the last second. It deflected the blow but the blade still cut me on the left side of my chest. I don't know where it came from, just an automatic reaction, but I swung the crowbar and took him out at the ankles. As he went down, I looked up and saw Cho-cho crawling out through an open window. I dropped the crowbar, grabbed the pillowcase tight, ran across the room, and dove head-first right behind him.

"Man, I wasn't even on my feet before Desnia was sticking his bald head out the window, getting ready to leap through after us. We ran into the backyard, to a corner where there was a shed with a light over it, but there was that damn ten-foot fence. My first thought was to try to jump it, but forget it, Desnia was already there behind us. He would have just slashed our asses. We backed against the fence and got ready to brawl.

"He walked slowly up to us, with the blade at his side. In the light from over the shed, I could see he had lost his glasses, and I don't know how he could have swung that sword the way he did, because his eyes weren't just fucked up, he had none. No eyes, just two puckered little assholes in his head.

"When Desnia was no more than three feet away, Cho-cho held up the crucifix that hung around his neck, like in a vampire movie, to protect himself. The old guy laughed without hardly a sound. Then he lifted the sword slowly, brought it to Cho-cho's neck, and with a flick of the wrist just nicked him so he started to bleed. With that, Desnia dropped the sword and turned around. He took two steps away from us and his legs buckled. He went down like a sack of turnips. In the distance I could hear Johnny still screaming like mad, and above his racket the sound of the police siren. Cho-cho and I used the side of the shed to scrabble up over the fence, and we got away with the gold.

"Sounds crazy, right? The old man turning into fucking Zorro at the drop of a hat? But I'm telling you it was serious. The Martian died that night on the old man's living room rug. The blade had sliced an artery and he bled out before the ambulance could get there. On top of that, the old man was found dead from a heart attack. But get this, Wolfey got away. While we were out in the backyard up against the fence, he came to, pulled the metal thing out of his head, and split before the cops got there.

"We left Mars's car where it was and he took the rap for the whole caper. Maria kept her mouth shut. We all went into hiding, laying low for a while. I had the chess pieces stashed under a loose floorboard in my mother's bedroom. What was good was that I was pretty sure no one else even knew Desnia had the chess pieces, so the cops didn't know they were stolen. I thought if we just chilled for a while, I could fence them and we'd be set. Still, I was spooked by what had happened, Johnny's death and the way it went down. I could feel something wasn't right.

"About two months after the heist, I got a call at like three in the morning from Cho-cho. He said he knew he wasn't supposed to call but he couldn't take it anymore. He was having these dreams that scared him so much he couldn't sleep. I asked him what he was dreaming about and he just said, 'Really evil shit.' A month after that, I heard from someone that he'd finished the job they started on him in Brooklyn when he was a kid. He'd hung himself in his mother's attic.

"The year wasn't out before both Maria and Wolfe went down too. I'd heard that he'd taken to staying in his grandfather's shed all the time. She was joining him now on a regular basis, and they had begun taking pills, ludes and Darvon, and drinking while huffing the Zippoway, and that just ate what little there was of their brains, melted that Swiss cheese like acid one night. I should have been sadder at losing all my friends, but instead I was just scared to death and started living the clean life, laying off the booze and dope and getting to my crappy job at the metal shop every day on time. I never even went to Cho-cho's funeral.

"After that year ended, I let another six months go by before I started looking around for a fence. I knew it would have to be somebody high class, who dealt in antiques but was willing to look the other way when it came to how you acquired what you were selling. I did some studying up on the way it worked and spoke to a few connections. Eventually, I got the phone number of a guy in New York and the green light to give him a call. Nothing in person until he checked out you and the goods you claimed to have.

"I got the pieces out from under the floorboards and really looked at them for the first time. The bigger pieces were about four inches tall, and the smaller ones, which I guessed were pawns—I didn't know shit then about chess—were three inches. They definitely seemed to be made of solid gold. Half of them were figures of monsters, each one different, the work on them really detailed. The other half, I don't know what they were, but I recognized one as being Christ. The smaller ones looked like angels. I couldn't make heads or tails of it.

"The day finally came when I was supposed to call the guy, which I did, from the pay phone in the back of Phil's barbershop. I was nervous, you know, sweating how much I was gonna get and still scared at all the ill stuff that had gone down. Well, the phone rings, a guy answers, he tells me, 'No names. Describe what you have.' So I told him, 'Gold chess set from the sixteenth century.' But the minute I started describing the individual pieces, the line went dead. That was it. At first I thought it was just a bad connection, or I needed more change. I called back, but no one would pick up.

"Then shit started to really slide. Dreams like Cho-cho described, and I took to drinking again, but drinking in a way I never did before. I lost my job, and on top of it all my mother got the cancer. I was reeling and it took me a while, like two years, to get it together to deal with the damn gold again. Just by luck, I guess, I ran into a guy who knew this guy, a Dominican, who fenced stuff from break-ins out in the Hamptons. I met him one winter afternoon over in the parking lot at Jones Beach. Thinking it might be a setup, I only took three pieces with me.

"The wind was blowing like a motherfucker that day. It was like a sandstorm even in the parking lot. The guy was there when I pulled up, sitting in a shiny black Cadillac. We got out of the cars. He was short, dark-skinned, wore sunglasses and a raincoat. We shook hands, and he asked to see what I had. I took two of the pieces out and held them up for him to see. He took one look at them and said, 'Isiaso,' and then made a face like I was holding a couple of turds. The guy didn't say anything else, he just turned around, got in his car, and drove away.

"And that's the way it went trying to fence them. I'd give it a shot, be turned down, and then get swamped in a lot of bad circumstance. Then I just wanted to unload them and take whatever I could get. Even this guy, Bowes, who bought gold teeth down on Canal Street in the city wouldn't touch them. He called them *La Ventaja del Demonio*, and threatened to call the cops if I didn't leave his shop. It wasn't until after my mother passed away that I decided to try to find out about them.

"Imagine me, Bobby Lennin, failer of classes and king of detention, in the library. I don't think I'd ever been in the fucking place in my life. But I started there, and you know what? I discovered I wasn't as stupid as I looked. There was some real pleasure in researching them. It was the only thing that offset the depression of drinking. In the meantime, old man Ryan took pity on me and gave me a job bartending here at The Tropics. I barely managed to keep myself from getting too screwed up until he went home in the evening, so as to keep the job.

"Yeah, I scoured the library, got interlibrary loans, all that good stuff, and I started to crack the story on the chess set. Then, when the Internet came in, I got with that too, and over a period of long years, I put it together. The set was known as *The Demon's Advantage*. Scholars talked about it like it was more a legend than anything that actually existed. It was supposedly crafted by this goldsmith in Italy, Dario Foresso, in 1533, commissioned by a strange cat who went by the name of Isiaso. The dude had no last name as far as I could tell.

"Anyway, this Isiaso was from Hispaniola, now the Dominican Republic. In 1503, I think it was Pope Julius II declared Santo Domingo an official city of Christendom. It was the jumping-off place for European explorers who were headed to South and North America. Isiaso was born the year the pope gave the two-fingered salute to the city. Our boy's father was Spanish, an attaché to the crown, there to oversee the money to be spent on expeditions. You know, basically an accountant. But his mother was a native, and—here's where it gets creepy—said to be from a long line of sorcerers.

She was an adept of the island magic. Isiaso, who was supposed to be like a genius kid, learned the ways of both parents.

"When he was in his twenties, his old man ships him off to Rome to finish his education. He goes to the university and studies with the great philosophers and theologists of the time. It was during these years that he comes to see the battle between Good and Evil in terms of chess—the dark versus the light, etc., with the advantage going back and forth. Strategy was part of it, and mathematics along with faith, but, to tell you the truth, I never really completely understood what he was getting at.

"Somehow Isiaso gains wealth and power very quickly. Rises to the top of the heap. No one can figure out how he came by his wealth and those who cross him meet with weird and ugly deaths. Anyway, he has the funds to get Foresso to undertake the set. And Foresso is no slouch—an apprentice to Benvenuto Cellini, greatest goldsmith who ever lived. 'Many thought Foresso was his master's equal' was how one book put it.

"Okay, you with me? Enter Pope Paul III, a later successor to Julius II. He's this big patron of the arts. Michelangelo worked for him at one time. He hears tell of this incredible chess set being created by Foresso and goes to the guy's studio and checks it out. Later, he lets it be known to his underlings that he wants the chess set for himself. He sends someone to see Isiaso, and the guy tells him the pope wants to buy it off him. Isiaso has other plans. He knows the Vatican's going to be funding a university in Santo Domingo, and he tells him what he wants in exchange is passage home and a professor job at the university. I got the idea from my reading that it might have been difficult for him to get the job because he was half-native.

"He's surprised when the pope's go-between says, 'Cool, we'll cut the deal.' What Isiaso doesn't know is that the Vatican has had their eye on him as a troublemaker, and they want him out of Rome anyway. On the voyage home, the ship drops anchor for a day off a small, uninhabited island. Isiaso is asked if he would like to go ashore and witness a true paradise on Earth. Being a curious guy, he says yes. He and a sailor go to the island in a rowboat. They explore the place; but in the middle of looking around, Isiaso suddenly realizes that he's alone. When he makes it back to the beach, he sees the sailor in the rowboat heading back to the ship.

"The ship pulls up anchor and splits, stranding him there. It was the plan all along. They wanted him out of Rome, but they were too afraid of his supposed magic to come right out and boot his ass.

So they got the chess set *and* got rid of him, and the legend has it that he put a curse on the chess set. Legend also has it that if you play the demon side of the board, you can never lose. You could play fucking Gary Kasparov and not lose. But at the same time, the person who owns it is doomed, cursed, screwed, blued, and tattooed, and you can't give it away, you can't throw it away. Believe me, I've tried and it's a shit-storm of misery and the dreams just get too intense. The only way to unload it is to have it stolen from you, and in the process blood must be drawn. Die with it in your possession, and you ain't going to be seeing paradise.

"Now," said Lennin, "what do you think of that? I swear on my mother's grave that it's all completely true." He lifted the bottle and filled each of our glasses. "And the biggest kicker of all is that I dug all this up on my own. Man, I could have gotten through high school and college, for Christ sake."

"So, you believe in the curse?" I asked.

"I'm not gonna bore you with how many times I tried to dump the pieces," he said.

"You don't seem cursed, though," I said.

"Well, there's cursed and then there's cursed. Look at me. I'm a wreck. My liver is shot. I've been in and out of the hospital five times in the last year. They told me if I don't quit drinking, I'm gonna die very soon."

"What about some kind of addiction center where they can treat you?" I asked.

"I've tried it," he said. "I just can't stop. It's my part of the curse. I'm in here every day, throwing back the booze, it doesn't matter what kind it is, and staring at that mural, a castaway like Isiaso. It doesn't make any sense, but I swear that's his hand in the picture, down in the corner by the bathroom. All my attempts at relationships went south, all my plans to better myself dried up and blew away. I'm slowly killing myself. You see," he said, lifting his shirt to show me his sagging chest, "the scar is right here, over my heart, and my heart is poisoned."

"I don't know what to say," I told him. "You were always kind to me when I was a kid."

"Thanks," he said. "Maybe if I can unload the set eventually that'll be at least one thing on the scale in my favor." He got up then and went behind the bar. When he came back, he was carrying a chessboard and on it were the golden pieces. He laid it down on the table between us.

"Man, they're beautiful," I told him.

"Listen, you gotta get going home now," he said, the same as he had so many years ago. "I had a couple of rough-looking characters in here the other day, and I showed them the set, told them how much it was worth and that I kept it behind the bar all the time. It's getting past midnight, and there's a chance they'll show up. I know the old man let Maria see it and told her about it for the same reason I've been flaunting it lately. Maybe when they come for it, I'll get some of the old juice back like Desnia did, and we'll have a good brawl."

I stood up, a little wobbly from the bottle of VO we'd finished. "There's no other way?" I asked.

He shook his head.

I turned and took in the mural one last time, because I knew I would never come back again. Bobby looked it over too.

"You know," he said, "I bet you always thought that guy in the boat was trying to get to the island, right?"

"Yeah," I said.

"The truth is, he's been trying to escape all these years. Those women look like women to you, but count 'em—there are as many as there are pieces in a chess set."

"I hope he makes it," I said, and then reached out and shook Bobby's hand.

Leaving The Tropics behind, I stepped onto the sidewalk and stood there for a minute to get my bearings. The night was cold, and I realized autumn was only a week away. I turned my collar up and walked along, searching my mind, without success, for the warmth from that painted vision of paradise. Instead, all I could think of was my old man, sitting in his recliner, smiling like the Buddha, while the world he once knew slowly disintegrated around him. I turned off Higbee onto my block and was nearly home, when from somewhere away in the distance, I heard a gunshot.

A Night in the Tropics
Story Notes

I think I had my old boy, Kipling, in mind when I wrote this one. I'd been rereading a lot of my favorite stories of his, especially "The Gate of a Hundred Sorrows," just before I wrote it. "A Night in the Tropics" was populated with characters right out of central casting from my early days in West Islip. The bar and the painting actually did exist. I know the bar is still there. In fact, a guy I grew up with now owns it, but I haven't been in to check up on the painting in about fifteen years. The part about the gang robbing a blind man who pulled a sword on them is a true tale, as is a goodly portion of the rest of the story. Fellow writer, Rick Bowes, the Albert Schweitzer of story doctors, read the piece in an early draft and suggested a few key changes that really made a big difference. As a tip of the hat to him, I used his name for the guy in the story who buys gold teeth down on Canal Street. This story was written for Lou Anders for the first issue of the new Argosy Magazine. *No doubt by some enchantment of Isiaso's magic, the story clawed its way onto* Locus's Best of the Best *list for 2003.*

The Empire of Ice Cream

ARE YOU FAMILIAR WITH THE SCENT OF EXTIN-
guished birthday candles? For me, their aroma is superseded
by a sound like the drawing of a bow across the bass string of a violin. This note carries all of the melancholic joy I have been told the
scent engenders—the loss of another year, the promise of accrued
wisdom. Likewise, the notes of an acoustic guitar appear before my
eyes as a golden rain, falling from a height just above my head only
to vanish at the level of my solar plexus. There is a certain imported
Swiss cheese I am fond of that is all triangles, whereas the feel of
silk against my fingers rests on my tongue with the flavor and consistency of lemon meringue. These perceptions are not merely
thoughts, but concrete physical experiences. Depending upon how
you see it, I, like approximately nine out of every million individuals, am either cursed or blessed with a condition known as *synesthesia*.

It has only recently come to light that the process of synesthesia
takes place in the hippocampus, part of the ancient limbic system,
where remembered perceptions triggered in diverse geographical
regions of the brain as the result of an external stimulus come
together. It is believed that everyone, at a point somewhere below
consciousness, experiences this coinciding of sensory association,
yet in most it is filtered out and only a single sense is given predom-
inance in one's waking world. For we lucky few, the filter is broken

or perfected, and what is usually subconscious becomes conscious. Perhaps, at some distant point in history, our early ancestors were completely synesthetic and touched, heard, smelled, tasted, and saw, at once, each specific incident, the mixing of sensoric memory along with the perceived sense, without affording precedence to the findings of one of the five portals through which "reality" invades us. The scientific explanations, as far as I can follow them, seem to make sense now, but when I was young and told my parents about the whisper of vinyl, the stench of purple, the spinning blue gyres of the church bell, they feared I was defective and that my mind was brimming with hallucinations like an abandoned house choked with ghosts.

As an only child, I wasn't afforded the luxury of being anomalous. My parents were well on in years—my mother nearly forty, my father already forty-five—when I arrived after a long parade of failed pregnancies. The fact that, at age five, I heard what I described as an angel crying whenever I touched velvet would never be allowed to stand, but was seen as an illness to be cured by whatever methods were available. Money was no object in the pursuit of perfect normalcy. And so my younger years were a torment of hours spent in the waiting rooms of psychologists, psychiatrists, and therapists. I can't find words to describe the depths of medical quackery I was subjected to by a veritable army of so-called professionals who diagnosed me with everything from schizophrenia to bipolar depression to low IQ caused by muddled potty training. Being a child, I was completely honest with them about what I experienced, and this, my first mistake, resulted in blood tests, brain scans, special diets, and the forced consumption of a demon's pharmacopeia of mind-deadening drugs that diminished my will but not the vanilla scent of slanting golden sunlight on late autumn afternoons.

My only-child status along with the added complication of my "condition," as they called it, led my parents to perceive me as fragile. For this reason I was kept fairly isolated from other children. Part of it, I'm sure, had to do with the way my abnormal perceptions and utterances would reflect upon my mother and father, for they were the type of people who could not bear to be thought of as having been responsible for the production of defective goods. I was tutored at home by my mother instead of being allowed to attend school. She was actually a fine teacher, having a PhD in history and a firm grasp of classical literature. My father, an actuary, taught me math, and in this subject I proved to be an unquestionable failure until I reached college age. Although x=y might have been a suitable metaphor for the phenomenon of synesthesia, it made no sense on paper. The number 8, by the way, reeks of withered flowers.

What I *was* good at was music. Every Thursday at 3:00 in the afternoon, Mrs. Brithnic would arrive at the house to give me a piano lesson. She was a kind old lady with thinning white hair and the most beautiful fingers—long and smooth, as if they belonged to a graceful young giantess. Although something less than a virtuoso at the keys, she was a veritable genius at teaching me to allow myself to enjoy the sounds I produced. Enjoy them I did, and when I wasn't being dragged hither and yon in the pursuit of losing my affliction, home base for me was the piano bench. In my imposed isolation from the world, music became a window of escape I would crawl through as often as possible.

When I would play, I could see the notes before me like a fireworks display of colors and shapes. By my twelfth year I was writing my own compositions, and my notations on the pages accompanying the notes referred to the visual displays that coincided with them. In actuality, when I played, I was really painting—in midair before my eyes—great abstract works in the tradition of Kandinsky. Many times, I planned a composition on a blank piece of paper using the crayon set of sixty-four colors I'd had since early childhood. The only difficulty in this was with colors like magenta and cobalt blue, which I perceive primarily as tastes, so I would have to write them down in pencil as licorice and tapioca on my colorfully scribbled drawing where they would appear in the music.

My punishment for having excelled at the piano was to lose my only real friend, Mrs. Brithnic. I remember distinctly the day my mother let her go. She calmly nodded, smiling, understanding that I had already surpassed her abilities. Still, though I knew this was the case, I cried when she hugged me goodbye. When her face was next to mine, she whispered into my ear, "Seeing is believing," and in that moment I knew she had completely understood my plight. Her lilac perfume, the sound of one nearly inaudible B-flat played by an oboe, still hung about me as I watched her walk down the path and out of my life for good.

I believe it was the loss of Mrs. Brithnic that made me rebel. I became desultory and despondent. Then one day, soon after my thirteenth birthday, instead of obeying my mother, who had just told me to finish reading a textbook chapter while she showered, I went to her pocketbook, took five dollars, and left the house. As I walked along beneath the sunlight and blue sky, the world around me seemed brimming with life. What I wanted more than anything else was to meet other young people my own age. I remembered an ice-cream shop in town where, when passing by in the car returning from whatever doctor's office we had been to, there always seemed to be kids hanging around. I headed directly for that spot while wondering if my mother would catch up to me before I made it. When I pictured her drying her hair, I broke into a run.

Upon reaching the row of stores that contained The Empire of Ice Cream, I was out of breath as much from the sheer exhilaration of freedom as from the half-mile sprint. Peering through the glass of the front door was like looking through a portal into an exotic other world. Here were young people, my age, gathered in groups at tables, talking, laughing, eating ice cream—not by night, after dinner, but in the middle of broad daylight. I opened the door and plunged in. The magic of the place seemed to brush by me on its way out as I entered, for the conversation instantly died away. I stood in the momentary silence as all heads turned to stare at me.

"Hello," I said, smiling, and raised my hand in greeting, but I was too late. They had already turned away, the conversation resumed, as if they had merely afforded a grudging glimpse to see the door open and close at the behest of the wind. I was paralyzed by my inability to make an impression, the realization that finding friends was going to take some real work.

"What'll it be?" said a large man behind the counter.

I broke from my trance and stepped up to order. Before me, beneath a bubble dome of glass, lay the Empire of Ice Cream. I'd never seen so much of the stuff in so many colors and incarnations —with nuts and fruit, cookie and candy bits, mystical swirls the sight of which sounded to me like a distant siren. There were deep vats of it set in neat rows totaling thirty flavors. My diet had never allowed for the consumption of confections or desserts of any type, and rare were the times I had so much as a thimbleful of vanilla ice cream after dinner. Certain doctors had told my parents that my eating these treats might seriously exacerbate my condition. With this in mind, I ordered a large bowl of coffee ice cream. My choice of coffee stemmed from the fact that that beverage was another item on the list of things I should never taste.

After paying, I took my bowl and spoon and found a seat in the corner of the place from which I could survey all the other tables. I admit that I had some trepidations about digging right in, since I'd been warned against it for so long by so many adults. Instead, I scanned the shop, watching the other kids talking, trying to overhear snatches of conversation. I made eye contact with a boy my own age two tables away. I smiled and waved to him. He saw me and then leaned over and whispered something to the other fellows he was with. All four of them turned, looked at me, and then broke into laughter. It was a certainty they were making fun of me, but I basked in the victory of merely being noticed. With this, I took a large spoonful of ice cream and put it in my mouth.

There is an attendant phenomenon of the synesthetic experience I have yet to mention. Of course I had no term for it at this point in my life, but when one is in the throes of the remarkable transference of senses, it is accompanied by a feeling of "epiphany," a "eureka" of contentment that researchers of the anomalous condition would later term *noetic*, borrowing from William James. That first taste of coffee ice cream elicited a deeper noetic response than I'd ever before felt, and along with it came the appearance of a girl. She coalesced out of thin air and stood before me, obscuring my sight of the group that was still laughing. Never before had I seen through tasting, hearing, touching, smelling, something other than simple abstract shapes and colors.

She was turned somewhat to the side and hunched over, wearing a plaid skirt and a white blouse. Her hair was the same dark brown as my own, but long and gathered in the back with a green rubber band. There was a sudden shaking of her hand, and it became clear to me that she was putting out a match. Smoke swirled away from her. I could see now that she had been lighting a cigarette. I got the impression that she was wary of being caught in the act of smoking. When she turned her head sharply to look back over her shoulder, I dropped the spoon on the table. Her look instantly enchanted me.

As the ice cream melted away down my throat, she began to vanish, and I quickly lifted the spoon to restoke my vision, but it never reached my lips. She suddenly went out like a light when I felt something land softly upon my left shoulder. I heard the incomprehensible murmur of recrimination, and knew it as my mother's touch. She had found me. A great wave of laughter accompanied my removal from The Empire of Ice Cream. Later I would remember the incident with embarrassment, but for the moment, even as I spoke words of apology to my mother, I could think only of what I'd seen.

The ice-cream incident—followed hard by the discovery of the cigar box of pills I hid in my closet, all of the medication that I'd supposedly swallowed for the past six months—led my parents to believe that heaped upon my condition was now a tendency toward delinquency that would grow, if unchecked, in geometrical proportion with the passing of years. It was decided that I should see yet another specialist to deal with my behavior, a therapist my father had read about who would prompt me to talk my willfulness into submission. I was informed of this in a solemn meeting with my parents. What else was there to do but acquiesce? I knew that my mother and father wanted, in their pedestrian way, what they believed was best for me. Whenever the situation would infuriate me, I would go to the piano and play, sometimes for three or four hours at a time.

Dr. Stullin's office was in a ramshackle Victorian house on the other side of town. My father accompanied me on the first visit, and, when he pulled up in front of the sorry old structure, he checked the address at least twice to make sure we'd come to the right place. The doctor, a round little man with a white beard and glasses with small circular lenses, met us at the front door. Why he laughed when we shook hands at the introductions, I hadn't a clue, but he was altogether jolly, like a pint-sized Santa Claus dressed in a wrinkled brown suit one size too small. He swept out his arm to usher me into his house, but when my father tried to enter, the doctor held up his hand and said, "You will return in one hour and five minutes."

My father gave some weak protest and said that he thought he might be needed to help discuss my history to this point. Here the doctor's demeanor instantly changed. He became serious, official, almost commanding.

"I'm being paid to treat the boy. You will have to find your own therapist."

My father was obviously at a loss. He looked as if he was about to object, but the doctor said, "One hour and five minutes." Following me inside, he quickly shut the door behind him.

As he led me through a series of unkempt rooms lined with crammed bookshelves, and one in which piles of paper covered the tops of tables and desks, he said, laughing, "Parents—so essential, yet sometimes like something you have stepped in and cannot get off your shoe. What else is there but to love them?"

We wound up in a room at the back of the house made from a skeleton of thin steel girders and paneled with glass panes. The sunlight poured in, and surrounding us, at the edges of the place, and also hanging from some of the girders, were green plants. There was a small table on which sat a teapot and two cups and saucers. As I took the seat he motioned for me to sit in, I looked out through the glass and saw that the backyard was one large, magnificent garden, blooming with all manner of colorful flowers.

After he poured me a cup of tea, the questioning began. I'd had it in my mind to be as recalcitrant as possible, but there was something in the manner in which he had put my father off that I admired about him. Also, he was unlike other therapists I had been to, who would listen to my answers with complete reservation of emotion or response. When he asked why I was here and I told him it was because I had escaped in order to go to the ice-cream shop, he scowled and said, "Patently ridiculous." I was unsure if he meant me or my mother's response to what I'd done. I told him about playing the piano, and he smiled warmly and nodded. "That is a good thing," he said.

After he asked me about my daily routine and my home life, he sat back and said, "So, what's the problem? Your father has told me that you hallucinate. Can you explain?"

No matter how ingratiating he had been, I'd already decided that I would no longer divulge any of my perceptions to anyone. Then he did something unexpected.

"Do you mind?" he asked as he took out a pack of cigarettes.

Before I could shake my head no, he had one out of the pack and lit. Something about this, perhaps because I'd never seen a doctor smoke in front of a patient before, perhaps because it reminded me of the girl who had appeared before me in the ice-cream shop, weakened my resolve to say nothing. When he flicked his ashes into his half-empty teacup, I started talking. I told him about the taste of silk, the various corresponding colors for the notes of the piano, the nauseating stench of purple.

I laid the whole thing out for him and then sat back in my chair, now somewhat regretting my weakness, for he was smiling and the smoke was leaking out of the corners of his mouth. He exhaled, and in that cloud came the word that would validate me, define me, and haunt me for the rest of my life—*synesthesia*.

By the time I left Stullin's office that day, I was a new person. The doctor spoke to my father and explained the phenomenon to him. He cited historical cases and gave him the same general overview of the neurological workings of the condition. He also added that most synesthetes don't experience the condition in such a variety of senses as I did, although it was not unheard of. My father nodded every now and then but was obviously perplexed at the fact that my long-suffered *condition* had, in an instant, vanished.

"There's nothing wrong with the boy," said Stullin, "except for the fact that he is, in a way, exceptional. Think of it as a gift, an original way of sensing the world. These perceptions are as real for him as are your own to you."

Stullin's term for my condition was like a magic incantation from a fairy tale, for through its power I was released from the spell of my parents' control. In fact, their reaction to it was to almost completely relinquish interest in me, as if after all of their intensive care I'd been found out to be an imposter now unworthy of their attention. When it became clear that I would have the ability to go about my life as any normal child might, I relished the concept of freedom. The sad fact was, though, that I didn't know how to. I lacked all experience at being part of society. My uncertainty made me shy, and my first year in public school was a disaster. What I wanted was a friend my own age, and this goal continued to elude me until I was well out of high school and in college. My desperation to connect made me ultimately nervous, causing me to act and speak without reserve. This was the early 1960s, and if anything was important in high school social circles at the time, it was remaining *cool*. I was the furthest thing from cool you might imagine.

For protection, I retreated into my music and spent hours working out compositions with my crayons and pens, trying to corral the sounds and resultant visual pyrotechnics, odors, and tastes into cohesive scores. All along, I continued practicing and improving my abilities at the keyboard, but I had no desire to become a performer. Quite a few of my teachers through the years had it in their minds that they could shape me into a brilliant concert pianist. I would not allow it, and when they insisted, I'd drop them and move on. Nothing frightened me more than the thought of sitting in front of a crowd of onlookers. The weight of judgment lurking behind even one set of those imagined eyes was too much for me to bear. I'd stayed on with Stullin, visiting once a month, and no matter his persistent proclamations as to my relative normalcy, it was impossible for me, after years of my parents' insisting otherwise, to erase the fact that I was, in my own mind, a freak.

My greatest pleasure away from the piano at this time was to take the train into the nearby city and attend concerts given by the local orchestra or small chamber groups that would perform in more intimate venues. Rock and roll was all the rage, but my training at the piano and the fact that calm solitude, as opposed to raucous socializing, was the expected milieu of the symphony drew me in the direction of classical music. It was a relief that most of those who attended the concerts were adults who paid no attention to my presence. From the performances I witnessed, from the stereo I goaded my parents into buying for me, and my own reading, I, with few of the normal distractions of the typical teenager, gathered an immense knowledge of my field.

My hero was J. S. Bach. It was from his works that I came to understand mathematics and, through a greater understanding of math, came to a greater understanding of Bach—the golden ratio, the rise of complexity through the reiteration of simple elements, the presence of the cosmic in the common.

Whereas others simply heard his work, I could also feel it, taste it, smell it, visualize it, and in doing so was certain I was witnessing the process by which all of Nature had moved from a single cell to a virulent, diverse forest. Perhaps part of my admiration for the good cantor of Leipzig was his genius with counterpoint, a practice where two or more distinct melodic lines delicately join at certain points to form a singularly cohesive listening experience. I saw in this technique an analogy to my desire that some day my own unique personality might join with that of another's and form a friendship. Soon after hearing the fugue pieces that are part of *The Well-Tempered Clavier*, I decided I wanted to become a composer.

Of course, during these years, both dreadful for my being a laughingstock in school and delightful for their musical revelations, I couldn't forget the image of the girl who momentarily appeared before me during my escape to The Empire of Ice Cream. The minute that Dr. Stullin pronounced me sane, I made plans to return and attempt to conjure her again. The irony of the situation was that just that single first taste of coffee ice cream had ended up making me ill, either because I'd been sheltered from rich desserts my whole life or because my system actually was inherently delicate. Once my freedom came, I found I didn't have the stomach for all of those gastronomic luxuries I had at one time so desired. Still, I was willing to chance the stomachache in order to rediscover her.

On my second trip to The Empire, after taking a heaping spoonful of coffee ice cream and experiencing again that deep noetic response, she appeared as before, her image forming in the empty space between me and the front window of the shop. This time she seemed to be sitting at the end of a couch situated in a living room or parlor, reading a book. Only her immediate sur-roundings within a foot or two of her body were clear to me. As my eyes moved away from her central figure, the rest of the couch and the table beside her, holding a lamp, became increasingly ghost-like; images from the parking lot outside the shop window showed through. At the edges of the phenomenon there was nothing but the merest wrinkling of the atmosphere. She turned the page, and I was drawn back to her. I quickly fed myself another bit of ice cream and marveled at her beauty. Her hair was down, and I could see that it came well past her shoulders. Bright green eyes, a small, perfect nose, smooth skin, and full lips that silently moved with each word of the text she was scanning. She was wearing some kind of very sheer, powder-blue pajama top, and I could see the presence of her breasts beneath it.

I took two spoonfuls of ice cream in a row, and, because my desire had tightened my throat and I couldn't swallow, their cold burned my tongue. In the time it took for the mouthful of ice cream to melt and trickle down my throat, I simply watched her chest subtly heave with each breath, her lips move, and I was enchanted. The last thing I noticed before she disappeared was the odd title of the book she was reading: *The Centrifugal Rickshaw Dancer*. I'd have taken another spoonful, but a massive headache had blossomed behind my eyes, and I could feel my stomach beginning to revolt against the ice cream. I got up and quickly left the shop. Out in the open air I walked for over an hour, trying to clear my head of the pain while at the same time trying to retain her image in my memory. I stopped three times along my meandering course, positive I was going to vomit, but never did.

My resistance to the physical side effects of the ice cream never improved, but I returned to the shop again and again, like a binge drinker to the bottle, hangover be damned, whenever I was feeling most alone. Granted, there was something of a voyeuristic thrill underlying the whole thing, especially when the ice cream would bring her to me in various states of undress—in the shower, in her bedroom. But you must believe me when I say that there was much more to it than that. I wanted to know everything about her. I studied her as assiduously as I did *The Goldberg Variations* or Shoenberg's serialism. She was, in many ways, an even more intriguing mystery, and the process of investigation was like constructing a jigsaw puzzle, reconfiguring a blasted mosaic.

I learned that her name was Anna. I saw it written on one of her sketchpads. Yes, she was an artist, and I believe she had great aspirations in this direction as I did in music. I spent so many spoonfuls of coffee ice cream, initiated so many headaches, just watching her draw. She never lifted a paintbrush or pastel, but was tied to the simple tools of pencil and paper. I never witnessed her using a model or photograph as a guide. Instead she would place the sketchpad flat on a table and hunker over it. The tip of her tongue would show itself from the right corner of her lips when she was in deepest concentration. Every so often she would take a drag on a cigarette that burned in an ashtray to her left. The results of her work, the few times I was lucky enough to catch a glimpse, were astonishing. Sometimes she was obviously drawing from life, the portraits of people whom she must have known. At other times she would conjure strange creatures or mandala-like designs of exotic blossoms. The shading was incredible, giving weight and depth to her creations. All of this from the tip of a graphite pencil one might use to work a calculation or jot a memo. If I did not adore her, I might've envied her innate talent.

To an ancillary degree, I was able to catch brief glimpses of her surroundings, and this was fascinating for she seemed to move through a complete, separate world of her own, some kind of *other* reality that was very much like ours. I'd garnered enough to know that she lived in a large old house with many rooms, the windows covered with long drapes to block out the light. Her work area was chaotic, stacks of her drawings covering the tops of tables and pushed to the sides of her desk. A black-and-white cat was always prowling in and out of the tableau. She was very fond of flowers and often worked in some sun-drenched park or garden, creating painstaking portraits of amaryllis or pansies, and although the rain would be falling outside my own window, there the skies were bottomless blue.

Although over the course of years I'd told Stullin much about myself, revealed my ambitions and most secret desires, I had never mentioned Anna. It was only after I graduated high school and was set to go off to study at Gelsbeth Conservatory in the nearby city that I decided to reveal her existence to him. The doctor had been a good friend to me, albeit a remunerated one, and was always most congenial and understanding when I'd give vent to my frustrations. He persistently argued the optimistic viewpoint for me when all was as inky black as the aroma of my father's aftershave. My time with him never resulted in a palpable difference in my ability to attract friends or feel more comfortable in public, but I enjoyed his company. At the same time, I was somewhat relieved to be severing all ties to my troubled past and escaping my childhood once and for all. I was willing to jettison Stullin's partial good to be rid of the rest.

We sat in the small sunroom at the back of his house, and he was questioning me about what interests I would pursue in my forthcoming classes. He had a good working knowledge of classical music and had told me at one of our earliest meetings that he had studied the piano when he was younger. He had a weakness for the Romantics, but I didn't hold it against him. Somewhere in the midst of our discussion I simply blurted out the details of my experiences with coffee ice cream and the resultant appearances of Anna. He was obviously taken aback. He leaned forward in his chair and slowly went through the procedure of lighting a cigarette.

"You know," he said, releasing a cascade of smoke, the aroma of which always manifested itself for me in the faint sound of a mosquito, "that is quite unusual. I don't believe there has ever been a case of a synesthetic vision achieving a figurative resemblance. They are always abstract. Shapes, colors, yes, but never an image of an object, not to mention a person."

"I know it's the synesthesia," I said. "I can feel it. The exact same experience as when I summon colors from my keyboard."

"And you say she always appears in relation to your eating ice cream?" he asked, squinting.

"Coffee ice cream," I said.

This made him laugh briefly, but his smile soon diminished, and he brought his free hand up to stroke his beard. I knew this action to be a sign of his concern. "What you are describing to me would be, considering the current medical literature, a hallucination."

I shrugged.

"Still," he went on, "the fact that it is always related to your tasting the ice cream, and that you can identify an associated noetic feeling, I would have to agree with you that it seems related to your condition."

"I knew it was unusual," I said. "I was afraid to mention it."

"No, no, it's good that you did. The only thing troubling me about it is that I am too aware of your desire to connect with another person your age. To be honest, it has all the earmarks of wish fulfillment that points back to a kind of hallucination. Look, you don't need this distraction now. You are beginning your life, you are moving on, and there is every indication that you will be successful in your art. When the other students at the conservatory understand your abilities, you will make friends, believe me. It will not be like high school. Chasing this insubstantial image could impede your progress. Let it go."

And so, not without a large measure of regret, I did. To an extent, Stullin was right about Gelsbeth. It wasn't like high school, and I did make the acquaintance of quite a few like-minded people with whom I could at least connect on the subject of music. I wasn't the only odd fish in that pond, believe me. To be a young person with an overriding interest in Bach or Mozart or Scriabin was its own eccentricity for those times. The place was extremely competitive, and I took the challenge. My fledgling musical compositions were greeted with great interest by the faculty, and I garnered a degree of notoriety when one day a fellow student discovered me composing a chamber piece for violins and cello using my set of crayons. I would always work in my corresponding synesthetic colors and then transpose the work, scoring it in normal musical notation.

The years flew by, and I believe they were the most rewarding of my entire life. I rarely went home to visit, save on holidays when the school was closed, even though it was only a brief train ride from the city. The professors were excellent but unforgiving of laziness and error. It wasn't a labor for me to meet their expectations. For the first time in my life, I felt what it meant to play, an activity I'd never experienced in childhood. The immersion in great music, the intricate analysis of its soul, kept me constantly engaged, filled with a sense of wonder.

Then, in my last year, I became eligible to participate in a competition for composers. There was a large cash prize, and the winner's work would be performed by a well-known musician at a concert in the city's symphony hall. The difficulty of being a composer was always the near-impossibility of getting one's work performed by competent musicians in a public venue. The opportunity presented by the competition was one I couldn't let slip away. More important than the money or the accolades would be a kind of recognition that would bring me to the attention of potential patrons who might commission a work. I knew that it was time to finally compose the fugue I'd had in mind for so many years. The utter complexity of the form, I believed, would be the best way to showcase all of my talents.

When it came time to begin the composition of the fugue, I took the money I'd made tutoring young musicians on the weekends and put it toward renting a beach house out on Varion Island for two weeks. In the summer the place was a bustling tourist spot for the wealthy, with a small central town that could be termed quaint. In those months, I wouldn't have been able to touch the price of the lowliest dwelling for a single day's rent. It was the heart of winter, though, when I took a leave from the school, along with crayons, books, a small tape player, and fled by way of bus and cab to my secret getaway.

The house I came to wasn't one of the grand wooden mansions on stilts that lined the road along the causeway, but instead a small bungalow, much like a concrete bunker. It was painted an off-putting yellow that tasted to me for all the world like cauliflower. It sat atop a small rise, and its front window faced the ocean, giving me a sublime view of the dunes and beach. What's more, it was within walking distance of the tiny village. There was sufficient heat, a telephone, a television, a kitchen with all the appliances, and I instantly felt as at home there as I had anywhere in my life. The island itself was deserted. On my first day I walked down to the ocean, along the shore the mile and a half to the eastern point, and then back by way of the main road, passing empty houses, and I saw no one. I'd been told over the phone by the realtor that the diner in town and a small shop that sold cigarettes and newspapers stayed open through the winter. Thankfully, she was right, for without the diner, I would have starved.

The setting of the little bungalow was deliciously melancholic, and for my sensibilities that meant conducive to work. I could hear the distant breaking of waves and, above that, the winter wind blowing sand against the window glass, but these were not distractions. Instead, they were the components of a silence that invited one to dream wide awake, to let the imagination open, and so I dove into the work straightaway. On the first afternoon, I began recording in my notebook my overall plan for the fugue. I'd decided that it would have only two voices. Of course, some had been composed with as many as eight, but I didn't want to be ostentatious. Showing reserve is as important a trait of technical mastery as is that of complexity.

I already had the melodic line of the subject, which had been a castoff from another project I'd worked on earlier in the year. Even though I decided it wasn't right for the earlier piece, I couldn't forget it and kept revising it here and there, playing it over and over. In the structure of a fugue, one posits the melodic line or subject, and then there is an answer (counterpoint), a reiteration of that line with differing degrees of variation, so that what the listener hears is like a dialogue (or a voice and its echo) of increasing complexity. After each of the voices has entered the piece, there is an episode that leads to the reentry of the voices and given answers, now in different keys. I had planned to use a technique called *stretto*, in which the answers, as they are introduced, overlap somewhat the original subject lines. This allows for a weaving of the voices so as to create an intricate tapestry of sound.

All this would be difficult to compose but nothing outlandishly original. It was my design, though, to impress the judges by trying something new. Once the fugue had reached its greatest state of complication, I wanted the piece to slowly, almost logically at first, but then without rhyme or meter, crumble into chaos. At the very end, from that chaotic cacophony, there would emerge one note, drawn out to great length, which would eventually diminish into nothing.

For the first week, the work went well. I took a little time off every morning and evening for a walk on the beach. At night I would go to the diner and then return to the bungalow to listen to Bach's *Art of the Fugue* or *Toccata and Fugue in D Minor*, some Brahms, Haydn, Mozart, and then pieces from the inception of the form by composers like Sweelinck and Froberger. I employed the crayons on a large piece of good drawing paper, and although to anyone else it wouldn't look like musical notation, I knew exactly how it would sound when I viewed it. Somewhere after the first week, though, I started to slow down, and by Saturday night my work came to a grinding halt. What I'd begun with such a clear sense of direction had me trapped. I was lost in my own complexity. The truth was, I was exhausted and could no longer pick apart the threads of the piece — the subject, the answer, the counter-subject snarled like a ball of yarn.

I was thoroughly weary and knew I needed rest, but even though I went to bed and closed my eyes, I couldn't sleep. All day Sunday I sat in a chair and surveyed the beach through the front window. I was too tired to work but too frustrated about not working to sleep. That evening, after having done nothing all day, I stumbled down to the diner and took my usual seat. The place was empty, save for one old man sitting in the far corner reading a book while eating his dinner. This solitary character looked somewhat like Stullin for his white beard, and at first glance, had I not known better, I could've sworn the book he was reading was *The Centrifugal Rickshaw Dancer*. I didn't want to get close enough to find out for fear he might strike up a conversation.

The waitress came and took my order. When she was finished writing on her pad, she said, "You look exhausted tonight."

I nodded.

"You need to sleep," she said.

"I have work to do," I told her.

"Well, then, let me bring you some coffee."

I laughed. "You know, I've never had a cup of coffee in my life," I said.

"Impossible," she said. "It looks to me like tonight might be a good time to start."

"I'll give it a try," I told her, and this seemed to make her happy.

While I ate, I glanced through my notebook and tried to re-establish the architecture of the fugue. As always, when I looked at my notes, everything was crystal clear, but when it came time to continue on the score, every potential further step seemed the wrong way to go. Somewhere in the midst of my musing, I pushed my plate away and drew toward me the cup and saucer. My usual drink was tea, and I'd forgotten I had changed my order. I took a sip, and the dark, bitter taste of black coffee startled me. I looked up, and there was Anna, staring at me, having just lowered a cup away from her lips. In her eyes I saw a glint of recognition, as if she were actually seeing me, and I'm sure she saw the same in mine.

I whispered, "I see you."

She smiled. "I see you too," she said.

I would have been less surprised if a dog had spoken to me. Sitting dumbfounded, I reached slowly out toward where she seemed to sit across from me in the booth. As my hand approached, she leaned back away from it.

"I've been watching you for years," she said.

"The coffee?" I said.

She nodded. "You are a synesthete, am I right?"

"Yes," I said. "But you're a figment of my imagination, a product of a neurological anomaly."

Here she laughed out loud. "No," she said, "you are."

After our initial exchange, neither of us spoke. I was in a mild state of shock, I believe. *This can't be*, I kept repeating in my mind, but there she was, and I could hear her breathing. Her image appeared even sharper than it had previously under the influence of the coffee ice cream. And now, with the taste that elicited her presence uncompromised by cream and sugar and the cold, she remained without dissipating for a good few minutes before beginning to mist at the edges and I had to take another sip to sharpen the focus. When I brought my cup up to drink, she also did at the same exact time, as if she were a reflection, as if I were her reflection, and we both smiled.

"I can't speak to you where I am. They'll think I've lost my mind," I whispered.

"I'm in the same situation," she said.

"Give me a half-hour and then have another cup of coffee, and I'll be able to speak to you in private."

She nodded in agreement and watched as I called for the check.

By the time the waitress arrived at my booth, Anna had dissolved into a vague cloud, like the exhalation of a smoker. It didn't matter, as I knew she couldn't be seen by anyone else. As my bill was being tallied, I ordered three cups of coffee to go.

"That coffee is something, isn't it?" said the waitress. "I swear by it. Amazing you've never had any up to this point. My blood is three-quarters coffee, I drink so much of it," she said.

"Wonderful stuff," I agreed.

Wonderful it was, for it had awakened my senses, and I walked through the freezing, windy night, carrying in a box my containers of elixir, with all the joy of a child leaving school on Friday afternoon. The absurdity of the whole affair didn't escape me, and I laughed out loud remembering my whispered plan to wait a half-hour and then drink another cup. The conspiratorial nature of it excited me, and I realized for the first time since seeing her that Anna had matured and grown more beautiful in the years I had forsaken her.

Back at the bungalow, I put the first of the large Styrofoam containers into the microwave in the kitchen and heated it for no more than thirty seconds. I began to worry that perhaps in Anna's existence time was altogether different and a half-hour for me might be two or three or a day for her. The instant the bell sounded on the appliance, I took the cup out, seated myself at the small kitchen table, and drank a long draught of the dark potion. Before I set the cup down, she was there, sitting in the seat opposite me.

"I know your name is Anna," I said to her. "I saw it on one of your drawing pads."

She flipped her hair behind her ear on the left side and asked, "What's yours?"

"William," I said. Then I told her about the coffee ice cream and first time I encountered her image.

"I remember," she said, "when I was a child of nine, I snuck a sip of my father's coffee he had left in the living room, and I saw you sitting at a piano. I thought you were a ghost. I ran to get my mother to show her, but when I returned you had vanished. She thought little of it since the synesthesia was always prompting me to describe things that made no sense to her."

"When did you realize it was the coffee?" I asked.

"Oh, some time later. I again was given a taste of it at breakfast one morning, and there you were, sitting at our dining room table, looking rather forlorn. It took every ounce of restraint not to blurt out that you were there. Then it started to make sense to me. After that, I would try to see you as much as possible. You were often very sad when you were younger. I know that."

The look on her face, one of true concern for me, almost brought tears to my eyes. She was a witness to my life. I hadn't been as alone as I'd always thought.

"You're a terrific artist," I said.

She smiled. "I'm great with a pencil, but my professors are demanding a piece in color. That's what I'm working on now."

Intermittently in the conversation we'd stop and take sips of coffee to keep the connection vital. As it turned out, she too had escaped her normal routine and taken a place in order to work on a project for her final portfolio review. We discovered all manner of synchronicities between our lives. She admitted to me that she had also been a loner as a child and that her parents had a hard time dealing with her synesthetic condition. As she put it, "Until we discovered the reality of it, I think they thought I was crazy." She laughed, but I could tell by the look in her eyes how deeply it had affected her.

"Have you ever told anyone about me?" I asked.

"Only my therapist," she said. "I was relieved when he told me he had heard of rare cases like mine."

This revelation brought me up short, for Stullin had told me he had never encountered anything of the sort in the literature. The implications of this inconsistency momentarily reminded me that she was not real, but I quickly shoved the notion from my thoughts and continued the conversation.

That night, by parsing out the coffee I had, and she doing the same, we stayed together until two in the morning, telling each other about our lives, our creative ideas, our dreams for the future. We found that our synesthetic experiences were similar and that our sense impressions were often transposed with the same results. For instance, for both of us, the aroma of new-mown grass was circular and the sound of a car horn tasted of citrus. She told me that her father was an amateur musician who loved the piano and classical music. In the middle of my recounting for her the intricacies of the fugue I was planning, she suddenly looked up from her cup and said, "Oh no, I'm out of coffee." I looked down at my own cup and realized I'd just taken the last sip.

"Tomorrow at noon," she said as her image weakened.

"Yes!" I yelled, afraid she would not hear me.

Then she became a phantom, a miasma, a notion, and I was left staring at the wall of the kitchen. With her gone, I could not sit still for long. All the coffee I'd drunk was coursing through me, and because my frail system had never before known the stimulant, my hands literally shook from it. I knew sleep was out of the question, so after walking around the small rooms of the bungalow for an hour, I sat down to my fugue to see what I could do.

Immediately, I picked up the trail of where I had been headed before Saturday's mental block had set in. Everything was piercingly clear to me, and I could hear the music I was noting in various colors as if there were a tape of the piece playing as I created it. I worked like a demon, quickly, unerringly, and the ease with which the answers to the musical problems presented themselves gave me great confidence and made my decisions ingenious. Finally, around eight in the morning (I hadn't noticed the sunrise), the coffee took its toll on me, and I became violently ill. The stomach pains, the headache, were excruciating. At ten, I vomited, and that relieved the symptoms somewhat. But by eleven A.M. I was at the diner buying another four cups of coffee.

The waitress tried to interest me in breakfast, but I said I wasn't hungry. She told me I didn't look well, and I tried to laugh off her concern. When she pressed the matter, I made some surly comment to her that I can't now remember, and she understood I was interested in nothing but the coffee. I took my hoard and went directly to the beach. The temperature was milder that day and the fresh air cleared my head. I sat in the shelter of a deep hollow amidst the dunes to block the wind, drank, and watched Anna at work, wherever she was, on her project—a large, colorful abstract drawing. After spying on her for a few minutes, I realized that the composition of the piece, its arrangement of color, presented itself to me as the melodic line of Symphony no. 8 in B Minor by Franz Schubert. This amused me at first, to think that my own musical knowledge was inherent in the existence of her world, that my imagination was its essence. What was also interesting was that such a minor interest of mine, Schubert, should manifest itself. I supposed that any aspect of my life, no matter how minor, was fodder for this imaginative process. It struck me just as quickly, though, that I didn't want this to be so. I wanted her to be apart from me, her own separate entity, for without that, what would her friendship mean? I physically shook my head to rid myself of the idea. When at noon she appeared next to me in my nest among the dunes, I'd already managed to forget this worm in the apple.

We spent the morning together talking and laughing, strolling along the edge of the ocean, climbing on the rocks at the point. When the coffee ran low around three, we returned to the diner for me to get more. I asked them to make me two whole pots and just pour them into large, plastic takeout containers. The waitress said nothing but shook her head. In the time I was on my errand, Anna, in her own world, brewed another vat of it.

We met up back at my bungalow, and as evening came on, we took out our respective projects and worked together, across from each other at the kitchen table. In her presence my musical imagination was on fire, and she admitted to me that she saw for the first time the overarching structure of her drawing and where she was headed with it. At one point I became so immersed in the work, I reached out and picked up what I thought would be one of my crayons but instead it turned out to be a violet pastel. I didn't own pastels, Anna did.

"Look," I said to her, and at that moment felt a wave of dizziness pass over me. A headache was beginning behind my eyes.

She lifted her gaze from her work and saw me holding the violet stick. We both sat quietly, in awe of its implications. Slowly, she put her hand out across the table toward me. I dropped the pastel and reached toward her. Our hands met, and I swear I could feel her fingers entangled with mine.

"What does this mean, William?" she said with a note of fear in her voice and let go of me.

As I stood up, I lost my balance and needed to support myself by clutching the back of the chair. She also stood, and as I approached her, she backed away. "No, this isn't right," she said.

"Don't worry," I whispered. "It's me." I took two wobbly steps and drew so close to her I could smell her perfume. She cringed but did not try to get away. I put my arms around her and attempted to kiss her.

"No," she cried. Then I felt the force of both her hands against my chest, and I stumbled backward onto the floor. "I don't want this. It's not real," she said, and began to hurriedly gather her things.

"Wait, I'm sorry," I said. I tried to scrabble to my feet, and that's when the sum total of my lack of sleep, the gallons of caffeine, the fraying of my nerves came together like the twining voices in a fugue and struck me in the head as if I'd been kicked by a horse. My body was shaking, my vision grew hazy, and I could feel myself phasing in and out of consciousness. I managed to watch Anna turn and walk away as if passing through the living room. Somehow I got to my feet and followed her, using the furniture as support. The last thing I remember was flinging open the front door of the small house and screaming her name.

I was found the next morning lying on the beach, unconscious. It was the old man with the white beard from the diner, who, on his daily early-morning beachcombing expedition, came across me. The police were summoned. An ambulance was called. I came to in a hospital bed the next day, the warm sun, smelling of antique rose, streaming through a window onto me.

They kept me at the small shore hospital two days for psychological observation. A psychiatrist visited me, and I managed to convince him that I'd been working too hard on a project for school. Apparently the waitress at the diner had told the police that I'd been consuming ridiculous amounts of coffee and going without sleep. Word of this had gotten back to the doctor who attended to me. When I told him it was the first time I had tried coffee and that I'd gotten carried away, he warned me to stay off it, telling me they found me in a puddle of my own vomit. "It obviously disagrees with your system. You could have choked to death when you passed out." I thanked him for his advice and promised him I'd stay well away from it in the future.

In the days I was at the hospital, I tried to process what had happened with Anna. Obviously, my bold advance had frightened her. It crossed my mind that it might be better to leave her alone in the future. The very fact that I was sure I'd made physical contact with her was, in retrospect, unsettling. I wondered if perhaps Stullin was right, and what I perceived to be a result of synesthesia was actually a psychotic hallucination. I left it an open issue in my mind as to whether I would seek her out again. One more meeting might be called for, I thought, at least to simply apologize for my mawkish behavior.

I asked the nurse if my things from the beach house had been brought to the hospital, and she told me they had. I spent the entirety of my last day there dressed and waiting to get the okay for my release. That afternoon, they brought me my belongings. I went carefully through everything, but it became obvious to me that my crayon score for the fugue was missing. Everything else was accounted for, but there was no large sheet of drawing paper. I asked the nurse, who was very kind, and actually reminded me somewhat of Mrs. Brithnic, to double-check and see if everything had been brought to me. She did and told me there was nothing else. I called the Varion Island police on the pretense of thanking them and asked if they had seen the drawing. My fugue had vanished. I knew a grave depression would descend upon me soon due to its disappearance, but for the moment I was numb and slightly pleased to merely be alive.

I decided to return to my parents' house for a few days and rest up before returning to the conservatory in order to continue my studies. In the bus station near the hospital, while I was waiting, I went to the small newspaper stand in order to buy a pack of gum and a paper with which to pass the time. As I perused the candy rack, my sight lighted upon something that made me feel the way Eve must have when she first saw the apple, for there was a bag of Thompson's Coffee-Flavored Hard Candy. The moment I read the words on the bag, I reached for them. There was a spark in my solar plexus, and my palms grew damp. *No Caffeine* the package read, and I was hard-pressed to believe my good fortune. I looked nervously over my shoulder while purchasing three bags of them, and when, on the bus, I tore a bag open, I did so with such violence, a handful of them scattered across the seat and into the aisle.

I arrived by cab at my parents' house and had to let myself in. Their car was gone, and I supposed they were out for the day. I hadn't seen them in some months and almost missed their presence. When night descended and they didn't return, I thought it odd but surmised they were on one of the short vacations they often took. It didn't matter. I sat at my old home base on the piano bench and sucked on coffee-flavored hard candies until I grew too weary to sit up. Then I got into my childhood bed, turned to face the wall as I always had when I was little, and fell asleep.

The next day, after breakfast, I resumed my vigil that had begun on the long bus trip home. By that afternoon my suspicions as to what had become of my fugue were confirmed. The candy didn't bring as clear a view of Anna as did the ice cream, let alone the black coffee, but it was focused enough for me to follow her through her day. I was there when she submitted my crayon score as her art project for the end-of-the-semester review. How she was able to appropriate it, I have no idea. It defied logic. In the fleeting glimpses I got of the work, I tried to piece together how I had gone about weaving the subjects and their answers. The second I would see it, the music would begin to sound for me, but I never got a good-enough look at it to sort out the complex structure of the piece. The two things I was certain of were that the fugue had been completed right up to the point where it was supposed to fall into chaos, and that Anna did quite well with her review because of it.

By late afternoon, I'd come to the end of my Thompson's candies and had but one left. Holding it in my hand, I decided it would be the last time I would conjure a vision of Anna. I came to the conclusion that her theft of my work had canceled out my untoward advance and we were now even, so to speak. I would leave her behind as I had before, but this time for good. With my decision made, I opened the last of the hard confections and placed it on my tongue. That dark, amber taste slowly spread through my mouth and, as it did, a cloudy image formed and crystallized into focus. She had the cup to her mouth, and her eyes widened as she saw me seeing her.

"William," she said. "I was hoping to see you one more time."

"I'm sure," I said, trying to seem diffident, but just hearing her voice made me weak.

"Are you feeling better?" she asked. "I saw what happened to you. I was with you on the beach all that long night, but couldn't reach you."

"My fugue," I said. "You took it."

She smiled. "It's not yours. Let's not kid ourselves, you know you are merely a projection of my synesthetic process."

"Who is a projection of whose?" I asked.

"You're nothing more than my muse," she said.

I wanted to contradict her, but I didn't have the meanness to subvert her belief in her own reality. Of course, I could have brought up the fact that she was told that figurative synesthesia was a known version of the disease. This was obviously not true. Also, there was the fact that her failed drawing, the one she had abandoned for mine, was based on Schubert's Eighth, a product of my own knowledge working through her. How could I convince her she wasn't real? She must've seen the doubt in my eyes because she became defensive in her attitude. "I'll not see you again," she said. "My therapist has given me a pill he says will eradicate my synesthesia. We have that here, in the true reality. It's already begun to work. I no longer hear my cigarette smoke as the sound of a faucet dripping. Green no longer tastes of lemon. The ring of the telephone doesn't feel like burlap."

This pill was the final piece of evidence. A pill to cure synesthesia? "You may be harming yourself," I said, "by taking that drug. If you cut yourself off from me, you may cease to exist. Perhaps we are meant to be together." I felt a certain panic at the idea that she would lose her special perception and I would lose the only friend I'd ever had who understood my true nature.

"Dr. Stullin says it will not harm me, and I will be like everyone else. Goodbye, William," she said, and pushed the coffee cup away from her.

"Stullin," I said. "What do you mean, Stullin?"

"My therapist," she said, and although I could still see her before me, I could tell I had vanished from her view. As I continued to watch, she lowered her face into her hands and appeared to be crying. Then my candy turned from the thinnest sliver into nothing but saliva, and I swallowed. A few seconds more, and she was completely gone.

It was three in the afternoon when I put my coat on and started across town to Stullin's place. I had a million questions, and foremost was whether or not he treated a young woman named Anna. My thoughts were so taken by my last conversation with her that when I arrived in front of the doctor's walkway, I realized I hadn't noticed the sun go down. It was as if I had walked in my sleep and awakened at his address. The street was completely empty of people or cars, reminding me of Varion Island. I took the steps up to his front door and knocked. It was dark inside except for a light on the second floor, but the door was slightly ajar, which I thought odd given it was the middle of the winter. Normally, I would have turned around and gone home after my third attempt to get his attention, but there was too much I needed to discuss.

I stepped inside, closing the door behind me. "Dr. Stullin?" I called. There was no answer. "Doctor?" I tried again and then made my way through the foyer to the room where the tables were stacked with paper. In the meager light coming in through the window, I found a lamp and turned it on. I continued to call out as I went from room to room, turning on lights, heading for the sunroom at the back of the place where we always had our meetings. When I reached that room, I stepped inside, and my foot came down on something alive. There was a sudden screech that nearly made my heart stop, and then I saw the black-and-white cat whose tail I had trod upon, race off into another room.

It was something of a comfort to be again in that plant-filled room. The sight of it brought back memories of it as the single safe place in the world when I was younger. Oddly enough, there was a lit cigarette in the ashtray on the table between the two chairs that faced each other. Lying next to it, opened to the middle and turned down on its pages, was a copy of *The Centrifugal Rickshaw Dancer*. I'd have preferred to see a ghost to that book. The sight of it chilled me. I sat down in my old seat and watched the smoke from the cigarette twirl up toward the glass panes. Almost instantly a great weariness seized me, and I closed my eyes.

That was days ago. When I discovered the next morning that I could not open the doors to leave, that I could not even break the glass in order to crawl out, it became clear to me what was happening. At first I was frantic, but then a certain calm descended upon me, and I learned to accept my fate. Those stacks of paper in that room on the way to the sunroom — each sheet held a beautiful pencil drawing. I explored the upstairs, and there, on the second floor, found a piano and the sheet music for Bach's *Grosse Fugue*. There was a black-and-white photograph of Mrs. Brithnic in the upstairs hallway and one of my parents standing with Anna as a child.

That hallway, those rooms, are gone, vanished. Another room has disappeared each day I have been trapped here. I sit in Stullin's chair now, in the only room still remaining (this one will be gone before tonight), and compose this tale — in a way, my fugue. The black-and-white cat sits across from me, having fled from the dissipation of the house as it closes in around us. Outside, the garden, the trees, the sky have all lost their color and now appear as if rendered in graphite—wonderfully shaded to give them an appearance of weight and depth. So too with the room around us: the floor, the glass panels, the chairs, the plants, even the cat's tail and my shoes and legs have lost their life and become the shaded gray of a sketch. I imagine Anna will soon be free of her condition. As for me, who always believed himself to be unwanted, unloved, misunderstood, I will surpass being a mere artist and become instead a work of art that will endure. The cat meows loudly, and I feel the sound as a hand upon my shoulder.

The Empire of Ice Cream

Story Notes

*I initially got the idea for this story by reading a book about the phenomenon of synesthesia—*The Man Who Tasted Shapes *by Richard E. Cytowic. While reading, I came across a passage that stated that when synesthetes experienced visual manifestations in response to sensory stimulation, these images were always abstract shapes, never figures. I thought to myself,* What would it be like if the visual manifestations did take figurative form, like furniture or birds or, even better, people? *I wrote up a proposal and tried to sell the idea as a novel. When the idea got shot down, I filed it away. Then Jeff VanderMeer told me he was about to embark on an editing project with Mark Roberts—an anthology of fake illnesses called* The Thackery T. Lambshead Pocket Guide to Eccentric & Discredited Diseases—*and he asked me to come up with a couple of my own diseases. I remembered my idea for "Figurative Synesthesia" and turned that into one of the maladies; and I wrote up another one called "Radical Lordosis." I banged them out in a matter of about two hours, sent them in, and got word back later that day that they would be in the guide. After writing up the disease, though, it got me thinking about the story I had wanted to write using the idea. After a few days, I found I couldn't stop thinking about it, and Jeff and Mark said they didn't mind if I turned the idea into a longer story for another magazine. The story, when it was finished, was nothing like my medical guide entry. I eventually sold the story to Ellen Datlow for* SCIFICTION, *and, as always, she provided me with a lot of good editorial advice. When the story appeared on the SCI-FICTION website, I added a footnote that referenced the* Lambshead Pocket Guide *as the source where I first discovered figurative synesthesia. Later on, I was accused by a reader of having ripped off the concept from whoever had written the entry for that disease in the guide.*

A *few interesting things about this piece: The novel that continuously crops up throughout the story,* The Centrifugal Rickshaw Dancer, *is an actual book written by my teaching colleague, friend, and mentor William Jon Watkins, and has some bearing on the story. There's a glaring mistake in the musical history part of the story, which only one person caught as far as I know—an Israeli editor who was translating the story into Hebrew. He also showed me how to effectively argue the point of this mistake so that my gaff could be seen as logical to the fiction. I was not aware, until long after the piece was published, that the structure of the plot emulated the shape of the fugue that the narrator plans to compose. And many people have commented that the story has something to do with Wallace Stevens's poetry and, beyond that, William Carlos Williams as well, but the title was chosen merely as an interesting name for the ice-cream parlor the narrator visits in the course of the story and was never intended to be any kind of literary allusion.*

A lot of readers seemed to really dig this story as it was nominated for the Hugo, the Nebula, the World Fantasy Award, and the Theodore Sturgeon Memorial Award. It won the Nebula Award for best novelette.

The Beautiful Gelreesh

HIS FACIAL FUR WAS A SWIRLING WONDER OF
blond and blue with highlights the deep orange of a
November sun. It covered every inch of his brow and cheeks, the
blunt ridge of his nose, even his eyelids. When beset by a bout of
overwhelming sympathy, he would twirl the thicket of longer
strands that sprouted from the center of his forehead. His bright
silver eyes emitted invisible beams that penetrated the most
guarded demeanors of his patients and shed light upon the condition of their souls. Discovering the essence of an individual, the
Gelreesh would sit quietly, staring, tapping the black enamel nails
of his hirsute hands together in an incantatory rhythm that would
regulate the heartbeat of his visitor to that of his own blood muscle.

"And when, may I ask, did you perceive the first inklings of your
despair?" he would say with a sudden whimper.

Once his question was posed, the subject was no longer dis-
tracted by the charm of his prominent incisors. He would lick his
lips once, twice, three times, with diminishing speed, adjusting the
initiate's respiration and brain pulse. Then the loveliness of his
pointed ears, the grace of his silk fashions would melt away, and his
lucky interlocutor would have no choice but to tell the truth, even
if in her heart of hearts she believed herself to be lying.

"When my father left us," might be the answer.

"Let us walk, my dear," the Gelreesh would suggest.

The woman or man or child, as the case might be, would put a hand into the warm hand of the heart's physician. He would lead them through his antechamber into the hallway and out through a back entrance of his house. To walk with the Gelreesh, matching his languorous stride, was to partake in a slow, stately procession. His gentle direction would guide one down the garden path to the hole in the crumbling brick and mortar wall netted with ivy. Before leaving the confines of the wild garden, he might pluck a lily to be handed to his troubled charge.

The path through the woods snaked in great loops around stands of oak and maple. Although the garden appeared to be at the height of summer life, this adjacent stretch of forest, leading toward the sea, was forever trapped in autumn. Here, just above the murmur of the wind and just below the rustle of red and yellow leaves, the Gelreesh would methodically pose his questions designed to fan the flames of his companion's anguish. With each troubled answer, he would respond with phrases he was certain would keep that melancholic heart drenched in a black sweat. "Horrible," he would say in the whine of a dog dreaming. "My dear, that's ghastly." "How can you go on?" "If I were you I would be weeping," was one that never failed to turn the trick.

When the tears would begin to flow, he'd reach into the pocket of his loose-fitting jacket of paisley design for a handkerchief stitched in vermillion, bearing the symbol of a broken heart. Handing it to his patient, he would again continue walking and the gentle interrogation would resume.

An hour might pass, even two, but there was no rush. There were so many questions to be asked and answered. Upon finally reaching the edge of the cliff that gave a view outward of the boundless ocean, the Gelreesh would release the hand of his subject and say with tender conviction, "And so, you see, this ocean must be for you a representation of the overwhelming, intractable dilemma that gnaws at your heart. You know without my telling you that there is really only one solution. You must move toward peace, to a better place."

"Yes, yes, thank you," would come the response followed by a fresh torrent of tears. The handkerchief would be employed, and then the Gelreesh would kindly ask for it back.

"The future lies ahead of you and the troubled past bites at your heels, my child."

Three steps forward and the prescription would be filled. A short flight of freedom, a moment of calm for the tortured soul, and then endless rest on the rocks below surrounded by the rib cages and skulls of fellow travelers once pursued by grief and now cured.

The marvelous creature would pause and dab a tear or two from the corners of his own eyes before undressing. Then, naked but for the spiral pattern of his body's fur, he would walk ten paces to the east where he kept a long rope tied at one end to the base of a mighty oak growing at the very edge of the cliff. His descent could only be described as acrobatic, pointing to a history with the circus. When finally down among the rocks, he would find the corpse of the new immigrant to the country without care and tidily devour every trace of flesh.

Later, in the confines of his office, he would compose a letter in turquoise ink on yellow paper, assuring the loved ones of his most recent patient that she or he, seeking the solace of a warm sun and crystal sea, had booked passage for a two-year vacation on the island of Valshavar—a paradisiacal atoll strung like a bead on the necklace of the equator. *Let not the price of this journey trouble your minds, for I, understanding the exemplary nature of the individual in question, have decided to pay all expenses for their escape from torment. In a year or two, when next you meet them, they will appear younger, and in their laughter you will feel the warmth of the tropical sun. With their touch, your own problems will vanish as if conjured away by island magic.* This missive would then be rolled like a scroll, tied fast with a length of green ribbon, and given into the talon of a great horned owl to be delivered.

And so it was that the Gelreesh operated, from continent to continent, dispensing his exquisite pity and relieving his patients of their unnecessary mortal coils. When suspicion arose to the point where doubt began to negate his beauty in the eyes of the populace, then, by dark of night, he would flee on all fours, accompanied by the owl, deep into the deepest forest, never to be seen again in that locale. The pile of bones he'd leave behind was undeniable proof of his treachery, but the victims' families preferred to think of their loved ones stretched out beneath a palm frond canopy on the pink beach of Valshavar, being fed peeled grapes by a monkey valet. This daydream in the face of horror would deflate all attempts at organizing a search party to hunt him down.

Although he would invariably move on, setting up a practice in a new locale rich in heavy hearts and haunted minds, something of him would remain behind in the form of a question, namely, "What was The Beautiful Gelreesh?" Granted, there were no end of accounts of his illusory form—everything from that of a dashing cavalry officer with waxed mustache to the refined blond impertinence of a symphony conductor. He reminded one young woman

whom he had danced with at a certain town soiree as being a blend
of her father, her boss, and her older brother. In fact, when notes
were later compared, no two could agree on the precise details of
his splendor.

He was finally captured during one of his escapes, found with
his leg in a fox trap only a mile from the village he had last
bestowed his pity upon. This beast in pain could not fully concentrate on creating the illusion of loveliness, and the incredulous
chicken farmer who discovered him writhing in the bite of the steel
jaws witnessed him shifting back and forth between suave charm
and gnashing horror. The poor farmer was certain he had snared
the devil. A special investigator was sent to handle the case. Blind
and somewhat autistic, the famous detective, Gal de Gui, methodically put the entire legacy together as if it was a child's jigsaw
puzzle. Of course, in the moments of interrogation by de Gui, the
Gelreesh tried to catch him up with a glamorous illusion. The
detective responded to this deception with a yawn. The creature
later told his prison guards that de Gui's soul was blank as a white
wall and perfect. De Gui's final comment on the Gelreesh was,
"Put down some newspaper and give him a bone. Here is the clas-
sic case of man's best friend."

It was when the Gelreesh related his own life story to the court,
eliciting pity from a people who previously desired his, that he
allowed himself to appear as the hominid-canine entity that had
always lurked behind his illusion. As the tears filled the eyes of the
jury, his handsome visage wavered like a desert mirage and then
lifted away to reveal fur and fangs. No longer were his words the
mellifluous susurrations of the sympathetic therapist, but now came
through as growling dog-talk in a spray of spittle. Even the huge owl
that sat on his shoulder in the witness stand shrunk and darkened
to become a grackle.

As he told it, he had been born to an aristocratic family, the
name of which everyone present would have known, but he would
not mention it for fear of bringing reprisals down upon them for
his actions. Because of his frightening aspect at birth, his father
accused his mother of bestiality. The venerable patriarch made
plans to do away with his wife, but she saved him the trouble by poisoning herself with small sips of opium and an arsenic pastry of her
own recipe. The strange child was named Rameau after a distant
relation on the mother's side, and sent to live in a newly constructed barn on the outskirts of the family estate. At the same time
that the father ordered the local clergy to try to exorcise the beast
out of him, there was a standing order for the caretaker to feed him

nothing but raw meat. As the Gelreesh had said on the witness stand, "My father spent little time thinking about me, but when he did, the fact of my existence twisted his thinking so that it labored pointlessly at cross-purposes."

The family priest taught the young Rameau how to speak and read, so that the strange child could learn the Bible. Through this knowledge of language he was soon able to understand the holy man's philosophy, which, in brief, was that the world was a ball of shit adrift in a sea of sin and the sooner one passed to heaven the better. As the Gelreesh confessed, he took these lessons to heart, and so later in life when he helped free his patients' souls from excremental bondage, he felt he was actually doing them a great favor. It was from that bald and jowly man of God that the creature became acquainted with the power of pity.

On the other hand, the caretaker who daily brought the beef was a man of the world. He was very old and had traveled far and wide. This kindly aged vagabond would tell the young Rameau stories of far-off places—islands at the equator and tundra crowded with migrating elk. One day, he told the boy about a fellow he had met in a far-off kingdom that sat along the old Silk Road to China. This remarkable fellow, Ibn Sadi was his name, had the power of persuasion. With subtle movements of his body, certain tricks of respiration in accordance with that of his audience, he could make himself invisible or appear as a beautiful woman. It was an illusion, of course, but to the viewer it seemed as real as the day. "What was his secret?" asked Rameau. The old man leaned in close to the boy's cage and whispered, "Listen to the rhythm of life and, when you look, do not accept but project. Feel what the other is feeling and make what they have felt what you feel. Speak only their own desire to them in a calm, soft voice, and they will see you as beautiful as they wish themselves to be."

The Gelreesh had time, days on end, to mull over his formula for control. He worked at it and tried different variations, until one day he was able to look into the soul of the priest and discover what it was—a mouse nibbling a wedge of wooden cheese. Soon after, he devised the technique of clicking together his fingernails in order to send out a hypnotic pulse, and with this welded the power of pity to the devices of the adept from the kingdom along the old Silk Road. Imagine the innate intelligence of this boy they considered a beast. A week following, he had escaped. For some reason, the priest had opened the cage, and, for his trouble, was found by the caretaker to have been ushered into the next and better world minus the baggage of his flesh.

The jury heard the story of the Gelreesh's wanderings and the perfection of his art, how he changed his name to that of a certain brand of Mediterranean cigarettes he had enjoyed. "I wanted to help the emotionally wounded," he had said to his accusers, and all grew sympathetic, but when they vented their grief for his solitary life and saw his true form, they unanimously voted for his execution. Just prior to accepting, against his will, the thirty bullets from the rifles of the firing squad marksmen, the Gelreesh performed a spectacular display of metamorphosis, becoming, in turn, each of his executioners. Before the captain of the guard could shout the order for the deadly volley, the beautiful one became, again, himself, shouted, "I feel your pain," and begged for all in attendance to participate in devouring him completely once he was dead. This final plea went unheeded. His corpse was left to the dogs and carrion birds. His bones were later gathered and sent to the Museum of Natural Science in the city of Nethit. The grackle was released into the wild.

Once he had been disposed of and the truth had been circulated, it seemed that everyone on all continents wanted to claim some attachment to the Gelreesh. For a five-year period there was no international figure more popular. My god, the stories told about him: women claimed to have had his children, men claimed they were him or his brother or at least the son of the caretaker who gave him his first clues to the protocol of persuasion. Children played Gelreesh, and the lucky tyke who got to be his namesake retained for the day ultimate power in the game. An entire branch of psychotherapy had sprung up called Non-Consumptive Gelreeshia, meaning that the therapists swamped their patients with pity but had designs not on the consumption of their flesh, merely their bank accounts. There were studies written about him, novels and plays and an epic poem entitled *Monster of Pity*. The phenomenon of his popularity had given rise to a philosophical reevaluation of *Beauty*.

Gelreesh mania died out in the year of the great comet, for here was something even more spectacular for people to turn their attention to. With the promise of the end of the world, mankind had learned to pity itself. Fortunately or unfortunately, however one might see it, this spinning ball of shit, this paradisiacal Valshavar of planets, was spared for another millennium in which more startling forms of anomalous humanity might spring up and lend perspective to the mundane herd.

And now, ages hence, recent news from Nethit concerning the

Gelreesh. Two years ago, an enterprising graduate student from Nethit University, having been told the legends of the beautiful one when he was a child, went in search through the basement of the museum to try to uncover the box containing the creature's remains. The catacombs that lay beneath the imposing structure are vast. The records kept as to what had been stored where have been eaten by an unusual mite that was believed to have been introduced into the environs of the museum by a mummy brought back from a glacier at the top of the world. Apparently, this termitic flea species awoke in the underground warmth and discovered its taste for paper, so that now the ledgers are filled with sheets of lace, more hole than text.

Still, the conscientious young man continued to search for over a year. His desire was to study the physiological form of this legend. Eventually, after months of exhaustive searching, he came upon a crate marked with grease pencil: *Gelreesh*. Upon prying open the box, he found inside a collection of bones wrapped in a tattered garment of maroon silk. There was also a handkerchief bearing the stitched symbol of a broken heart. When he uncovered the bones, he was shocked to find the skeleton of a very large bird instead of a mutant human. A professor of his from the university determined upon inspection that these were indeed the remains of a great horned owl.

The Beautiful Gelreesh

Story Notes

I don't remember what dark basement of my imagination this story crawled out of, but when it finally showed itself in the daylight I was enchanted by it. I can tell you that a good many editors were not. Who can blame them? There's a brutal irony to it that verges on cynicism, something that usually doesn't find a home in my fiction. I don't know what it was, but I felt that in this story's darkness it still pointed the way to some truth. What that truth might be, I couldn't tell you if you put a gun to my head. Jeff VanderMeer published it in his anthology, Album Zutique, *where it was surrounded by other work that made it feel at home. A story needs the right residence. To my surprise, this piece made the 2003 Locus Awards recommended reading list, which led me to wonder if there were not perhaps some readers out there with mutant entities lurking in the basements of their own imaginations.*

Boatman's Holiday

BENEATH A BLAZING ORANGE SUN, HE MANEU-vered his boat between the two petrified oaks that grew so high their tops were lost in violet clouds. Their vast trunks and complexity of branches were bone white, as if hidden just below the surface of the murky water was a stag's head the size of a mountain. Thousands of crows, like black leaves, perched amidst the pale tangle, staring silently down. Feathers fell, spiraling in their descent with the slow grace of certain dreams, and he wondered how many of these journeys he'd made or if they were all, always, the same journey.

Beyond the oaks, the current grew stronger, and he entered a constantly shifting maze of whirlpools, some spinning clockwise, some counter, as if to negate the passage of Time. Another boatman might have given in to panic and lost everything, but he was a master navigator and knew the river better than himself. Any other craft would have quickly succumbed to the seething waters, been ripped apart and its debris swallowed.

His boat was comprised of an inner structure of human bone lashed together with tendon and covered in flesh stitched by his own steady hand, employing a thorn needle and thread spun from sorrow. The lines of its contours lacked symmetry, meandered, and went off on tangents. Along each side, worked into the gunwales well above the waterline, was a row of eyeless, tongueless faces—

the empty sockets, the gaping lips, portals through which the craft breathed. Below, in the hold, there reverberated a heartbeat that fluttered randomly and died every minute only to be revived the next.

On deck, there were two long rows of benches fashioned from skulls for his passengers, and at the back, his seat at the tiller. In the shallows, he'd stand and use his long pole to guide the boat along. There was no need of a sail as the vessel moved slowly forward of its own volition with a simple command. On the trip out, the benches empty, he'd whisper, "There!" and on the journey back, carrying a full load, "Home!" and no river current could dissuade its progress. Still, it took a sure and fearless hand to hold the craft on course.

Charon's tall, wiry frame was slightly but irreparably bent from centuries hunched beside the tiller. His beard and tangled nest of snow-white hair, his complexion the color of ash, made him appear ancient. Yet when in the throes of maneuvering around Felmian, the blue serpent, or in the heated rush along the shoals of the Island of Nothing, he'd toss one side of his scarlet cloak back over his shoulder, and the musculature of his chest, the coiled bulge of his bicep, the thick tendon in his forearm, gave evidence of the power hidden beneath his laconic facade. Woe to the passenger who mistook those outer signs of age for weakness and set some plan in motion, for then the boatman would wield his long shallows pole and with one mighty swing shatter every bone in their body.

Each treacherous obstacle, the clutch of shifting boulders, the rapids, the waterfall that dropped into a bottomless star-filled space, was expertly avoided with a skill born of intuition. Eventually a vague but steady tone like the uninterrupted buzz of a mosquito came to him over the water; a sign that he drew close to his destination. He shaded his eyes against the brightness of the flaming sun and spotted the dark, thin edge of shoreline in the distance. As he advanced, that distant, whispered note grew steadily into a high keening, and then fractured to reveal itself a chorus of agony. A few more leagues and he could make out the legion of forms crowding the bank. When close enough to land, he left the tiller, stood, and used the pole to turn the boat so it came to rest sideways on the black sand. Laying down the pole, he stepped to his spot at the prow.

Two winged, toad-faced demons with talons for hands and hands for feet, Gesnil and Trinkthil, saw to the orderliness of the line of passengers that ran from the shore back a hundred yards into the writhing human continent of dead. Every day there were more travelers, and no matter how many trips Charon made, there was no hope of ever emptying the endless beach.

Brandishing cat-o'-nine-tails with barbed tips fashioned from incisors, the demons lashed the "tourists," as they called them, subduing those unwilling to go.

"Another load of the falsely accused, Charon," said Gesnil, puffing on a lit human finger jutting from the corner of his mouth.

"Watch this woman, third back, in the blue dress," said Trinkthil, "her blithering lamentations will bore you to sleep. You know, she never *really* meant to add belladonna to the recipe for her husband's gruel."

Charon shook his head.

"We've gotten word that there will be no voyages for a time," said Gesnil.

"Yes," said Charon, "I've been granted a respite by the Master. A holiday."

"A century's passed already?" said Gesnil. "My, my, it seemed no more than three. Time flies . . ."

"Traveling?" asked Trinkthil. "Or staying home?"

"There's an island I believe I'll visit," he said.

"Where's it located?" asked Gesnil.

Charon ignored the question and said, "Send them along."

The demons knew to obey, and they directed the first in line to move forward. A bald, overweight man in a cassock, some member of the clergy, stepped up. He was trembling so that his jowls shook. He'd waited on the shore in dire fear and anguish for centuries, milling about, fretting as to the ultimate nature of his fate.

"Payment," said Charon.

The man leaned his head back and opened his mouth. A round shiny object lay beneath his tongue. The boatman reached out and took the gold coin, putting it in the pocket of his cloak. "Next," called Charon as the man moved past him and took a seat on the bench of skulls.

Hell's orange sun screamed in its death throes every evening, a pandemonium sweeping down from above that made even the demons sweat and set the Master's three-headed dog to cowering. That horrendous din worked its way into the rocks, the river, the petrified trees, and everything brimmed with misery. Slowly it diminished as the starless, moonless dark came on, devouring every last shred of light. With that infernal night came a cool breeze whose initial tantalizing relief never failed to deceive the damned, though they be residents for a thousand years, with a false promise of Hope.

That growing wind carried in it a catalyst for memory, and set all who it caressed to recalling in vivid detail their lost lives—a torture individually tailored, more effective than fire.

Charon sat in his home, the skull of a fallen god, on the crest of a high flint hill overlooking the river. Through the skull's left eye socket, glazed with transparent lies, he could be seen sitting at a table, a glutton's fat tallow burning, its flame guttering in the night breeze let in through the gap of a missing tooth. Laid out before him was a curling width of tattooed flesh skinned from the back of an ancient explorer who'd no doubt sold his soul for a sip from the Fountain of Youth. In the boatman's right hand was a compass and in his left a writing quill. His gaze traced along the strange parchment the course of his own river, Acheron, the River of Pain, to where it crossed paths with Pyriphlegethon, the River of Fire. That burning course was eventually quelled in cataracts of steam where it emptied into and became the Lethe, River of Forgetting.

He traced his next day's journey with the quill tip, gliding it an inch above the meandering line of vein blue. There, in the meager width of that last river's depiction, almost directly halfway between its origin and end in the mournful Cocytus, was a freckle. Anyone else would have thought it no more than a bodily blemish inked over by chance in the production of the map, but Charon was certain after centuries of overhearing whispered snatches of conversation from his unlucky passengers that it represented the legendary island of Oondeshai.

He put down his quill and compass and sat back in the chair, closing his eyes. Hanging from the center of the cathedral cranium above, the wind chime made of dangling bat bones clacked as the mischievous breeze that invaded his home lifted one corner of the map. He sighed at the touch of cool wind as its insidious effect reeled his memory into the past.

One night, he couldn't recall how many centuries before, he was lying in bed on the verge of sleep, when there came a pounding at the hinged door carved in the left side of the skull. "Who's there?" he called in the fearsome voice he used to silence passengers. There was no verbal answer, but another barrage of banging ensued. He rolled out of bed, put on his cloak, and lit a tallow. Taking the candle with him, he went to the door and flung it open. A startled figure stepped back into the darkness. Charon thrust the light forward and beheld a cowed, trembling man, his naked flesh covered in oozing sores and wounds.

"Who are you?" asked the boatman.

The man stared up at him, holding out a hand.

"You've escaped from the pit, haven't you?"

The backside of the flint hill that his home sat atop overlooked the enormous pit, its circumference at the top, a hundred miles across. Spiraling along its inner wall was a path that led down and down in ever decreasing arcs through the various levels of Hell to end at a pinpoint in the very mind of the Master. Even at night, if Charon were to go behind the skull and peer out over the rim, he could see a faint reddish glow and hear the distant echo of plaintive wails.

The man finally nodded.

"Come in," said Charon, and held the door as the stranger shuffled past him.

Later, after he'd offered a chair, a spare cloak, and a cup of nettle tea, his broken visitor began to come around.

"You know," said Charon, "there's no escape from Hell."

"This I know," mumbled the man, making a great effort to speak as if he'd forgotten the skill. "But there is an escape *in* Hell."

"What are you talking about? The dog will be here within the hour to fetch you back. He's less than gentle."

"I need to make the river," said the man.

"What's your name?" asked Charon.

"Wieroot," said the man with a grimace.

The boatman nodded. "This escape in Hell, where is it, what is it?"

"Oondeshai," said Wieroot, "an island in the River Lethe."

"Where did you hear of it?"

"I created it," he said, holding his head with both hands as if to remember. "Centuries ago, I wrote it into the fabric of the mythology of Hell."

"Mythology?" asked Charon. "I suppose those wounds on your body are merely a myth?"

"The suffering's real here, don't I know it, but the entire construction of Hell is, of course, man's own invention. The pit, the three-headed dog, the rivers, you, if I may say so, all sprung from the mind of humanity, confabulated to punish itself."

"Hell has been here from the beginning," said Charon.

"Yes," said Wieroot, "in one form or another. But when, in the living world, something is added to the legend, some detail to better convince believers or convert new ones, here it leaps into existence with a ready-made history that instantly spreads back to the start and a guaranteed future that creeps inexorably forward." The escapee fell into a fit of coughing, smoke from the fires of the pit issuing in small clouds from his lungs.

"The heat's made you mad," said Charon. "You've had too much time to think."

"Both may be true," croaked Wieroot, wincing in pain, "but listen for a moment more. You appear to be a man, yet I'll wager you don't remember your youth. Where were you born? How did you become the boatman?"

Charon strained his memory, searching for an image of his past in the world of the living. All he saw was rows and rows of heads, tilting back, proffering the coin beneath the tongue. An image of him setting out across the river, passing between the giant oaks, repeated behind his eyes three dozen times in rapid succession.

"Nothing there, am I correct?"

Charon stared hard at his guest.

"I was a cleric, and in copying a sacred text describing the environs of Hell, I deviated from the disintegrating original and added the existence of Oondeshai. Over the course of years, decades, centuries, other scholars found my creation and added it to their own works and so, now, Oondeshai, though not as well known as yourself or your river, is an actuality in this desperate land."

From down along the riverbank came the approaching sound of Cerberus baying. Wieroot stood, sloughing off the cloak to let it drop into his chair. "I've got to get to the river," he said. "But consider this. You live in the skull of a fallen god. This space was once filled with a substance that directed the universe, no, was the universe. How does a god die?"

"You'll never get across," said Charon.

"I don't want to. I want to be caught in its flow."

"You'll drown."

"Yes, I'll drown, be bitten by the spiny eels, burned in the River of Fire, but I won't die, for I'm already dead. Some time ages hence, my body will wash up on the shore of Oondeshai, and I will have arrived home."

"What gave you cause to create this island?" asked the boatman.

Wieroot staggered toward the door. As he opened it and stepped out into the pitch black, he called back, "I knew I would eventually commit murder."

Charon followed out into the night and heard the man's feet pacing away down the flint hill toward the river. Seconds later, he heard the wheezing breath of the three-headed dog. Growling, barking, sounded in triplicate. There was silence for a time, and then finally . . . a splash, and in that moment, for the merest instant, an image of a beautiful island flashed behind the boatman's eyes.

He'd nearly been able to forget the incident with Wieroot as the centuries flowed on, their own River of Pain, until one day he heard one of his passengers whisper the word "Oondeshai" to another. Three or four times this happened, and then, only a half-century past, a young woman, still radiant though dead, with shiny black hair and a curious red dot of a birthmark just below her left eye, was ushered onto his boat. He requested payment. When she tilted her head back, opened her mouth, and lifted her tongue, there was no coin but instead a small, tightly folded package of flesh. Charon nearly lost his temper as he retrieved it from her mouth, but she whispered quickly, "A map to Oondeshai."

These words were like a slap to his face. He froze for the merest instant, but then thought quickly and, nodding, stepped aside for her to take a seat. "Next," he yelled and the demons were none the wiser. Later that night, he unfolded the crudely cut rectangle of skin, and after a close inspection of the tattoo cursed himself for having been duped. He swept the map onto the floor and the night breeze blew it into a corner. Weeks later, after finding it had been blown back out from under the table into the middle of the floor, he lifted it and searched it again. This time he noticed the freckle in the length of Lethe's blue line and wondered.

He kept his boat in a small lagoon hidden by a thicket of black poplars. It was just after sunrise, and he'd already stowed his provisions in the hold below deck. After lashing them fast with lengths of hangman's rope cast off over the years by certain passengers, he turned around to face the chaotically beating heart of the craft. The large blood organ, having once resided in the chest of the Queen of Sirens, was suspended in the center of the hold by thick branch-like veins and arteries that grew into the sides of the boat. Its vasculature expanded and contracted, and the heart itself beat erratically, undulating and shivering, sweating red droplets.

Charon waited until after it died, lay still, and then was startled back to life by whatever immortal force pervaded it chambers. Once it was moving again, he gave a high-pitched whistle, a note that began at the bottom of the register and quickly rose to the top. At the sound of this signal, the wet red meat of the thing parted in a slit to reveal an eye. The orb swiveled to and fro, and the boatman stepped up close with a burning tallow in one hand and the map, opened, in the other. He backlit the scrap of skin to let the eye read its tattoo. He'd circled the freckle that represented Oondeshai with his quill, so the destination was clearly marked. All he'd have to do is steer around the dangers, keep the keel in deep water, and stay awake. Otherwise, the craft now knew the way to go.

Up on deck, he cast off the ropes, and instead of uttering the word "There," he spoke a command used less than once a century —"Away." The boat moved out of the lagoon and onto the river. Charon felt something close to joy at not having to steer between the giant white oaks. He glanced up to his left at the top of the flint hill and saw the huge skull, staring down at him. The day was hot and orange and all of Hell was busy at the work of suffering, but he, the boatman, was off on a holiday.

On the voyage out, he traveled with the flow of the river, so its current combined with the inherent, enchanted propulsion of the boat made for swift passage. There were the usual whirlpools, out-croppings of sulfur and brimstone to avoid, but these occasional obstacles were a welcome diversion. He'd never taken this route before when on holiday. Usually, he'd just stay home, resting, mak-ing minor repairs to the boat, playing knucklebones with some of the bat-winged demons from the pit on a brief break from the gruel-ing work of torture.

Once, as a guest of the Master during a holiday, he'd been in-vited into the bottommost reaches of the pit, transported in a winged chariot that glided down through the center of the great spiral. There, where the Czar of the Underworld kept a private palace made of frozen sighs, in a land of snow so cold one's breath fractured upon touching the air, he was led by an army of living marble statues, shaped like men but devoid of faces, down a tunnel that led to an enormous circle of clear ice. Through this transparent barrier he could look out on the realm of the living. Six days he spent transfixed between astonishment and fear at the sight of the world the way it was. That vacation left a splinter of ice in his heart that took three centuries to melt.

None of his previous getaways ever resulted in a tenth the sense of relief he already felt having gone but a few miles along the nauti-cal route to Oondeshai. He repeated the name of the island again and again under his breath as he worked the tiller or manned the shallows pole, hoping to catch another glimpse of its image as he had the night Wieroot dove into the Acheron. As always, that men-tal picture refused to coalesce, but he'd learned to suffice with its absence, which had become a kind of solace in itself.

To avoid dangerous eddies and rocks in the middle flow of the river, Charon was occasionally forced to steer the boat in close to shore on the port side. There, he glimpsed the marvels of that remote, forgotten landscape: a distant string of smoldering volca-noes; a thundering herd of bloodless behemoths, sweeping like a white wave across the immensity of a fissured salt flat; a glittering forest of crystal trees alive with long-tailed monkeys made of lead. The distractions were many, but he struggled to put away his curiosity and concentrate for fear of running aground and ripping a hole in the hull.

He hoped to make the River of Fire before nightfall, so as to have light with which to navigate. To travel the Acheron blind would be sheer suicide, and unlike Wieroot, Charon was uncertain as to whether he was already dead or alive or merely a figment of Hell's imagination. There was the possibility of finding a natural harbor and dropping the anchor, but the land through which the river ran had shown him fierce and mysterious creatures stalking him along the banks, and that made steering through the dark seem the fairer alternative.

As the day waned, and the sun began to whine with the pain of its gradual death, Charon peered ahead with a hand shading his sight in anticipation of a glimpse at the flames of Pyriphlegethon. During his visit to the palace of frozen sighs, the Master had let slip that the liquid fire of those waters burned only sinners. Because the boat was a tool of Hell, made of Hell, he was fairly certain it could withstand the flames, but he wasn't sure if at some point in his distant past he had not sinned. If he were to blunder into suffering, though, he thought that he at least would learn some truth about himself.

In the last moments of light, he lit three candles and positioned them at the prow of the boat. They proved ineffectual against the night, casting their glow only a shallows pole length ahead of the craft. Their glare wearied Charon's eyes and he grew fatigued. To distract himself from fatigue, he went below and brought back a dried, salted Harpy leg to chew on. In recent centuries the winged creatures had grown scrawny, almost thin enough to slip his snares. The meat was known to improve eyesight and exacerbate the mind. Its effect had nothing to do with clarity, merely a kind of agitation of thought that was, at this juncture, preferable to slumber. Sleep was the special benefit of the working class of Hell, and the boatman usually relished it. Dreams especially were an exotic escape from the routine of work. The sinners never slept, nor did the Master.

It was precisely at the center of the night that Charon felt some urge, some pull of intuition to push the tiller hard to the left. As soon as he'd made the reckless maneuver, he heard from up ahead the loud gulping sound that meant a whirlpool lay in his path. The sound grew quickly to a deafening strength, and only when he was upon the swirling monster, riding its very lip around the right arc, was he able to see its immensity. The boat struggled to free itself from the draw, and instead of being propelled by its magic it seemed to be clawing its way forward, dragging its weight free of the hopeless descent. There was nothing he could do but hold the tiller firm and stare with widened eyes down the long, treacherous tunnel. Not a moment passed after he was finally free of it than the boat entered the turbulent waters where Acheron crossed the River of Fire.

He released his grip on the tiller and let the craft lead him with its knowledge of the map he'd shown it. His fingers gripped tightly into the eyeholes of two of the skulls that formed his seat, and he held on so as not to be thrown overboard. Pyriphlegethon now blazed ahead of him, and the sight of its dancing flames, some flaring high into the night, made him scream, not with fear but exhilaration. The boat cleaved the burning surface, and then was engulfed in a yellow-orange brightness that gave no heat. The frantic illumination dazed Charon, and he sat as in a trance, dreaming wide-awake. He no longer felt the passage of Time, the urgency to reach his destination, the weight of all those things he'd fled on his holiday.

Eventually, after a prolonged bright trance, the blazing waters became turbulent, lost their fire, and a thick mist rose off them. That mist quickly became a fog so thick it seemed to have texture, brushing against his skin like a feather. He thought he might grab handfuls until it slipped through his fingers, leaked into his nostrils, and wrapped its tentacles around his memory.

When the boatman awoke to the daily birth cry of Hell's sun, he found himself lying naked upon his bed, staring up at the clutch of bat bones dangling from the cranial center of his skull home. He was startled at first, grasping awkwardly for a tiller that wasn't there, tightening his fist around the shaft of the absent shallows pole that instead rested at an angle against the doorway. As soon as the shock of discovery that he was actually home had abated, he sighed deeply and sat up on the edge of the bed. It struck him then that his entire journey, his holiday, had been for naught.

He frantically searched his thoughts for the slightest shred of a memory that he might have reached Oondeshai, but every trace had been forgotten. For the first time in centuries, tears came to his eyes, and the frustration of his predicament made him cry out. Eventually, he stood and found his cloak rolled into a ball on the floor at the foot of his bed. He dressed and without stopping to put on his boots or grab the shallows pole, he left his home.

With determination in his stride, he mounted the small rise that lay back behind the skull and stood at the rim of the enormous pit. Inching to the very edge, he peered down into the spiraled depths at the faint red glow. The screams of tortured sinners, the wailing laments of self-pity, sounded in his ears like distant voices in a dream. Beneath it all he could barely discern, like the buzzing of a fly, the sound of the Master laughing uproariously, joyously, and that discordant strain seemed to lace itself subtly into everything.

Charon's anger and frustration slowly melted into a kind of numbness as cold as the hallways of Satan's palace, and he swayed to and fro, out over the edge and back, not so much wanting to jump as waiting to fall. Time passed, he was not aware how much, and then as suddenly as he had dressed and left his home, he turned away from the pit.

Once more inside the skull, he prepared to go to work. There was a great heaviness within him, as if his very organs were now made of lead, and each step was an effort, each exhalation a sigh. He found his eelskin ankle boots beneath the table at which he'd studied the flesh map at night. Upon lifting one, it turned in his hand, and a steady stream of blond sand poured out onto the floor. The sight of it caught him off guard and for a moment he stopped breathing.

He fell to his knees to inspect the little pile that had formed. Carefully, he lifted the other boot, turned it over, and emptied that one into its own neat little pile next to the other. He reached toward these twin wonders, initially wanting to feel the grains run through his fingers, but their stark proof that he had been to Oondeshai and could not recall a moment of it ultimately defeated his will and he never touched them. Instead, he stood, took up the shallows pole, and left the skull for his boat.

As he guided the boat between the two giant oaks, he no longer wondered if all his journeys across the Acheron were always the same journey. With a dull aspect, he performed his duties as the boatman. His muscles, educated in the task over countless centuries, knew exactly how to avoid the blue serpent and skirt the whirlpools without need of a single thought. No doubt it was these same unconscious processes that had brought Charon and his craft back safely from Oondeshai.

Gesnil and Trinkthil inquired with great anticipation about his vacation when he met them on the far shore. For the demons, who knew no respite from the drudgery of herding sinners, even a few words about a holiday away would have been like some rare confection, but he told them nothing. From the look on Charon's face, they knew not to prod him and merely sent the travelers forward to offer coins and take their places on the benches.

During the return trip that morning, a large fellow sitting among the passengers had a last second attack of nerves in the face of an impending eternity of suffering. He screamed incoherently, and Charon ordered him to silence. When the man stood up and began pacing back and forth, the boatman ordered him to return to his seat. The man persisted moving about, his body jerking with spasms of fear, and it was obvious his antics were spooking the other sinners. Fearing the man would spread mutiny, Charon came forth with the shallows pole and bringing it around like a club, split the poor fellow's head. That was usually all the incentive a recalcitrant passenger needed to return to the bench, but this one was now insane with the horror of his plight.

The boatman waded in and beat him wildly, striking him again and again. With each blow, Charon felt some infinitesimal measure of relief from his own frustration. When he was finished, the agitator lay in a heap on deck, nothing more than a flesh bag full of broken bones, and the other passengers shuffled their feet sideways so as not to touch his corpse.

Only later, after he had docked his boat in the lagoon and the winged demons had flown out of the pit to lead the damned up the flint hill and down along the spiral path to their eternal destinies, did the boatman regret his rage. As he lifted the sack of flesh that had been his charge and dumped it like a bale of chum over the side, he realized that the man's hysteria had been one and the same thing as his own frustration.

The sun sounded its death cry as it sank into a pool of blood that was the horizon and then Hell's twilight came on. Charon dragged himself up the hill and went inside his home. Before pure night closed its fist on the riverbank, he kicked off his boots, gnawed on a haunch of Harpy flesh, and lit the tallow that sat in its holder on the table. Taking his seat there he stared into the flame, thinking of it as the future that constantly drew him forward through years, decades, centuries, eons, as the past disappeared behind him. "I am nothing but a moment," he said aloud and his words echoed around the empty skull.

Some time later, still sitting at his chair at the table, he noticed the candle flame twitch. His eyes shifted for the first time in hours to follow its movement. Then the fire began to dance, the sheets of flesh parchment lifted slightly at their corners, the bat bones clacked quietly overhead. Hell's deceptive wind of memory had begun to blow. He heard it whistling in through the space in his home's grin, felt its coolness sweep around him. This most complex and exquisite torture that brought back to sinners the times of their lives, now worked on the boatman. He moved his bare feet beneath the table and realized the piles of sand lay beneath them.

The image began in his mind no more than a dot of blue and then rapidly unfolded in every direction to reveal a sky and crystal water. The sun there in Oondeshai had been yellow and it gave true warmth. This he remembered clearly. He'd sat high on a hill of blond sand, staring out across the endless vista of sparkling water. Next to him on the left was Wieroot, legs crossed, dressed in a black robe, and sporting a beard to hide the healing scars that riddled his face. On the right was the young woman with the shining black hair and the red dot of a birthmark beneath her left eye.

". . . And you created this all by writing it in the other world?" asked Charon. There was a breeze blowing and the boatman felt a certain lightness inside as if he'd eaten of one of the white clouds floating across the sky.

"I'll tell you a secret," said Wieroot, "although it's a shame you'll never get a chance to put it to use."

"Tell me," said the boatman.

"God made the world with words," he said in a whisper.

Charon remembered that he didn't understand. He furrowed his brow and turned to look at the young woman to see if she was laughing. Instead she was also nodding along with Wieroot. She put her hand on the boatman's shoulder and said, "And man made God with words."

Charon's memory of the beach on Oondeshai suddenly gave violent birth to another memory from his holiday. He was sitting in a small structure with no door, facing out into a night scene of tall trees whose leaves were blowing in a strong wind. Although it was night, it was not the utter darkness he knew from his quadrant of Hell. High in the black sky there shone a bright disk, which cast its beams down onto the island. Their glow had seeped into the small home behind him and fell upon the forms of Wieroot and the woman, Shara was her name, where they slept upon a bed of reeds. Beneath the sound of the wind, the calls of night birds, the whirr of insects, he heard the steady breathing of the sleeping couple.

And one last memory followed. Charon recalled Wieroot drawing near to him as he was about to board his boat for the return journey.

"You told me you committed murder," said the boatman.

"I did," said Wieroot.

"Who?"

"The god whose skull you live in," came the words, which grew faint and then disappeared as the night wind of Hell ceased blowing. The memories faded and Charon looked up to see the candle flame again at rest. He reached across the table and drew his writing quill and a sheaf of parchment toward him. Dipping the pen nib into the pot of blood that was his ink, he scratched out two words at the top of the page. *My Story*, he wrote, and then set about remembering the future. The words came, slowly at first, reluctantly, dragging their imagery behind them, but after a short while their numbers grew to equal the number of sinners awaiting a journey to the distant shore. He ferried them methodically, expertly, from his mind to the page, scratching away long into the dark night of Hell until down at the bottom of the spiral pit, in his palace of frozen sighs, Satan stopped laughing.

Boatman's Holiday

Story Notes

Neil Ayres, a writer from the UK, contacted me about an anthology he was involved with, entitled Book of Voices, *to be published by Flame Books. The proceeds of the book will support writers in Sierra Leone, part of PEN's Africa 05 project. I was thankful for the opportunity to have a chance to submit a story, and I congratulate Neil, editor Mike Butscher, and the other authors for devoting their time and energy to a worthwhile cause. The loose theme of the book was* imprisonment. *At first, I had a hard time coming up with a story. Just thinking about what's gone on politically and socially in Sierra Leone in the past few years, and then comparing that to what I saw outside the window in my sleepy little South Jersey town, I became aware of a rather large disconnect. I realized that for me to come up with anything that would bear some meaning for those to whom the book's efforts are dedicated, the story would have to tend toward the mythic. Before I had any story at all, I had a title rolling around in my head for a while, which I didn't associate with this project. I don't know where "Boatman's Holiday" came from, but every once in a while I'd take that title out in my mind and roll it around a little. One day, I was looking at a book of illustrations by Doré, which contained a few plates from his illustrated* Dante. *One was of Charon, the boatman of Hell. The idea for the title and the picture collided in my head, and I saw this story all at once. I meant to use some of the images I still remembered from having read* The Inferno, *but I also wanted to customize this vision to suit myself. The prospect of messing with this rich mythical figure and landscape got me excited and, after that, I wrote the piece pretty quickly.*

Botch Town

IT ALL BEGAN IN THE LAST DAYS OF AUGUST WHEN the leaves of the elm in the front yard had curled into crisp, brown tubes and fallen away to litter the lawn. I remember I sat at the curb that afternoon, waiting for Mr. Softee to round the bend at the top of Pine Avenue, listening carefully for that mournful knell, each measured *ding* both a promise of ice cream and a pinprick of remorse. Taking a castoff leaf into each hand, I made double fists. When I opened my fingers, brown crumbs fell and scattered on the road at my feet. Had I been waiting for the arrival of the stranger, I might have understood the sifting debris to be symbolic of the end of something. Instead, I waited for the eyes.

That morning, I'd left the house early under a blue sky, walked through the woods and crossed the railroad tracks away from town, where the third rail hummed and lay in wait, like a snake, for an errant ankle. Then, along the road by the fastener factory, back behind the grocery, and up and down the streets, I searched for discarded glass bottles in every open garbage can, dumpster, forgotten corner. By early afternoon, I'd found three soda bottles and a half-gallon milk bottle. At the grocery store, I turned them in for the refund and walked away with a quarter.

All summer long, Mr. Softee had this contest going. With each purchase of twenty-five cents or more, he gave you a card: on the front was a small portrait of the waffle-faced cream being pictured on the side of the truck. On the back was a piece of a puzzle that, when joined with seven other cards, made the same exact image of the beckoning soft one but eight times bigger. I had the blue lapels and red bow tie, the sugar-cone-flesh lips parted in a pure white smile, the exposed, towering brain of vanilla, cream kissed at the top into a pointed swirl, but I didn't have the eyes.

A complete puzzle won you the Special Softee, like Coney Island in a plastic dish—four twirled Softee loads of cream, chocolate sauce, butterscotch, marshmallow goo, nuts, party-colored sprinkles, raisins, M&M's, shredded coconut, bananas, all topped with a cherry. You couldn't purchase the Special Softee, you had to win it, or so said John, who, through the years, had come to be known simply as Softee.

Occasionally John would try to be pleasant, but I think the paper canoe of a hat he wore every day had soured his disposition irreparably. He also wore a blue bow tie, a white shirt, and white pants. His face was long and crooked, and, at times, when the orders came too fast and the kids didn't have the right change, the bottom half of it would slowly melt—a sundae abandoned at the curb. His long ears sprouted tufts of hair as if his skull contained a hedge of it, and the lenses of his glasses had internal flaws like diamonds. In a voice that came straight from his freezer, he called my sister, Mary, and all the other girls, "Sweetheart."

Earlier in the season, one late afternoon, my brother, Jim, said to me, "You wanna see where Softee lives?" We took our bikes. He led me way up Higbee Lane, past the shoe store and Paumonok School, up beyond Our Lady of Lourdes. After an hour of riding, he stopped in front of a small house. As I pulled up, he pointed to the place and said, "Look at that dump."

Softee's truck was parked on a barren plot at the side of the place. I remember ivy and a one-story house, no bigger than a good-sized garage. Shingles showed their zebra stripes through fading white. The porch had obviously sustained a meteor shower. There were no lights on inside, and I thought this strange because twilight was mixing in behind the trees.

"Is he sitting in there in the dark?" I asked my brother.

Jim shrugged as he got back on his bike. He rode in big circles around me twice and then shot off down the street, screaming over his shoulder as loud as he could, "Softee sucks!" The ride home was through true night, and he knew that without him I would get lost, so he pedaled as hard as he could.

We had forsaken the ostentatious jingle bells of Bungalow Bar and Good Humor all summer in an attempt to win. By the end of

July, though, each of the kids on the block had at least two near-complete puzzles, but no one had the eyes. I had heard from Tim Caliban, who lived in the development on the other side of the school field, that the kids over there got fed up one day and rushed the truck, jumped up and swung from the bar that held the rearview mirror, invaded the driver's compartment, all the while yelling, "Give us the eyes. The fuckin' eyes." When Softee went up front to chase them, Tim's brother, Bill, leaped up on the sill of the window through which Softee served his customers, leaned into the inner sanctum, unlatched the freezer, and started tossing Italian Ices out to the kids standing at the curb.

Softee lost his glasses in the fray, but the hat held on. He screamed, "You little bitches!" at them as they played him back and forth from the driver's area to the serving compartment. In the end, Bill got two big handfuls of cards and tossed them out on the lawn. "Like flies on dogshit," said Tim, describing the scene. By the time they realized there wasn't a pair of eyes in the bunch, Softee had turned the bell off and was coasting silently around the corner.

I had a theory, though, that day at summer's end when I sat at the curb, waiting. It was my hope that Softee had been holding out on us until the close of the season, and then, in the final days before school started and he quit his route till spring, some kid was going to have bestowed upon him a pair of eyes. I had faith like I never had at church that something special was going to happen that day to me. It did, but it had nothing to do with ice cream. I sat there at the curb, waiting, until the sun started to go down and my mother called me in for dinner. Softee never came again, but as it turned out, we all got the eyes.

My mother was a better painter than she was a cook. I loved her landscape of the snow-covered peak of Mount Kilimanjaro, rising above the clouds while gazelles grazed in the savannah of the foreground, but I wasn't much for her spaghetti with tomato soup.

She stood at the kitchen stove over a big pot of it, glass of cream sherry in one hand, burning cigarette with a three-quarter-inch ash in the other. When she turned and saw me, she said, "Go wash your hands." I headed down the hall toward the bathroom and, out of the corner of my eye, caught sight of that ash falling into the pot. Before I opened the bathroom door, I heard her mutter, "Could you possibly . . ." followed hard by the mud-sucking sounds of her stirring the orange glug.

When I came out of the bathroom, I got the job of mixing the powdered milk and serving each of us kids a glass. At the end of the meal there would be three full glasses of it sitting on the table. Unfortunately, we still remembered real milk. The mix-up kind tasted like sauerkraut, and looked like chalk water with froth on the top. It was there merely for show, a kind of stage prop. As long as no one mentioned that it tasted horrible, my mother never forced us to drink it.

In the dining room where the walls were lined with grained paneling, the knots of which always showed me screaming faces, Jim sat across the table from me, and Mary sat by my side. My mother sat at the end of the table beneath the open window. Instead of a plate she had the ashtray and her wine in front of her.

"It's rib stickin' good," said Jim, and added a knifeful of margarine to his plate. When the orange stuff started to cool, it was in need of constant lubrication to prevent it from seizing.

"Shut up and eat," said my mother.

Mary said nothing. I could tell by the way she quietly nodded her head that she was being Mickey.

"Softee never came today," I said.

My brother looked up at me and shook his head in disappointment. "He'll be out there at the curb in a snow drift," he said to my mother.

She laughed without a sound and swatted the air in his direction. "You've got to have faith," she said. "Life's one long son of a bitch."

She took a drag on her cigarette and a sip of wine, and Jim and I knew what was coming next.

"When things get better," she said. "I think we'll all take a nice vacation."

"How about Bermuda?" said Jim.

In her wine fog, my mother hesitated an instant, not sure if he was being sarcastic, but he knew how to keep a straight face. "That's what I was thinking," she said. We knew that, because once a week, when she hit just the right level of intoxication, that's what she was always thinking. It had gotten to the point that when Jim wanted me to do him a favor and I asked how he was going to pay me back, he'd say, "Don't worry, I'll take you to Bermuda."

She told us about the water, crystal blue. So clear you could look down a hundred yards and see schools of manta rays flapping their wings. She told us about the pure white beaches with palm trees swaying in a soft breeze filled with the scent of wildflowers. We'd sleep in hammocks on the beach. We'd eat pineapples we cut open with a machete. Swim in lagoons. Washed up on the shore, amidst the chambered nautilus, the sand dollars, the shark teeth, would be pieces of eight from galleons wrecked long ago.

That night, as usual, she told it all, and she told it in minute detail, so that even Jim sat there listening with his eyes half-closed and his mouth half-open.

"Will there be clowns?" asked Mary in her Mickey voice.

"Sure," said my mother.

"How many?" asked Mary.

"Eight," said my mother.

Mary nodded in approval and went back to being Mickey.

When we got back from Bermuda, it was time to do the dishes. From the leftovers in the pot, my mother heaped a plate with spaghetti for my father for when he got home from work. She wrapped it in wax paper and put it in the center of the stove where the pilot light would keep it warm. Whatever was left over went to George the dog. My mother washed the dishes, smoking and drinking the entire time. Jim dried, I put the plates and silverware away, and Mary counted everything a few dozen times.

The garage of our house had, five years earlier, been converted into an apartment and my grandparents, Nan and Pop, lived in there. A door separated our house from their rooms. My mother knocked, and Nan called out for us to come in.

Pop took out his mandolin and played us a few songs: "Apple Blossom Time," "Show Me the Way to Go Home," "Good Night Irene." All the while he played, Nan chopped cabbage on a flat wooden board with a one-handed guillotine. My mother rocked in the rocking chair and drank and sang. The trilling of the double-stringed instrument accompanied by my mother's voice was beautiful to me.

Over at the little table in the kitchenette area, Mary sat with the Laredo machine, making cigarettes. My parents didn't buy their smokes by the pack. Instead they got this machine that you loaded with a piece of paper and a wad of loose tobacco from a can. Once it was all set up, there was a little lever you pulled forward and back, and presto. It wasn't an easy operation. You had to use just the right amount to get them firm enough so the tobacco didn't fall out the end.

When my parents had first gotten the Laredo, Mary watched them perform the process and was fascinated. She was immediately expert at measuring out the brown shag and never got tired of it. A regular cigarette factory once she got going; Pop called her R. J. Reynolds. He didn't smoke them, though. He smoked

Lucky Strikes, and he drank Old Grand-Dad, which seemed fitting.

Jim and I, we watched the television with the sound turned down. Dick Van Dyke mugged and rubber-legged and did pratfalls in black and white, perfectly synchronized to the strains of "Shanty Town" and "I'll Be Seeing You in All the Old Familiar Places." Even if they weren't playing music, we wouldn't have been able to have the sound up, since Pop hated Dick Van Dyke more than any other person on Earth.

My room was dark, and though it had been warm all day, a cool end of summer breeze now filtered in through the screen of the open window. Moonlight also came in, making a patch on the bare, painted floor. From outside, I could hear the chug of the Farleys' little pool filter next door, and beneath that, the sound of George's claws, tapping across the kitchen linoleum downstairs.

Jim was asleep in his room across the hall. Below us, Mary was also asleep, no doubt whispering the times tables into her pillow. My mother, in the room next to Mary's, I could picture, lying in bed, her reading light on, her mouth open, her eyes closed, and the thick, red volume of Sherlock Holmes stories with the silhouette cameo of the detective on the spine, open and resting on her chest. All I could picture of Nan and Pop was a darkened room and the tiny, glowing bottle of Lourdes Water in the shape of the Virgin that sat on the dresser.

I was thinking about the book I had been reading before turning out the light—another in the series of adventures of Perno Shell. This one was about a deluge, like Noah's flood, and how the old wooden apartment building he lived in had broken away from its foundation and he and all of the other tenants were sailing the giant ocean of the world, having adventures.

There was a mystery about the Shell books, because they were each published with a different author's name, sometimes by different publishing companies, but all you had to do was read a few pages and it was easy to tell that they were all written by the same person. I would never have discovered this if it wasn't for Mary.

Occasionally, I would read to her, snatches from whatever book I was working through. We'd sit in the corner of the backyard on the lower boards of the fence, in the bower made by forsythia bushes. In there, amidst the yellow flowers one day, I read to her from the first Shell book I had taken out: *The Stars Above* by Mary Holden. There were illustrations in it, one per chapter. When I was done reading, I handed the book to her so she could look at the pictures. While paging through it, she held it up to her face, sniffed it, and said, "Pipe smoke." Back then, my father smoked a pipe once in a while, so we knew the aroma. I took the book from her and smelled it up close, and she was right, but it wasn't the kind of tobacco my father smoked. It had a darker, older smell, something like a horse and a mildewed wool blanket, a captain's cabin. I got an image of the silhouette of Holmes on the binding of my mother's book. His pipe had a stem that dipped in a curve like an S and the bowl had a belly.

When I walked to the library downtown, Mary would walk with me. She usually never said a word during the entire trip, but a few weeks after I had returned *The Stars Above*, she came to me while I was searching through the four big stacks that lay in the twilight zone between the adult and children's sections. She tugged at my shirt, and when I turned around, she handed me a book: *The Enormous Igloo* by Duncan Main.

"Pipe smoke," she said.

Opening the volume to the first page, I read to myself, "*Perno Shell was afraid of heights and could not for the world remember why he had agreed to a journey in the Zeppelin that now hovered above his head.*" Another Perno Shell novel by someone completely different. I lifted the book, smelled the pages, and nodded.

I wanted Perno Shell to stay in my imagination until I dozed off, but my thoughts of him soon grew as thin as paper, and then the persistent theme of my wakeful nights alone in the dark, namely *Death*, came clawing through. Jimmy Bonnel, a boy who'd lived up the block, two years younger than me and two years older than Mary, had been struck by a car on Montauk Highway one night in late spring. The driver was drunk and swerved onto the sidewalk. According to his brother, Teddy, who was with him, Jimmy was thrown thirty feet in the air. I always tried to picture that: twice again the height of the basketball rim. We had to go to his wake. The priest said he was at peace, but he didn't look it. Lying in the coffin, his skin was yellow, his face was bloated, and his mouth was turned down in a bitter frown.

All summer, he came back to me from where he lay under the ground. I imagined him suddenly waking up, clawing at the lid as in a story Jim had once told me. I dreaded meeting his ghost on the street at night when I walked George around the block alone. I'd stop under a streetlight and listen hard, fear would build in my chest until I shivered, and then I'd bolt for home. In the lonely backyard at sundown, in the darkened woods behind the school field, in the corner of my night room, he was waiting, jealous and angry.

George came up the stairs and stood beside my bed. He looked at me with his bearded face, eyes glinting in the moonlight, and then jumped aboard. He was a small, schnauzer-type mutt but fearless, and having him there made me less scared. Slowly, I began to doze. I had a memory of riding waves at Fire Island and it blurred at the edges, slipping into a dream. Next I knew, I suddenly fell from a great height and woke to hear my father coming in from work. The front door quietly closed. I could hear him moving around in the kitchen. George got up and left.

I contemplated going down to say hello. The last I saw him was the previous weekend. The bills forced him to work all day. There were three jobs: a part-time machining job in the early morning, then his regular job as a gear cutter, and then nights, part-time as a janitor in a department store. He left the house before the sun came up every morning and didn't return until very near midnight. Through the week, I would smell a hint of machine oil, here and there, on the cushions of the couch, on a towel in the bathroom, as if he were a ghost leaving vague traces of his presence.

Eventually, the sounds of the refrigerator opening and closing and the water running stopped, and I realized he must be sitting in the dining room, eating his pile of spaghetti, reading the newspaper by the light that shone in from the kitchen. I heard the big pages turn, the fork against the plate, a match being struck, and that's when it happened. There came from somewhere outside the house the shrill scream of a woman, so loud it tore open the night.

When I came downstairs the next morning, the door to Nan and Pop's was open. I stuck my head in and saw Mary sitting at the table in the kitchenette where the night before she had made cigarettes. She was eating a bowl of Cheerios. Pop sat in his usual seat next to her, the horse paper spread out in front of him. He was jotting down numbers with a pencil in the margins, murmuring a steady stream of bloodlines, jockeys' names, weights, speeds, track conditions, ciphering what he called the *McGinn System*, named after himself. Mary nodded with each new factor added to the equation.

My mother came out of the bathroom down the hall in our house, and I turned around. She was dressed for work in her turquoise outfit with the big star-shaped pin that was like a stained-glass window. I went to her and she put her arm around me, enveloped me in a cloud of perfume that was too much powder, and kissed my head. We went into the kitchen, and she made me a bowl of cereal with the mix-up milk, which wasn't as bad that way, because we were allowed to put sugar on it. I sat down in the dining room and she joined me, carrying a cup of coffee. The sunlight poured in the window behind her. She lit a cigarette and dragged the ashtray close to her.

"Friday, last day of vacation," she said. "You better make it a good one. Monday is back to school."

I nodded.

"Watch out for strangers," she said. "I got a call from next door this morning. Mrs. Kelty said that there was a prowler at her window last night. She was changing into her nightgown, and she turned and saw a face at the glass."

"Did she scream?" I asked.

"She said it scared the crap out of her. Bill was downstairs watching TV. He jumped up and ran outside, but whoever it was had vanished."

Jim appeared in the living room. "Do you think they saw her naked?" he asked.

"A fitting punishment," she said. And as quickly added, "Don't repeat that."

"I heard her scream," I said.

"Whoever it was used that old ladder Pop keeps in the backyard. Put it up against the side of the Keltys' house and climbed up to the second-floor window. So keep your eyes out for creeps wherever you go today."

"That means he was in our backyard," said Jim.

My mother took a drag of her cigarette and nodded. "I suppose."

Before she left for work, she gave us our list of jobs for the day — walk George, clean our rooms, mow the back lawn. Then she kissed Jim and me, and went into Nan's to kiss Mary. I watched her car pull out of the driveway. Jim came to stand next to me at the front window.

"A prowler," he said, smiling. "We better investigate."

A half-hour later, Jim and Mary and I, joined by David Kelty, sat back amidst the forsythias.

"Did the prowler see your mother naked?" Jim asked David.

David had a hairdo like Curly from the Three Stooges, and he rubbed his head with his fat, blunt fingers. "I think so," he said, wincing.

"A fitting punishment," said Jim.

"What do you mean?" asked David.

"Think about your mother's ass," said Jim, laughing.

David sat quietly for a second and then said, "Yeah," and nodded.

Mary took out a Laredo cigarette and lit it. She always stole one or two when making them. No one would have guessed. Mary was sneaky in a way, though. The favorite song of her life would end up being "Time of the Season" by The Zombies, so that gives you a clue. Jim would have told on me if I'd smoked one. All he did was tell her, "You'll stay short if you smoke that." She took a drag and said, "Could you possibly . . ." in a flat voice.

Jim, big boss that he was, laid it out for us. "I'll be the detective and you all will be my team. Jeff," he said, pointing to me, "you have to write everything down. Everything that happens has to be recorded. I have a notebook upstairs to give you. Don't be lazy."

"Okay," I said.

"Mary," he said. She just kept nodding as she had been. "You count shit. And none of that Mickey stuff."

"I'm counting now," she said in her Mickey voice.

We cracked up, but she didn't laugh.

"David, you're my right-hand man. You do whatever the hell I tell you."

David agreed, and then Jim told us the first thing we needed to do was look for clues.

"Did your mother say what the prowler's face looked like?" I asked.

"She said it was no one she ever saw before. Big eyes, big teeth, and really white, like he hadn't seen the sun all summer."

"Could be a vampire," I said.

"It wasn't a vampire," said Jim, "it was a pervert. If we're going to do this right, it's got to be like Science. There are no such things as vampires."

Our first step was to investigate the scene of the crime. Beneath the Keltys' second-floor bedroom window, on the side of their house next to ours, we found a good footprint. It was big, much larger than any of ours when we measured next to it, and it had a design on the bottom of lines and circles.

"You see what that is?" asked Jim, squatting down and pointing to the design.

"It's from a sneaker," I said.

"Yeah," he said.

"I think it's Keds," said David.

"What does that tell you?" asked Jim.

"What?" asked David.

"Well, it's too big to be a kid, but grown-ups usually don't wear sneakers. It might be a teenager. We better save this for if the cops ever come to investigate."

"Did your dad call the cops?" I asked.

"No, he said that if he ever caught who it was, he'd shoot the son of a bitch himself."

It took us about a half-hour to dig the footprint up, carefully loosening all around it and scooping way down beneath it with the shovel. We went to Nan's side door and asked her if she had a box. She gave us a round, pink hatbox with a lid that had a picture of a poodle and the Eiffel Tower on it.

Jim told David, "Carry it like it's nitro," and we took it into our yard and stored it in the toolshed back by the fence. When David slid it into place on the wooden shelf next to the bottles of bug killer and the shears, Mary said, "One."

Nan made lunch for us when the fire whistle blew at noon. She served it in our house at the dining room table. Her sandwiches always had butter, no matter what else she put on them. Sometimes, like that day, she just made butter and sugar sandwiches. We also had barley soup. Occasionally she would make chocolate pudding for us, the kind with a two-inch vinyl skin on top, but usually dessert was just a sugar-calloused digit she called a ladyfinger.

Nan had gray, wire-hair like George's, big bifocals, and a brown mole on her temple that looked like a squashed raisin. Her small stature, her dark and wrinkled complexion, the silken black strands at the corners of her upper lip, her high-pitched laughter made her seem to me at times like some ancient monkey king. When she'd fart while standing, she'd kick her left leg up in the back, and say, "Shoot him in the pants, the coat and vest are mine." Every morning she'd say the rosary, and at night sometimes; in the afternoon when the neighborhood ladies came over to drink wine from teacups, she'd read the future in a pack of playing cards.

Each day at lunch that summer, along with the butter sandwiches, she'd also serve up a story from her life. That first day of our investigation, she chose to tell us one from her childhood, at the turn of the century, in Whitestone. Through the hot high noons of June and July, we had come to know that town out of her distant past where her father was the editor of the local paper, the fire engines were pulled by horses, Moisha Pipick, the strongest man alive, ate twelve raw eggs every morning for breakfast, Clementine Cherenete, whose hair was a waterfall of gold, fell in love with a blind man who could not see her beauty, and John Hardy Farty, a wandering vagrant, strummed a harp and sang, "Damn the rooster crow." All events, both great and small, happened within sight of a much-referred-to landmark, Nanny Goat Hill.

"A night visitor," she said when we told her about the footprint we had found and preserved in the hatbox she had given us. "Once there was a man who lived in Whitestone, a neighbor of ours. His name was Mr. Weeks. He had a daughter, Luqueer, who was in my grade at school."

"Luqueer?" said Jim, and he and I laughed. Mary looked up from her soup to see what was funny.

Nan smiled and nodded. "She was a little odd. Spent all her time staring into a mirror. She wasn't vain but was looking for something. Her mother told my mother that at night the girl would wake up choking, blue in the face, from having dreamt she was swallowing a thimble."

"That wasn't really her name," said Jim.

"As God is my judge," said Nan. "Her father took the train every day to work in the city and did not come home until very late at night. He always got the very last train that stopped in Whitestone, just before midnight, and would walk home through the streets from the station, stumbling drunk and singing in a loud voice. It was said that when he was drunk at a bar, he was happy-go-lucky, not a care in the world, but when drunk at home, he hit his wife and cursed her.

"One night in the fall, around Halloween time, he got off the train onto the platform at Whitestone. The wind was blowing and it was cold. The station was empty but for him. He started walking toward the steps that led down to the street, when from behind him he heard a noise like a voice in the wind. *OOOOoooo* was what it sounded like. He turned around, and at the far end of the platform was a giant ghost, eight feet tall, its white form rippling in the breeze.

"It scared the bejesus out of him. He ran home, screaming. The next day, which was Saturday, he told my father that the train station was haunted. My father printed the story as a kind of joke. No one believed Mr. Weeks because everyone knew he was a drunk. Still, he tried to convince people by swearing to it and saying he knew what he saw and it was real.

"At the end of the following week, on the way into the city on Friday, he told one of the neighbors, Mr. Hardy, who rode in with him at the same time, that the ghost had been there on both Monday and Wednesday nights. On these occasions it had called his name. Weeks was a nervous wreck, stuttering and shaking while he told of his latest encounters. Mr. Hardy said Weeks was a man on the edge, but before getting off the train in the city, Weeks leaned in close to our neighbor and whispered to him that he had a plan to deal with the phantom. It was eight o'clock in the morning, and Mr. Hardy said he already smelled liquor on Weeks's breath.

"That night, Weeks returned from the city on the late train. When he got off onto the platform at Whitestone, it was deserted as usual. The moment he turned around, there was the ghost, moaning, calling his name, and now, for the first time, coming at him. But that day, in the city, Weeks had bought a pistol for four dollars. That was his plan. He took it out of his jacket, and tried to aim it, even though his hand was wobbling terribly from fear. He shot four times, and the ghost collapsed on the platform."

"How can you kill a ghost?" asked Jim.

"It was eight feet," said Mary.

"It wasn't a ghost," said Nan. "It was his wife in a bed sheet, standing on stilts. Her brother had been a performer, who had a pair of stilts, and she borrowed them from him for the get-up. She wanted to scare her husband into coming home on time and not drinking. But he killed her."

"Did he get arrested for murder?" I asked.

"No," said Nan. "He wept bitterly when he found out it was his wife. When the police investigation was over and he was shown to have acted in self-defense, he abandoned his home and Luqueer, and went off to live as a hermit in a cave in a field of wild asparagus at the edge of town. I don't remember why, but he eventually became known as Bedillia, and kids would go out to the cave and scream, 'Bedillia, we'd love to steal ya!' and run when he chased them. Luqueer got sent to an orphanage and I never saw her again."

"What happened to the hermit?" asked Jim.

"During a bad winter, someone found him in the middle of the field by his cave, frozen solid. In the spring, they buried him there among the wild asparagus."

After lunch, we put George on the leash and took him out in the backyard. Mary didn't go with us because she decided to have a session with her make-believe friends, Sally O'Mally and Sandy Graham, who lived in the closet in her room. Once in a while, she'd let them out and she would become Mickey and they would go to school together down in the cellar.

Jim had the idea that we could use George to track the pervert. We'd let him smell the ladder, he'd pick up the scent, and we'd follow along. David Kelty joined us in our backyard where the ladder again lay propped against the side of the toolshed. For a while, we just stood there waiting for the dog to smell the ladder. Then I told Jim, "You better rev him up." To rev George up all you had to do was stick your foot near his mouth. If you left it there long enough, he'd start to growl. Jim stuck his foot out and made little circles with it in the air near George's mouth. "*Geooorgieeee*," he sang very softly. When the dog had enough, he went for the foot, growling like crazy, and fake biting all over it—a hundred fake bites a second. He never really chomped down, but he worked a sneaker over pretty thoroughly.

When he was revved, he moved to the ladder, smelled it a few times, and then pissed on it. We were ready to do some tracking. George started walking and so did we. Out of the backyard we went through the gate by Nan's side of the house, over the slates and under the pink blossoms of the prehistoric mimosa tree to the front yard, and then down the block.

Around the corner was Southgate school, a one-story structure of red brick, which was a big rectangle of classrooms with a court-yard of grass at its center. On the right-hand side was an alcove that held the playground for the kindergarten—monkey bars, swings, a seesaw, a sandbox, and one of those round, turning platform things that if you got it circling fast enough, all the kids would fly off. The gym was attached on the left-hand side; a giant, windowless box of brick that towered over the squat main building.

The school had a circular drive in front with an elongated, high-curbed oval of grass at its center. Just west of the drive and the little parking lot there were two asphalt basketball courts; and then a vast field with a baseball backstop and bases, where on windy days the powdered dirt of the baselines would rise in cyclones. At the border of the field was a high barbed-wire-topped fence to prevent kids from climbing down into a crater-like sump. Someone long ago had used a chain cutter to make a slit in the fence that a small person could pass through. Down there in the early fall, among the golden rod stalks and dying weeds, it was a kingdom of crickets.

Behind the school were more vast fields of sunburnt summer grass cut by three asphalt bike paths. At the back, the school fields were bounded by another development, but to the east lay the woods: a deep oak forest that stretched well into the next town and south as far as the railroad tracks. Streams ran through it, as well as some rudimentary paths that we knew better than the lines on our own palms. A quarter-mile in, there lay a small lake that we had been told was bottomless.

That day, George led us to the boundary of the woods, near the pregnant swelling of the ground known as Sewer Pipe Hill. We stood on the side of the hill where the round, dark circle of the pipe faced the tree line. Some days a trickle of water flowed from the pipe, but now it was bone dry. Jim walked over to the round opening, three feet in circumference, leaned over, and yelled, "*Helloooooo.*" His word echoed down the dark tunnel beneath the fields of the school. George pissed on the concrete facing that held the end of the pipe.

"X marks the spot," said Jim. He turned to David. "You better crawl in there and see if the prowler is hiding underground."

David rubbed his head and stared at the black hole.

"Are you my right-hand man?" asked Jim.

"Yes," said David. "But what if he's in there?"

"Before he touches you, just say you're making a citizen's arrest."

Kelty thought about this for a moment.

"Don't do it," I said.

Jim glared at me. Then he put his hand on David's shoulder and said, "He saw your mom's ass."

David nodded and moved toward the pipe. He bent down, got on his knees at the opening, and then shuffled forward into the dark a little way before stopping. Jim went over and lightly tapped him in the rear end with the toe of his sneaker. "You'll be a hero if you find him. They'll put you in the newspaper." David started crawling slowly forward and in seconds was out of sight.

"What if he gets lost in there?" I said.

"We'll just have everyone in town flush at the same time and he'll ride the wave out into the sump behind the baseball field," said Jim.

Every few minutes, one of us would lean into the pipe and yell to David, and he would yell back. We couldn't make out what he was saying, and his voice came smaller and smaller. Then we called a few times and there was no answer.

"What do you think happened to him?" I asked.

"Maybe the pervert got him," said Jim, and he looked worried. "He could be stuck in there."

"Should I run home and get Pop?" I asked.

"No," said Jim, "go up to that manhole cover on the bike path by the playground and call down through the little hole. Then put your ear over the hole and see if you hear him. Tell him to come back."

I took off running up the side of Sewer Pipe Hill and then across the field as fast as I could. Reaching the manhole cover, I got on all fours and leaned my mouth down to the neat round hole at the edge of it. "Hey," I yelled. I then turned my head and put my ear to it.

His voice came up to me quite clearly but with a metallic ring to it, as if he were a robot. "What?" he said. "I'm here." It sounded as if he was right beneath me.

"Come out," I called. "Jim says to come back."

"I like it in here," he said.

In that moment, I pictured his house, his sister Jean with the crossed eyes, his mother's prominent jaw and horse teeth, her crazy red hair, the little man figures his father fashioned out of the wax from his own enormous ears. "You gotta come back," I said.

A half-minute passed in silence, and I thought maybe he had moved on, continuing through the darkness. Finally his voice sounded. "Okay," he said, and then, "Hey, I found something."

I found Jim sitting on the lip of the sewer pipe, reading a magazine, while George sat at his feet, staring up at him. As I eased down the side of the hill, he said, "Look what George tracked down over by that fallen tree." He pointed into the woods. "There were some crushed beer cans and cigarette butts there too."

I came up next to him and looked over his shoulder at the magazine. It was wrinkled from having been rained on and there was mud on the cover. He turned the page he was looking at toward me, and on it I saw a woman with red hair, black stockings, high heel shoes, a top hat, and an open jacket but nothing else.

"Look at the size of those tits," said Jim.

"She's naked," I whispered.

Jim picked the magazine up to his mouth, positioning it right in the middle of her spread-out legs, where the little hedge of red hair grew over her pussy, and yelled, "*Hellooooooo.*"

We laughed.

I forgot to tell Jim that I had made contact with David. Instead, we moved on to the centerfold. Three full pages of a giant blonde, bending over a piano bench.

"Aye, aye, Captain," said Jim, and rapidly saluted her ass four times. Then we flipped the pages quickly to the next naked woman, only to stare and swoon.

As I reached down to pet the dog for his discovery, we heard David inside the pipe. Jim got up and turned around and we both stared into the opening. Slowly, the soles of his shoes appeared out of the dark, then his rear end, as he backed out into daylight. When he stood up and turned to face us, he was smiling.

"What's your report?" asked Jim.

"It was nice and quiet in there," said David.

Jim shook his head. "Anything else?"

David held out his hand and showed Jim what he had found. It was a green plastic soldier, carrying a machine gun in one hand and a grenade in the other. I moved closer to see the detail and noticed that the figure wore no helmet, which was unusual for an army man. He wore strings of big bullets over his shoulders and his mouth was open so that you could see his teeth gritted together.

Jim took the soldier out of David's hand, looked at it for a second, said, "Sergeant Rock," and then put it in his pocket.

David's brow furrowed. "Give it back," he said. His hands balled into fists and he took a step forward as a challenge.

Jim said, "Let me ask you a question. When the prowler saw your mother's ass—"

"Stop saying my mother's ass," said David, and took another step forward.

"—did it look like this?" asked Jim, and flipped the magazine so that the centerfold opened.

David saw it and went slack. He slowly brought his hand up to rest with his palm on his cheek and his fingers partially covering his right eye. "Oh, no," he said, and stared.

"Oh, yes," said Jim, and then took the magazine and ripped off the bottom fold of the center section, the page containing the big ass, and handed the sheet to David. "This is your reward for bravery in the sewer pipe."

David took the torn page in his trembling hands, his gaze fixed on the picture. Then he looked up and said, "Let me see the magazine."

"I can't," said Jim, "it's exhibit A. Evidence. You'll get your fingerprints on it." He rolled it up and put it under his arm the way Mr. Mardinella carried the newspaper as he walked down the street on his way home from work every evening.

We spent another couple of hours looking for clues all around the school fields and through the woods, but George lost the scent and we eventually headed home. Every other driveway we passed, David would take his piece of centerfold out of his back pocket and stop and stare at it. We left him standing in front of Mrs. Grimm's house, petting the image as if it were flesh instead of slick paper.

When we got home, Jim made me go in first and see if the coast was clear. My mother wouldn't be home for about two hours and Nan and Pop were in their place. I didn't see Mary around, but that didn't matter anyway.

Up in his room, Jim slid the loose floorboard back and stowed the magazine. Then he got up and went to his desk. "Here," he said, and turned around holding a black-and-white-bound composition book. "This is for the investigation." He walked over and handed it to me. "Write down everything that happened so far."

I took the book from him and nodded.

"What are you gonna do with the soldier?" I asked.

Jim took the green warrior out of his pocket and held it up. "Guess," he said.

"Botch Town?" I asked.

"Precisely," he said.

I followed him out of the room, down the stairs, through the living room, to the hallway that led to the first-floor bedrooms. At the head of this hall there was a door. He opened it, and we descended on the creaking wooden steps into the dim, mildew waft of the cellar.

The cellar was lit by one bare bulb with a pull string and whatever light managed to seep in from outside through the four window wells. The floor was unpainted concrete, as were the walls. The staircase separated the layout between a right and left side, and there was an area behind the steps that allowed access from one side to the other. Six metal poles, four inches thick and six feet apart, supported the ceiling, positioned in a row across the center of the house.

It was warm in the winter and cool in the summer down there in the underground twilight where the aroma of my mother's oil paints and turpentine mixed with the pine and glittering tinsel scent of Christmas decorations heaped up in one corner. It was a treasure vault of the old, the broken, the forgotten. Stuff lay on shelves or stacked along the walls covered with a thin layer of cellar dust, the dandruff of concrete, and veiled in cobwebs hung with spider eggs.

On Pop's heavy wooden workbench, complete with crushing vise, there sat coffee cans of rusted nuts and bolts and nails, planes, rasps, wrenches, levels with little yellow bubbles encased to live forever. Riding atop this troubled sea of strewn tools, seemingly abandoned in the middle of the greatest home repair job ever attempted, was a long curving Chinese junk carved from the horn of an ox, sporting sails the color of singed paper created from thin sheets of animal bone, and manned by a little fellow, carved right out of the black horn, who wore a field worker's hat and kept a hand on the tiller. Pop told me he had bought it in Singapore, when he traveled the world with the Merchant Marine, from a woman who showed him my mother as a little girl, dancing, years before she was born, in a piece of crystal shaped like an egg.

Leaning against the pipe, that ran along the back wall and then out of the house to connect with the sewer line, were my mother's paintings: *The Snows of Kilimanjaro*; a self-portrait of her standing in a darkened hallway, holding me when I was a baby; the flowering bushes of the Bayard Cutting Arboretum; a seascape and view of Captree Bridge. All of her colors were subdued, and the images came into focus slowly, like a phantom approaching out of a fog.

Crammed into and falling out of one tall bookcase that backed against the stair railing on the right-hand side were my father's math books and used notebooks, every inch filled with numbers and weird signs, in his hand, in pencil, as if through many years he had been working the equation to end all equations. I remember a series of yellow journals each displaying in a circle on the cover the bust of some famous, long-dead genius I would have liked to know more about, but when I pulled one journal off the shelf and opened it that secret language told me nothing.

In the middle of the floor on the right-hand side of the cellar sat an old school desk, with wooden chair attached, and a place to put your books underneath. Around this prop, Mary created the school that her alter ego, Mickey, attended. Sometimes, when I knew she was playing this game, I would open the door in the hallway and listen to the strangely different voices of the teacher, Mrs. Harkmar, her classmates, Sally O'Mally and Sandy Graham, and, of course, Mickey, who knew all the answers.

Back in the shadows where the oil burner clanked and whirred and gibbered, there stood a small platform holding the Extreme Unction box, a religious artifact with hand-carved doors and a brass cross protruding from the top. We had no idea what *unction* was, so could not conceive of it in the extreme state, but Jim told me it was "holy as hell" and that if you opened the door, the Holy Ghost would come out and strangle you, making it look like you just swallowed your tongue the wrong way.

To the left of the stairs, beneath the single bare bulb, like a sun, lay Jim's creation, the sprawling burg of Botch Town. At one point my father was thinking of getting us an electric train set. He went out and bought four sawhorses and the most enormous piece of plywood. He set these up as a train table, but then the financial trouble descended and it sat for quite a while, smooth and empty. One day, Jim brought a bunch of cast-off items home with him from his early morning paper route. It had been junk day and the garbage men had not yet come. With coffee cans, old shoeboxes, pieces from broken appliances, Pez dispensers, buttons, Dixie cups, ice cream sticks, bottles, and anything else you could possibly imagine being pitched out, he began to build a facsimile of our development and the area around it. It became a project that he worked on a little here, a little there, continuously adding details.

He'd started by painting the road (a battleship gray) that came down straight from Higbee Lane and then curved around to the school, which was a shoebox with windows cut in it, a flag pole outside, the circular drive, basketball courts, and fields. Neatly written on the building, in black magic marker above the front doors was *Retard Factory.* The rest of the board he painted green, for grass, of course, with the exception of the lake in the woods, whose blue oval was covered with glitter.

I sat at the desk in my room, the open notebook in front of me, a pencil in my hand, and stared out the window, trying to recall all of the details surrounding the prowler. There was the old ladder and the footprint, sitting, like a dirt layer cake, in a pink hatbox in the shed. I could have started with Mrs. Kelty and her ass, or just her scream in the night.

In fact, I didn't know where to start and, although from the time I was six, I had always loved writing and reading, I didn't feel much like recording evidence. Then, through the open window, from over at the Farleys', I heard the back screen door groan open and slam shut. I stood and looked to see what was going on. It was Mr. Farley, carrying a highball in one hand and a towel in the other. He was dressed in his swimming trunks, his body soft and yellow-white. His head seemed too heavy for the muscles of his neck, and it made him look as if he was searching for something he had dropped in the grass.

The Farleys' pool was a child's pool, larger than the kind you blow up but no bigger than three-feet deep and no wider than eight across. He set his drink down on the picnic table, draped his towel over the thickest branch of the cherry tree, shuffled out of his sandals, and then stepped gently over the side into the glassy water.

He trolled the surface, inspecting every inch for beetles and bees that had escaped the draw of the noisy little filter that ran constantly. He fetched up blackened cherry leaves from off the bottom with his toes and tossed them into the yard. Only then did he sit, slowly, cautiously, the liquid rising to accommodate his paunch, his sagging chest, and rounded shoulders, until his head bobbed on the surface. Slowly, he dipped forward, bringing his legs underneath him. His arms stretched out at his sides, his legs straightened behind him, his back broke the surface, and his face slipped beneath the water, leaving one bright bubble behind in its place.

He floated there for a moment or two, his body stretched tautly across the center of the pool, and then there came an instant when the rigid raft of his form gave way to death. His arms floated down, and his body curled like a piece of dough in the deep fry. Mr. Farley could really do the dead man's float. I wondered if he left his eyes open, letting them burn with chlorine, or if he closed them in order to dream more deeply into himself.

I sat back down at my desk, and instead of writing about the investigation, I wrote about Mr. Farley. After describing him getting into the pool and fake drowning on the water, I wrote about two other incidents I remembered about him. The first was about his older son, who had since moved away from home. When the boy was younger, Farley, an engineer who made tools for flights into outer space, tried to get his son interested in astronomy and science. Instead, the kid, Gregory, wanted to become an artist. Mr. Farley didn't approve. Before the kid left home for good, he created a giant egg out of plaster of Paris and set it up in the middle of the garden in the backyard. It sat there through months of wind and rain and sun and eventually turned green. On the day after the astronauts walked on the moon, Mr. Farley sledgehammered the thing into oblivion.

The second incident happened one day when I was raking leaves on the front lawn with my father. Suddenly the door over at the Farleys' opened and there he stood, weaving slightly, highball in hand. My father and I both stopped raking. Mr. Farley started down the steps slowly, and with each step his knees buckled a little more until upon reaching the walkway, he stumbled forward, his knees landing on the grass of the lawn. He remained kneeling for an instant, and then tipped forward, falling face first onto the ground. Throughout all of this, and even when he lay flat, he held his drink up above his head like a man trying to keep a pistol dry while crossing a river. I noticed that not a drop was spilled, as did my father, who looked over at me and whispered, "Nice touch."

I put the pencil down and closed the notebook with a feeling that I had accomplished something. It was hard to believe how much I had enjoyed capturing Mr. Farley on paper. I thought to myself, *Perhaps this writing is something that could be mine.* Jim had Botch Town, Mary had her imaginary world, my mother had her wine, my father, his jobs, Nan, the cards, and Pop, his mandolin. Instead of writing about the footprint or Mrs. Kelty's scream, I planned to fill the notebook with the lives of my neighbors, creating a Botch Town of my own between two covers.

When I went down into the cellar to tell Jim about my decision,

I found him holding the plastic soldier up to the light bulb. He showed me what he had done to the figure. Big white circles had been painted over his eyes, and his hands, which had once held the machine gun and grenade, had been chopped off and replaced with straight pins that jutted dangerously point out from the stubs of his arms.

"Watch this, glow in the dark paint," said Jim, standing the figure upright on the board between our house and the Keltys'. He then leaned way out over Botch Town and pulled the light bulb string. The cellar went dark.

"The eyes," he said, and I looked down to see the twin circles on the soldier's face glowing in the night of the handmade town. The sight of him there, like a specter from a nightmare, gave me a chill.

Jim stood quietly, admiring his creation, and I told him what I had decided to do with the notebook. I thought he would be mad at me for not following his orders.

"Good work," he said. "Everyone is a suspect."

Saturday afternoon, I sat with Mary back amidst the forsythias and read to her the descriptions of the people I had so far written about in my notebook. That morning I had gone out on my bike early, scouring the neighborhood for likely suspects to turn into words, and had caught sight of Mrs. Ryan, whom I named The Colossus for her mesmerizing girth, and Mitchell Potaney, a kid who shared my same birthday and who, for every school assembly and holiday party, played "Lady of Spain" on his accordion.

I doled them out to Mary, starting with Mr. Farley, reading with the same rapid whisper and grave import as I used when relaying a chapter of a Perno Shell adventure. Mary was a good audience. She sat still, only nodding her head occasionally as she did when sitting with Pop while he figured the horses. Each nod told me that she had taken in and understood the information up to that point. She was not obviously saddened when Mrs. Ryan's diminutive, potato-head husband died nor did she laugh at my description of Mitchell's simpering smile when bowing to scanty applause. Her nod told me she was tabulating the results of my effort, though, and that was all I needed.

When I was done and had closed the notebook, she sat for a moment in silence. Finally, she looked at me and said, "I'll take Mrs. Ryan to place."

Our mother called us in then. My father had just gotten home from work (Saturdays he only went to the shop until 12:30), and it was time for us to visit our Aunt Laura at the T. B. hospital. We piled into the white Biscayne, Jim and me in the back with Mary between us. My father drove with the window open, his elbow leaning out in the sun, a cigarette going between his fingers. I hadn't seen him all week until just then, and he looked tired. Adjusting the rearview mirror, he peered back at us and smiled. "All aboard," he said.

St. Anselm's was somewhere on the north shore of Long Island, nearly an hour drive from our house. The ride was usually solemn, but my father sometimes played the radio for us, or if he was in a particularly good mood, he'd tell us a story about when he was a boy. Our favorites were about the ancient, swaybacked plough horse, Pegasus, dirty white and ploddingly dangerous, he and his brother kept as kids in Amityville. Those stories had wings and he managed to end them just as we pulled in through the tall iron gates of the place.

This hospital was not a single modern building, painted white inside and smelling vaguely of Lysol and piss. St. Anselm's was like a small town of stone castles set amidst the woods; a fairy tale place of giant granite steps, oaken doors, stained glass, dim, winding corridors that echoed in their emptiness. There was a spot set amidst a thicket of poplars where a curved concrete bench lay before a fountain whose statuary was a pelican piercing its own chest with its beak. Water geysered forth from the wound. And the oddest thing of all—everyone there, save for old, bent Doctor Hasbith of the bushy white sideburns, was a nun.

I'd never seen so many nuns before, all of them dressed in their black flowing robes and tight headgear. When one of them came toward you from out of the cool shadows and your eyes weren't yet adjusted to inside, it was like a disembodied face floating in midair. They moved about in utter silence and only rarely would one smile in passing. The place, haunted by God and his mysteries, was both a dream and a nightmare. I couldn't help thinking that our aunt was being held prisoner there, enchanted like Sleeping Beauty, and that on some lucky Saturday we would rescue her.

As was usual, we were not allowed to accompany our parents to the place where Aunt Laura was being kept. Jim was left in charge, and we were each given a quarter to buy a soda. We knew that if we went down a set of winding steps that led into what I thought of as a dungeon, we would find a small room with a soda machine and two tables and chairs. Our usual routine was to descend, have a drink, and then go and sit on the bench by the fountain to watch the pelican bleed water for two hours. But that day, after we'd finished our sodas, Jim pointed into the shadow off to the left side of the small canteen at a door I'd never noticed before.

"What do you think is in there?" he asked.

"Hell," said Mary.

Jim got up and went over to it. I watched as he turned the knob. He flung the door open and jumped back. Mary and I left our seats and stood behind him. From there, you could see a set of stone steps leading down, walls close on either side like a brick gullet. There was no light in the stairway itself, but a vague glow shone up from the bottom. Jim turned to look at us briefly. "I order you to follow me."

At the bottom of the long flight of steps, we found a room with a low ceiling, a concrete floor, and a row of pews that disappeared into darkness toward the back. Up front, near the entrance to the stairway, was a small altar and above it a huge painting in an ornate gilt frame. The dim light we had seen from above was a single bulb positioned to illuminate the picture, which showed a scene of Jesus and Mary sitting next to a pool in the middle of a forest. The aquamarine of Mary's gown was resilient, and both her and Christ's eyes literally shone. The figures were smiling, and their hair along with the leaves in the background appeared to be moving in a light breeze.

"Let's go back," I said.

Mary inched away toward the stairs, and I started to follow her.

"One second," said Jim. "Look at this, the holy fishing trip."

We heard a rustle of material and something clunk against the heavy wood of one of the pews behind us. I jumped and even Jim spun around with a look of fright on his face.

"It's a lovely scene, isn't it?" said a soft, female voice. Then from out of the dark came a nun, whose face, pushing through the black mantle of her vestments, was so young and beautiful, it confused me. She was smiling and her hands were pale and delicate. She lifted one as she passed by us and climbed onto the altar. "But you mustn't miss the idea of the painting," she said, pointing.

"Do you see here?" she asked, and turned to look at us.

We nodded and followed her direction to gaze into the woods behind where Mary and Jesus were sitting.

"What do you see?"

Jim stepped closer and a few seconds later said, "Eyes and a smile."

"Someone is there in the woods," I said as the figure became evident to me.

"A dark figure, spying from the woods," said the nun. "Who is it?"

"The Devil," said Mary.

"You're a smart girl," said the nun. "Satan. Do you see how much this looks like a scene from the Garden of Eden? Well, the painter is trying to show that just as Adam and Eve were subject to temptation, to Death, so were the Savior and his mother. So are we all."

"Why is he hiding?" asked Jim.

"He's waiting and watching for the right moment to strike. He's clever."

"But the Devil isn't real," said Jim. "My father told me."

She smiled sweetly at us. "Oh, the Devil is real, child. I've seen him. If you don't pay attention, he'll take you."

"Goodbye now," whispered Mary, who took my hand and pulled me toward the steps.

"What does he look like?" asked Jim.

I wanted to flee, but I couldn't move. I thought the nun would get angry, but instead her smile intensified, and that same face went from pleasant to scary.

Mary pulled my arm, and we took off up the stairs. Not bothering to stop in the canteen, we kept going up the next set of steps to the outside and only rested when we made it to the bench by the fountain. We waited there for some time, hypnotized by the cascading water, before Jim finally showed up.

"You chickens should be hung for mutiny," he said as he approached.

"Mary was afraid," I said. "I had to get her out of there."

"Check your own shorts," he said. "Anyway, get this. That nun's name was Sister Joseph."

"You mean she was a guy?"

"I don't know," he said, shaking his head. "But she told me a secret."

"What?" I asked.

"How to spot the Devil when he walks the Earth. That's what Sister Joe said, 'When he walks the Earth,' " said Jim, and started laughing.

"She was the Devil," said Mary, staring into the water.

That night, back at home, the wine flowed, and my parents danced in the living room to The Ink Spots on the Victrola. Something dire was up, I could tell, because they didn't talk and there was a joyless gravity to their spins and dips.

Before we turned in, Nan came from next door and told us that while we were out she had heard from Rose across the street that the prowler had struck again. When her husband, Dan, had gone out late on Friday night to throw away the trash, he heard something moving back in their grape arbor. He called out, "Who's there?" Of course there was no answer, but he saw a shadow and a pair of eyes. Dan was an airline pilot who flew all over the world, and one of his hobbies was collecting old weapons. He ran inside and fetched a long knife from Turkey that had a wriggled blade like a flat, frozen snake. Rose had told Nan that he charged out the back door toward the arbor, but halfway there, tripped on a divot in the lawn, fell, and stabbed his own thigh. By the time he was able to hobble back beneath the hanging grapes, the prowler had vanished.

While my mother sat in her rocker, eyes closed, rocking to the music, Jim and I arm-wrestled my father a few times and then Mary danced with him, her bare feet on his shoes. "Bed," my mother finally said, her eyes still closed. At the top of the stairs before Jim and I went into our separate rooms, he said to me, "He walks the Earth." I laughed but he didn't. George followed me to bed and lay at the bottom, falling instantly asleep. He kicked his back leg three times and growled in his dreams. I stayed awake for a while, listening to my parents' hushed conversation down in the living room, but I couldn't make anything out.

I wasn't the least tired, so I got up and went over to my desk. Nan's talking about Rose and Dan gave me the idea to capture them in my notebook before I forgot. What I found interesting was that Dan could only be defined by the things that he owned: the leopard skin rug, the shrunken head, the axes and knives and ancient pistols. Otherwise, he was a pretty blank person, save for his toupee, which sat on his head like a doily. Rose, on the other hand, had been born in Ireland, in the town of Cork, and had the most beautiful way of talking. She had grown up with the actor Richard Harris, who sang the song about the cake in the rain. I could not write about her without recounting some of the ghost stories she had told Jim and me.

In one, her father was coming home from a neighboring town one evening, and just before crossing the bridge into their hometown, he was confronted by a funeral procession. He thought it an odd time for a funeral and he asked each of the long train of mourners preceding the funeral carriage who had died. The strangers, dressed in stiff, black crepe and tall hats, none of whom he recognized, refused to acknowledge him. Only the carriage driver would answer, and he told Rose's father that John Connely had passed away. Her father couldn't believe it, because he had just seen John the night before and he had been drinking and laughing. The eerie procession passed by and he continued over the bridge. Upon arriving home, he saw John coming out of his own house to go to the pub. Rose's father waved and wondered what sort of madness he had been subject to, but later that week, his poor neighbor, John, dropped over stone-cold dead from heart failure at dinner in the middle of a sentence.

I wrote it up in detail and also added the one about the giant black dog that haunted the abandoned abbey. It didn't surprise me that the visit from the prowler had frightened Rose. Nothing ever happened by chance for her. Banshees, little people, fetches, you name it and she'd seen it. She was devoted to the tea leaves, and because Nan could read the cards, Rose respected her more than anyone else on the block.

By the time I was done, it had grown quiet downstairs, and I knew my parents had finally gone to bed. Still, I wasn't tired, and on top of that I was a little spooked by remembering Rose's stories. Any meditation on Death was capable of conjuring the angry spirit of Jimmy Bonnel. To dispel his gathering presence, I got out of bed and tiptoed quietly down the stairs. In the kitchen, I stole a cookie and that's when I decided to descend and review Jim's recent progress with Botch Town.

Every old wooden step on the way to the cellar groaned miserably, but my father's snoring, rolling out from the bedroom at the back of the house, covered my own prowling. Once below, I inched blindly forward and when my hip touched the edge of the plywood world, I leaned way out and grabbed the pull string. The sun came out in the middle of the night in Botch Town. I half-expected the figures to all be moving of their own volition, but no, they must have heard me coming and froze on cue. Jim was right, there was a sense of being God, hovering above the clouds and peering down on the minute lives. It also made me think for an instant about my own smallness.

Scanning the board, I found the prowler, with his straight-pin hands, on the prowl, hiding in the toothpick grape arbor netted with vines of green thread behind the Curdmeyers' house across the street from ours, his clever, glowing eyes, like beacons, searching the dark for lost souls.

School started on a day so hot it seemed stolen from the heart of summer. The tradition was that if you got new clothes for school, you wore them the first day. My mother made Mary a couple of dresses on the sewing machine. Because he had outgrown what he had, Jim got shirts and pants from Gertz department store. I got his hand-me-downs, but I did also get a new pair of dungarees. They were stiff as concrete and, after months of nothing but cutoffs, seemed to weigh fifty pounds. I sweated like the Easter pig, shuffling through school zombie style, to the library, the lunchroom, on the playground, and all day long that burlap scent of new denim smelled like the spirit of Work.

Jim was starting junior high and, going to a different school, he had to take a bus to get there. Mary and I were still stuck at the Retard Factory around the corner. None of us were good students. I spent most of my time in the classroom either completely confused or daydreaming. Mary was in a special class, basically because they couldn't figure out if she was really smart or really simple. The kids they couldn't figure out, they put in room X. Although all of the other rooms had numbers, this one just had the letter that signaled something cut-rate, like on the TV commercials: Brand X. When I'd pass by that room, I'd look in and see these wacky kids hobbling around or mumbling or crying, and there would be Mary, sitting straight up, focused, nodding every once in a while. Her teacher, Mrs. Rockhill, whom we called Rockhead, was no Mrs. Harkmar and didn't have the secret to draw the Mickey of all right answers out of her. I knew Mary was really smart, though, because Jim had told me she was a genius.

As for Jim, no one knew what the hell he was up to. He had a history of putting obviously wrong answers down on his tests and homework assignments. "What's 6 apples and 3 apples?" they'd asked him in third grade. Jim's answer: "4 tin cans." In an essay question dealing with the Navajo boy, Joe Mannygoats, we had to read about in fifth grade social studies, Jim ignored the question about Navajo family life, and created a scenario where Joe stole a gun and shot his goats. Then he cooked them and invited everyone to a barbecue. How Jim stayed out of room X was a room-X mystery no one could solve.

Once they called him into the psychologist's office and made my mother go over to the school and witness the tests they gave him. They showed him pages of paint blobs and asked him what he saw in them. "I see a spider, biting a woman's lip," he said. "That's a sick, three-legged dog, eating grass." Then they asked him to put pegs of various shapes into appropriate holes in a block of wood. He shoved all the wrong pegs in the wrong holes. Finally my mother smacked him in the back of the head, and then he and she started laughing hysterically. Throughout sixth grade, he incorporated something about Joe Mannygoats into all of his test answers, no matter the subject, and signed all yearbooks with that name. Still, he never failed a grade, and this gave me hope that I too would someday leave Southgate.

My teacher for sixth grade was the fearsome Mr. Krapp. To borrow a phrase from Nan, "as God is my judge," that was his name. He was a short guy with a big nose and a crew cut so flat you could land a helicopter on it. Jim had had him and told me he screamed a lot. My mother had diagnosed Krapp with a Napoleonic complex. "You know," she said, "he's a little general." He assured us on the first day that he "wouldn't stand for any of it." The third time he repeated the phrase, Tim Caliban, who sat behind me, leaned forward and whispered, "He'd rather get down on all fours." Krapp had big ears too, and he heard Tim, who he made get up in front of the classroom and repeat for everyone what he'd said. That day we all learned an important lesson in how not to laugh no matter how funny something is.

School brought a great heaviness to the hours of my days as if they had put on new dungarees. By that year, though, it was business as usual, so I weathered it with a grim resignation. The only thing drastic that happened in that first week was on the way home one afternoon: Will Hickey, a kid with a bulging Adam's apple and big, curly hair, challenged me to a fight. I tried to walk away, but before I knew what was going on, a bunch of kids surrounded us and Hickey started pushing me. The whirl of voices and faces, the evident danger, made me lightheaded and what little strength I had quickly evaporated. Mary was with me and she started crying. I was not popular and had no friends there to help me; instead everyone was cheering for me to get beat up.

After a lot of shoving and name calling and me trying to back out of the circle and getting thrown into the middle again, he hit me once in the side of the head and I was dazed. Putting my hands up, I assumed the position I had seen on TV and when other kids fought, and he circled around me. I tried to follow his movements, but he darted in quickly and his bony knuckle split my lip. There was little pain, just an overwhelming sense of embarrassment, because I felt tears welling in the corners of my eyes.

As Hickey came toward me again, I saw Jim pushing through the crowd. He came up behind Hickey, reached around, and grabbed him by the throat with one hand. In a second, Jim wrestled him to the ground where he proceeded to punch him again and again in the face. When Jim got up, blood was running from Hickey's nose and he was quietly whimpering. All of the other kids had taken off. Jim lifted my book bag and handed it to me.

"You're such a pussy," he said.

"How?" was all I could manage, I was shaking so badly.

"Mary ran home and told me," he said.

"Did you kill him?"

He shrugged.

Hickey lived, and his mother called our house that night complaining that Jim was dangerous, but Mary and I had already told our mother what had happened. I remember her telling Mrs. Hickey over the phone, "Well, you know, you play with fire, you're liable to get burned." When she hung up the phone, she flipped it the middle finger, and then told us she didn't want us fighting anymore. She made Jim promise he would apologize to Hickey. "Sure," he said, but later, when I asked him if he was really going to apologize, he said, "Yeah, I'm going to take him to Bermuda."

In reality, the start of school was an afterthought, because the prowler had surfaced twice again. The Graves's teenage daughter, Marci, spotted him spotting her sitting on the toilet late one night. The Stutton kid, Kenny, who regularly proclaimed in school that he would someday be president, found the shadow man in their darkened garage, crouching in the corner behind the car when he went out there with the empty milk bottles after dinner. As he told Jim and me later when we went to talk to him about it, "He ran by me so fast, I didn't see him, but his air was cold."

"What do you mean his air was cold?" asked Jim.

"It smelled cold."

"Unlike yours?" said Jim.

Kenny nodded.

That evening, down in the cellar, Jim made tiny, red flags out of sewing needles and construction paper, and stuck them into the turf of Botch Town at all the spots where we knew the prowler had been. When he was done, we stepped back and he said, "I saw this on *Dragnet* once. Just the facts. It's supposed to show the criminal's plan."

"Do you see any plan?" I asked.

"They're all on our block," he said, "but otherwise it's just a mess."

Apparently, we weren't the only ones concerned about the prowler, because somebody called the cops. Thursday afternoon, a police officer walked down the block, knocking on people's doors, asking if they had seen anything suspicious at night or if they had heard someone in their backyard. When he got to our house, he spoke to Nan. As usual, Nan knew everything that happened on the street and she gave him an earful. We hid in the kitchen and listened, and in the process learned a tidbit we had been unaware of. It so happened that the Farleys had found human shit at the bottom of their swimming pool, as if someone had sat on the rim and dropped it.

When the cop was getting ready to leave, Jim stepped out of hiding and told him we had a footprint we thought belonged to the prowler. He smiled at us and winked at Nan, but asked to see it. We led him back to the shed, and Jim went in and brought out the hatbox. He motioned for me to take the lid off and I did. The cop bent over and peered inside.

"Nice job, fellas," he said, and took the box with him, but later on, when I walked George around the block that night, I saw the pink cardboard, the poodle, and the Eiffel Tower jutting out of the Mardinellas' open garbage can at the curb. I went over to it and peeked under the lid. The footprint was ruined, so I decided not to tell Jim.

As George and I continued on our rounds, the autumn came. We were standing at the entrance to Southgate; there was a full moon, and suddenly a great burst of wind rushed by. The leaves of the trees at the boundary of the woods over beyond Sewer Pipe Hill rattled, some flying free of their branches in a dark swarm. Just like that, the temperature dropped, I realized the crickets had gone silent, and I smelled a trace of Halloween.

Down the block a wind chime that had been silent all summer sounded its cowbell call, and I turned and looked over at the Fuscias' house; the last one before the school. Their lighted window brought me a memory of their pet rabbit, Dibby, who had chewed through its wooden crate and then chewed a hole in the wall. It was never found and now either lived or died somewhere inside the darkness behind the walls of their house. Mrs. Farley had announced, at one of the wine-in-a-teacup afternoon gatherings of the ladies, presided over by Nan, that Amy Fuscia, who was in Mary's grade, lived in fear that the creature would crawl out of the wall some night and seek revenge on her, and she wet her bed every night since its escape.

I looked up at the stars and felt my mind start to wander, so I sat down at the curb and George sat next to me. That day in school they had herded us into the cafeteria and showed us a movie, *The Long Way Home from School*. It was about kids playing on the train tracks and getting killed by speeding trains or electrocuted on the third rail. The guy who spoke the stories looked like the father from *Leave It to Beaver*. He told one about kids thinking it was fun climbing onto train cars and running across the tops. Little did they know that the train was about to pull out, and when they showed it start to move, he said, "Oops, Johnny fell in between the cars and was crushed to death by tons of steel. It's not so much fun when you're flat as a pancake." After that came a scene of a kid shooting a slingshot at a moving train, that jumped right into another scene of a little girl on board in a passenger compartment with her hand covering her eye and blood dripping down across her face while the landscape rolled by. "Nice shooting, Cowboy," the guy said.

After the movie, they made us line up out in the hallway on our knees with our heads down and pressed into the angle where the floor met the wall. "Cover the back of your head by locking your fingers behind it. This will protect you from flying debris," said Mr. Tary, the principal, as he rubbed his throat. He was always rubbing his throat. We were led to believe, without anyone coming right out and making the claim, that this maneuver on the floor would save us if the Russians dropped an atomic bomb on our town.

My mother had told us if the air raid siren ever really went off, I was to get home. She and my father had devised a plan. The minute the siren sounded someone was supposed to shovel dirt into the window wells of the cellar and then get all the mattresses from the house and lay them out on the first floor to block the radiation from seeping down. At one time they had stocked a bunch of cans of food in the cellar and gallons of water with a drop of bleach in each one to keep them fresh. But as time went on, the supplies dwindled to a single can of Spam and a bottle of water that had gone green. As George and I got up and headed back, I daydreamed a *Twilight Zone* scenario of us projecting ourselves into the world of Botch Town to escape the horrible death of atomic bombs in the wider world.

At home, the wine bottle sat on the kitchen counter, empty, and my mother had passed out on the couch. There was a cigarette between her fingers with an ash almost as long as a cigarette. Jim pointed it out to me. Then he went and got an ashtray that was half a giant clamshell we had found on the beach the previous summer, and Mary and I watched as he positioned it under the ash. He gave my mother's wrist the slightest tap, and the ash dropped perfectly into the shell.

I wedged a pillow under her head as Jim took her by the shoulders and laid her down more comfortably on the couch. Mary fetched the *Sherlock Holmes*. Jim opened it to "The Hound of the Baskervilles," the story that obsessed her as a writer, and gently placed the volume, binding up, its wings open like those of a giant red moth, on her chest.

We went next door to say goodnight to Nan and Pop.

"Where's your mother?" asked Nan.

"She's out cold," said Jim.

Nan's lips did that kissing fish thing, in and out, that they did whenever she was about to try to trick you into ignoring the truth. I noticed it first that past summer on the day the ladies came over and she read the cards for them. The widow, old Mrs. Ripici, who lived by herself next to the Curdmeyers on the left, across the street, drew the ace of spades. Nan's lips started going, and she quickly pulled the card from the table and claimed, "Misdeal." There was a moment where the room went stone quiet and then, like someone flipped a switch, the ladies started chattering again.

"Your mother works hard for you kids and she's very tired," Nan told us the night autumn came.

Mary was always upset when my mother didn't tuck her in at night, so to create a diversion, Pop brought out the band. He collected windup toys that played musical instruments, and he had seven of them. One was an Indian who beat a tom-tom, one, an elephant that blew a horn, a clown that played the tambourine, and more. He took out his mandolin, and Nan and Mary and Jim and I madly wound the toys to get them all ready to play at the same time, but at the same time could not let any of them start to unwind. Then Pop gave the signal and we released the keys at their backs. They banged and tooted and jangled away while he strummed and sang "When the Saints Go Marching In." Somehow that crazy music blended together and it all sounded just right.

The first Saturday morning after school started, I followed Pop around the yard, holding a colander, as he harvested the yield of the trees. Before he picked each piece of fruit, he'd take it lightly in his hand as if it were a live egg with the most fragile shell imaginable.

As we moved from tree to tree, he told me things about them. "Never put a peach leaf near your mouth." he said. "They're poisonous." Or when we came to the yellow apple tree: "This tree grew from seeds that no one sells anymore. It's called Miter's Sun, and I bought the sapling from an old coot who told me there were less than a dozen of them left in the world. It's important to take care of it, because if it and the couple of others that remain die, it will be gone from the face of the Earth for all of eternity." He picked a small, misshapen yellow apple from a branch, rubbed it on his shirt, and handed it to me. "Take a bite of that," he said. From that ugly marble came a wonderful, sweet taste.

We continued on to the plum tree, and he said to me, "I heard you were in a fight this week."

I nodded.

"Do you want me to teach you how to box?" he asked.

I thought about it for a while. "No," I said, "I don't like to fight."

He laughed so loud that the crow sitting on the TV antenna atop the house was frightened into flight. I felt embarrassed for a moment, but then he reached down and put his hand on my head. "Okay," he said, and laughed more quietly.

After retiring from the Big A, Aqueduct Race Track, where he had worked in the boiler room for years, Pop took up an interest in trees, especially ones that gave fruit. On our quarter-acre of property, he planted quite a few—a peach, a plum, three apple, a cherry, an ornamental crab apple, and something called a Smoke Bush that kept the mosquitoes away—and spent the summer months tending to them; spraying them for bugs, digging around their bases, pulling up saplings, getting rid of dead branches. I'd never seen him read a book about the subject or study it in any way, he just started one day the first week after he had left his job.

I guess it was something he had done before at some point in his long life. Nan had shown us old, yellowing newspaper clippings from when he was a boxer and photographs of him standing on the deck of a ship with an underwater suit on and a metal diving helmet with a little window in it. Once when my parents thought I was asleep on the couch but I just had my eyes closed, I learned that he had spent time in a mental institution where they had given him electroshock therapy. Supposedly, when he was fifteen, his mother had sent him out around the corner for a loaf of bread. He went and joined the Merchant Marine, lying about his age, and returned home three years later, carrying the loaf of bread. When asked how his mother reacted, his answer was, "She beat the shit out of me."

He was powerfully built with a huge chest and wide shoulders. Even in old age, his biceps took three of my hands to fit around. Every once in a while, we'd ask to see his tattoos, vein-blue drawings he could make dance by flexing his muscle: a naked woman on his left forearm; an eagle on his chest; and a weird, fire-breathing dragon-dog, all curly cue fur and huge lantern eyes, on his back that he had gotten in Java from a man who used whale bone needles to render the design. He told Jim and me that the dog creature was named Chimto, and that it watched behind him for his enemies.

The trees may have been Pop's hobby, a way to fill up the hours of retirement, but his art and his love were the horses. He studied the *Daily Telegraph*, the horse paper, as if it were a sacred text. When he was done with it, the margins would be filled with the scribble of horses' names, jockeys' names, times, claiming purses, stacks of simple arithmetic, and strange symbols that looked like Chinese writing. Whatever it all stood for, it allowed him to pick a fairly high percentage of winners. There was one time when he went to the track and came home in a brand new car, and another when he won so much he took us all on vacation to Niagara Falls. Pop's best friend was his bookie, Bill Pharo, and Pop drove over to Babylon to see him almost every day.

Saturday afternoon, when my father returned home from work, he called us kids into the living room and made us sit before him on the love seat. My mother and he sat on the couch across the marble coffee table from us. Before they spoke, my mind raced back through the recent weeks to try to remember if we could be in trouble for something.

All I could think of besides the incident with Hickey, which seemed to have blown over by then, was a night sometime before school started when we made a dummy out of old clothes—shirt and pants—stuffed with newspapers and held together with safety pins. The head was from a big, mildewed doll, an elephant stuffed with sawdust someone had won at a fair or the circus, that had been lying around in the cellar for as long as I could remember. We decapitated it, removed some of the sawdust, tied the neck in a knot, and pinned it to the collar of the shirt. The figure was crude, but we knew it would serve our purposes, especially in the dark and when people were driving in their cars. We got it out of the cellar unseen by lifting it through one of the windows into the backyard.

We'd named our floppy elephant guy, Mr. Blah-blah, and tied a long length of fishing line around his chest under the arms of the shirt. We laid him at the curb on one side of the street and then doled out the fishing line over to the other side of the street and through the bottom of the hedges in front of the empty house that had, until recently, belonged to the Holsters. We knew it wouldn't pay to do what we were planning in front of our own house, and the one we chose had the benefit of having a southern extension of the woods right behind it in the backyard. We could move along the trails in the pitch black and anyone who tried to chase us would have to turn back.

Hiding behind the hedges, we waited until we saw the lights of a car coming down the street. Just when the car got close to where the hedges started, we reeled the bum in, pulling on the line, and in the dark he looked like he was crawling across the road in fits and starts, sort of like he'd already been hit once by a car.

The car's brakes screeched and it swerved, almost driving up on the curb and nearly hitting the telephone pole before it stopped. The instant I heard the brakes, I realized the whole thing was a big mistake. Jim and I ran like hell, bent in half to gain cover from the hedges. We stopped at the corner of the house, in the shadows.

"If they come after us, run back and jump the stream, and I'll meet you at the fork in the main path," Jim whispered.

I nodded.

From where we stood, we had a good view of the car. I was relieved to see it was not one I recognized as belonging to one of our neighbors. It was an old model, from before I was born, shiny white, with a kind of bubble roof and fins that stuck up in the back like a pair of goal posts. The door creaked open and a man dressed in a long, white trench coat got out. It was too dark and we were too far away to see his features, but he came around the side of the car and obviously discovered Mr. Blah-blah in the road. He must have seen the fishing line, because he looked up and stared directly at us. Jim pulled me back deeper into the shadows. The man didn't move for the longest time, but his face was pointing exactly at where we stood. My heart was pounding, and only Jim's hand on the back of my shirt kept me from running. Finally, the man got back in the car and drove away. When we were sure the car was gone, we got Blah-blah and threw him back in the woods.

My father cleared his throat, and I looked at Jim, who sat on the other side of Mary, and he looked at me, and I knew that his memory was stuffed with that mildewed elephant head.

"We just wanted to tell you that we don't think Aunt Laura is going to be with us much longer," said my father. His elbows were on his knees and he was looking more at our feet than at us. He rubbed his hands together as if he were washing them.

"You mean she's going to die?" said Jim.

"She's very sick and weak. In a way, it will be a blessing," said my mother. I could see the tears forming in the corners of her eyes.

We nodded, but I was unsure if that was the right thing to do. That phrase, "a blessing," stuck in my mind, and I wondered how dying could be a good thing. Then my father told us, "Okay, go and play." Mary went over to where my mother was sitting and climbed into her lap. I left before the tears really started rolling.

That afternoon, I took George and my notebook and we traveled far. When I started I felt the weight of a heavy thought in my head. I could feel it roosting, but when I tried to realize it, reach for it with my mind, it proved utterly illusive, like trying to catch a killifish in the shallows with your bare hands. On my way up to Higbee Lane, I witnessed a scene involving Mr. and Mrs. Wilson being screamed at by their ten-year-old tyrant son, Reggie; passed by Nick, the janitor from Southgate, who was fixing his car out in his driveway; saw the lumbering, moon-eyed Milton kid, Peter, big and slow as a mountain, riding a bike whose seat seemed to have disappeared up his ass.

We crossed Higbee Lane and went down the street lined on both sides with giant sycamores; leaves gone yellow and brown. To the left of me was the farm, cows grazing in the field, to the right was a ploughed expanse of bare dirt where they had begun to frame a line of new houses. Beyond that another mile, down a hill, amidst a thicket of trees, next to the highway, we came to a stream I knew about where no one ever went.

I sat with my back to an old telephone pole someone had dumped there and wrote up the neighbors I'd seen on my journey —told about how Mrs. Wilson had Reggie when she was forty-one; told about how the kids at school would try to fool Nick, who was Yugoslavian and didn't speak English very well, and his response to them: "Boys, you are talking dogshit"; told about the weird redneck Miltons, who I had overheard described by Mrs. Kelty once as "incest from the hills."

When I was finished writing, I put my pencil in the notebook and drew George close to me. I petted his head and told him, "It's gonna be okay." The thought I'd been carrying finally broke through, and I saw a figure, like a human shadow, leaning over Aunt Laura's bed in the otherwise empty room at St. Anselm's and lifting her up. He held her to him, pressed her inside of him, into the dark, and then, like a bubble of ink bursting, vanished.

That night, my mother, well into her bottle of wine, erupted, spewing anger and fear in loud, slurred tones. During these episodes, she was another person, and when they were done I could never remember what the particulars of her rage were, just that the experience seemed to suck the air out of the room and leave me unable to breathe. The image that came to my mind was of the evil queen gazing into her talking mirror, and I tried to rebuff it by conjuring the memory of a snowy day when I was little and she rode Jim and me to school on the sled, running as fast as she could. We laughed, she laughed, and the world was covered in white.

We kids abandoned our father, leaving him to take the brunt of the attack. Jim fled down the cellar to lose himself in Botch Town. Mary went instantly Mickey, encircled herself with a whispered string of numbers for protection, and snuck next door to Nan's house. As I headed up the stairs to the refuge of my own room, I heard the sound of a smack and then something skittered across the kitchen floor. I knew it was either my father's glasses or his teeth, but I wasn't going back to find out. While he sat there, stoically, waiting for the storm to pass, I shoved off with Perno Shell down the Amazon in search of El Dorado.

Sometime later, just after Shell had taken a curare dart in the neck and paralysis was setting in, there was a knock on my door. I said to come in and Mary entered. She curled up at the bottom of my bed and lay there staring at me.

"Hey," I said, "want me to read you some people from my note-book?"

She sat up and nodded.

So I read her all the ones I had recently added, up to the Milton kid on his bike. I recounted my findings at a slow pace in order to kill time and allow her a long stint of the relief she found in the mental tabulation of my findings. When we finished, the house was silent.

"Any winners in that bunch?" I asked.

"Nick the janitor," she said.

"Go to bed now," I told her.

When she opened the door to leave, George was sitting there, waiting to accompany her to her room.

Sunday morning, at the breakfast table, a phone call came in after we had pretty much finished eating and my father was re-counting some of his stories from the army. I wondered if my mother's assault the night before had put him in mind of other con-flagrations. My mother, now light and smiling, as if suffering amnesia of her Mr. Hyde nature, answered the phone. When she hung up, she told us the news—Charlie Eddisson, who was in my class at Southgate, had gone out to play on Saturday afternoon and had never returned. At dinnertime, when he didn't appear, his mother started to worry. When night fell and he still hadn't gotten home, his father called the police. My mother said, "Either some-thing has happened to him or he's been abducted." Nan's lips moved in and out, and she said, "Maybe he'll show up for lunch."

Charlie Eddisson was even more weak and meek than me. We'd had the same teachers all the way up from kindergarten. In class photographs, he came across as the runt of the collective litter. His arms were as thin as pipe cleaners, and he was short and skinny with a pencil neck and face that looked like Tommy the Turtle from the old cartoons. His glasses were so big, it was as if he had stolen them from his old man, and every time I tried to picture him, I'd see him pushing those huge specs up on the bridge of his nose with one extended finger. Charlie's daily project was trying to achieve invisibility, because the meaner kids liked to pick on him. My feelings for him were ones of sympathy and also relief that he existed, since without him, those same kids would probably have been picking on me.

For gym, we had a teacher, Coach Cambell, who for some reason always had at least one hand in his sweat pants, and I'm not talking about the pockets. When it rained or the weather was too cold to go outside, we'd stay in the gym and play dodge ball. There were two teams, one on either side of the gym. You couldn't cross the dividing line and you had to bean someone on the other side with one of those hard, red gym balls in order to get them out. If they managed to catch the ball, then you were out and had to sit on the side.

One day, right before Christmas, Cambell got that glint in his eye and called for dodge ball. The usual game ensued, and Charlie managed to hide out and practice his powers of invisibility long enough so he was the last one left on his side of the line. On the other side of the line, the last one left was Jake Harweed. No one knew how many times he'd been left back, but it was certain he'd already been arrested once before he'd made it to fifth grade. His arm muscles were like smooth rocks and he had a tattoo he had given himself with a straight pin and India ink: the word *Shit*, scrawled across the calf of his left leg. When Cambell saw the final match-up, he blew the whistle and instituted a new rule: the two remaining players could go anywhere they wanted, the dividing line no longer mattered.

Charlie had the ball, but Jake stalked toward him, unworried. Charlie threw it with all his might, but it just kind of floated on the air, and Jake grabbed it like he was picking an apple off a tree. That should have been the end of the game, but Cambell didn't blow the whistle. Everyone in the gym started chanting Jake's name. Then Jake wound up, and as he did, Charlie backed away until he was almost to the wall. He brought his hands up to cover his face. When it came, the ball hit him with such force in the chest it knocked the air out of him and slammed him backward so that his head hit the concrete wall. His glasses flew off, cracked in half on the hardwood floor, and he slumped down unconscious. An ambulance was called, and for that Christmas, Charlie got a broken rib.

My father and Pop went out in the car to join the search for Charlie, and Jim and I hooked up George and headed for the woods to see if we could track him there. On the way, we passed a lot of parents and kids from the neighborhood either in their cars or on bikes out looking for him too.

Jim told me, "He must have just gotten lost somewhere and couldn't remember how to get home. You know Charlie."

I didn't say anything as my imagination was spinning with images of myself lost, unable to find my way home, or worse, being tied up and taken away to a place where I would never see my parents or home again. I was frightened, and the only thing that prevented me from running back to the house, besides the daylight, was that we had George with us. My thoughts concerning recent events and the new terror I felt for poor Charlie's situation eventually twined together behind my eyes, and I said, "Maybe the prowler took him."

We were, by then, at the entrance to the school, and Jim stopped walking. He turned and looked at me. "You know what?" he said. "You might be right."

"Do you think they thought of it?"

"Of course," he said, but I remembered the hatbox in the garbage can and had my doubts.

Our tour of the woods was brief. It was a beautifully clear and cool day, the trees all turning red, but the idea that the prowler was now doing more than just looking kept us on edge. We only ventured in as far as the bend in the stream where the sassafras grew, before giving up. Once out from under the trees, we peered in the sewer pipe, inspected the basketball courts, gazed briefly down into the sump, and followed the perimeter of the fence around the schoolyard back to the entrance.

"I have thirty cents," said Jim. "You want to go to the deli and get a soda?"

There were cops all over the neighborhood for the next week or so, interviewing people about the disappearance of Charlie Eddisson and trying to piece together what might have happened to him. The story was on the nightly news, and they showed a shot of Southgate in the report. It looked different in black and white, almost like some other school a kid would want to go to. Then they flashed a photo of Charlie, smiling, from behind his big glasses, and I had to look away, aware of what he'd been through since I'd known him.

There had been honest grief over his absence and the anguish it caused his family, but at the end of the second week, the town started to slip into its old ways as if some strong current was pulling us back to normalcy. It distressed me, though I couldn't so easily put my finger on the feeling then, how readily we were to leave Charlie behind and continue with the business of living. I can't say I was any different. My mind turned to worrying about Krapp's math homework and the tribulations of my own family. I suppose the investigation into Charlie's disappearance continued, but it no longer involved the neighborhood at large.

Even though the hubbub surrounding the tragedy was quickly receding, I'd still get a chill when, at school, I'd look over to Charlie's place and see an empty chair, or when out on my bike, I'd pass by his mother, who had certainly lost her mind when losing her son. Every day she'd wander the neighborhood, traipsing through people's backyards, inspecting the dumpsters behind the stores downtown, staggering along the railroad tracks. She had been one of the youngest mothers on the block, but the loss had drained her overnight and she became haggard; her blonde hair frizzed and her expression blank.

In the evenings, she'd walk around to the schoolyard and stand by the playground, calling Charlie's name. One night, as darkness came and we were sitting, eating dinner, my mother, quite a few glasses of sherry on her way to Bermuda, looked up and saw, through the front window, Mrs. Eddisson heading home from Southgate. She stopped talking and got up, walked through the living room and out the door. Jim and Mary and I went to the window to watch. She met Mrs. Eddisson in the street and said something to her. She then stepped closer and put her arms around the smaller woman and held her. They stood like that for a very long time, swaying slightly, until true night came, and every now and then my mother would lightly pat her back.

Since it involved him going out in the early morning before the sun came up, Jim was made to quit his paper route, and certain precautions were taken as far as now locking the front and back door at night. We weren't allowed to go anywhere off the block without another kid with us, and if I went to the woods, I'd have to get Jim to go with me. Still, I walked George by myself at night, and now had another specter lurking behind the bushes, along with Jimmy Bonnel, to contend with.

On the first really cold night, near the end of September, the wind blowing dead leaves down the block, I went out with George and started around the bend toward the school. As we passed Mrs. Grimm's darkened house, I heard a whisper: "Is that you?" The sudden sound of a voice made me jump and George gave a low growl. I looked over at the yard, and there, standing amidst the barren rosebushes, was Mrs. Eddisson dressed in white.

"Charlie, is that you?" she said, and put her hand out toward me.

The sudden sight of her there scared the hell out of me, and I turned, unable to answer, and ran as fast as I could back to the house. When I got home, my mother was asleep on the couch, so just to be near someone else I went down in the cellar to find Jim. He was there, sitting beneath the sun of Botch Town, fixing the roof on Mrs. Ripici's house. On the other side of the stairs, Mickey and Sandy Graham and Sally O'Mally were working hard in Mrs. Harkmar's class.

"What do you want?" asked Jim.

My heart was still beating fast, and I realized it wasn't so much the sight of Mrs. Eddisson that had scared me, since we were used to her now popping up anywhere at just about any time, but it was the fact that she thought I was Charlie. I didn't want to tell Jim what was wrong, as if to speak it would make the connection between me and the missing boy a real one.

"I guess the prowler is gone now," I said to him. There had been no reported sightings of him since Charlie's disappearance. I scanned the board to find the shadow man's figure, those painted eyes and straight-pin hands, and found him standing behind the Miltons' shack of a place up near Higbee Lane.

"He's still around, I bet," said Jim. "He's laying low because of all the police on the block in the last couple weeks."

My eyes kept moving over the board as he spoke. Botch Town always drew me in. There was no glancing quickly at it. I followed Pine Avenue down from Higbee and around the corner. When I got to Mrs. Grimm's house on the right side of the street, I was brought up short. Standing in her front yard was the clay figure of Mrs. Eddisson.

"Hey," I said, and leaned out over the board to point, "did you put her there?"

"Why don't you go do something," he said.

"Just tell me, did you put that there?"

I knew he could tell from the tone of my voice that I wasn't kidding.

"No," he said. "Why?"

" 'Cause I was just out with George, and that's exactly where I saw her a few minutes ago."

"Maybe she walked over there after I turned the lights out last night," said Jim.

"Come on," I said, "did you move her?"

"I swear I didn't touch her," he said. "I haven't moved any of them in a week."

We looked at each other, and out of the silence that followed, we heard, from the other side of the cellar, the voice of Mrs. Harkmar say, "Mickey, you have scored a 100 on your English test."

A few seconds passed and then I called out, "Hey, Mary, come here."

The voice of Sally O'Mally said, "I'll have to do better next time."

Jim got up and took a step toward the stairs. "Mickey, we need you over here," he said.

A moment later, Mary came around the stairs and over to where we were standing.

"I'm not going to be mad at you if you did, but did you touch any of the stuff in Botch Town?" he asked, smiling.

"Could you possibly . . . ?" she said in her Mickey voice.

"Did you move Mrs. Eddisson, here?" I asked, and pointed to where the figure stood.

She stepped up to the board and looked down at the town.

"What do you think?" asked Jim, resting his hand lightly on her shoulder.

She stared intently and then nodded.

The next day on the playground at school, I overheard Peter Milton telling Chris Hacket that there had been someone at his mother's window the night before.

"Who was it?" asked Chris. "Batman?"

Peter thought for some time and then laughed so his whole giant body jiggled. "No, course not," he said. "She thought she was lookin' at a full moon, but then it was a face."

"What a dip," said Chris.

Peter thought just as long again, and then said, "Hey," reaching out one of his man-sized hands for Chris's throat. Hacket took off, though, running across the field, yelling, "Your mom's got a fart for a brain." Milton ran four steps and then either forgot why he was running or became winded.

The minute I heard what Peter had said, I thought back to the board the previous night and remembered the shadow man's pins scratching the back wall of the Miltons' house. When I got home that afternoon, I told Jim and we went to find Mary. At first, she was nowhere to be found, but then we saw little clouds of smoke rising from the forsythias in the corner of the backyard. We went back there and crawled in to sit on either side of her.

"How do you know where to put the people in Botch Town?" asked Jim.

Mary flicked the ash off her cigarette exactly the way my mother did and said, "Ciphering the McGinn System."

"You're handicapping them?" I asked.

"From your Morning Line," she said.

"What do you mean?" I asked.

"You read them to me," she said.

"My notebook?"

She nodded.

"A town full of horses," said Jim.

"It's not a race," I said.

"Yes it is, in the numbers," she said, staring ahead.

"Do you figure it in your head or on paper?" I asked.

"Sometimes," she said.

Mary stamped out her cigarette. We sat there quiet for a time, the wind blowing the branches of the bushes around us. Above, the dying leaves of the oak tree scraped together. I tried to understand what she was doing with the information I was giving her, but couldn't stretch my imagination around it.

"Where's Charlie Eddisson?" asked Jim.

"Gone," said Mary.

"But where does he belong on the board?"

"I don't know. You never read him to me," she said.

"I never read you his mother either," I said.

"I saw her," said Mary. "Saw her on the street and saw her with Mommy."

For the next fifteen minutes we told her everything we knew about Charlie Eddisson; all of his trials and tribulations in school, what color bike he rode, what team insignia was on his baseball hat (the Cleveland Indians), and so on. She nodded as we fed her the information. When we were done, she said, "Goodbye, now," and got up and left the forsythias.

Jim started laughing. "It's all luck," he said. "There's only so much space in Botch Town and if you place the figures down, they have to go somewhere. There's a good chance you'll get it right sometimes."

"I don't know," I said.

"You think she's Doctor Strange," he said, and laughed so hard at me, I was convinced I'd been a fool. For my trouble, he gave me a Fonseca Pulverizer in the side muscle of my right arm that deadened it for a good five minutes. As he left me behind in the bushes, he called back, "You'll believe anything."

In silent revenge, I thought back a few winters to the night when my parents told Jim and me that there was no Santa Claus. Just that afternoon, Jim had me next to him out in the backyard. The cellar had been off-limits since a week after Thanksgiving. We were lying on our stomachs in the snow, peering through the cellar window. "I see a bike," said Jim. "Christ, I think I see Robot Commando." But when my mother dropped the bomb that there was no Santa Claus after dinner, I was the one who simply nodded. Jim went to pieces. He sat down in the rocking chair by the front window, the snow falling in huge flakes outside in the dark, and he rocked and sobbed with his hands covering his face for the longest time.

I left the bushes and went inside to dig around in the couch cushions for change. I found a nickel and decided to ride to the store and get a couple pieces of Bazooka. There was still an hour left before my mother got home from work and made dinner. The sun was already setting when I left the house. Night was coming sooner and sooner with each day, and I rode along wondering what I should be for Halloween. I took the back way to the store, down Jean Road, and wasn't paying much attention to what was going on around me, when I suddenly woke up to the scent of a vaguely familiar aroma.

A few feet in front of me, parked next to the curb of the sidewalk I rode along, was a white car. I knew I had seen it before, but couldn't remember where right away. Only when I was next to it, and looked in the open passenger-side window to see a man sitting in the driver's seat, did I remember. The fins, the bubble top, the old curved windshield—it was the car that had stopped the night we dragged Mr. Blah-blah across the street. As I passed by, the man inside, wearing a white trench coat and smoking a pipe, turned and stared at me. His hair was close cut, salt-and-pepper, his face, thin with a thin, sharp nose, and his eyes were squinted as if he was studying me.

I panicked and took off. Behind me, I heard the car start up, and that pushed me to peddle even faster. I made it around the turn that led to the stores, but didn't stop. Instead of heading left to the deli, I made a right on Higbee and rode all the way down to Pine and back home. When I almost got to the house, I was winded. Finally I stopped and turned around to see if he was still behind me. The street was empty all the way to the end, and night was only a few minutes away.

I didn't want to tell Jim about what had happened, because I knew he would laugh at me, but I couldn't shake the memory of the way that guy had stared. It took a lot of effort to put him out of my mind. We had dinner and did our homework and went next door to listen to Pop play the mandolin, and only after a few hours was I able to forget him. When I went to bed, though, and opened the novel about Perno Shell in the Amazon, that face came floating back. Pipe smoke! The same exact scent that had made me look up during the bike ride, now emanated from the pages of my book.

The next day, Pop had to drive over to the school and pick Mary up. She was running a high fever and feeling sick to her stomach. Something was definitely making the rounds at Southgate. When my class was in the library that afternoon, Johnny March, the boy who smelled like ass, puked without warning all over the giant dictionary old Mr. Rogers, the librarian, kept on a pedestal by the window. Johnny was escorted to the nurse's office, and Nick the janitor was called in, pushing his barrel of red stuff and carrying a broom. I don't know what that red stuff was, but in my imagination it was composed of grated pencil erasers and its special properties absorbed the sins of children. He used about two snow-shovels full in the library that day. As Nick disposed of the ruined dictionary, much to Mr. Rogers's obvious sadness, he diagnosed the problem. "It must have been the black olives," he said.

Back in Krapp's classroom, though, after library, Patricia Trepedino puked, and then after watching her, Felicia Barnes puked. Nick and his barrel of red stuff were in hot demand, because reports of more puking came in from all over the school, and his call of the black olives was obviously found to be an instance of his "talking dogshit." Krapp was visibly shaken, his nostrils flaring, his eyes darting. After everything was cleaned up, a lingering vomit funk pervading the room, he opened all the windows and put on a filmstrip for us about the uses of fossil fuels, featuring a talking charcoal briquette. He sat in the last row in the dark, dabbing his forehead with a handkerchief.

When I got home, Doctor Geller was there. He had pulled the rocker over by the living room couch where Mary was sleeping wrapped in a blanket with a bed pillow under her head. A big steel pot we knew as "the puke bucket" was on the floor next to her. He opened his eyes and waved to me when I came through the door.

He was smoking a cigar, which he took out of his mouth momentarily to put his finger to his lips and caution me to be quiet.

Doctor Geller was everybody's doctor in town. He was a heavyset man, with a thick wave of black hair, a wide face, and glasses. I never saw him without his black suit on and his black bag sitting next to him or in his hand. He gave us kids all of our shots, choked us on flat sticks, rubber hammered our knees, listened to our hearts, and came when we were really sick and couldn't make it to his office. When my mother first brought Mary, small and weak, home from the hospital, he came every day for a month to help her get used to administering a special medicine and to assure her our sister would live. It was not unusual to find him, morning or night, dozing for a few minutes in the living room rocking chair, his pocket watch in his hand. He was constantly tired, dark circles under his eyes, and always due at another sick neighbor's house.

Once, during a snowstorm, when it was impossible to drive, and my mother thought Jim was having an appendicitis attack because of the pains in his stomach, Geller came the half-mile from his office on foot, trudging through the snow. When the doctor discovered Jim only had a bad case of gas, he shook his head and laughed. Then he went next door to see Pop, with whom he shared an interest in the horses, had a glass of Old Grand-Dad and a cigar, and was off. I watched him through the front window when he left, the dark coming on and the snow still driving down.

He didn't stay long the day Mary was sick, but told Nan, who was in and out from her apartment, leaving the door open to listen, that he had another dozen kids to see, who all had the same thing. When he left, I sat at the end of the couch and watched cartoons on TV with the sound off. Just when I was about to get up and go outside, Mary opened her eyes. She was shivering slightly. Her mouth started to move and she mumbled something to me. I got up and went to the hall closet where the towels were kept. Taking a washrag, I wet it with cold water and placed it on her forehead. She grabbed my hand as I pulled it back and her eyes opened wide.

"The boy," she said. "He's to show. I found him." She pointed one finger down at the floor.

"Okay," I said. "Okay."

She soon returned to a deep sleep and seemed to be more comfortable. I told Nan, who had come to the door every few minutes to check on Mary, that I was going outside. She came in then, her cleaning done, and took my place at the end of the couch. I went out into the yard and looked for something to do. Jim, I knew, would not be home soon, as he had joined the wrestling team and now took the late bus. In the middle of smacking the cherry tree trunk with an old, yellow whiffle-ball bat, it suddenly came to me what Mary was signaling.

I ran back inside and went down into the cellar. Leaning out over Botch Town, I pulled the string for the bulb. I started at Higbee Lane and scanned down the block, looking for the clay figure of Charlie Eddisson. Mrs. Ryan was standing, round as a marble, in her front yard. Nick was turned, facing his house. Mr. Kelty was out of place, standing next to Mrs. Graves in the Graveses' backyard. Mr. Stutton had fallen over in his driveway. I did find Mrs. Eddisson on her way down Pine Street toward the school, but didn't see Charlie anywhere. Most of the characters usually just milled around by their houses, but Charlie was no longer there. I thought maybe Mary or Jim had taken him from the board because he was missing.

I was about to turn the light out and give up my search when I finally saw him. All the way on the other side of the board, beyond the school field and the trees that represented the woods, his figure lay on its side, directly in the center of the glittering blue waters of the lake.

Back upstairs, I put the leash on George and we were out the door in a second. Down the block and around the corner we went, moving quickly toward the school. It was getting late in the afternoon and the temperature had dropped. The woods were somewhat forbidding to me after Charlie had gone missing, and I wasn't supposed to go in them alone, but I only hesitated for a moment before plunging in beneath the trees.

We took the main trail, and ten minutes of fast walking later, stood at the edge of the lake. I'm not sure it was really a lake or just a very large pond, but I know that it was supposed to be very deep in places. All of the kids' parents told them it was bottomless, whatever that meant, but the older I got the more I suspected it was a story concocted to keep us from swimming in it or trying to set sail on a raft. My father added to the story for us. He had said that the corpse of someone who had drowned in it once was found months later, floating over in the bay. In circumference the lake could easily have fit the entire structure of the school within its boundaries.

Its surface was littered with fallen leaves, and in those places where just the water showed through, the reflection of the surrounding trees was scattered by the wind moving over its surface. It was so peaceful. I didn't know what I expected to find, maybe a body floating out in the middle, but it merely looked as it always did in autumn. I stood there for quite a while, listening to acorns and twigs falling in the woods around me, until I started thinking about Charlie. An image of him resting lightly on his back at the bottom, his eyes wide, mouth open as if he were crying out, his hands reaching up for the last rays of sunlight that came in over the treetops, cutting the water and revealing the way through his murky nightmare back to the world, spooked me. The gathering dusk chased George and me down the path and back out of the woods.

That night I woke from sleep, shivering. The wind was blowing and the antenna on the roof above my room vibrated with a high-pitched wail, like the very house was moaning. I made it to the bathroom, got sick, and staggered back to bed where I fell into feverish dreams—a tumbling whirl of images punctuated with scenes of the sewer pipe, the lake, the descending brick stairway at St. Anselm's. Jimmy Bonnel paid me a visit. Charlie, his mother, the man in the white car, a pale face at the window, and Perno Shell himself chased me, befriended me, betrayed me, until it all suddenly stopped. I heard the birds singing and opened my eyes to see a hint of red through the window. There was a wet cloth on my forehead, and then I noticed the shadowy form of my father, sitting at the end of my bed, hunched forward, eyes closed, one hand lying atop the covers over my ankle. He must have felt me stir. "It's okay," he whispered, "I'm here. Go back to sleep."

Although the fever had broken, and I was feeling much better by nine o'clock in the morning, the virus bought me a day off from school. Mary didn't go either, and my mother stayed home from work to take care of us. It was like the old days, before the drinking and the money trouble. Nan came in and we all sat for an hour after breakfast at the dining room table, playing cards: Old Maid and Casino. I had a great adventure with my plastic soldiers, which I hadn't bothered with for months, on the windowsill in the living room while the brilliant, cold day shone in around me. We watched a mystery movie on TV with Peter Lorre as the sauerkraut-eating detective, Mr. Motto, and my mother made white spaghetti with butter.

At around three o'clock, I lay back down on the couch and closed my eyes. Mary sat on the floor in the kitchen, putting together a puzzle, my mother sat in the rocker beside me and dozed. All was still save the murmur of the wind from outside making it sound as if the house was breathing.

I thought back to when I was in fourth grade and had stayed out of school off and on for forty-five days. My mother wasn't working then, and if I didn't feel like going to school, she let me stay home.

I had genuinely discovered reading that year, and I lay in bed much of the time, devouring one book after another: *Jason and the Argonauts*, *Treasure Island*, *The Martian Chronicles*, *Charlotte's Web*, to name just a few of my favorites. It didn't matter what type of story it was, the characters were more alive to me than all the students and teachers at Southgate.

At lunchtime I would come out into the living room and she would make the spaghetti, and we would watch an old movie. I was the only fourth grader who could identify Paul Muni or Leslie Howard on sight. I loved the mystery movies, their plots and the sense of suspense. My favorites were the ones with the Thin Man, and my mother, of course, was partial to Basil Rathbone as Holmes. Mr. Tary threatened to keep me from passing fourth grade, but she went over to the school and told him I was passing, and I did.

In remembering that year, I realized how different she was from other parents. That difference was like a light that always shone in the back of my mind no matter how dim things got when she'd drink the dark wine and become a vampire. She scared me and I hated what she became, but that light was like the promise of an eventual return to paradise. These memories protected me when suddenly I fell a thousand stories down into sleep. I didn't struggle or abruptly awaken in the descent, but let myself go, my breathing copying the breathing of the house.

I only woke from that peaceful nap of no dreams because Jim pried open my left eye with his thumb. "This one's dead, Doctor," he said. I came to and noticed twilight at the window, heard the sound of the wine bottle pinging the rim of a glass in the kitchen. The first thought I had was of Charlie at the bottom of the lake. Who could I tell that would believe what I thought I knew?

After dinner, my mother put the Kingston Trio on the Victrola and sat at the dining room table drinking and reading the newspaper. Mary was in roller skates, going round and round, following the outer curve of the braided rug in the living room. Inside her orbit, Jim showed me some of his wrestling moves.

"Could you possibly . . ." I heard my mother say, and then she called us over to her.

Jim and I each went to one side of her chair. She pointed at a small photograph on the page. "Look who that is," she said.

I didn't recognize him at first because he wasn't wearing his paper hat, but Jim finally said, "Hey, it's Softee."

Then that long, haggard face came into focus, and I could just about hear him say, *What'll it be, sweetheart?*

My mother told us that the news story was about him recently being arrested because he was wanted for child molestation in another state. For a while, they suspected him in the disappearance of Charlie Eddisson, but he was cleared of that suspicion.

"What's child molestation?" I asked.

"It means he's a creep," said my mother, and turned the page.

"He gave some kid a Special Softee," said Jim.

My mother lifted the paper and swung it at him, but he was too fast.

"What's the world coming to?" she said, and took a sip of wine.

That night, I couldn't get to sleep, partly because I had slept during the day and partly because my thoughts were full of all the dark things that had burrowed into my world. I pictured a specimen of Miter's Sun fresh from the branch but riddled with wormholes. The antenna moaned in the wind, and it didn't matter how close Perno Shell was to the golden streets of El Dorado, the aroma of pipe smoke made it impossible to concentrate on the book.

I got up and went to my desk, opened the drawer, and took out the stack of Softee cards. The living vanilla-cone head now struck me as sinister; leering with that frozen smile. I took them over to the garbage pail and dropped them in. Back in bed, though, all I could think of was the one card that I had never owned. Unable to throw it out, bury it, burn it with the rest of the deck, those eyes gained an illusive power, and they watched me from inside my own head. They were Charlie's drowned eyes, the eyes of the prowler, the eyes of the man in the white car, my mother's eyes when the anger was upon her. I hunkered down under the covers and waited to hear my father come in from work.

Instead, I heard a scream, Mary downstairs, and the sound of George barking. I jumped out of bed and took the steps. Jim was up in a flash, right behind me. When I got to her darkened room, she was sitting upright in bed with a terrified look on her face.

"What?" said Jim.

"Someone is outside," she said. "There was a face at the window."

George snorted and growled.

I felt someone right behind me and turned quickly. It was Nan, standing there in her quilted bathrobe and hairnet, holding a blackjack in her hand. The weapon—a slim sack of stitched leather, like a long, black teardrop, with lead sewn into it—had belonged to her first husband, who had been a motorcycle cop in New York City. She'd told me once that you could break bones with it and leave no bruises.

Jim took George by the collar and led him to the kitchen. "Get 'em, George," he said, and opened the back door. The dog ran out, growling. Mary, Nan, Jim, and I waited to hear if he caught anyone. After some time passed, Nan told us to stay put and went out, holding the blackjack at the ready. A few seconds later, she came back with George following her.

"Whoever it was is gone," she said. She sent Jim and me back to bed and told us she'd sit with Mary until our father got home. My mother had never even opened an eye, and as I passed by her bedroom, next to Mary's, I saw her lying there, mouth open, the weight of *Holmes* holding her down.

By the time I was in the kitchen the next morning, fixing a bowl of cereal, Jim had already been out in the backyard, studying the scene of the crime.

"The ladder was up against the house," he said.

"Any footprints?" I asked.

He shook his head.

"Your father is calling the police about it from work today," said my mother from the dining room.

Jim leaned in close to me and whispered, "We gotta catch this guy."

I nodded.

I went to school, my head full of worry, only to learn a piece of information that almost made me laugh with joy. At recess, Tim Caliban told me that he had heard from his father that on the coming Saturday the police were going to dredge the lake for Charlie Eddisson. I couldn't believe how lucky I was. It was as if someone had read my mind, and not only that, they were doing something about it. I suppose it only made sense, given the circumstances of Charlie's disappearance, but for me it was an enormous relief.

That afternoon, Krapp announced that the police were going to be "searching" the lake for Charlie on Saturday, and they had asked him to make an announcement that no kids were allowed near the school field or in the woods. Part of our homework assignment was to tell our parents.

"We'll go into the woods behind the Hossetters' house," Jim said later that day after I'd told him. We were in his room, and he was supposed to be doing his homework. "The cops will have guys at the school field and maybe over on Minerva, but they probably won't be that far into the woods. We'll take the binoculars."

I nodded.

"Can you imagine if they pull him out of the lake?" he said, staring at the floor as if he were seeing it before his eyes. "We'll have to get up and go early."

I wasn't so sure I wanted to see them dredge Charlie up, but I knew I had to go. "If they find him, does that mean he fell in or someone threw him in there?" I asked.

"What do I look like, Sherlock Holmes?" he said.

After that he gave me instructions to rig the ladder the next day after school. "Get two old soda cans and fill them with pebbles," he said. "Tie one to one end of the ladder with fishing line and one to the other end the same way. If he comes at night and tries to take it, we'll hear him, and let George out."

The week dragged in anticipation of the Saturday dredging. Mary sat with me the following afternoon as I worked at setting up the ladder. It lay along the fence on the right-hand side of the yard, near the clothesline. She had counted the number of pebbles I put into the first can and would not let me tie the second one on until I had evened up the number in that one.

"Two more," she said when I tried to add just one extra pebble and leave it at that. I looked over at her, and she lifted her hand. First the index finger came up and then, slowly, the thumb. I laughed and put the other two in.

"So, Charlie's in the lake," I said as I tied the second can in place. I had not yet spoken to her about her Botch Town revelation.

"He'll be in the lake," she said.

"Are you sure?" I asked.

"He'll be in the lake."

I went out on my bike looking for someone to write about and passed Mr. Barzita's yard. He was such a quiet old man, I'd almost forgotten he lived on our block. There he was, though, raking leaves in his front yard. He lived alone since his wife had died back when I was only seven. His property was surrounded by a chain-link fence, and instead of going for the usual open lawn, he had long ago planted rows of fig trees, so that the front of his house was obscured by a small orchard. Even though he lived in solitude, rarely coming out of the front gate, he always smiled and waved to us kids when we rode by on our bikes, and he would come to the fence to talk to grown-ups.

Mr. Barzita was one of those old people who seemed to be shrinking, and would eventually disappear instead of die of old age. During the winter, I never saw him, but in spring, he would emerge from his house shorter, more wizened than the year before. On the hottest days of the summer, he would sit in his chaise longue among the fig trees, sipping wine, holding a loaded pellet pistol in his lap. When the squirrels would invade his yard to get at the figs, he'd shoot them. In passing his house, if you yelled to him, "How many?" he'd hold whatever his kill was up by the tails.

One Sunday when just my father and I were in the car, and we passed the old man's house, I asked what he thought of Barzita killing the squirrels. My father shrugged. He told me, "That old man, he was in the medical corps in the army during the Second World War. At the place where he was stationed, a very remote mountain base in Europe, there was an outbreak of meningitis—a brain disease, very catching, very deadly. They asked for volunteers to take care of the sick. He volunteered. They put him and another guy in a locked room with fifteen infected soldiers. When it was over, he was the only one who came out alive."

I tried to imagine what it must have been like in that room, the air stale with the last exhalations of the dying, but didn't get very far.

"A lot of these old farts you see scrabbling around town . . ." he said. "You'd be surprised."

Jim looked both ways up and down Pine to check for cars or anyone who might be watching, and then he and I ducked into the Hossetters' driveway and behind the hedges. We ran around the side of the house, through the backyard, and down a slope that led to a branch of the stream. Jumping the stream, we moved in under the trees. It was a little before eight o'clock on Saturday morning. The sky was overcast and there was a cold breeze that occasionally gusted, lifting the dead leaves off the floor of the woods and loosing more from the branches above.

We moved along the winding path to where it led back behind Southgate. Jim suggested we not take the most direct route that passed closest to the schoolyard, but that we arc out on the less used trail that went through the moss patches and the low scrub. He had Pop's old binoculars around his neck, and he made me carry the Brownie camera. When we came to the split in the path, one direction leading away south toward the railroad tracks and one directly to the lake, he told me to move quietly and that if we got chased we should split up. He'd head for the tracks, and I was supposed to go back the way we came. I nodded and from that point on we only whispered.

After jumping the snaking stream twice more, from mossy hillock to root bole, from sand bank to solid dirt, we came in view of the lake. Jim motioned for me to get down and I did.

"The cops are there already," he said. "We'll have to crawl."

We made our way to within thirty yards of the southern bank of the lake, and moved in behind a fallen oak with some tall stickers forming a kind of blind between us and the view the police had. My heart was pounding, and my hands were shaking. Jim peeked up over the trunk and put the binoculars to his eyes.

"It looks like they just got started," he said. "There's five guys. Two on the bank and three in a flat-bottom boat with a little electric motor."

I looked and saw what he had described. Coming off the back of the boat were two ropes attached to winches with hand cranks. The boat was moving along slowly, trolling the western side of the lake. Then I noticed that on the opposite bank there stood some of the neighbors. Mr. Eddisson was there, a big man with a bald head and a mustache. He wore his gas station uniform and stood, head down, arms folded across his chest. It was the first I'd seen of him since Charlie had gone missing. Beside him was his next-door neighbor, Mr. Gelimina. There were a few other people I didn't recognize, but when one of them moved to the side, I caught sight of Krapp. There he stood, dressed in his usual short-sleeve white shirt and tie, his hairdo flatter than his personality.

"Krapp's here," I whispered.

Jim turned the binoculars to focus on the crowd I had been looking at. "Jeez, you're right," he said.

"Wonder what he's doing here?" I said.

"I think he's crying," said Jim. "Yeah, he's drying his eyes. Man, I always knew he was a big pussy."

"Yeah," I said, but the thought of Krapp both showing up and crying struck me.

Jim swung the binoculars back to see what the cops were doing. He reported to me that at the ends of those ropes they had these big steel hooks with four claws each. Every once in a while, they'd stop moving and reel them in by turning the hand cranks. He gave me an inventory of what they brought up—pieces of trees, the rusted handlebars of a bike, the partial skeleton of either a dog or fox . . . and it went on and on. They slowly covered the entire lake and then started again.

"He's not down there," said Jim. "So much for Mary's predictions."

I peered back over the fallen trunk and watched for a while, braver now that I probably wasn't going to see Charlie. We sat there in the cold for two straight hours and I was starting to shiver. "Let's go home," I whispered.

"Okay," said Jim. "They're almost done." Still he sat watching, and our hiding and spying reminded me of the prowler.

From out on the lake, one of the cops yelled, "Hold up, there's something here." I stuck my head up to watch. The cop started turning the crank, reeling in the rope. "Looks like clothing," he called to the other cops on the bank. "Wait a second . . ." he said. He reeled more quickly then.

Something broke the surface of the water near the back of the boat. It looked like a soggy body at first, but it was hard to tell. There were definitely pants and a shirt. Then the head came into view, big and gray, with a trunk.

"Shit," said Jim.

"Mr. Blah-blah," I whispered.

"Hand me the camera," said Jim. "I gotta get a picture of this."

He snapped it, handed me back the camera, and then motioned for me to follow him. We got down on all fours and crawled slowly away from the fallen tree. Once our escape was covered by enough trees and bushes, we got to our feet and ran like hell.

We stood behind the Hossetters' place, still in the cover of the woods, and worked to catch our breath.

"Blah-blah," said Jim, and laughed.

"Did you put him in there?" I asked.

"Blah," he said, and shook his head. "Nah, Softee molested him and threw him in there."

"Get out," I said.

"Probably Stutton and his horrible dumpling sisters found him and took him to the lake. They're always back here in the woods," he said. "We should have had Mary predict where Mr. Blah-blah would be."

"But then where's Charlie?" I asked.

He brushed past me and jumped the stream.

I followed him across the stream and stayed close as we moved through the backyard and around the house to the street.

When we arrived home, I was relieved to find that my mother wasn't sitting at the dining room table. We had a chance to stash the camera and binoculars. The door to Nan's was open. I could hear Pop in their figuring his system out loud and, without looking, knew Mary was beside him. Jim took our spying implements upstairs, and I walked down the hallway toward my parents' room to see if my mother was up yet. She wasn't in her bed, but when I passed by the bathroom door, I heard her in there retching.

I knocked once. "Are you okay?" I called.

"I'll be right out," she said.

It had been obvious since the start of the school year that Mr.

Rogers, the librarian, had been losing his mind. During his lunch break, when we were usually laboring over math in Krapp's class, the old man would be out on the baseball diamond, walking the bases in his rumpled suit, hunched over, talking to himself, as if he were reliving some game from the distant past. That loose dirt that collected around the bases, the soft brown powder that Stinky Steinmacher ate with a spoon, would lift up in a strong wind, circling around Rogers, and he'd clap as if the natural commotion was really the roar of the crowd. Krapp would look over his shoulder from where he stood at the blackboard and see us all staring out the window, shake his head, and then go and lower the blinds.

The loss of his giant dictionary seemed to be the last straw for Rogers, as if it was an anchor that kept him from floating away. With that gone, as my father would say, "He dipped out." Each week we would be delivered to the library by Krapp and spend a half-hour there with Rogers. Of late, the old man had been smiling a lot like a dog on a hot day, and his eyes were always busy, shifting back and forth. Sometimes he'd stand for minutes on end, staring into a beam of light shining in through the window, and sometimes he'd be frantic, moving here and there, pulling books off the shelves and shoving them into kids' hands.

Jake Harweed was brutal to him, making hand motions behind the librarian's back, coaxing everyone to laugh (and you had to laugh if Jake wanted you to). Jake would knock books off the shelf onto the floor and just leave them there. For Rogers to see a book on the floor was a heart-rending experience, and one day Harweed had him nearly in tears. I secretly liked Rogers, because he loved books and had a sense that there was something alive in them between the covers, but I couldn't let on that I wished the others would just leave him alone. Still, he was beginning to put even me off with his weirdness.

On the Monday morning following the dredging, we had library. Rogers sat in his little office nearly the entire time we were there, bent over his desk with his face in his hands. Harweed started the rumor that he kept *Playboy* magazines in there. When the time was almost up, he came out to stamp the books kids had chosen. Before he sat down at the table with his stamp, he walked up behind where I was standing, put one hand on my shoulder, and then reached up over my head to the top shelf where he pulled a thin volume from the row.

"You'll need this," he said, and handed it to me. He walked away to the table then, the kids lined up with their selections, and he began stamping them.

I looked down at the book he had handed me. On the cover, behind the library plastic, was a drawing of a mean-looking black dog. Above the creature in two rows of words, yellow letters made of lines like saber blades, was the title: *The Hound of the Baskervilles*. I wanted to ask him what he meant, but I never got the chance. News spread quickly through the school the next day that he had been fired because he was so old he went nuts. Having the *Baskervilles* in my possession was, at first, an unsettling experience. It felt like I had taken some personal belonging of my mother's, just as if I had appropriated my father's watch or Nan's hairnet. The book itself had an aura of power around it that prevented me from simply opening the cover and beginning. I hid it in my room, between the mattress and box spring of the bed. For the next few days, I'd take it out every now and then and hold it, look at the cover, gingerly flip the pages. Although by this time my mother only used the big, red volume of *The Complete Sherlock Holmes* as an anvil in her sleep, there was a time when she had avidly read it over and over. She read a wide range of other books as well, everything from Tchaikovsky's *Letters To His Family* to *The Naked Ape*, but always returned to detective stories. She loved them in every form, and before we went broke, spent Sunday mornings consuming five cups of coffee and a dozen cigarettes, solving the mystery of the *New York Times* crossword puzzle.

Painting, playing the guitar, making bizarre collages were mere hobbies compared to my mother's desire to be a mystery writer. Before work became a necessity for her, she'd sit at the dining room table all afternoon, the old typewriter in front of her, composing her own mystery novel. I remembered her having read me some of it. The title was *Something by the Sea*, and it involved her detective Milo, a farting dog, a blind heiress, and a stringed instrument to be played with different colored glass tubes that fit over one's fingers. Something by the Sea was the name of the resort where the story took place. All the while she wrote it, she kept *Holmes* by her side, opened to "The Hound of the Baskervilles."

My fear of starting the library book lasted nearly a week until one night at dinner when my mother told a story about a friend of hers when she was younger. From the state she was in, I was sure her conversation was headed directly toward Bermuda but instead it veered off into an odd detour about Kenny Boucher. He was a boy in her class in grade school, and he stuttered and was very timid, but she involved him as a co-conspirator in all of her evil plots. One was the distribution of Ex-Lax to the kids in the neighborhood under the false claim that it was free chocolate. "It was a shit storm," she said, laughing into her wine.

Another had to do with a giant box they had found at the curb on junk day. They cut a little door out of it and then strung the inside with wads of chewed gum that they stretched into spider webs. When their work was done, they invited friends to enter their clubhouse. Kids emerged covered in gum, their clothes ruined, their hair matted with it.

When Jim and I asked to hear more of her adventures with Kenny Boucher, she shook her head and looked sad. "He died," she said. "He had this disease called Saint Vitus Dance that would make him spin around out of control every once in a while. He had an attack of it one day, fell down in the street, and drowned in a puddle before anyone found him." She fell into a sullen silence and said nothing else for the rest of the night until she sent us to bed.

Upstairs, I thought about the affect her memory had on her and realized that maybe there was something in *The Hound of the Baskervilles* that could tell me a secret about her. I passed up Perno Shell and pulled the book out from under the mattress. That night I stayed up late and read the first few chapters. In them I met Holmes and Watson. The book was not hard to read. I was used to the British voice in it as my father, when we were younger, read us a lot of books by Kipling and Rider Haggard. I was interested in the story, and liked the character of Watson very much, but Holmes was something else.

The great detective came across to me like a snob, the type my father once described as "believing the sun rose and set from his asshole." The picture of him in my mind was something like a mix between Perno Shell and Phineas Fogg, but his personality was pure Krapp. When told about the demon hound, Holmes replied that it was an interesting story for those who believed in fairy tales. He was obviously, "not standing for it." Still, I was intrigued by his voluminous smoking and the fact that he played the violin.

The days sank deeper into autumn, rotten to their cores with twilight. The bright warmth of the sun only lasted about as long as we were in school, and then once we were home, an hour later, the world was briefly submerged in a rich, golden aura, a honey glow, that was both beautiful and sad, gilding everything, from the barren branches of willows to the old wreck of a Pontiac parked alongside the Miltons' garage. A minute after that, the tide turned, the sun suddenly appeared a distant star, and in rolled a dim gray wave of neither here nor there that seemed to last a week each day, its shadows enhanced by our steamy exhalations and the smoke of burning leaves.

The wind of this in-between time made me always want to curl up inside a memory and sleep with eyes open. Dead leaves rolled across lawns, scraped along the street, quietly tapped the windows. Jack-o'-lanterns with luminous triangle eyes and jagged smiles turned up on front steps and in windows. Rattle-dry cornstalks bore half-eaten ears of brown and blue kernels like teeth gone bad, as if they had eaten themselves, the way kids wore and then chewed the ultimately unsatisfying licorice/root beer gunk of wax teeth. Scarecrows hung from lawn lampposts or stoop railings, listing forward, disjointed and drunk, dressed in the rumpled plaid shirts of long-gone grandfathers and jeans tied up with a length of rope. In the true dark, when walking George after dinner, these shadow figures often startled me when their stitched and painted faces took on the features of Charlie Eddisson or Jimmy Bonnel.

Halloween was close, our favorite holiday because it carried none of the pain-in-the-ass holiness of Christmas and still there was free candy. The excitement of it crowded all problems to the side. The prowler, Charlie, school work were overwhelmed by hours of decision as to what we would be for that one night—something or someone who wasn't us, but who we wished to be, which I suppose ended up being us in some way. I could already taste the candy corn and feel my teeth aching. My father had given me a dollar and with it I'd bought a molded plastic skeleton mask that smelled like fresh BO and made my cheeks sweat.

At the time, the only thought I had about that leering bone face was that it was cool as hell, but maybe, in the back of my mind, I was thinking of all those eyes out there trying to look into me, and it was a good disguise because it let them think they were seeing deep under my skin even though it was only an illusion. I showed the mask to Jim, and he told me, "This is the last year you can wear a costume. You're getting too old. Next year you'll have to go as a bum." All the older kids went around trick-or-treating as bums— a little charcoal on the face and some ripped up, baggy clothes.

Mary decided she would be the jockey, Willie Shoemaker. She modeled her outfit for Jim and me one night. It consisted of baggy pants tucked into a pair of white go-go boots, a baseball cap, a baggy, patchwork shirt, and a piece of thin curtain rod for a jockey's whip. She walked past us once and then looked over her shoulder. In the high nasal voice of the TV race announcer, she said, "And they're off . . ." We clapped for her, but the second she turned away again, Jim raised his eyebrows and whispered, "And it's Cabbage by a head."

Then, only three days from the blessed event, Krapp threw a wet blanket on my daydreams of roaming the neighborhood by moonlight, gathering, door-to-door, a Santa sack of candy, turning the joyous sparks of my imagination to smoke, which leaked out my ears and mixed with the twilight. He assigned a major report that was to be handed in the day after Halloween. Each of us in the class was given a different country, and we had to write a five-page report about it. Krapp presented me with Greece, as if he were dropping a steaming turd into my open Halloween sack.

I should have gotten started that afternoon when school let out, but instead I just sat in my room staring out the window. When Jim got home from wrestling, he came into my room and found me still sitting there like a zombie. I told him about the report.

"You're going to be doing it on Halloween if you don't get started," he said. "Here's what you do. Tomorrow, right after school, ride down to the library. Get the G volume of the encyclopedia, open it to Greece, and just copy what they have there. Write big, but not too big or he'll be on to you. If it doesn't look like what's written there will fill five pages, add words to the sentences. If the sentence says, 'The population of Greece is one million,' instead you write like, 'There are approximately one million Greeks in Greece. As you can see, there are many, many Grecians.' You get it? Use long words like 'approximately' and say stuff more than once in different ways."

"Krapp warned us about plagiarism, though," I said.

Jim made a face. "What's he gonna do, go read the encyclopedia for every paper?"

The next afternoon I was in the public library, copying from the G volume. With the exception of the fact that it said the people there ate goat cheese, none of the information in the book got into my head, as I had become merely a writing machine, dashing down one word after the next. The further I got into the report, the harder it was to concentrate. My mind wandered for long stretches at a time and I stared at the design of the weave in my balled up sweater that lay on the table in front of me. Then I'd look over at the window and see that the twilight was giving way to night. I was determined to finish even if I got yelled at for coming home late for dinner. When I hit the fourth page, I could tell the information in the encyclopedia was running out, and so I started adding filler the way Jim described. The last page and a half of my report was based on about five sentences from the book and was infused with so much hot air I thought it would float away.

I didn't know how late it was when I finished, but I was so relieved I began to sweat. I rolled up the five written pages and shoved them in my back pocket. Closing the big, green tome, I lifted it and took it back in the stacks to reshelve it. As I was coming out of the stacks, I suddenly remembered my sweater and pencil and looked over at the table by the magazine section where I'd been working. Sitting there in my chair was the man in the white trench coat. My heart instantly began pounding. I was stunned for a second, but as soon as I came to, I ducked out of the aisle in behind the row of shelves to my right.

I raced down the row, and, once in the middle, pulled a book off the third shelf from the top and then reached through and pushed the books on the other side over so I could see what he was doing. He was sitting there, reading a magazine, or pretending to. Every couple of seconds he looked up and turned to scan the library. The woman who'd been reading the newspaper in one of the big chairs while I finished the last pages of my report, got up, laid the paper down on the table, and walked away. The man in the white trench coat looked around and, seeing no one near him, lifted my balled up sweater and sniffed it. His beady eyes closed and his head cocked back a bit as if my sweater funk was crumb cake day at McGill's Bakery. A shiver ran through me. Still clutching it in his hand, he stood up and started heading for me.

I ran down to the center aisle and made for the back of the stacks. I was pretty sure that when he came looking for me, he would head up the center aisle so that he could look down each row. Once I reached the back wall, I moved all the way along it to the side of the building that held the front door. Checking my pocket, I touched the rolled up report. I didn't care about leaving the sweater and pencil behind. I waited, while in my mind I pictured him walking slowly toward me, peering down each row. My breathing was shallow, and I didn't know if I would have the power to scream if he somehow cornered me. Then I saw the sleeve of his trench coat, the sneaker of his left foot, before he came fully into view, and I bolted.

I was down the side aisle and out the front door in a flash. I knew that whereas a kid might run in a library, an adult would be expected not to, which might give me a few extra seconds. Outside, I sprinted around to the side of the building where my bike was chained up. Whatever time I saved was spent fumbling with the lock. Just when I had the bike free and got my ass on the seat,

I saw him coming around the side of the building. My only route to Higbee was now cut off. Instead of trying to ride around him, I turned and headed back behind the library, into the woods that led to the railroad tracks.

I carried my bike over the tracks in the dark, listening to the deadly hum of electricity coursing through the third rail and watching both ways for the light of a train in the distance. Although the wind was cold, I was sweating, trying not to lose my balance on the dew-covered wooden ties. All the time I cautiously navigated, grim scenes from *The Long Way Home from School* played in my memory. At any second, I expected to feel upon my shoulder the bony hand of the man in the white coat.

On the other side of the tracks there was another narrow barrier of woods, and I searched along it, walking my bike, until I found a path. I wasn't actually sure what street it would lead me to since I had never gone that way before. We occasionally crossed back and forth over the tracks, but always in daylight and always over on the other side of town behind the woods that started at the schoolyard. This was uncharted territory for me.

I walked clear of the trees onto a road that didn't seem to have any houses. My mind was a jumble, and I was on the verge of tears, but I controlled myself by trying to think through where I was in relation to the library and home. I had an idea I was west of Higbee and just had to follow that street around to find the main road. Getting on my bike, I started off, following my best guess.

No sooner had I pedaled twenty feet before I saw, way up ahead, the lights of a car that had just turned onto the street. It was moving slowly, and I immediately feared it was the man in the white coat, searching for me. At the same time that I saw the car coming toward me, I noticed there was another one parked on the right-hand side only a few more feet up the road. I would have taken to the woods, but there was no path immediately there and it was too dark to find one. Once off my bike, I gave it a good shove and it wheeled into the tall grass and bushes and fell over, pretty well covered from sight. I got low and ran up to hide close against the side of the parked car, which was an old station wagon with wood paneling like our next door neighbor's, Mr. Kelty's.

The headlights of the car approaching drew slowly closer, and the low speed that it traveled at could easily have been an indication that the driver was looking for something or someone. By the time it passed the parked car I was hiding behind, I was hunkered down, my hands covering my head air-raid style, my right leg off the curb and under the station wagon. The vehicle moved very slowly by and then picked up speed, almost disappearing around the bend at the opposite end of the road before I could get a look at it. No mistaking, though, I saw the fins of the old white car. I wasn't sure whether to sit tight in case the stranger reached a dead end somewhere and came back or get on my bike and make a run for it.

Then I felt the car I was next to begin to gently rock. From inside there came a muffled moan. I lifted my head up carefully and peered in the window. Only then did I notice that the glass of all the windows was fogged over. It was dark inside, but the dashboard was glowing. I found a small spot where the glass was clear. Lying on the wide front seat was Mrs. Graves, her blouse open, one big, pale breast visible in the shadows, and one bare leg wrapped around the back of a small man. After observing his grease-slicked hair and flapping ears I didn't have to see his face to know that it was Mr. Kelty.

I ran over to where my bike had fallen in the weeds and lifted it. In a second I was on it and peddling like a maniac up the street.

As it turned out, I found Higbee and made it back to the house safely, never seeing the white car along my way. When I pulled up in the front yard, I knew I was late and would get yelled at, perhaps sent to my room. Luckily, through all of the turmoil, my report on Greece still stuck out of my back pocket, and my hope was that this document could be used as proof that I wasn't just goofing off. I was sweating and dirty from kneeling in the road next to the car. When I opened the front door, and stepped into the warmth of the living room, I remembered that I had left my sweater at the library and had not concocted an excuse for its absence.

The house was unusually quiet, and I was inside no more than a few seconds when I could feel something wasn't normal. The light in the dining room, where my mother usually sat drinking in the evenings, was off. The kitchen was also dark. I walked over and knocked on Nan's door. She opened it, and the aroma of fried pork chops came wafting out around us. Her hairnet was in place and she wore her yellow quilted bathrobe.

"You're mother's gone to bed already," she said.

I knew what she meant by this and pictured the empty bottle in the kitchen garbage.

"She told me to give you a kiss, though," she said. She came close and gave me one of those protracted Nan kisses that sounded like air escaping from the pulled-taut, wet mouthpiece of a balloon. "Jim told me you were at the library doing your homework. I left food for you in the oven."

And that was it. She went back into her house and closed the door. Like my father, I was left to get my own dinner, alone. It was all too quiet, too stark. I sat in the dining room by myself and ate. Nan wasn't a much better cook than my mother. Every dinner she made had some form of cabbage in it. Only George happened by while I sat there. I cut him a piece of meat and he looked up at me as if wondering why I hadn't taken him out yet.

When I had finished eating and put my plate in the kitchen sink, Jim came down from upstairs.

"Did you get your paper finished?" he asked.

"Yeah," I said.

"Let me see it," he said, and held his hand out.

I pulled it out of my back pocket and handed the rolled up pages to him.

"You shouldn't have bent it all up. What was your country again?" he said, sitting down at the dining room table in my mother's chair.

"Greece."

He read through it really quickly, obviously skipping half the words. When he got to the end, he said, "This last page is a hundred percent double talk. Nice work."

"The Greece part in the encyclopedia ran out," I said.

"You stretched it like Mrs. Ryan's underwear," he said. "There's only one thing left to do. You gotta spice it up a little for the big grade."

"What do you mean?" I asked.

"Let's see," he said, and went back through it. "It says the exports are cheese, tobacco, olives, and cotton. I saw a kid do this thing once for a paper and the teacher loved it. He taped samples of the exports onto a sheet of paper. We've got all these things. Get me a blank sheet of paper and the tape."

Jim went to the refrigerator and took out a slice of cheese and the bottle of olives. I fetched the tape for him, and then he told me to get a copy of a magazine and start looking for a picture about Greece in it for the cover of the report. Fifteen minutes later, as I sat paging through an old issue of *Life*, he turned the sheet of paper he had been working on around to show me.

"Feast your eyes," he said. The page had the word *EXPORTS* written across the top in block letters. Below that title, a square of American cheese, a half an olive (with pimento), an old, crumpled cigarette butt from the dining room ashtray, and a Q-tip head were affixed with three pieces of tape for each. Under these items appeared their names.

"Wow," I said.

"No applause, just throw money," said Jim. "Did you find a picture for the cover?"

"There's nothing Greek in here," I said, "but this old woman's face looks kind of Greek." I showed him a picture of a woman who was probably about a hundred years old. She was in profile, wore a black shawl, and her face was a prune with eyes. "She's from Mexico, though," I said.

"It's Joe Mannygoats's grandmother," said Jim. "I heard she was half Greek. Cut her out."

I did, pretty well too, except that I hacked the tip of her nose off. He then told me to tape her face to a piece of paper and write the title of the report coming out of her mouth as if she was saying it. There was a subheading in the encyclopedia entry—The Glory That Was Greece—that he told me to use as the title of my paper. "Do it in block letters," he said. "Then take the whole thing and put six books on top of it to flatten it out and you're all set. Krapp's gonna be caught between a shit and a sweat when he sees this one."

Mary cried at bedtime because my mother wasn't awake to tuck her in. Instead, Nan sat with her until she dozed off. Jim and I were sent upstairs. After it got quiet downstairs, I got out of bed and snuck over to Jim's room and knocked on the open door. It was dark in there and from the light shining in from the hallway it looked like he was already asleep.

"Yeah?" he said, and opened one eye.

"I think I know who the prowler is," I whispered.

He told me to come in. I sat at the bottom of his bed and told him about the man in the white car and recounted what had happened at the library that night. When I told him about the old man sniffing my sweater, he breathed deeply through his nostrils, rolled his eyes upward, and said, "Delicious."

"I'm telling you, it's him," I said. "He travels around during the daytime in that old white car and then at night he sneaks through the backyards, looking for kids to steal. I bet he took Charlie."

"What's he using him as, an air freshener?" asked Jim.

"Not only that, but I think he might be some kind of evil spirit," I said.

"If he's an evil spirit," said Jim, "I doubt he'd be driving a car."

"Yeah, but remember, the nun said that the evil one walks the Earth. Maybe he gets tired of walking and needs to drive some."

"Hey," said Jim, "you said he always smells like smoke? That the books from the library he probably touched smell like smoke?

That's what Sister Joe told me was the secret to knowing him when he came. She said he'd smell like the fires of hell. Fire doesn't smell, though, except for the smoke."

This revelation made me shiver and I felt unsafe, even inside the house with Jim there. The old man could be anywhere, listening at the glass, sneaking in the cellar window, anywhere. I swallowed hard.

"So who is this guy?" asked Jim. "Where's he live?"

"I don't know his name," I said. "Do you remember the night we dragged Mr. Blah-blah across the street? The guy who stopped and got out of his car? That's the guy."

"He was kind of creepy looking," said Jim, "and I never saw him around here before." He yawned and lay back on the pillow. "We'll have to find out who he is."

"How?" I asked. I sat there for a long time, waiting for his answer.

"Somehow," he said, and turned over. I knew he was almost asleep.

The antenna cried mercilessly all night, and I tossed and turned, thinking of the man in the white car, my fear in the library, and spying Mrs. Graves's tit. I could sense the evil as it crept forward day by day, dismantling my world, like a very slow explosion. I woke and slept and woke and slept, and it was still dark. The third time I awoke to the same night, I thought I heard the sound of pebbles jangling in soda cans. The plan had been to let George out after whoever it was taking the ladder, but I didn't move, save to curl up into a ball.

The next day, Halloween, was clear and cool and blue. My mother had to leave for work early, so Nan made us breakfast. Jim told Mary and me to request oatmeal instead of eggs, so the latter would be there to steal later on and use for ammo on the night streets. I could tell Mary was excited because she wasn't being Mickey and wasn't counting or doing any of her strange antics, but instead pumping Jim for a rundown on how the coming night would be. She had always before gone trick-or-treating with our mother and this was to be her first time on the loose with us. The ugly oatmeal came, lumps of steaming khaki, with raisins in it, no less, and we all forced it down. Meanwhile, Jim held forth on the strategies of the holiday.

"The idea," he told Mary, "is to get as much candy as possible. You want candy, wrapped candy. If you get a candy bar, that's the best—a Hershey bar or a Milky Way. Mary Janes are okay if you don't mind losing a few fillings, little boxes of Good & Plenty,

Dots, Chocolate Babies, packs of gum, all good. Then you've got your cheapskate single-wrapped candy—root beer barrels, butterscotches, licorice drops—not bad, usually given out by people who are broke, but what can they do? They're trying.

"You don't eat anything that's not wrapped, except for Mr. Barzita's figs. Some people drop an apple in your bag. You can't eat it, but you can throw it at someone, so that's okay. Once in a while a mother will bake stuff to give out. Don't eat it, you don't know what they put in it. It could be the best-looking cupcake you ever saw, with chocolate icing and a candy corn on top, but who knows, they might have crapped in the batter. I've seen where people will throw a penny in your sack. A penny's a penny.

"You always stay where we can see you. If someone invites you into their house, don't go. When we tell you to run, run, 'cause kids could be coming to throw eggs at us. If you hear someone shout 'Nair bomb,' run like hell—"

"What's a Nair bomb?" asked Mary.

"Nair is that chemical stuff women use to take the hair off their legs. Kids pour that stuff into balloons and then throw it at you. If you get hit on the head with it, all of your hair will fall out. If it gets in your eyes, it could blind you for a while."

Mary nodded.

"I'm going to give you two eggs tonight. Save them until you see someone you really want to get. Aim for the head, cause if it hits their coat, it will probably bounce off and smash on the ground. Or you can throw it at the house of someone you hate. Who do you hate?" Jim asked.

"Will Hickey," Mary said.

"Yeah," I said.

"We'll egg his house tonight for sure," said Jim. "Maybe I'll put one through his front window. One more thing: kids will try to steal your sack of candy. Don't let them. Scream and kick them if they try to. I'll come and help you."

"Okay," said Mary.

Then we went in and said goodbye to Nan before leaving for school. She was at her table in the little dining area. Heaped on the table were three enormous piles of candy—one, rolls of Sweet Tarts, another, Mary Janes, the last, miniature Butterfingers. She took one from each pile, stuffed them in a little orange bag with a picture of a witch on a broomstick on it, and twisted the top. Pop was sitting there in his underwear watching her, chewing a Mary Jane.

School was endless that day. We usually had a holiday party in the classroom on Halloween, but not that year. It was cancelled because Krapp had to give us a series of standardized intelligence tests. It was a day of filling in little bubbles with a number two pencil. The questions started off easy, but soon became impossibly strange. There were passages to be read about sardine fishing off the coast of Chile and math problems where they showed you a picture of a weird shape and asked you to turn it around in your mind 180 degrees before answering questions about it.

I realized right before handing one of the exams in that I'd meant to skip an answer I didn't know, but instead filled that bubble in by mistake, so that all my answers from then on would really be for the following question. I felt a fleeting moment of remorse as I put the test in Krapp's hand.

On the playground at lunch break, Tim Caliban told me his theory of taking those kinds of tests. "I don't even bother reading the questions," he said. "I just guess. I've got to get at least some of them right."

Back in the classroom, in the afternoon, Patricia Trepedino, the smartest girl in the class, referred Krapp to question number four. "It says," she said, "concrete is to peanut butter as . . ."

"Yes," said Krapp, checking his sheet.

"Chunky or plain?" she asked.

He stared at her with the same blank look that Marvin Gompers wore after telling us in third grade he was made of metal and then ran headfirst into the brick wall behind the gym. Finally, Krapp snapped out of it and said, "No talking or I will have to invalidate your test."

The lingering twilight finally breathed its last, and that first moment of true night was like a gunshot at the start of a race, for, instantly, frantic kids in costumes streamed from lit houses, beginning their rounds, not to return until they had reached the farthest place they could and still remember how to get home. My mother and Nan stood at the front door and waved to us as Jim led the way, dressed in a baggy flannel shirt, ripped dungarees, a black skullcap, and charcoal beard. Mary followed him in her jockey outfit, and I brought up the rear, stumbling on the curbs and across lawns because the slits in my skull mask drastically limited my view. Even though it was cold and windy, before we had climbed two front stoops and opened our bags, my face was sweating. I could hear every breath I took, and each was laced with the hair-raising stench of molded plastic. Finally, when I walked into a parked car, I decided to only pull the mask down when arriving on a house's front steps.

We traveled door-to-door around the block, joining with other groups of kids, splitting away and later being joined by others. David Kelty, dressed like a swami, with a bath towel wrapped in a turban around his head, eyeliner darkening his eyes, and a long, purple robe, followed along with us for a dozen houses. The Farley girls were angels or princesses, I couldn't tell which, but their costumes, made from flowing white material, glowed in the dark. President Kenny Stutton was dressed in his Communion suit, a button on the lapel that said VOTE FOR KENNY, and his sisters were ghosts with sheets over their heads. Reggie Wilson was a robot, wrapped in silver foil, wearing a hat with a light bulb sticking out the top that went on and off without a switch; and Chris Hacket wore the army helmet of his father, who'd gotten hand grenade shrapnel in his ass and lost three fingers in Korea.

We worked the trick-or-treat with a dedication that rivaled our father's for his three jobs, systematically moving up one side of the street and then down the other. Our pillowcases filled with candy. Old lady Ripici gave out Chinese handcuffs, a kind of tube woven from colored paper strips. You stuck a finger in each side and then couldn't pull them out. That's how we lost David Kelty. He was left behind, standing on the lawn, unable to figure out that you just had to twist your fingers to free them. The slow, the hobbled, the weak were all left behind as we blitzkrieged Pine Avenue, moved on to Sylvia, and covered Manhassett.

When we finished with the last house on the last street in that part of the development, we took the secret trail through the dirt hills, through the waist-high weeds, to the path that led around the high fence of the sump, and came out on the western field of Southgate, just beyond the basketball courts. In the moonlight, a strong wind whipping across the open expanse and driving tatters of dark clouds above, we met up with Tim Caliban and some of his friends. We rested for a while there and stuffed chocolate and licorice into ourselves as sustenance for the next leg of the journey.

Just as we were getting ready to head east toward Minerva Avenue on the other side of the school field over by the woods, we were attacked by Stinky Steinmacher, Justin Wunch, and about twenty other dirt eaters. The eggs flew back and forth. President Stutton took one in the face and went down on his knees in tears. Someone yelled that Wunch had Nair bombs and we fled. Jim had Mary by the hand, and I was right behind them. As we ran around the back of the school, I looked over my shoulder to see the enemy swarming toward Kenny. His sisters, the horrible dumplings, had also abandoned him and were gaining on me. We would learn the next day that they beat him with flour socks until he went albino, split his lip, and stole his sack of treasure. Then Stinky peed on him. Any other night of the year such brutality would have been considered an outrage, but not on Halloween when even our parents sided with Darwin.

We begged our way up Minerva and the street beyond that, and the farther we went away from our own neighborhood, kids would break off and head back toward more familiar ground. Once when we left Mary standing on the sidewalk by herself for a minute, a kid tried to steal her sack, but she was able to keep him off by swinging her curtain rod/jockey whip until Jim got to her and pummeled the kid. We ended up taking his sack and splitting it three ways. Still, the run-in had made Mary nervous and she had to sit down on the curb for a while, mumble some numbers, and have a cigarette. The rest of the group went on without us. While we were waiting for her to relax, a bunch of Jim's junior high friends came by, and, just like that, he left me in charge of Mary and went off with them.

By then it was late, and the street we were on, which I didn't know the name of, was deserted. Many of the houses had turned their lights out as a sign they had either gone to bed or were out of candy. That was the way Halloween always went, one minute it was a colorful celebration of chaos, candy gathering, and cruelty, and the next, when you weren't watching, it had laid back and gone to sleep. It was now far quieter, but more eerie, for in sleep, all that was left on the streets were its nightmares. I told Mary to get up and she did. I vaguely remembered the direction home, and we started off, walking quickly, sticking to the shadows so as not to be noticed. We passed darkened houses whose trees were hung with wind-whipped strands of white toilet paper, smashed jack-o'-lanterns in the road, broken shells and the iridescent film of egg splatter reflected under streetlights where a battle had taken place. The scarecrows again took on a sinister aspect, and every shadowy form startled me, brought to mind the prowler and Charlie and worse.

We traveled back three streets, turning right and left and right, trying to home in on the school as a point of orientation, while the temperature dropped drastically.

Mary hadn't worn a coat or a sweat shirt, having felt that without people seeing her baggy shirt, no one would be able to make out that she was Willie Shoemaker. It hadn't mattered, because kids kept asking me all night, "Hey, what's your sister supposed to be?" The guesses ranged from baseball player to clown to janitor, but no one hit on a jockey, even when she had heard one of them mention it and replied, "They're coming around the back turn . . ." Anyway, I stopped and gave her my hooded sweat shirt.

Crossing the school field was a harrowing event, and we kept to the dark of the perimeter fence, so as to remain inconspicuous. Instead of striking out across the field and the lit basketball courts and front drive, I opted for the path that went around the sump. It took a little longer, but that vision of Kenny Stutton being attacked and the fact that Mary was with me made me cautious. The over-grown weed lot was lonesome enough to make me shiver, and the dirt hills were a strange, barren moonscape, but once I saw the street on the other side, I felt we were going to be okay. It was right then, as we stepped down onto the pavement, that lurching into the glow of the streetlight came a true monster; a hulking form with a red and blistered face, its hair sloughing off, leaving huge bald spots. The creature whimpered as it tottered forward, its hands out in front of it. Mary put her arms around me, pressing her face to my side, and I stood, unable to move, my mouth open. Then I realized it was poor Peter Milton, half-blind and suffering the effects of a Nair attack, trying to grope his way home. We let him pass, and then continued on.

As we came down a side street that opened onto Pine Avenue, I finally relaxed. Mary wasn't holding my hand anymore as she could sense my ease and was more calm herself. All we had to do was get to Pine and turn left and walk down seven houses. I wondered where Jim had gone and what adventures he had met and then gave myself over to thinking about the moment when I would empty my sack onto the dining room table, spilling out all that was right and good into a huge pile.

Mary interrupted me by pulling on my shirt. "Pipe smoke," she said.

I stopped walking and looked up. At that very moment, down on Pine, I could see from the aura of a streetlight no more than twenty yards away, that old white car pull away from the curb in the direc-tion of our house. Grabbing Mary by the arm, I led her through a hole in the hedges we had been passing, and whispered to her, "Don't make a sound." We stood, motionless, and waited. Only when I heard the car turn around and recede into the distance toward Higbee did I motion to Mary to return to the street. "Run," I told her, and took her hand. We sprinted around the corner onto Pine and all the way home. She'd been right: pervading the air at the spot where the two roads intersected was that smoldering scent of the man with the white coat. A relentless spirit, it pursued us to our doorstep.

*   *   *

I sat at the dining room table, chewing away like a cow with its cud, on both a Mary Jane and the contents of a miniature box of Good & Plenty, feeling slightly nauseous. My mind was vacant and I was so weary I could hardly keep my eyes open. I had an animal fear that if I closed them, my pile of booty, which formed a small, colorful mountain, might disappear. Mary had already fallen asleep on the living room floor, a melting Reese's cup smearing her outstretched hand. My mother sat across from me, smoking a cigarette and picking through both my pile and Mary's for caramels, which, it was understood, were hers.

Jim finally came home, and my mother took Mary off to bed, telling Jim and me it was time to go up. We gathered all of the candy together and put it in the community pot, a huge serving bowl that otherwise only got used on Thanksgiving. As we headed up the stairs, Jim whispered behind me, "We egged the hell out of Hickey's house, and almost got away without anyone seeing us. But I saw Will's weasel face at the upstairs window. I doubt he'll tell his parents since we'd kick his ass, but watch out for him. I'm sure he saw me."

That was the news I was left with at my bedroom door, and suddenly I was no longer tired. The threat of Hickey's revenge was enough to revive me, but since he wasn't there at that moment with his sharp knuckles it eventually receded, and I lay in bed, reviewing the night, the costumes, the thrill of running away across the field at Southgate, the agonized form of Peter Milton, which had brought a sense of genuine horror to the holiday. Then, of course, I came to the incident with the pipe smoke, and the memory of the white car pulling away from the curb made me realize that something was missing. I got out of bed and quietly made my way down stairs to the dining room. There, I dug through the giant bowl of treats we had all three collected.

What was missing were the plump, ripe figs that each year Mr. Barzita wrapped in orange or black tissue paper and tied at the top with ribbon. I saw in my mind a fleeting image of his knotted old fingers, shaking slightly, making a bow. They were a Pine Avenue tradition, but this year there were none. I thought back through the night, and realized that his house had been dark, and he hadn't been at his front gate to meet us and drop one of his "beauties," as he called them, into our sacks. In the rush and fever of greed we hadn't noticed his absence but simply moved on to the Blairs' house. Then I worked away at a dark spot in my memory, clawing through the sugar haze, the night, the turmoil, trying to remember if the white car had been parked in front of his house when we had first passed it early on in our travels, for it was old man Barzita's place it had pulled away from when Mary and I noticed it this evening. Perhaps I had my mask on, or my thoughts were caught up still with the glittering handful of silver-wrapped Chunkies that Mrs. Ryan had dropped into my sack, but no matter how I tried I couldn't remember those minutes.

Instead, I pictured Barzita as a young man, stepping out of that disease-laden room during the war. I wondered if the prowler, the man in the white coat, who had become for me, Death himself, had appeared on Halloween to finally claim a man who by all accounts should have perished years before in another country, in a mountain base stricken with meningitis. The possibility scared me more than any threat posed by Will Hickey.

For solace, I walked down the hallway to my parents' bedroom, forgetting that my mother had passed out on the living room couch. My heart sank as I viewed the empty room. The light was on, as it always seemed to be, but the bed was unmade, my father's work clothes from earlier in the week lay in a pile on the floor.

As I stood there in the doorway, the weariness that had sway over me earlier returned and I yawned. I tottered forward into the room and crawled into my parents' bed on my mother's side. The mattress was soft and I sunk into it. Immediately I noticed the aromas of machine oil and my mother's deep powder, work perfume and these scents combined, their chemistry making me feel safe. I lifted the red, bug-crushing weight of *The Complete Sherlock Holmes* from the night table and turned to "The Hound of the Baskervilles." The print was very small and in double columns, the pages tissue thin. I found the place where I had left off in my own copy and started reading. Not even a minute went by and the tiny letters began moving like ants. Then gravity took over and my arms couldn't hold the volume up. As the open red book settled onto my chest, I settled into sleep.

I dreamed Halloween and an egg battle on the western field beneath the moon at Southgate. Stinky Steinmacher's little brother, Gunther, hit me in the head with an egg and knocked me over. When I opened my eyes, all the kids from both sides were gone, and the man in the white coat was leaning over me to lift me up. I pretended to still be asleep as he carried me, the wind blowing fiercely, toward his car parked by the basketball court. He said in an angry voice to me, "Come on, open your eyes," and then I did and it was morning and I realized his voice had been Jim's. "You'll be late for school." I was in my own bed, upstairs in my room.

It was a rush to get ready, and all three of us kids were groggy. I remembered at the last second to take my report for Krapp from beneath its tomb of six books. Mary and I made it to school just before the bell rang, and we hurried to our classrooms. I was in my seat no more than five minutes before Krapp stood up from his desk and said, with a grim smile on his face, "Hand me your reports." As soon as he said it, I looked around and could tell all of those who'd let Halloween enchant them into inaction by the flush of red that spread across their faces. "Who doesn't have it?" said Krapp. Five trembling hands went up. He lifted his grade book and recorded the zeros with excruciating precision, saying with each one, "A zero for you and two detentions." Someone behind me started crying, but I didn't dare turn around and look.

Krapp swept down the aisle, taking reports, and I held mine out to him. Just before his fingers closed on it, I noticed on the front cover, I had misspelled Greece. Instead of writing it the right way, I had written *The Glory That Was Grease*. He took it all in in a second, the cut out picture of the old Mexican woman in the shawl, the misspelling, and shook his head in disgust. He added the paper to the stack in his other hand, and what he didn't notice, I did. The back of the bottom page, which held the samples of exports, was completely discolored with huge dark stains.

That paper came back to me the next day, bearing an F grade and the words *plagiarism* and *a stinking mess* written across the woman's wrinkled cheek. Between the molded cheese, rotten olive, and cigarette stench, it smelled like shit. I brought it home and showed it to Jim. He shrugged and said, "That's the breaks." He told me not to tell our parents about it. "They won't even notice, they're so busy with work and—" He tilted his head back and brought his arm up as if drinking from a big bottle. "Take it outside and bury it," he said. "It smells like a dead man's feet." So I did, feeling betrayed and knowing that no good would come of it. Mary watched me dig a hole with the shovel. When I was done laying the foul muddle to rest and had tamped down the dirt, she put a rock on top to mark the grave.

I stood above Botch Town, surveying its length and breadth, and noticed that, since Jim had started wrestling, taken up with a new group of friends, stayed away from the house as much as possible, a thin film of dust had settled on his creation. At first I imagined it to be the result of a minor snow squall, the kind that had already happened in early November, but snow was white and I couldn't ignore that this film was gray. Then I imagined it to be a sleeping powder, like a sprinkling of magic dust from an evil magician in a fairy tale. The town appeared quiet, as if in sleep, and there was a certain loneliness that pervaded the entire expanse. Nothing much had moved since last I had looked down upon it before Halloween. Charlie still lay in the lake, Nick was still at work on his car, Mrs. Ryan, no doubt seized by weariness, had rolled forward onto her stomach to sleep.

The only change I noticed was that Mary, obviously out of fright at having seen the face at her window, put the prowler behind our own house. Of course, in reality he was long gone, and had probably spied on a dozen other families since he'd looked in on her. The repair to Mrs. Ripici's roof had still not been completed, and although the Hossetters had been gone for months, the figure of Raymond, the oldest boy, still lay, sleeping, behind the house. I wondered if this was to be the end of Botch Town. If Jim, getting older now, would forsake it, and it would continue to sleep and slowly decompose until the clay figures cracked and turned to dust and the cardboard houses wilted down and lost their forms. There was some connection between the sorry nature of Botch Town and our family, but whatever that connection was remained unclear to me and no manner of dredging with sharp hooks would bring it up.

I walked over to a corner of the cellar where there was a box of old toys we no longer played with. Searching through it, I found the item I remembered from long ago that I had once seen amidst its jumble. It was a Matchbox car, a reproduction of a hearse—long and black. The back doors opened and there had once been a little coffin that slid inside that you could close the doors on. Using Jim's supplies, I painted this car white and, while still wet, set it down on Pine Avenue, parked in front of Mr. Barzita's place. Then, after taking one more look at the entire board, I reached out over it and turned off the sun.

My father miraculously appeared in his bed Sunday morning. I happened to go down the hall to the bathroom and on my way out noticed him lying there asleep next to my mother. The sight of him startled me, and I went upstairs to tell Jim, who was still sleeping. He got up and followed me down the stairs. I went in and told Mary. Nudging her awake, I said, "Hey, Dad's home." She joined Jim and me, and we took up positions around the bed, staring and waiting. After quite a while, my father suddenly sat up and opened his eyes as if a nightmare had awakened him. He shook his head and breathed out, like a sigh of relief, and smiled at us.

We learned that not only was he there, but he would be home for the entire day. After he got up and had his coffee, he asked us if we wanted to go out for a drive. "Where?" asked Jim.

"I don't know. We'll find out when we get there," he said.

We went out and piled into his car, Jim in the passenger side of the front seat and Mary and me in the back. It was cold out, but they opened the windows up front and we drove along with the radio blaring and the wind blowing wildly around us. No one said anything. My father pulled over at a roadside hot dog stand. We ordered cream sodas and those hot dogs that snapped when you bit them, covered in cooked onions and mustard. Sitting on overturned milk crates a few feet from the hot dog stand, we ate in silence. Then we got back in the car and drove fast, and I had a feeling of freedom, of skipping school, of running away.

When we had gone many miles and there was no hope of turning back, Mary leaned over the front seat and said, "We didn't go to church today."

My father turned and looked at her for a second, smiling, "I know," he said, and laughed out loud.

We wound up at a huge park on the north shore. The parking lots were almost empty even though the day was beautifully clear. We parked in the middle of this concrete expanse, surrounded by woods on three sides.

"Which way will we walk?" my father asked me.

I pointed to the west because it seemed like it would take us the farthest from the road and away from the parking lots.

"Okay," he said, "and they're off . . ."

We got out of the car, zipped up our coats, and started in that direction. Jim moved right up next to our father and tried to match him step for step. I had wanted to be there, next to him, but I didn't make a fuss about it. Mary and I brought up the rear. We left the concrete behind and stepped into the shadows beneath the tall pines. There was a half-foot of fallen oak leaves and brown pine needles on the ground, and Mary and I shuffled our feet, occasionally kicking them into the air. She found a giant, yellow leaf as wide as her face, poked two eyeholes into it and held it up by the stem as a mask.

We walked along a path for quite a while, saw crows above in the treetops, and came to a clearing where my father held his hand up and then put his finger to his lips. We three kids stopped walking, and he crouched down and pointed into the trees on the other side of the clearing. Standing there staring at us was a huge deer with antlers. A whole minute went by, and then Mary said, "Hello," and waved to it. The deer sprang to the side and disappeared back into the woods.

In the clearing, we were standing on a patch of sand. My father looked down. "Tracks," he said. "A lot of them came through here in the last few hours." He then found a fox track and showed it to us as well. After the clearing, we changed direction, unanimously deciding, without saying so, that we'd follow the deer. We never saw it again for the rest of the day, but the trail we took led us to a huge hill. My father took Mary by the hand to help her and we all scrabbled up the hill, slipping on the fallen leaves and resting from time to time against the trunks of trees.

As it turned out, the deer had led us in the right direction, for as we crested the top of the rise, the trees disappeared and we could see out across the Long Island Sound all the way to the shore of Connecticut. The vast expanse of water was iron gray and choppy, dotted with white caps. A strong wind blew in our faces and it was exhilarating. The hill was covered in grass all the way down the other side and devoid of trees. At its base was a little inlet that, farther west, skirted the set of sand dunes between us and the sound. It was as wide as two football fields and as long as four, its surface rippling in the wind. An army of white birds stood along its shore, pecking at the wet sand.

My father sat down at the top of the hill and took out his cigarettes. As he lit a match and cupped it in his hands, catching its spark at the end of his smoke, he said, out of the side of his mouth, "You better go down there and investigate." We didn't need to be told twice, but charged down the hill, whooping, and the birds took off, lifting into the sky in waves. It felt for a second, as we charged downhill, like I could lift into the air, myself. Jim tripped and rolled a quarter of the way down, and, seeing him, Mary followed his lead, fell, and rolled the rest of the way.

We stayed down there, by the water, for a long time, skipping stones, dueling with driftwood swords, watching the killifish swarm in the shallows. An hour or two passed, and when Jim and Mary decided to try to catch one of the fish with an old Dixie cup they found in the sand, I looked up at my father just sitting there. I sidled away from them and went back up the hill. During the climb, I lost sight of him, as I could only see a few feet ahead of me with the steep incline, but when I got to the top and he came into view, I noticed that he had his glasses in his hand. I think he had been crying, because as soon as he saw me coming, he wiped his eyes and put the glasses back on.

"Come here," he said to me. "I need some help."

I walked over and stood next to him. He reached up, and placing a hand lightly upon my shoulder, stood, making believe he was using me as a crutch. "Thanks," he said, and for a brief moment, he put his arm around me and hugged me to him. My face went into the side of his coarse, plaid jacket, and I smelled the machine oil. Then he let go and called for Jim and Mary to come back.

We stopped on the way home and had dinner at a chrome diner. My father ordered meat loaf and we all ordered meat loaf too. No one spoke all through dinner, and when the ice cream came, he said to us, "How are you all doing in school?"

I felt Jim lightly kick my shin under the table as he said, "I'm doing great."

"Good," said Mary."

I said nothing at first, but Jim kicked me again, and I said, "Doing fine."

Mary, in her Mickey voice, said, "Could you possibly . . . ?" But my father didn't notice or chose not to notice and called for the check.

By the time we got back home it was dark out. We got ready for bed, and then sat in the living room. My mother was up and around and feeling good. She played the guitar and sang us a few songs. My father, like in the old days, read some poems to us from his collection of little red books—*The Charge of the Light Brigade*, *The Ballad of Reading Gaol*, and *Crossing the Bar*. That night, I slept well, no dreams, and the antenna whispered instead of moaned, like the music of a very small violin.

I looked up Mr. Barzita's phone number in the book, and began calling his house every day after school, but there was never an answer. I asked Nan and Pop if they had seen him, but they both told me no. Pop asked me why I wanted to know, and I just shrugged and said, "Because I haven't seen him around."

"Do you ever see him during the winter?" asked Nan.

It was true, he rarely showed himself after Halloween, and the weather had really gotten frigid. Mid-November and the temperature had dropped into the teens for a week straight. We prayed for a snowstorm, but it seemed like even the sky was frozen solid. Jim and I rode over to Babylon on our bikes on Saturday afternoon and went skating on Argyle Lake, but otherwise, I just stayed inside, reading and catching up on my journal, filling in those members of our neighborhood I'd yet to capture in words.

There was one old lady who lived over by Southgate, and I always forgot her name. It was written on her mailbox, but on the way home from school I kept forgetting to check it. I had a good story about her occasionally going door-to-door, like trick-or-treating, asking everyone on the block for a glass of gin. Her dog, Tatel, a vicious German shepherd, was worth a few lines, especially concerning the time it chased the mailman up the Grimms' elm tree. I had a fine description of this old woman's white, hag hair, her skeleton body, and how her sallow skin fit her skull like a rubber glove you could pick a dime up while wearing, but no name. The cold snap had broken and the temperature had risen slightly, so, to just get out of the house and get some fresh air, I put George on the leash and we took a quick walk around the block.

I wrote her name in my mind, in script, three times—*Mrs. Homretz*—while George peed on the post of her mailbox. The sky was overcast, and even though the wind blew, it was mild enough to keep my jacket open. When I was sure I had it memorized, I turned to start home. Lucky for me I looked around when I did, because just then, rounding the turn on Pine and heading straight for me were three kids on their bikes—Will Hickey, Stinky Steinmacher, and Justin Wunch.

"There he is!" cried Hickey, and I saw all three of them lift their asses off their seats and press down hard on their peddles for a burst of speed. Even before my heart started pounding, and I felt the fear explode inside me, I ran. They had blocked off my direct escape to home, and were gaining on me too fast for me to take the corner at Sylvia in order to make my way around the block back to Pine. They'd have been on me before I reached Tommy Brown's house in the middle of that street. Instead, I made a beeline for Southgate and the woods, thinking they might stop chasing me once they hit the tree line.

George easily kept pace with me as we made our way across the field and then down the slope of Sewer Pipe Hill. I chose the main path, thinking that if they did come after me, I'd get as far into the woods as possible before cutting into the trees and underbrush. At the last second I would head south toward that spit of woods that extended into the backyards of the Stuttons' and Hossetters'. If I could make it that far, I could get back on to Pine close to my house and be home before they caught me. I stopped on the path to listen for them. The pounding in my ears was too loud at first, but then I heard Stinky give a battle cry. The sound of bikes breaking twigs, rolling over fallen leaves, followed.

We were off again, down the trail, branches whipping my face, ruts stumbling me. I tried not to think about what would happen if they caught us. George would hold his own against them, but just picturing Hickey's fists made me go weak inside.

"He's right in front of us," Wunch yelled, and I knew they could see me. I left the path and cut into the trees. They continued behind me, but the underbrush and fallen logs slowed them down, and it sounded as if they had left their bikes behind. If you were a coward like I was, it was a good thing to be a fast runner, which I also was. I ran for another five minutes at top speed, and then I had to stop, not because I was winded, but the lake spread out in front of me. I'd trapped myself.

I knew that if I had to turn either right or left they would easily catch me. The lake was still frozen from the cold snap, but a thin layer of water covered the top as it had begun to thaw. I put a foot out onto the slippery surface and slowly eased my weight down. It held me. George was uncertain of the ice and I had to drag him along behind. I took slow, careful steps forward. By the time they'd broken through the trees at the edge of the lake, I was about fifteen feet from shore. I didn't look back, although they were calling my name and saying I was a "fairy" and a "scumbag" and a "piece of shit." George didn't like the situation at all and began to growl low in his throat.

"Egg my house?" I heard Hickey scream, and then I saw a rock whiz past my head, hit the ice and slide three quarters of the way to the opposite shore.

"Let's go get him," yelled Steinmacher, and they must have stepped onto the ice together, because I felt the entire surface of the lake undulate and make a growling sound like George just before he got down to business chewing a sneaker. Following that, there came from behind me a cracking noise, like a giant egg hatching, and a splash. I looked over my shoulder and saw Wunch standing three feet from shore, up to his waist in brown water. I kept going forward as they helped him out of his hole and retreated.

Their extra weight on the ice must have made it unstable, because now with each step I took I could hear tiny splintering noises and see fissures grow like veins in the clear, frozen green beneath each sneaker. The wind was blowing fiercely out there in the middle of the open expanse, and my sense of victory that they had turned back suddenly vanished, replaced by the prospect that the lake might, at any moment, open up and swallow me. That's when the rock hit me in the back of the head, and I went down hard on my chest and face. I heard a great fracturing sound and my mind went blank as much from fear as from the concussion.

When I finally opened my eyes, I remained splayed out, listening. I heard the wind, dead leaves blowing through the woods, George quietly whimpering, and a very distant sound of laughter, moving away. Every now and then the ice would make a cracking noise. I was soaked from having fallen in the film of water atop the frozen surface, and it came to me slowly that I was shivering. With the slowest and most cautious of movements, I got to my knees. Once I achieved that position, I rested for a moment, my head still hurting and dizzy. My next goal was to stand, and I told myself I would count to thirty and then just stand up and get to shore.

The moment I started counting, I thought of Mary. When I reached twenty-five, I happened to look down, and staring up at me through the green ice was a pair of eyes. At first I thought it was my reflection. I leaned down closer to the surface to see, and there, beneath the ice, was the pale, partially rotted face of Charlie Eddisson. His hair was fixed solid in a wild tangle, much of the whites of his eyes had gone brown, and they were big and round like fish eyes. His mouth was open in a silent scream. Next to his face was the palm of one hand, and I could barely see past his wrist as the forearm disappeared into the murk below. His glasses were missing and so was the flesh of his right cheek.

When I screamed, I felt as though he was screaming through me. Dropping George's leash, I scrabbled to my feet, and, slipping and sliding, ice cracking everywhere around me, I ran straight-forward toward the shore, twenty yards away. In the midst of one step I felt the ice crack and give way beneath my heel, but I was already gone. The dog and I reached the shore at the same moment and we both jumped the last few feet over the thin ice at the edge.

Chattering like mad and half-frozen, I came out of the woods through Hossetters' backyard. My pant legs were stiff as was the front of my shirt. When I walked through the front door of our house, the warmth thawed my fear and I began to cry. My mother was cooking dinner in the kitchen, but she just called, "Hello," and didn't come in. I went upstairs to my room, pulled off the wet things, and got into bed. Until I was called to dinner, I lay under the covers, shivering.

I never told anyone except Mary that I'd seen Charlie under the ice of the lake, and when I told her she'd been right the whole time, all she said was, "I know." I told her to keep the secret and she just nodded, which with Mary was as good as a written contract. The reason I never spoke up about it was that I couldn't bear the thought of Charlie's mother seeing him the way he was. I thought she would die on the spot if she did, so I held him in my mind, the way the lake held him, and most times he lay at the dark bottom, but sometimes he'd surface.

Two days later, Mr. Barzita's next-door neighbor, Mrs. Blair, suddenly realized that she'd not seen him since the day before Halloween and went to his house to check up on him. The doors were locked from the inside, so she looked in all the windows. It was while kneeling on the ground, staring down into one of the window wells, the same way Jim had spied what we'd gotten for Christmas, that she saw his shadowy figure hanging, a rope around his neck, from the ceiling rafters of his cellar.

I figured, after much thought, that the man in the white coat couldn't collect Barzita's soul unless he willingly committed suicide and that Charlie'd been killed because the old man had at first refused. I also realized the stranger had been after me next, the second weakest kid in town, but somehow Barzita had finally found the courage to pay up on the deal he'd made to avoid death in the mountains so long ago.

If this all sounds crazy, consider the fact: In the spring, when Barzita's son came to town to sell his father's house, he had a yard sale of all the stuff he'd found in it. I saw, while passing by on my bike, my sweater lying on a table by the curb.

That old white car was never seen again on Pine Avenue and the only smoke we smelled afterward was that of piles of leaves burning in subsequent autumns, not to mention the time Mrs. Kelty found out her husband was having an affair with Mrs. Graves and burned all of his belongings in a big blaze on the front lawn. The pale stranger's face never again showed itself at our night windows, but even though he was gone, I could feel his presence had changed me in some way. Maybe it was because of what I knew and couldn't tell but could only secretly write, which I did through the frozen, snowy days of winter; the antenna moaning above me.

As for Botch Town, it's still there, sitting in the cellar astride the sawhorses. Through the years, the clay citizens have carried on with their lives, and although the wizard's dust is deep and the sun no longer shines, they still, from time to time, stare up into the darkness, half-hoping, half-dreading, they'll see the eyes.

Botch Town

Story Notes

As a way to commemorate the publication of their twenty-fifth book, Golden Gryphon Press published an anthology with stories by most of the authors they'd worked with up to that point in time. That book is The Silver Gryphon, *and I had a story in it, "Present from the Past." If you were kind enough to have read that story, you'd know that at the end the narrator finds a black-and-white-bound notebook he'd hidden beneath a tree many years earlier when he was a child. "Botch Town" is the contents of that notebook. It's a story of another time and place, a homage of sorts to the town where I grew up and the people who lived there. Like any group of people from any time and place, they exhibited traits of courage and honesty and love and stupidity and selfishness and cruelty. In other words, they were all, in their own way, doing their best to live a life. They've stayed with me through the years and their acts and stories have fortified my own life, especially Jim and Mary and Dolores, for whom this piece is dedicated.*

A Man of Light

A S IF ARRANGED FOR A GAME OF MUSICAL CHAIRS, the furniture in the large parlor was all gathered in a tight oval at the center of the room where divan backs touched the backs of rockers. Between two chairs was a small table upon which the servant rested a tray of hors d'oeuvres and the sole guest his drink. Other than this clutch of seating and an opulent crystal chandelier of six lit candles and five hundred pendants hanging directly above it, the space was completely bare. The floor, consisting of cheap gray planks, the kind used to build fences against dunes near the seashore, was swept perfectly clean. The walls all around, interrupted only once by a small rectangular window that gave a view of the eastern side of the estate, reached to a height of fifteen feet and were devoid of paintings or bric-a-brac. Instead they were neatly covered, floor to ceiling, with a faux-velvet olive green paper.

A lone cellist played in the room above the parlor, and the quiet, contemplative tune seemed to filter down through the center of the chandelier and disperse itself in droplets of light. The servant retreated to some other room of the enormous house, and the single guest, a young man by the name of August Fell, a reporter from the *Gazette*, sat in a straight-backed chair, reviewing the list of questions he'd jotted in his notebook. The peaceful nature of the music's glow, the palliative effects of the wine, his awe at the prospect of having an audience with Larchcroft, caused him to whisper as he read aloud what he'd earlier written. If he managed to bring it off, this would be the only interview ever conducted with his host.

Young August knew as much as the man on the street about Larchcroft, who carried the moniker "Man of Light" precisely because he'd shown the world what could be accomplished by manipulating that most elemental of substances. For working his alchemy of luminescence, turning the grim beautiful, the thread-bare new, the physical spiritual, and the false true, the world had paid him handsomely. He'd come to the attention of the public while still in his twenties—not much older than August himself—by one night lighting, with five perfectly placed beacons, merely candlepower and large lenses, the local bank of his hometown so that the entire building, with its marble columns and decorative arch, appeared to float a good two feet off the ground. Since then he'd gained world renown as a visionary of illumination. Customers famous, infamous, and pedestrian patronized his services for a myriad of reasons. He utilized his expertise in all types of light imaginable, from sunlight to starlight, firefly to flame, to satisfy any and all requests.

One simple example of Larchcroft's magic was his personalized makeup regimen for discerning women. Of course this process didn't achieve the same level of international notoriety as his famous feat of having lit a battlefield to appear like Heaven—the corpses transformed into heaps of sleeping angels; an overturned war wagon taking on the very countenance of God—but he had revealed the secrets of his cosmetics whereas those of his more flamboyant efforts had not. Patrons had written to him with the sim-ple request that he use his art to make them appear younger.

He produced a makeup that directed light to magically vanish extra chins, smooth wrinkles, negate crow's feet, and offer up to the world the radiance of youth and health. The idea had come to him when his constant research led him to read that the old masters, in the production of their paints, ground substances to a certain coarseness or fineness with a mind toward how each would refract and reflect. These painters knew exactly what would happen to light when it came in contact with their homemade paint, and through well-wrought strategies of intersecting beams were able to make their images appear to glow from within.

Larchcroft did the same with powder and rouge and eyeliner and for his efforts achieved even more remarkable results. Each patron's features were assessed by his people and prescribed an idiosyncratic formulation of makeup and a special plan of application. Crones appeared coquettes, and the plain-faced were transformed into sultry temptresses, so that by the end of an evening of socializing many a man found himself smitten with someone's grandmother. This rarely became an issue, for as many men purchased the same service, and since the process negated the ravages of age equally at all ages, the man finding a grandmother was more than likely someone's grandfather.

August, his notebook closed now, sipping port amidst the aural rain of light, could hardly believe his good fortune. All he'd done to arrange the meeting was write a letter to Larchcroft and request an interview. When he'd told his boss this, the older man laughed at him and shook his head. "You're a fool, lad, to think this man will give you five minutes," said his boss. For three weeks he was the laughingstock of the *Gazette*, until one day a letter arrived with Larchcroft's name on the return address. When it was opened, the shiny material inside the flap of the envelope caught the ambient light from the gas lamps of the newspaper office and shone back so brightly into the room that all present were momentarily blinded.

An hour passed in the vast parlor and August began to wonder if perhaps the famous recluse had changed his mind. Then the music abruptly ceased. A door opened at the very northern end of the parlor and a gentleman in evening wear, sporting a bow tie and a red carnation in his lapel, entered. He stood still for a moment as if having forgotten something, and then, leaving the door open halfway, slowly walked toward the center of the room.

"Mr. Fell," he said and waited, even though he'd already captured August's attention. "Mr. Larchcroft will now speak to you."

There was a prolonged silence in anticipation of the great man's entrance through the far door, but seconds gave way to minutes. The gentleman with the carnation in his lapel stood perfectly still in a half-bow. Finally, August asked quietly, "Sir, are you Mr. Larchcroft?"

The gentleman sighed and said, "I am not. He is right over there." He turned and pointed behind him at a spot near the entrance. August's glance tracked the man's direction, and a moment later, two sounds followed. The first was a gasp, and the second, coming quickly after, was that of a wine glass smashing upon the wooden floor. The sudden panic that seized the young reporter found its impetus in the fact that floating gracefully through the room, close to the right-hand wall, was a disembodied head, its chestnut hair streaked with gray and combed back in waves, gathered behind by a length of silver ribbon.

August stood, took a step forward, and the head turned to take him in. The face wore a stern countenance, bearing a slight but by no means insignificant descent at the corners of the lips; a subtle arch of the brows. It was a generous head, with fleshy cheeks that sagged into jowls and a long nose—bridge arched outward, tip pointing at the floor. The eyes were dark, encircled in shadows cast by a prominent brow at the center of which was set a diamond-shaped, green jewel the size of a thumbnail.

The head finally stopped moving and came around to face August straight on. Its strict gaze shifted back and forth, as if sizing him up, and the young man believed he'd been, by his appearance alone, found wanting. Before he could look away, though, the face of Larchcroft broke into a huge smile. His teeth gleamed in the soft light from the chandelier, and the entirety of his visage seemed to shine. "Thank you very kindly for waiting," he said. "I had an engagement in town earlier this evening that took me longer than I'd wished." August smiled back and took another step.

"Come closer," said Larchcroft, "and mind that you watch the glass splinters."

August began to apologize, but the head of the great man said, "Nonsense. It's not the first time that's happened." Then he laughed heartily. "Come closer, away from the glass, and take a seat on the floor."

Like a child at nursery school, the reporter sat on the floor but a few feet from the hovering visage, crossing his legs Indian-style. Larchcroft's head descended two feet, as if his non-existent body was sitting in an invisible chair. He stared up for a moment at the chandelier and then spoke:

"It's a strange thing to set out to learn about a Man of Light at night when the world is dark. But all things begin in darkness and far too many end there."

August simply stared, unable to speak.

"I believe you have questions?" said Larchcroft.

The young man fumbled with his notebook, flipping through the pages so quickly a few were torn off at the corners. He licked his dry lips, and then repeated a question quietly to himself before voicing it. "Yes, sir," said August, trembling. "Where were you born?"

The head wagged slowly back and forth.

"No?" said August.

"No," said Larchcroft. "Everyone knows already where I was born. They've seen photographs of my parents in the newspapers. They've declared the hovel I grew up in a historic landmark, they wept at the early demise of my first wife, etc., etc. Look, son, if you want to get anywhere in life, you have to ask the big questions."

"You mean, like why are you only . . . a head?" asked August.

"Not bad for a start. Pay attention." Larchcroft's head turned to face the man with the red carnation in his lapel, who had gone to stand by the door at the far end of the room. "Baston," called the Man of Light.

"Sir," said the butler, looking up.

"Tell Hoates to play a few bars," Larchcroft called.

The man by the open door leaned through the entrance and yelled, "Hoates, a few bars, old boy."

A second later, the music again filtered down from the room upstairs. "Should I be listening for something?" asked August.

"No," said Larchcroft, "watching, and watching intently." He then closed his eyes and hummed along with the tune.

August watched but was confused as to what he was supposed to be watching. *This is certainly the strangest night of my life,* he thought. And then he began to see something he hadn't seen before. There was a very vague outline descending from the bottom of the great man's head, where, if it had a neck, that neck would be. August squinted and saw more of this line and a moment later saw a line descending on the other side from the bottom of the head. More seconds passed and it began to become clear to him—the vague shape of Larchcroft's body.

At that juncture, Larchcroft called out, "Enough," so loudly that the man with the carnation didn't have to transfer the message upstairs. The music ceased and when it did, the faint lines that had begun to define the Man of Light's body suddenly disappeared. August snapped his head back and blinked.

Larchcroft's eyelids lifted and he smiled. "What did you see?" he asked.

"I began to see *you*," said August.

"Very good. I'm wearing a suit: pants, jacket, shirt, gloves, shoes, and socks, all the exact same torpid velvet green as the wallpaper. The light acoustics in this room, if we can call them that—the barren space, the grayness of the floor, the height of the ceiling, our mass, and, of course, the glow of the chandelier, soft as liquid fire —conspire to make all but my head invisible against this background. But when Hoates plays his cello on the floor above, positioned directly over the chandelier, the vibration of the instrument travels through the ceiling and is picked up by the crystal pendants, which vibrate ever so slightly, altering the consistency of the light field and sundering the illusion."

"And you are sitting on a bench or chair upholstered in the same green?" asked August in an excited voice.

"Precisely," said Larchcroft.

"Ingenious," said the young man, and laughed.

Larchcroft laughed uncontrollably for a time, and August thought the sight of it was both wonderful and somewhat horrible.

"You're a smart lad," said the head, nodding in approval. "I have every bit of faith that you'll come up with the right question."

At first August felt confidant that he wouldn't disappoint. The question seemed right on the tip of his tongue, but after sitting with his mouth open for a time, he found it had never been there at all and the sensation of its presence dissolved.

Larchcroft rolled his eyes. His head lurched forward and lowered itself toward August. The mouth opened, and, when words came forth, the young reporter could smell the warm, garlic-laced breath of his subject. "The Creature of Night," came the great man's whispered message and was followed by a wink. Then the head ascended and moved back away.

"Can you please tell me about the creature of night?" asked August, bringing his pencil to the ready and resting his notebook on his knee.

Larchcroft sighed. "I suppose," he said, "although it's a very personal story, and I shan't tell it more than this one time. I will have to fill you in on some preliminaries first."

"I'm ready," said August.

"Well," said Larchcroft, closing his eyes briefly as if to gather his thoughts. "Light is a creative genius, an inventor, a sculptor. For proof of this we look no further than in the closest mirror at our own faces, and precisely into our own eyes. Can you think of anything, my dear Mr. Fell, more intricately complex, more perfectly compact and thoroughly functional than the human eye?"

"No, sir," said August.

"I thought not," said Larchcroft. "Consider this, though. Our eyes were created by light. Without the existence of light, we would not have eyes. Over the long course of man's evolutionary maturation to his modern condition, light sculpted these magical orbs, making subtle adjustments through the centuries, until now they are capable of the incredible process of sight. This most vital sense, not only a means of self-preservation but the single most important catalyst for culture, is a product of the inherent genius of light.

"In ancient times it was believed that our eyes were like beacons, generating beams that issued forth, mingling with the light of the sun as like is to like, to strike things and return to us a reflection that we would then register as sight. Now we understand that the eyes are only elaborate sensors by which light communicates with us. Make no mistake about it—light is sentient. It directs our will. Is both a taskmaster and a protective parent. This I understood very early in my investigation of it. From the time when I was five and I saw a beam of sunlight entering a room through a pinhole in a window blind, striking a goldfish bowl and being dispersed in the guise of its constituent colors, it was but a few short years of intellectual pursuit of the phenomenon before I realized that everything we see and seem is merely the detritus of pure light, or so I thought."

"One moment," said August as he scribbled madly. "You are saying that everything in existence is merely a product of the breakdown of light?"

"More or less," said Larchcroft. "This theory led me to a deep enough understanding of my subject to perform some feats of illusion that caught the attention of the public. But after I had gone to university and learned the mathematical formulas that neatly boiled down into numbers my youthful, groping discoveries, it seemed I could go no further with the subject. I'd come up against a kind of impenetrable wall, blocking me from the quintessential secrets. What it came to, I realized, is that light communicated with us through the eyes, but the eyes were merely receptors, so it could tell us, lecture us, demand of us, but there was no recourse for dialogue. I could manipulate the processes of light to some degree, as it would allow me, but the cold, hard fact remained: my relationship with the mind of light would always remain limited.

"Then one night, during the months in which I was suffering a kind of depression from the realization of this limitation, after a late dinner of curried lamb, I took to my bed and had a vivid dream. I found myself attending a party in the one-room schoolhouse I attended when I was a child. There were about a dozen guests, including myself, and the teacher, who was no teacher I remembered but a very lovely young woman with golden hair and a peaceful countenance. All of the desks had been removed and there was only one table with a punch bowl on it. We conversed for I'm not sure how long. The strange thing was, no candles had been lit, and we stood in the dim shadows, able only to see by the moonlight coming in through the windows. Then someone noticed that the teacher was missing. An old fellow with white hair went to search for her, and he soon came upon her lying next to a window, bathed in moonbeam. He called to us to come quickly for it was evident she'd been murdered. There was blood all over, but this was weird blood with the consistency of string or thread, and it wrapped around her like a web.

"All present somehow came to the conclusion that I had killed her. I didn't remember doing it but felt very guilty. While the rest stood in awe, staring down at the odd condition of the body, I very quietly sidled away, one small step at a time. Upon reaching the side door of the schoolhouse, I silently let myself out, walked down the steps, and fled. I didn't run, but I walked quickly. Instead of heading for the road, I went in the other direction, behind the school, through the trees, toward the river. There was snow on the ground. It was chilly, and the night sky was brilliant with the full moon and thousands of stars. The silhouettes of the tree trunks and barren branches were so visually crisp. I felt great remorse as I moved toward the riverbank.

"Once at the river, I removed all of my clothing. I now found myself holding a very large, round wicker basket without a handle, its circumference wide enough to cover the area from my head to my waist. I stepped into the water of the river, which came to my upper thighs, expecting it to be frigid. It was not. Then I leaned forward onto the basket and let myself be taken by the flow of the river. I passed beautiful snow-covered scenery lit by the resplendent night sky above. This smooth journey seemed to go on for hours, and then I watched the sun come up before me, as if the river was heading directly into its fiery heart. The light from the sun washed over me and whispered that all would be well. I stood up and left the river, and thought to myself, 'You've made it, Larchcroft, you're free.' Then I woke up.

"An odd dream, but no odder than most. The instant I opened my eyes, the thing I focused on was not its symbolic meaning. Instead I wondered, and this was the greatest revelation of my entire career as a lightsmith, 'Where does the light in dreams come from?' Within an hour of pondering this question, it came to me that there must be two types of light in the universe, the outer light of suns and candles, and the inner light, originating from our own idiosyncratic minds. Eureka! Mr. Fell. There it was!"

August wrote madly for a time, trying to catch up with his subject's story. When he was done, he looked up at Larchcroft's face and said, "Excuse my ignorance, sir, but there *what* was?"

"Don't you see? I knew that for me to plumb the depths of the soul of light, I needed to somehow intermingle my inner light with the outer light. In order to, as I said earlier, ask the big questions.

But how? That was the dilemma. As astonishing a creation as they are, eyes were no good for this effort, for they are strictly organs of reception. For a solid year, I researched this conundrum.

"Then one day while trying to rest my exhausted mind from the problem at hand, I flipped through a book of prints I'd purchased and never had time to peruse. There was one peculiar painting entitled *The Cure for Folly*. In this painting was a man sitting back upon a reclining chair, and standing behind him was what I took to be a physician. This physician seemed to be performing surgery, making a hole with a small instrument in the supine patient's forehead. A stream of blood was coursing down the patient's face, but despite this harrowing operation, he was completely wide-awake. It came to me eventually that this was a depiction of the ancient practice of trepanning."

"Trepanning?" asked August. "Making a hole in someone's head?"

"That's the long and short of it," said Larchcroft. "The practice goes back to the dawn of humanity. Its medical purpose is to alleviate pressure on the brain from either injury or disease. In occult circles though, in the rarified business of shamans, seers, visionaries, this same operation was performed with the design of opening a large direct conduit to the universe. Reports of these instances are rare, but I'd read a few by those who had undergone trepanning for these purposes. They attested to having experienced a continuous euphoria, an otherworldly energy, a deep, abiding confluence with all creation. As for myself, I didn't give a fig for euphoria. What I wanted was a way for my inner light to exit the cave of my cranium and join in conversation with the outer light of the universe.

"I made up my mind to undergo the surgery, and began searching about for a physician who could do it. In the meantime, I foresaw a problem. Once I had a hole in my head, how was I going to direct my inner light to flow outward? All of the testimony I'd read by patients of trepanning gave the impression that the aperture was a portal for the universe to *enter*. I needed some method of controlling my imagination. What I realized was that I needed to conceive of my messenger to the outside world in some symbolic sense, a figure for me to focus on and express my will through. So I sat down, and, with a modicum of grunting and a maximum of daydreaming, I impregnated my imagination with my desire." Here, Larchcroft went silent.

August looked up, scanned the room, and then directed his gaze back to the head. "Is something wrong?" he asked.

Larchcroft shook his head. "It's just that you must assure me that you won't take offense at what I'm about to say."

"Something about the nature of the messenger?" asked the young man.

"Well," said the Man of Light, "my imagination gave birth to the concept of a young man, much like you—inquisitive, prepared to ask the big questions, toting a notebook made, like himself, from the substance of dreams."

"I'm not offended by that," said August. "It makes sense."

"Yes, but I don't mean to imply that you are merely a messenger. You're a reporter, and proving to be a good one at that."

"Thank you," said August.

"That said, yes, my messenger was a young man much like you, and once he materialized, I began thinking about him constantly, so I would not forget him and I could call him forth at a moment's notice. I gave him a name, and then, over the course of many nights, trained myself to dream about him. Once I could insure his presence in my dreams, I worked on taking into sleep with me a command to give him. And so it was in my dreams that I'd see him, walking along a street, sitting at breakfast, lying in bed with a young woman, and I'd say in a low voice to him, 'Take your notebook, go to the Master of Light, and ask him the questions you have written down. Receive his answers and commit them to the notebook. Then bring them back to me.' He would dutifully do as I'd instructed, passing old acquaintances of mine, blue poodles, snarling beasts of the night's devising, and all manner of dream images. Nothing would dissuade his progress until he'd come to a door, painted black. Try as he might, turning the knob, pushing and kicking with all he was worth, he could not open the door. This he repeated every night, and every night, without frustration, he'd come to the door and try to pass through."

"There was no exit as of yet in your skull. Am I correct, Mr. Larchcroft?" asked August.

"Well put," said the Man of Light. "Meanwhile, as I was training my messenger, I was given, by one of my many contacts, the name of a fellow who might perform a trepanning for purposes other than medical. There were surgeons close by to where I was living at the time who knew the procedure, but when I told them why I desired it, they refused to do the surgery, certain I'd lost my mind. The fellow in question was not a doctor at all but had battlefield experience and, as I was told, would perform just about any operation requested of him."

"But what made him well-suited for your situation?" asked August.

"Nothing really, beyond the fact that he was down on his luck; an opium addict in need of ready cash. His experience having tended to the sick and dying in wartime inured him to the sight of carnage, left him with nerves of steel or such a lack of concern about the outcome that geysers of blood, gaping flesh wounds, and the ear-piercing screams of his patients never made him flinch. For all procedures, he'd offer the same anesthesia—a half bottle of Barcher's Yellow Gulley. Abortions and amputations for the frantic and destitute were his specialty.

"I met Frank Scatterill (an unfortunate name to be sure) on an overcast day in late autumn in the lobby of The Windsor Arms, a sort of house of prostitution/saloon/hotel. In describing him, the word that comes immediately to mind is *tired*. He appeared exhausted, his lids half-closed, his hands slightly trembling. Even his face sagged, adorned with a long, drooping mustache. With his sallow complexion and air of utter fatigue, he managed a yellow-toothed smile for me as I handed him the cash advance.

"He led me to a small third-floor flat, half of which he had rigged out as an operating den with a reclining barber's chair and a table full of instruments and candles and half-empty bottles of Barcher's. On the floor were old sheets, still bearing the dried tell-tale gore of his last operation. While I drank my half bottle of the Yellow Gulley, a piss concoction that never really dulled the pain but made me nauseous and tired, Scatterill explained the operation to me. He held up each of the tools he'd be using: the scalpel, for tissue incision, cutting and laying back the folds of forehead flesh; the trephine, like a corkscrew with a circular saw at the bottom; a Hey saw, which appeared a tiny hatchet with one serrated edge; a file for smoothing the edges of the opening; a bone brush for removing the skull dust.

"I asked him where the incision is usually made, and he pointed to a spot somewhat higher up on the forehead than I'd imagined, near the hairline. I told him I wanted it lower, directly at the center of my forehead in the indentation between the two ridges of brow. 'Whatever you like, Captain,' he said in response. I also told him I wanted the edges of flesh cauterized so they would not grow back. I then took from my pocket the emerald you now see embedded in my forehead and instructed him to use it to stopper the hole once the entire operation had been completed—"

"Excuse me, Mr. Larchcroft, but the emerald—where did you come by that?" asked August.

"It was given to me in exchange for a lighting job I once did for a dead woman. A wealthy matriarch requested that I light her casket so that it appeared her cadaver's eyes were still moving back and forth during her wake. She wanted to give the impression to her grasping children that though she was gone she would always be watching them. The job was easily done with a couple of flame-powered paddle fans and the surreptitious placement of reflectors." Larchcroft pursed his lips and squinted, trying to remember where he'd been in the larger story.

"The trepanning . . ." said August.

"Oh, yes, Scatterill shook like a dried corn stalk in a January gale," said Larchcroft. "It was obvious this was not from any nervousness associated with the task but from some physical ailment as a result of his affair with the poppy. He was so long at screwing that trephine, I thought he was heading to China. I can't recall the pain, although I know there was some. My blood flowed freely, and the Yellow Gulley nearly left the gulley of my stomach on more than one occasion. I passed out near the end of the procedure and woke a few minutes later to the fetid smell of my own seared flesh. As I roused, Scatterill positioned a hand mirror in front of my face and I beheld my blood-drenched countenance now transformed with a third eye of brilliant green.

"Baston ferried me home in a hired cab, and I took to my bed, sleeping straight through for three days. This time was not fallow though, for while I slept I dreamed constantly of my messenger, following him through his days, his comings and goings on the street, drinking in the ale house, quietly jotting notes for his future interview, and wooing a beautiful young woman named May. Funny thing, this figure of May was the same as the schoolteacher whom I'd supposedly murdered in the earlier dream. 'Soon, very soon,' I promised the messenger as he went about his mundane life."

"May?" said August quietly, staring at the wall behind the floating head.

"A common enough name," said Larchcroft. "And so the time finally came to intermingle my inner light with that of the universe." Here, he cleared his throat and waited for the young reporter to snap out of the sudden trance.

"Very good," said August, looking back at Larchcroft and applying his pencil to the notebook.

"On a gloriously bright day in December, I dressed warmly—mittens and scarf, leggings, three shirts beneath my coat—and stepped out onto the second-floor balcony of my home. There, I lay down on my back in the direct sunlight, unstoppered my head by removing the emerald, and fell into a deep sleep. As soon as my first dream coalesced, I caught sight of my messenger, notebook at the ready, heading down a long alleyway toward that door, which was no longer black but now a bright green. He had a look of determination upon his face and his stride was all business. As he approached the door, it swung open and a bright light filled the frame. He stepped through, into the light of the universe, and from that point onward I was filled with the most excruciating sensation of ecstasy.

"I awoke on the balcony after dark, shivering so badly I could barely fit the emerald back into the hole in my forehead. No matter all of the clothes I'd put on; while I'd slept, the temperature had dropped drastically with the onset of night. My joints had seized from the cold, and it was a struggle just to get to all fours, open the balcony doors, and crawl into the warmth of the house. A half-hour later, once the more temperate conditions of the upstairs parlor had a chance to work on my bones, I was able to get to my feet. I struggled to be sure, but the only thing I could think about was going back to sleep, locating my messenger in the dream realm, and discovering what revelations he'd brought back from his interview.

"Once I'd removed all of my extra clothing and had a small glass of rye, I began to feel the effects of my foolish tactic of lying outside all of a winter's day. Although I was wide-awake, I felt feverish, and regardless of how well my plan had worked, a vague sense of depression and angst gathered around me like an autumn fog. To clear my mind, I decided to work on my accounts, the simple process of seeing which of my patrons had paid up and which had not, but I found the light of the candle I worked by irritated my eyes to the point where I couldn't concentrate. Instead, I retired to a dark corner of my office along with the bottle of whiskey.

"I drank in order to quell the rising sense of foreboding and to again achieve sleep. The former was undaunted and the latter was reluctant to come. I sat in a stupor until the sun showed itself through my office window, and the sight of it frightened me. I fled slowly to my bedroom, pulled the blinds down, the drapes over, and lay in darkness. I tossed and turned for another eight hours or so, shivering and sweating, before sleep finally descended.

"Once in dreams, I searched for my messenger—by then this process had become second nature—and found him, his collar turned up, walking along a cobblestone lane at night, toting his notebook beneath his arm. A wintry wind blew from behind and pushed him down the street along with old scraps of newspaper and dead leaves. I saw him stop and spin around to listen intently.

Behind him, from the shadows, came the sound of footsteps. He turned and doubled his speed.

"There followed a period of time where the dream was unclear to me, and then it returned and I saw him again. He'd reached the front door of his boarding house. Opening it, he entered and quietly, as to not disturb the other boarders sleeping in their rooms, took the two flights of steps to his own. He entered and locked the door behind him. Once his coat was off, he lit a candle and sat at his desk, the notebook in front of him. He turned back the cover and a few blank pages, and at this point I was able to swoop down behind him and look over his shoulder at the results of his interview. To my surprise, and I could tell to his as well, the pages were perfectly black, as if covered from margin to margin with a layer of soot. He cursed loudly and slammed the notebook shut. The slap of it closing woke me."

"Something had gone wrong," said August, ceasing his writing for a moment.

Larchcroft nodded and his countenance became stern. "Oh, something had gone wrong, all right. The worst of it wasn't blackened pages, I can assure you. When I woke from that dream, I stumbled out of bed and left my room. Out in the hallway, I was struck by the sunlight coming in the large window in front of me and I let out a cry like a dying animal. The pain was intolerable, all over, and especially in my head where it felt like my brain was on fire. I ran, growling and whimpering, down two flights of stairs to the cellar. There, in the darkness, I huddled in a corner trembling. It was as if I'd awoken from a dream into a nightmare.

"There I stayed. The thought of the merest spark of light filled me with paroxysms of fear. I slid to the floor and remained, passing in and out of consciousness. Baston, who had been searching for me, finally came to the cellar door and called down. The light that seeped in from the upper floors of the house clawed at my eyes, and the pain brought me around. I screamed at him to shut the door quickly. He brought me my meals down there. And it was only once the sun had set that my mind returned to its usual abilities of cogitation.

"After I'd eaten my dinner and drank two cups of strong coffee, I began trying to cipher out the meaning of my transformation. Retracing the events of the previous days, I believed I finally understood what had happened, and the realization, though in a way marvelous, was also quite disturbing. During my attempt to send the messenger of my dreams out into the world of light, I'd left the aperture in my head open too long. Night had fallen, and some creature of darkness had crawled inside of me, like a mouse through a split in the clapboard on a winter's day, looking for warmth. Yes, the dark was inside of me, and it was growing, taking control.

"If any proof of my theory was needed, it was provided by the current plight I found my messenger in when I fell into a fitful sleep later on. The day had broken in his dream world, but I found him and the other citizens of his town frantic, because although the sun shone there, a sinister phenomenon had occurred. Pitch-blackness, darker than night, had encircled the town and was closing in. The things it covered were not merely cast in shadow but were consumed. People had been swallowed, buildings negated, the landscape blotted out.

"Upon waking, I thought a cure might be, no matter how painful, removing the jewel from my forehead and subjecting my mind to an antidote of unfiltered sunlight. The problem with my plan soon became evident when I tried but found I could not command my hand to perform the task. The creature of the dark had insinuated its tentacles into the mechanisms of my brain and would not allow itself to be destroyed. I fell into the most abject depression and was powerless to conceive of any thought other than that of suicide. I cringe now at the thought of revealing this to you and ultimately your readers, but I actually began banging my head against one of the cellar's wooden beams, hoping to do myself in through severe head trauma. Ridiculous, no?" Larchcroft shook his head, smiling.

"Not at all," said August. "A desperate situation, I understand."

"Bless you," said the Man of Light. "I managed only to knock myself unconscious and back into the dream of my messenger. I found him at a bizarre juncture. Hand in hand with May, he ran through the streets of town. A crowd of those who had not as of yet been taken by the dark also fled to the center of the ever-diminishing circle of light. I watched this all with a placid sense of disinterest. At first I thought the young man and his girlfriend were running for their lives, but it soon became clear to me that he had a destination in mind, for he was searching the addresses of the buildings they passed.

"I realized he must have found the place, because he and May rushed up a set of steps and inside a dilapidated old structure of five stories and crumbling brickwork. As they ran past the entrance, I read the chipped and fading sign: THE WINDSOR ARMS. I tell you, my interest was roused. Without stopping, they ran through the empty lobby and took to the staircase. Up three flights they sped and came to a halt outside a familiar green door. The messenger knocked, and there was no answer. Without hesitating, he turned the knob and pushed open the door. Inside the dimly lit room, they found a dream-world Frank Scatterill sitting in a chair, puffing away at an opium pipe, a blue cloud surrounding his head.

"What followed next was difficult to discern, as it happened in a blur. There was a great commotion out on the street, a chorus of abbreviated screams of anguish. Then total silence. The young woman, May, for some reason had disrobed and was standing, shivering, in the cold off to the side of the operating area. The messenger was reclining in the barber chair, importuning Scatterill to hurry. The dreary addict fumbled with some tools on his worktable. I believe I was the first to notice it—the dark began flowing into the room, like water, from the space beneath the door.

" 'There's no time for that,' said the messenger just before he lay back and fell instantly asleep. May cried once and was consumed by the dark, which was filling the room. Scatterill lifted something off the table. I only caught the glint of it in the light from the single remaining candle. By this point he and the messenger on the chair were enclosed in a mere bubble of light. The surgeon held his hand out, aiming at the young man's forehead. I saw he held a derringer. As the dark's five hundred tentacles began to wrap themselves around Scatterill, he pulled the trigger, and his death cry was masked by the report of the weapon. A neat, bloodless, smoking hole had appeared in the center of the messenger's forehead.

"The dark closed in, but before it could eradicate the young man, a bright beam shot forth from the hole in his head as if his cranium had become a lighthouse. This brilliant light gathered itself together into a human figure without features. Its powerful glow pushed back the dark. The dark, for its part, sent forth a large glob of night, which also quickly took the form of a human figure but remained connected to the greater darkness by a kind of umbilical cord. The light and the dark then came together and met in combat.

"My experience of this battle was hallucinatory, to say the least. Even in sleep I could feel my mind buzzing, my skull vibrating. I don't know how long the match lasted, but it was a brutal struggle for victory. Finally, after they had each managed to get the other in a stranglehold, their bodies thrust so tightly together parts of them appeared gray, there came an audible pop, and a moment later all was returned to normal in the dream world. I looked out the window of Scatterill's room and saw a placid twilight. The dream citizens below on the street were passing to and fro on their normal business. The messenger awoke then, even though the bullet wound remained in his head. He sat up, and, when he looked around, I could tell he was actually seeing me. He scrabbled forward to the floor and found the surgeon's derringer, aiming it at me. I put my hands up in front of my face. He must have pulled the trigger then, because I heard a click. The weapon only carried a single shot and that had been spent, but that distinct sound woke me. I called for Baston, and he helped me up the stairs and into the light of day."

"A perfect ending," said August, and reached inside his jacket. Larchcroft's eyes flashed, following the reporter's movement, and his mouth tightened. The young man slowly drew a handkerchief from his inner pocket and applied it to his forehead. Larchcroft gave a sigh of relief.

"If you don't mind, I'd like to inspect your notes," said the Man of Light.

August held his notebook forward. The head leaned closer, and there appeared a green-gloved hand against the back cover of the book as it was lifted away. As Larchcroft flipped the pages, evidently reading, he passed his other green-gloved hand once over each page as if giving his blessing to what had been written there.

"You never did get the answers to your questions, did you?" said August.

The eyes of the Man of Light remained focused on the pages, but he answered. "I gained answers to questions I never conceived of asking."

"May I inquire as to what you learned?" asked the reporter. "Or do you count this information a trade secret?"

"I learned that light is not the sole proprietor of the universe. One must count the dark as equally powerful. Knowing this made me more expert at my work than any specific answers the messenger might have returned with. If you want to know the truth about the light, you must ask the dark. Since this incident, I've become a willing student of the night, of shadows, of the cavernous recesses of my own mind. Terrible things lurk there, but terrible beauty as well. All this has made me the lightsmith I am today."

"The dark is half the story then," said August.

"Yes," said Larchcroft, "it's a willing teacher. All it asks is the occasional sacrifice." He let go of the notebook then, and it fell to the floor in front of August.

The reporter did not reach for it, as he was too deeply immersed in trying to encompass all he'd learned that night. Thought led onto thought and drew him spiraling down into his imagination. He couldn't tell how long he'd sat contemplating the struggle between light and dark.

"This interview is now ended," said Larchcroft, bringing August back to full consciousness. The reporter looked up to see that the room was now filled with the early light of day.

"What type of sacrifices?" August asked the visage.

"The dearest kind, my boy," said Larchcroft, laughing as a beam of morning sun shot through the single window across the room and struck him full in the face. He stared momentarily into August's eyes and then abruptly and completely disappeared. The laughter lingered for a brief time, quickly diminished to a whisper, and then vanished.

August grabbed his notebook, stood up, stretched his aching legs, and left the room by the way he'd come in. As he walked the hallways toward the front entrance of the mansion, the sound of his footsteps echoed throughout the stillness of the massive building. He wondered where Larchcroft and Baston and the servant had gone. When he reached the door, he noted with a smile that it was bright green, something he'd not remembered from the previous night upon his arrival.

August walked the entire mile and a half from Larchcroft's estate into town, and when he arrived at the office of the *Gazette*, he found it already abuzz with the day's activity. Because of the interview he now carried in his notebook, he felt none of the usual hesitancy in approaching his boss. He rapped on the old man's office door, and a gruff voice commanded him to enter.

"Where were you last night?" asked the editor. There were dark pouches beneath his eyes, and what hair he possessed was askew with wispy eruptions. It was unusual for him to be seen without jacket and tie, but August noticed both were missing. His white shirt was rumpled and ink-stained; one sleeve turned up in a sloppy cuff as the other was turned down and unbuttoned.

"I had the interview with Larchcroft," said August. "I'm sure you'll want it for the front page."

The boss shook his head, his expression grim. "Sorry, kid, but you've been trumped."

"What do you mean?" asked August.

"Early in the evening last night, just after dark, a young woman was murdered in town. The third floor of a dump over on Paine Street. The Windsor Arms. Nobody was around, I couldn't find you, so I had to go. Brutal. Somebody opened a hole in this girl's head, right here, and poured in a pint of India ink," said the old man, pointing to the center of his forehead. "Blood everywhere."

August sat slowly down in the chair across the desk from his boss. "What was the girl's name?" he asked.

"May Lofton. We don't know much more about her yet."

"Was she a schoolteacher?" asked August.

"She might have been. She definitely didn't seem to be the type to frequent a place like that. Why, you know her?"

"No."

"The constable found something interesting near the body, though. Maybe they'll catch the killer . . ." The editor closed his eyes and stretched. "I could fall asleep right now. Anyway, what did you get?"

August reached across the desk to lay his notebook in front of the editor and then sat back into his chair. "This still might make the front page," said August. "A long and detailed recounting, basically a confession from the Man of Light."

The editor sat up straight and leaned over the desk, drawing the notebook to him. He yawned wearily, opened the cover, and flipped past the first few blank pages. A moment passed, and then his eyes fiercely focused, as if what he was reading had fully awoken him. He turned two pages. "Fascinating," he said. "You see this?" He lifted the open notebook and turned it to August.

The young man's jaw dropped and the color drained from his face as the editor flipped slowly through the pages for him. Each and every page he'd committed the interview to was covered from top to bottom, side to side, with pitch-black, not the least speck of white showing.

The editor cocked his head to the side and paused before speaking. "I guess you know the clue the constable found with the dead girl was a sheet of paper, like this, but instead of writing, it was completely black."

August wanted to protest his innocence but found himself suddenly speechless due to an unfounded yet overwhelming sense of guilt. The editor's bleak stare seemed to drill straight into him, while outside the sky had darkened even more than was usual for a winter's day. Feeling the night closing in on him, he stood, turned, and fled the office. The editor yelled behind him for his other workers to stop the young reporter. Still August managed to escape their clutches and the confines of the *Gazette*. Outside, an angry crowd pursued, following him to the riverbank, where they found his discarded clothes, and later, at dusk, after searching all day, his lifeless, frozen body, pale as the light of the moon.

A Man of Light

Story Notes

The idea for this story came from a visit to my friend Barney, who is a painter and an alternative comics artist (see "Coffins on the River"). I was visiting him in his studio one day, and while we were looking at his latest paintings and shooting the breeze, two things conspired to later give me the beginning idea for this story. The first was that he had just finished a painting for a Halloween show at a local gallery. The picture was sort of a takeoff on a work by an Early American painter, Charles Willson Peale, of a man ascending a staircase and looking back over his shoulder. Perhaps you've seen it; it's very famous. What Barney did was create a similar figure, carrying a cane, also ascending a staircase. The difference was that only the figure's head, gloves, socks, and shoes were rendered. Because of the manner in which he'd placed the figure, the green wallpaper behind seemed at first to be a green suit the man was wearing. On closer inspection, it was evident that the suit was an illusion and there was only the green wall. It was a very cool effect, and I laughed when I realized how my eyes had initially duped me. The face of the man on the stairs was very forbidding, and I told Barney that it looked like Ray Milland sniffing shit. He said, "Sort of, but you know who it really looks like?" "Who?" I asked. "Tell me that doesn't look like John Ashcroft," he said. And, man, I'll be damned if it didn't. He told me he hadn't intended for the figure to look like anyone, it just came out that way. A little while after that, we were looking at another painting of his, and I told him I liked the way the light shone in it. He said, "I'm the man of light," and then proceeded to tell me about some popular contemporary painter who billed himself as "The Man of Light." The guy painted these saccharine-sweet landscapes and added painted light to them in any amount the customer wanted. Barney said this artist had stores in malls and had become a franchise. From these two things, the initial idea of "A Man of Light" was born. I was going to call the character in the story Ashcroft, but I figured that would have made it a political allegory, so I changed the name to Larchcroft. There was actually another story Barney told me that day that I tried to work into my tale, but I found it really had no place. He kept all of his drawings and comics in this flat file he had in his studio. I'd asked him about some old drawing he'd done years back, and he nodded toward the flat file and said, "What's left of it is in there." I said, "What do you mean, 'what's left of it'?" He told me that mice had gotten in the file and ate through a lot of his work and crapped all over it. "When I'm out here late at night, I hear them chewing through it," he said. "That sucks," I said. "No great loss," he told me. "Strange thing is, some of the drawings they eat to smithereens and some they won't touch." "Why?" I asked. "Even the mice are critics," he said. "I've been meaning to compare the ones they've left with the one's they've chewed. I think they're trying to tell me something."

Ellen Datlow published this story on SCIFICTION. Luckily, in publishing it on the web, the mice couldn't touch it. Some readers gave it a pretty good chewing, though.

The Green Word

O N THE DAY THAT MOREN KAIRN WAS TO BE EXE-
cuted, a crow appeared at the barred window of his tower cell.
He lay huddled in the corner on a bed of foul straw, his body covered with bruises and wounds inflicted by order of the king. They had demanded that he pray to their God, but each time they pressed him, he spat. They applied the hot iron, the knife, the club, and he gave vent to his agony by cursing. The only thing that had prevented them from killing him was that he was to be kept alive for his execution.

When he saw the crow, his split lips painfully formed a smile, for he knew the creature was an emissary from the witch of the forest. The black bird thrust its head between the bars of the window and dropped something small and round from its beak onto the stone floor of the cell. "Eat this," it said. Then the visitor cawed, flapped its wings, and was gone. Moren held out his hand as if to beg the bird to take him away with it, and for a brief moment, he dreamed he was flying out of the tower, racing away from the palace toward the cool green cover of the trees.

Then he heard them coming for him, the warder's key ring jangling, the soldiers' heavy footsteps against the flagstones of the circular stairway. He ignored the pain of his broken limbs, struggled to all fours, and crept slowly across the cell to where the crow's gift lay. He heard the soldiers laughing and the key slide into the lock as he lifted the thing up to discover what it was. In his palm he held a round, green seed, the likes of which he had never before seen. When the door opened, so did his mouth, and as the soldiers entered, he swallowed the seed. No sooner was it in his stomach than he envisioned a breezy summer day in the stand of willows where he had first kissed his wife. She moved behind the dangling green tendrils of the trees, and when a soldier spoke his name it was in her voice, calling him to her.

With a gloved hand beneath each arm, they dragged him to his feet, and he found that his pain was miraculously gone. The noise of the warder's keys had somehow become the sound of his daughter's laughter, and he too laughed as they pulled him roughly down the steps. Outside, the midsummer sunlight enveloped him like water, and he remembered swimming beneath the falls at the sacred center of the forest. He seemed to be enjoying himself far too much for a man going to his death, and one of the soldiers struck him across the back with the flat side of a sword. In his mind, though, that blow became the friendly slap of his fellow warrior, the archer Lokush. Moren had somehow forgotten that his best bowman had died not but a week earlier, along with most of his other men, on the very field he was now so roughly escorted to.

The entirety of the royal court, the knights and soldiers and servants, had gathered for the event. To Kairn, each of them was a green tree and their voices the wind rippling through the leaves of that human thicket. He was going back to the forest now, and the oaks, the alders, the yews parted to welcome him.

The prisoner was brought before the royal throne and made to kneel.

"Why is this man smiling?" asked King Pious, casting an accusatory glance at the soldiers who had accompanied the prisoner. He scowled and shook his head. "Read the list of grievances and let's get on with it," he said.

A page stepped forward and unfurled a large scroll. Whereas all in attendance heard Kairn's crimes intoned—sedition, murder, treachery—the warrior heard only the voice of the witch, chanting the beautiful poetry of one of her spells. In the midst of the long list of charges, the queen leaned toward Pious and whispered, "Good lord, he's going green." Sure enough, the prisoner's flesh had darkened to a deep hue the color of jade.

"Finish him before he keels over," said the king, interrupting the page.

The soldiers spun Moren Kairn around and laid his head on the chopping block. From behind the king stepped a tall knight encased in gleaming red armor. He lifted his broadsword as he approached the kneeling warrior. When the deadly weapon was at its apex above his neck, Kairn laughed, discovering that the witch's spell had transformed him into a seedpod on the verge of bursting.

"Now," said the king.

The sharp steel flashed as it fell with all the force the huge knight could give it. With a sickening slash and crunch of bone, Kairn's head came away from his body and rolled onto the ground. It landed, facing King Pious, still wearing that inscrutable smile. In his last spark of a thought, the warrior saw himself, a thousandfold, flying on the wind, returning to the green world.

All but one who witnessed the execution of Moren Kairn that day believed he was gone for good and that the revolt of the people of the forest had been brought to an end. She, who knew otherwise, sat perched in a tree on the boundary of the wood two hundred yards away. Hidden by leaves and watching with hawklike vision, the witch marked the spot where the blood of the warrior had soaked into the earth.

Arrayed in a robe of fine purple silk and wearing his crown of gold, King Pious sat by the window of his bedchamber and stared out into the night toward the tree line of the forest. He had but an hour earlier awakened from a deep sleep, having had a dream of that day's execution—Kairn's green flesh and smile—and called to the servant to come and light a candle. Leaning his chin on his hand and his elbow on the arm of the great chair, he raked his fingers through his white beard and wondered why, now that he had successfully eradicated the threat of the forest revolt, he could not rest easily.

For years he had lived with their annoyance, their claims to the land, their refusal to accept the true faith. To him they were godless heathens, ignorantly worshiping trees and bushes, the insubstantial deities of sunlight and rain. Their gods were the earthbound, corporeal gods of simpletons. They had the audacity to complain about his burning of the forest to create new farmland, that his hunting parties were profligate and wasted the wild animal life for mere sport, that his people wantonly fished the lakes and streams with no thought of the future.

Had he not been given a holy edict by the pontiff to bring this wild territory into the domain of the church, convert its heathen tribes, and establish order amidst this demonic chaos? All he need do was search the holy scripture of the Good Book resting in his lap and in a hundred different places he would find justification for his actions. Righteous was his mission against Kairn, whom he suspected of having been in league with the devil.

Pious closed the book and placed it on the stand next to his chair. "Be at ease, now," he murmured to himself, and turned his mind toward the glorious future. He had already decided that in midwinter, when what remained of the troublesome rabble would be hardest pressed by disease and hunger, he would send his soldiers into the maze of trees to ferret out those few who remained and return them to the earth they claimed to love so dearly.

As the candle burned, he watched its dancing flame and decided he needed some merriment, some entertainment to wash the bad taste of this insurrection from his palate. He wanted something that would amuse him, but also increase his renown. It was a certainty that he had done remarkable things in the territory, but so few of the rulers of the other kingdoms to the far south would have heard about them. He knew he must bring them to see the extraordinary palace he had constructed, the perfect order of his lands, the obedience of his subjects.

While he pondered, a strong wind blew across the fields from out of the forest, entered the window by which he sat, and snuffed the flame of the candle. At the very moment in which the dark ignited in his room and swiftly spread to cover everything in shadow, the idea came to him: a tournament. He would hold a tournament and invite the knights from the southern kingdoms to his palace in the spring. He was sure that his own Red Knight had no equal. The challenge would go out the following morning, and he would begin preparations immediately. The invitation would be so worded to imply that his man could not be beaten, for he, Pious, had behind him the endorsement of the Almighty. "That should rouse them enough to make the long journey to my kingdom," he whispered. Then he saw the glorious day in his imagination and sat for some time, laughing in the dark. When he finally drifted off to sleep, he fell into another nightmare in which a flock of dark birds had rushed into his bedchamber through the open window.

The witch of the forest, doubly wrapped in black, first by her long cloak and then by night, crouched at the edge of the tree line, avoiding the gaze of the full autumn moon, and surveyed with a keen eye the field that lay between herself and the palace. She made a clicking noise with her tongue, and the crow that had perched upon her shoulder lit into the sky and circled the area in search of soldiers. In minutes it returned with a report, a low gurgling sound that told her the guards were quite a distance away, just outside the protective walls. She whistled the song of a nightingale, and a large black dog with thick shoulders padded quietly to her side over fallen leaves.

She pulled the hood of the cloak over her head, tucking in her long, white hair. Although she had more years than the tallest of trees looming behind her had rings, she moved with perfect grace, as if she was a mere shadow floating over the ground. The dog followed close behind and the crow remained on her shoulder, ready to fly off into a soldier's face if need be. The same memory that gave her the ability to recall, at a moment's notice, spells containing hundreds of words, all the letters in the tree alphabet, the languages of the forest creatures, and the recipes for magical concoctions, worked now to help her pinpoint the very spot where Moren Kairn's blood had soaked the earth three months earlier.

When she knew she was close, she stopped and bent over to search through the dark for new growth. Eventually she saw it, a squat, stemless plant, bearing the last of its glowing berries and yellow flowers into the early weeks of autumn. She dropped down to her knees, assuming the same position that Kairn had the day of his execution, and with her hands, began loosening the dirt in a circle around the plant's thick base. The ground was hard, and an implement would have made the job easier, but it was necessary that she use her hands in order to employ the herb in her magic.

Once the ground had been prepared, she started on a circular course around the plant, treading slowly and chanting in whispers a prayer to the great green mind that flows through all of nature. As she intoned her quiet plea in a singsong melodic voice, she thought of poor Kairn and her tears fell, knowing she would soon join him.

From within her cloak she retrieved a long length of rope woven from thin vines. Taking one end, she tied it securely around the base of the plant. With the other end in hand, she backed up twenty paces and called the dog to her with the same whistled note she had used earlier. He walked over to her and sat, letting her tie that end of the rope around his neck. Once the knot was tight, she petted the beast and kissed him atop the head. "Stay now, Mahood," she whispered. Then she took four small balls of wild sheep wool from a pouch around her waist. Carefully, she stuffed one into each of the dog's ears and one in each of her own. When the witch backed farther away now, the dog did not move.

The moon momentarily passed behind a cloud, and as she waited for it to reappear, the crow left her shoulder. Eventually, when the moon had a clear view of her again, she motioned with both hands for the dog to join her. Mahood started on his way and then was slowed by the tug of the plant. She dropped to her knees, opened her arms wide, and the dog lurched forward with all his strength. At that moment, the root of the plant came free from the ground, and its birth scream ripped through the night, a piercing wail like a pin made of sound for bursting the heart. Both witch and dog were protected from its cry by the tiny balls of wool, but she could see the effects the terrible screech still had on Mahood, whose hearing was more acute. The dog stopped in his tracks as if stunned. His eyes went glassy, he exhaled one long burst of steam, and then sat down.

The witch did not hesitate for a heartbeat but began running. As she moved, she reached for the knife in her belt. With a smooth motion she lifted the exposed root of the plant and tugged once on the vine rope to warn Mahood to flee. Then she brought the knife across swiftly to sever the lead, and they were off across the field like flying shadows. She made for the tree line with the crow flapping in the air just above her left shoulder. The bird cawed loudly, a message that the soldiers had heard and were coming on horseback. The hood fell from her head, and her long, white hair flew out behind her, signaling to her pursuers.

When she was a hundred yards from the boundary of the forest, she could hear the hoofbeats closing fast. The mounted soldier in the lead yelled back to those who followed, "It's the crone," and then nocked an arrow in place on his bow. He pulled back on the string and aimed directly for her back. Just as he was about to release, something flew into his face. A piece of night with wings and sharp talons gouged at his right eye. The arrow went off and missed its mark, impaling the ground in the spot where the witch's foot had been but a second before.

Mahood had bounded ahead and already found refuge in among the trees of the forest. The crow escaped and the witch ran on, but there was still fifty yards of open ground to cover and now the other horsemen were right on her heels. The lead soldier drew his sword and spurred his horse to greater speed. Once, twice, that blade cut the air behind her head and on both passes severed strands of her long hair. Just when the soldier thought he finally had her, they had reached the boundary of the trees. He reared back with the sword to strike across her back, but she leaped before he could land the blow. The height of her jump was miraculous. With her free hand, she grabbed the bottom branch of the closest tree and swung herself up with all the ease of a child a hundred years younger. The other soldiers rode up to join their companion at the tree line just in time to hear her scampering away, like a squirrel, through the dark canopy of the forest.

The black dog was waiting for her at her underground cave, whose entrance was a hole in the ground amidst the vast stand of willows. Once safely hidden in her den, she reached beneath her cloak and pulled out the root of the Mandrake. Holding it up to the light from a burning torch, she perused the unusual design of the plant's foundation. Shaped like a small man, it had two arms extending from the thick middle part of the body and at the bottom a V shape of two legs. At the top, where she now cut away the green part of the herb, there was a bulbous lump, like a rudimentary head. This root doll, this little wooden manikin, was perfect.

She sat on a pile of deerskins covering a low rock shelf beneath the light of the torch. Taking out her knife, she held it not by the bone handle but at the middle of the blade, so as to have finer control over it. The technique she employed in carving features into the Mandrake root was an ancient art called *simpling*. First, she carefully gouged out two eyes, shallow holes precisely equidistant from the center of the head bump. An upward cut beneath the eyes raised a partial slice of the root. This she delicately trimmed the corners off of to make the nose. Next, she made rudimentary cuts where the joints of the elbows, knees, wrists, and ankles should be on the limbs. With the tip of the blade, she worked five small fingers into the end of each arm to produce rough facsimiles of hands. The last, but most important job was the mouth. For this opening, she changed her grip on the knife and again took it by the handle. Applying the sharp tip to a spot just below the nose, she spun the handle so as to bore a deep, perfect circle.

She laid the knife down by her side and took the Mandrake into the crook of her arm, the way in which one might hold a baby. Rocking forward and back slightly, she began to sing a quiet song in a language as old as the forest itself. With the thumb of her free hand she persistently massaged the chest of the plant doll. Her strange lullaby lasted nearly an hour, until she began to feel a faint quivering of the root in response to her touch. As always with this process, the life pulse existed only in her imagination at first, but as she continued to experience it, the movement gradually transformed from notion to actuality until the thing was verily squirming in her grasp.

Laying the writhing root in her lap, she lifted the knife again and carefully sliced the thumb with which she had kneaded life into it. When she heard the first peep of a cry come from the root child, she maneuvered the self-inflicted wound over the round mouth of the thing and carefully let three drops of blood fill the orifice. When the Mandrake had tasted her life, it began to wriggle and coo. She lifted it in both hands, rose to her feet, and carried it over to a diminutive cradle she had created for it. Then looking up at the crow, who perched on a deer skull resting atop a stone table on the other side of the vault, she nodded. The bird spoke a single word and flew up out of the den. By morning, the remaining band of forest people would line up before the cradle and each offer three drops of blood for the life of the strange child.

King Pious hated winter, for the fierce winds that howled outside the palace walls in the long hours of the night seemed the voice of a hungry beast come to devour him. The cold crept into his joints and set them on fire, and any time he looked out his window in the dim daylight all he saw was his kingdom buried deeply beneath a thick layer of snow the color of a bloodless corpse. During these seemingly endless frigid months, he was often beset by the thought that he had no heir to perpetuate his name. He slyly let it be known that the problem lay with the queen, who he hinted was obviously barren, but whom, out of a keen sense of honor, he would never betray by taking another wife. The chambermaids, though, knew for certain it was not the queen who was barren, and when the winds howled so loudly in the night that the king could not overhear them, they whispered this fact to the pages, who whispered it to the soldiers, who had no one else to tell but each other and their horses.

To escape the beast of winter, King Pious spent much of the day in his enclosed pleasure garden. Here was summer confined within four walls. Neat, perfectly symmetrical rows of tulips, hyacinths, roses, tricked into growth while the rest of nature slept, grew beneath a crystal roof that gathered what little sunlight there was and magnified its heat and light to emulate the fair season. Great furnaces beneath the floor heated the huge chamber, and butterflies, cultivated for the purpose of adding a touch of authenticity to the false surroundings, were released daily. Servants skilled in the art of recreating bird sounds with their voices were stationed in rooms adjoining the pleasure garden, and their mimicked warblings were piped into the chamber through long tubes.

In the afternoon of the day on which the king was given the news that the first stirrings of spring had begun to show themselves in the world outside the palace walls, he was sitting on his throne in the very center of the enclosed garden, giving audience to his philosopher.

On a portable stand before him lay a device that the venerable academician had just recently perfected, a miniature model with working parts that emulated the movement of the heavens. The bearded wise man in tall pointed hat and starry robe lectured Pious on the Almighty's design of the universe. The curious creation had a long arm holding a gear train attached to a large box with a handle on the side. At the end of the arm were positioned glass balls connected with wire, representative of the Sun and Earth and other planets. Pious watched as the handle was turned and the solar system came to life, the heavenly bodies whirling on their axes while at the same time defining elliptical orbits.

"You see, Your Highness," said the philosopher, pointing to the blue ball, largest of the orbs, "the Earth sits directly at the center of the universe, the Almighty's most important creation, which is home to his most perfect creation, mankind. All else, the Sun, the Moon, the planets and stars, revolve around us, paying homage to our existence as we pay homage to God."

"Fascinating," said the king as he stared intently at the device that merely corroborated for him his place of eminence in the far-flung scheme of things.

"Would you like to operate the device?" asked the philosopher.

"I shall," said the king. He stood up and smoothed out his robes. Then he advanced and placed his hand on the handle of the box. He gently made the world and the heavens spin and a sense of power filled him, easing the winter ache of his joints and banishing, for a moment, the thought that he had no heir. This feeling of new energy spread out from his head to his arm, and he began spinning the handle faster and faster, his smile widening as he put the universe through its paces.

"Please, Your Highness," said the philosopher, but at that instant something came loose and the entire contraption flew apart, the glass balls careening off through the air to smash against the stone floor of the garden.

The king stood, looking perplexed, holding the handle, which had broken away from the box, up before his own eyes. "What is this?" he shouted. "You assassinate my senses with this ill-conceived toy of chaos!" He turned in anger and beat the philosopher on the head with the handle of the device, knocking his pointed hat to the floor.

The philosopher would have lost more than his hat that afternoon had the king's anger not been interrupted. Just as Pious was about to order a beheading, the captain of the guard strode into the garden carrying something wrapped in a piece of cloth.

"Excuse me, Your Highness," he said, "but I come with urgent news."

"For your sake, it had better be good," said the king, still working to catch his breath. He slumped back into his chair.

"The company that I led into the forest last week has just now returned. The remaining forest people have been captured and are in the stockade under guard. There are sixty of them, mostly women and children and elders."

Pious straightened up in his seat. "You have done very well," he told the soldier. "What of the witch?"

"We came upon her in the forest, standing in a clearing amidst a grove of willows with her arms crossed as if waiting for us to find her. I quietly called for my best archer and instructed him in whispers to use an arrow with a poison tip. He drew his bow and just before he released the shaft, I saw her look directly at us, where we were hiding beneath the long tendrils of a willow thirty feet from her. She smiled just before the arrow pierced her heart. Without uttering a sound, she fell forward, dead on the spot."

"Do you have her body? I want it burned," said Pious.

"There is no body, Your Highness."

"Explain," said the king, beginning to lose his patience.

"Once the bowman hit his mark, we advanced from the trees to seize her, but before we could lay hands on her, her very flesh, every part of her, became a swirling storm of dandelion seeds. I swear to you, before my very eyes, she spiraled like a dust devil three times and then the delicate fuzz that she had become was carried up and dispersed by the wind."

"Well," said the king, looking skeptically at the captain, "you had better pray that I do not see or hear of her again."

"The remaining people of the forest lamented her death so genuinely, I believe that she is gone for good," said the soldier.

Pious nodded, thought for a second, and then said, "Very well. What is that you carry?"

The soldier unwrapped the bundle and held up a book for the king to see. "We found this in her cave," he said.

The king cleared his eyes with the backs of his hands. "How can this be?" he asked. "That is the copy of the Good Book I keep in my bedchamber. What kind of trickery is this?"

"Perhaps she stole it, Your Highness."

Pious tried to think back to the last time he had picked the book up and studied it. Finally he remembered it was the night of Kairn's execution. "I keep it near the open window. My God, those horrid birds of my dream." The king looked quickly over each shoulder at the thought of it. "A bag of gold to the bowman who felled her," he added.

The captain nodded. "What of the prisoners, Your Highness?" he asked.

"Execute the ones who refuse to convert to the faith, and the others I want taught a hymn that they will perform on the day of the tournament this spring. We'll show our visitors how to turn heathens into believers."

"Very good, Your Highness," said the captain, and then handed the book to the king. With this, he turned and left the garden.

By this time the philosopher had crept away to hide, and Pious was left alone in the pleasure garden. "Silence!" he yelled in order to quell the bird song, which now sounded to him like the whispers of conspirators. He rested back in his throne, exhausted from the day's activities. Paging through the Good Book, he came to his favorite passage—one that spoke elegantly of vengeance. He tried to read, but the idea of the witch's death so relaxed him that he became drowsy. He closed his eyes and slept with the book open on his lap while that day's butterflies perished and the universe lay in shards scattered across the floor.

The tournament was held on the huge field that separated the palace from the edge of the forest. Spring had come, as it always did, and that expanse was green with new-grown grass. The days were warm and the sky was clear. Had it not been for the tumult of the event, these would have been perfect days to lie down beneath the sun and daydream up into the bottomless blue. As it was, the air was filled with the cheers of the crowd and the groans of agony from those who fell before the sword of the Red Knight.

Pious sat in his throne on a dais beneath a canvas awning, flanked on the right and left by the visiting dignitaries of the southern kingdoms. He could not recall a time when he had been more pleased or excited, for everything was proceeding exactly as he had imagined it. His visitors were obviously impressed with the beauty of his palace and the authority he exhibited over his subjects. He gave orders a dozen an hour in an imperious tone that might have made a rock hop to with a "Very good, Your Highness."

Not the least of his pleasures was the spectacle of seeing the Red Knight thrash the foreign contenders on the field of battle. That vicious broadsword dislocated shoulders, cracked shins, and hacked appendages even through the protective metal of opponents' armor. When one poor fellow, the pride of Belthaena, clad in pure white metal, had his heart skewered and crashed to the ground dead, the king leaned forward and, with a sympathetic smile, promised the ambassador of that kingdom that he would send a flock of goats to the deceased's family. So far it had been the only fatality of the four-day-long event, and it did little to quell the festivities.

On the final day, when the last opponent was finished off and lay writhing on the ground with a broken leg, Pious sat up straight in his chair and applauded roundly. As the loser was carried from the field, the king called out, "Are there any other knights present who would like to test our champion?" Since he knew very well that every represented kingdom had been defeated, he made a motion to one of his councilors to have the converted begin singing. The choir of forest people, chained at the ankles and to each other, shuffled forward and loosed the first notes of the hymn that had been beaten into their memories over the preceding weeks.

No sooner did the music start, though, than the voice of the crowd overpowered its sound, for now there was a new contender on the tournament field. He stood, tall and gangly, not in armor, but wrapped in a black, hooded cloak. Instead of a broadsword or mace or lance, he held only a long stick fashioned from the branch of a tree. When the Red Knight saw the surprised face of the king, he turned to view this new opponent. At this moment, the crowd, the choir, and the dignitaries became perfectly quiet.

"What kind of mockery is this?" yelled Pious to the figure on the field.

"No mockery, Your Highness. I challenge the Red Knight," said the stranger in a voice that sounded like a limb splintering free from an oak.

The king was agitated at this circumstance that had been no part of his thoughts when he had imagined the tournament. "Very well," he called, and to his knight said, "Cut him in half."

As the Red Knight advanced, the stranger undid the clasp at the neck of his cloak and dropped it to the ground. The crowd's response was a uniform cry torn between a gasp and a shriek of terror, for standing before them now was a man made entirely of wood. Like a tree come to life, his branch-like limbs, though fleshed in bark, somehow bent pliantly. His legs had the spring of saplings, and the fingers with which he gripped his paltry weapon were five-part pointed roots trailing thin root hairs from the tips of the digits. The gray bark of his body held bumps and knots like a log, and in certain places small twigs grew from him, covered at their ends with green leaves. There was more foliage simulating hair upon his pointed head and a fine stubble of grass across his chin. Directly in the center of his chest, beneath where one's heart might hide, there grew from a protruding twig a large blue fruit.

The impassive expression that seemed crudely chiseled into the face of the wooden man did not change until the Red Knight stepped forward and, with a brutal swing of the broadsword, lopped off the tree-root hand clutching the stick. Then that dark hole of a mouth stretched into a toothless smile, forming wrinkles of joy beneath the eyes. The Red Knight stepped back to savor the pain of his opponent, but the stranger exhibited no signs of distress. He held the arm stump up for all to see and, in a blur, a new hand grew to replace the one on the ground.

The Red Knight was obviously stunned, for he made no move as the tree man came close to him and placed that new hand up in front of his enemy's helmeted face. When the king's champion finally meant to react, it was too late. For as all the crowd witnessed, the five sharp tips of the root appendage grew outward as swiftly as snakes striking and found their way into the eye slits of the knight's helmet. Ghastly screams echoed from within the armor as blood seeped out of the metal joints and onto the grass. The knight's form twitched and the metal arms clanked rapidly against the metal sides of the suit. The broadsword fell point first and stuck into the soft spring earth. When the stranger retracted his hand, the fingers growing back into themselves, now wet with blood, the Red Knight tipped over backward and landed with a loud crash on the ground.

Pious immediately called for his archers. Three of them stepped forward and fired at the new champion. Each of the arrows hit its mark, thunking into the wooden body. The tree man nonchalantly swept them off of him with his arm. Then he advanced toward the dais, and the crowd, the soldiers, the visiting dignitaries fled. The king was left alone. He sat, paralyzed, staring at the advancing creature. So wrapped in a rictus of fear was Pious that all he could manage was to close his eyes. He waited for the feel of a sharp root to pierce his chest and puncture his heart. Those moments seemed an eternity to him, but eventually he realized nothing had happened. When he could no longer stand it, he opened his eyes to an amazing scene. The tree man was kneeling before him.

"My liege," said the stranger in that breaking voice. Then he stood to his full height, and said, "I believe as winner of the tournament, I am due a feast."

"Quite right," said Pious, trembling with relief that he would not die. "You are an exceptional warrior. What is your name?"

"Vertuminus," said the tree man.

*   *   *

A table had been hastily brought into the pleasure garden and laid with the finest place settings in the palace. The feast was prepared for only Pious and the wooden knight. The visiting ambassadors and dignitaries were asked if they would like to attend, but they all suddenly had pressing business back in their home kingdoms and had to leave immediately after the tournament.

The king dined on roasted goose, whereas Vertuminus had requested only fresh water and a large bucket of soil to temporarily root his tired feet in. Soldiers were in attendance, lining the four walls of the garden, and were under orders to have their swords sharp and to keep them drawn in case the stranger's amicable mood changed. Pious feared the tree man, but was also curious as to the source of his animation and bizarre powers.

"And so my friend, you were born in the forest, I take it?" asked the king. He tried to stare into the eyes of the guest, which blinked and dilated in size though they were merely gouges in the bark that was his face.

"I was drawn up from the earth by the witch," he said.

"The witch," said Pious, pausing with a leg of goose in his hand.

"Yes, she made me with one of her spells, but she has abandoned me. I do not know where she has gone. I have been lonely and needed other people to be with. I have been watching the palace from a distance, and I wanted to join you here."

"We are very glad you did," said the king.

"The witch told me that you lived by the book. She showed me the book and taught me to read it so that I would know better how to wage war on you."

"And do you wish me harm?" asked Pious.

"No, for when I read the book it started to take hold of me and drew me to its thinking away from the forest. I joined the tournament so that I could win a place at the palace."

"And you have," said Pious. "I will make you my first knight."

Here Vertuminus recited the king's favorite passage from the Good Book. "Does it not make sense?" he asked.

Pious slowly chewed and shook his head. "Amazing," he said, and for the first time spoke genuinely.

"You are close to the Almighty?" asked Vertuminus.

"Very close," said the king.

There was a long silence, in which Pious simply sat and stared as his guest drank deeply from a huge cup.

"And if you don't mind my asking," said the king, pointing, "what is that large, blue growth on your chest?"

"That is my heart," said Vertuminus. "It contains the word."

"What word?" asked Pious.

"Do you know in the book, when the Almighty creates the world?"

"Yes."

"Well, how does he accomplish this?" asked the tree man.

"How?" asked the king.

"He speaks these things into creation. He says, 'Let there be light,' and there is. For everything he creates, he uses a different word. This fruit contains the green word. It is what gives me life."

"Is there a word in everything?" asked Pious.

"Yes," said Vertuminus, whose index finger grew out and speared a pea off the king's platter. As the digit retracted, and he brought the morsel to his mouth, he said, "There is a word in each animal, a word in each person, a word in each rock, and these words of the Almighty make them what they are."

Suddenly losing his appetite, the king pushed his meal away. He asked, "But if that fruit of yours contains the green word, why is it blue?"

"Only its skin is blue, the way the sky is blue and wraps around the Earth."

"May I touch it?" asked Pious.

"Certainly," said Vertuminus, "but please be careful."

"You have my word," said Pious, as he stood and slowly reached a trembling hand across the table. His fingers encompassed the blue fruit and gently squeezed it.

The wooden face formed an expression of pain. "That is enough," said the tree man.

"Not quite," said the king, and with a simple yank, pulled the fruit free from its stem.

Instantly, the face of Vertuminus went blank, his branch arms dropped to his sides, lifeless, and his head nodded.

Pious sat back in his throne, unable to believe that defeating the weird creature could have been so easy. He held the fruit up before his eyes, turning it with his fingers, and pondered the idea of the word of God trapped beneath its thin, blue skin.

Minutes passed as the ruler sat in silent contemplation, and in his mind formulated a metaphor in which the acquisition of all he desired could be as easy as his plucking this blue prize. It was a complex thought for Pious, one in which the blue globe of the world from the philosopher's contraption became confused with the fruit.

He nearly dropped the precious object when suddenly his lifeless guest gave a protracted groan. The king looked up in time to see another blue orb rapidly growing on the chest of the tree man. It quickly achieved fullness, like a balloon being inflated. He gave a gasp of surprise when his recently dead guest smiled and brought his branch arms up.

"Now it is my turn," said Vertuminus, and his root fingers began to grow toward the king.

"Guards," called Pious, but they were already there. Swords came down on either side, and hacked off the wooden limbs. As they fell to the ground, Pious wasted no time. He dove across the table and plucked the new blue growth. Again, Vertuminus fell back into his seat, lifeless.

"Quickly, men, hack him to pieces and burn every twig!" In each of his hands he held half of his harvest. He rose from his throne and left the pleasure garden, the sound of chopping following him out into the corridor. Here was a consolation for having lost his Red Knight, he thought—something that could perhaps prove far more powerful then a man encased in metal.

When Pious ordered that one of the forest people be brought to him, he had no idea that the young woman chosen was the daughter of Moren Kairn. She was a tall, willowy specimen of fifteen with long, blonde hair that caught the light at certain angles and appeared to harbor the slightest hues of green. Life in the stockade, where the remaining rebels were still kept, was very difficult. For those who did not willingly choose the executioner over conversion to the faith, food was used as an incentive to keep them on the path to righteousness. If they prayed they ate, but never enough to completely satisfy their hunger. And so this girl, like the others, was exceedingly thin.

She stood before the king in his study, a low table separating her from where he sat. On that table was a plate holding the two blue orbs that had been plucked from Vertuminus.

"Are you hungry, my dear?" asked the king.

The girl, frightened for her life, knowing what had become of her father and having witnessed executions in the stockade, nodded nervously.

"That is a shame," said Pious. "In order to make it up to you, I have a special treat. Here is a piece of fruit." He waved his hand at the plate before him. "Take one."

She looked to either side where soldiers stood guarding her every move.

"It's quite all right," said Pious in as sweet a tone as he was capable.

The girl reached out her hand and carefully lifted a piece of fruit. She brushed her hair away from her face with her free hand as she brought the blue food to her mouth.

The king leaned forward with a look of expectation on his face as she took the first bite. He did not know what to expect and feared for the worst. But the girl, after tasting a mouthful, smiled, and began greedily devouring the rest of it. She ate it so quickly he barely had time to see that its insides, though green, were succulent like the pulp of an orange.

When she had finished and held nothing but the pit in her hand, Pious asked her, "And how was that?"

"The most wonderful thing I have ever tasted," she whispered.

"Do you feel well?" he asked.

"I feel strong again," she said, and smiled.

"Good," said Pious. He motioned to one of the soldiers to escort her back to the stockade. "You may go now," he said.

"Thank you," said the girl.

Once she and the soldier had left the room, the king said to the remaining guard, "If she is still alive by nightfall, bring me word of it."

It tasted, to him, something like a cool, wet ball of sugar, and yet hidden deeply within its dripping sweetness there lay the slightest trace of bitterness. With each bite he tried to fix more clearly his understanding of its taste, but just as he felt on the verge of a revelation, he found he had devoured the entire thing. All that was left in his hand was the black pit, shaped like a tiny egg. Since the blue-skinned treat had no immediate effect on him, he thought perhaps the secret word lay within its dark center and he swallowed that also. Then he waited. Sitting at the window in his bedchamber, he stared out into the cool spring night, listening, above the din of his wife's snoring, to the sound of an unseen bird calling plaintively off in the forest. He wondered what, if anything, the fruit would do for him. At worst he might become sick unto death, but the fact that the girl from the forest was still alive but an hour earlier was good insurance that he would also live. At best, the risk was worth the knowledge and power he might attain. To know the secret language of the Almighty, even one green word, could bring him limitless power and safety from age and death.

Every twinge of indigestion, every itch or creak of a joint, made him think the change was upon him. He ardently searched his mind, trying to coax into consciousness the syllables of that sacred word. As it is said of a drowning man, his life passed before the inner eye of his memory, not in haste but as a slow, stately procession. He saw himself as a child, he saw his parents, his young wife, the friends he had had when he was no older than the girl he had used to test the fruit. Each of them beckoned to him for attention, but he ignored their pleas, so intent was he upon owning a supreme secret.

The hours passed and instead of revelation, he found nothing but weariness born of disappointment. Eventually, he crawled into bed beside his wife and fell fast asleep. In his dreams he renewed his quest, and in that strange country made better progress. He found himself walking through the forest, passing beneath the boughs of gigantic pines. In those places where the sunlight slipped through and lit the forest floor, he discovered that the concept of the green word became clearer to him.

He went to one of these pools of light and as he stood in it, the thought swirled in his head like a ghost as round as the fruit itself. It came to him that the word was a single syllable comprised of two entities, one meaning life and one death, that intermingled and intertwined and bled into each other. This knowledge took weight and dropped to his tongue. He tried to speak the green word, but when he opened his mouth, all that came out was the sound of his own name. Then he was awake and aware that someone was calling him.

"King Pious," said the captain of the guard.

The man was standing next to his bed. He roused himself and sat up.

"What is it?" he asked.

"The forest people have escaped from the stockade."

"What?" he yelled. "I'll have your head for this!"

"Your Highness, we found the soldiers who guard them enmeshed in vines that rooted them to the ground and, impossible as it sounds, a tree has grown up in the stockade overnight and the branches bend down over the high wall to touch the ground. The prisoners must have climbed out in the night. One of the horseman tried to pursue them but was attacked by a monstrous black dog and thrown from his mount."

Pious threw back the covers and got out of bed. He meant to give orders to have the soldiers hunt them down and slay them all, but suddenly a great confusion clouded his mind. That ghost of the green word floated and turned again in his mind, and when he finally opened his mouth to voice his command, no sound came forth. Instead, a leafed vine snaked up out of his throat, growing with the speed of an arrow's flight. He clutched his chest, and the plant from within him wound itself around the soldier's neck and arms, trapping him. Another vine appeared and another, until the king's mouth was stretched wide with virulent strands of green life growing rapidly out and around everything in the room. At just this moment, the queen awoke, took one look at her husband, and fled, screaming.

By twilight, the palace had become a forest. Those who did not flee the onslaught of vegetation but stayed and tried to battle it were trapped alive in its green web. All of the rooms and chambers, the kitchen, the tower cell, the huge dining hall, the pleasure garden, and even the philosopher's hiding place were choked with a riot of leafy vine. The queen and those others who had escaped the king's virulent command traveled toward the south, back to their homes and roots.

Pious, still planted where he had stood that morning, a belching fountain of leaf and tendril, was now the color of lime. Patches of moss grew upon his face and arms, and his already arthritic hands had spindled and twisted into branches. In his beard of grass, dandelions sprouted. On the pools that were his staring eyes, miniscule water lilies floated. When the sun slipped out of sight behind the trees of the forest, the last of that part of the green word he knew to be *life*, left him and all that remained was *death*. A stillness descended on the palace that was now interrupted only by the warblings of real nightingales and the motion of butterflies escaped from the pleasure garden into the wider world.

It was obvious to all of the forest people that Moren Kairn's daughter, Alyessa, who had effected their escape with a startling display of earth magic, was meant to take the place of the witch. When they saw her moving amidst the trees with the crow perched upon her shoulder, followed by Mahood, they were certain. Along with her mother, she took up residence in the cave beneath the stand of willows and set to learning all that she could from what was left behind by her predecessor.

One day near the end of spring, she planted in the earth the seed from the blue fruit, the origin of her magic, that Pious had given her. What grew from it was a tree that in every way emulated the form of Vertuminus. It did not move or talk, but just its presence was a comfort to her, reminding her of the quiet strength of her father. With her new powers came new responsibilities as the forest people looked to her to help them in their bid to rebuild their village and their lives. At the end of each day, she would come to the wooden knight and tell him of her hopes and fears, and in his silence she found excellent council and encouragement.

She was saddened in the autumn when the tree man's leaves seared and fell and the bark began to lift away from the trunk, revealing cracks in the wood beneath. On a cold evening, she trudged through orange leaves to his side, intending to offer thanks before winter devoured him. As she stood before the wooden form, snow began to lightly fall. She reached out her hand to touch the rough bark of his face, and just as her fingers made contact, she realized something she had been wondering about all summer.

It had never been clear to her why the fruit had been her salvation and gift and at the same time had destroyed King Pious. Now she knew that although the king had the green word, he had no way to understand it. "Love," she thought, "so easy for some and for others so impossible." In the coming years, through the cycle of the seasons, she planted the simple seed of this word in the hearts of all who knew her, and although, after a long life, she eventually passed on, she never died.

The Green Word
Story Notes

"The Green Word" was my first attempt at writing for a young adult audience. Terri Windling and Ellen Datlow were starting an anthology series, the first volume of which would deal with the folkloric figure of the Green Man, and they kindly invited me to submit a story. I'd never written with a specific age range in mind, so the prospect of doing so was a little daunting at first. Luckily, my two sons were in the demographic the book was aimed at, so I thought about the kinds of things that they liked to read themselves or have me read to them. I also tried to think back into the distant, misty past of my own youth and remember what it was like. Here are a few of the items that appeared on my inventory —magic, weird creatures, sword battles, good witches, evil kings . . . With these and a few more in mind, I began.

My story of the Green Man was going to borrow some ideas from the legend of the mystical mandrake plant. I hit a roadblock, though, when the mandrake was about to enter the story. The legend has it that the mandrake plant only grows at the foot of the gallows, planted from the ejaculated seed of hung men. It is a fact that when men are hung and the neck is broken they automatically ejaculate. This fact seemed a little too much for a young adult story, but I was unsure because I knew that young adult fiction, in recent years, had been taking on some very adult subject matter, as well it should. In addition, I knew that Terri Windling is a real expert on folklore. I convinced myself that I was in a jam. If I have a dead man ejaculating in my story for kids, I was afraid my editors would think me a creep. On the other hand, I was worried that if I left this detail out Terri might think I was lame, trying to meddle with the integrity of the legend just because I was dealing with younger readers. So I wrote to Ellen and asked her what she thought. She wisely told me to bypass the gallows ejaculation, which I did. I came up with a solution that everyone could live with, except the poor character. Instead, he simply gets his head cut off, and his spilled blood carries the seed that gives birth to the plant, which grows into the Green Man figure.

When I finished the story, I realized that there was something to this writing for young people and, in the process, for my younger self. Kids are not unaware of the darkness in the world, the tragedy and evil that lurks outside their doors or sometimes behind them, but recognizing this, they have a tendency to have their antennae always up for those instances of wonder, miracles of humanity, and mysteries of nature that we lose track of as we get older. The story made The Green Man *anthology and featured a great illustration by artist Charles Vess, as did all the other pieces in the volume. It's since been reprinted in Datlow and Windling's* The Year's Best Fantasy and Horror: Sixteenth Annual Collection *and in Hartwell and Cramer's* Year's Best Fantasy 3. The Green Man: Tales from the Mythic Forest *went on to win (in a tie) the World Fantasy Award for best anthology.*

Giant Land

ONCE A GIANT KEPT THREE PEOPLE IN A BIRD-
cage. It was made of twigs from the trees of Giant Land and it
hung in the corner of his kitchen over the rotisserie. Steam was
always rising and sometimes sparks would jump up and set the
peoples' clothes on fire. They thought they might be dreaming, but
still they frantically slapped at the flames with their coats to smother
them.

The giant had captured them, two men and a woman, at night
—snatched their cars right off the interstate and stuffed them in a
burlap sack. By sunrise he had made his way back up the mountain
unseen. He took them, wriggling like earthworms, out of their cars
and put them in the birdcage. Every day he fed them bowls of
grease soup, potatoes, and chocolate. When they got fat enough, he
intended to eat them.

One night when the woman was sleeping and the giant was put-
tering around his kitchen, the two men in the cage called him over.
The giant was not averse to speaking with his captives; most times
he was even civil. "Yes, gentlemen," he said in a whisper that blew
their hair back.

"Isn't she a beauty?" the tall one said, pointing to the sleeping
woman.

The giant stared hard and eventually smiled.

"We can set it up so that she'll be willing to marry you in
exchange for our freedom."

"How will you work such a miracle?" asked the giant.

"We'll talk you up for a couple of weeks," said the man with white hair, "make you seem like a prince."

"You've got two weeks," said the giant.

As soon as the woman awoke, they started to work on her. "You've got to say one thing for that giant . . ." "It must be pretty satisfying to be a giant . . ." "Did you see him punch that goat . . . ?" "His gold could sink a fleet of ships . . ."

Every time the tall man and the man with white hair got on the subject of the giant, though, the woman would say, "I don't care, I hate that bastard." She was always at the bars screaming at him, "You're a big loaf of shit!"

The giant would watch her body tense against the wooden bars, smile, and go about his business. In the mornings, after a breakfast of calf kidney pie, he'd count his gold. At midday, he'd dress in a tweed suit, take his tall hat and cane, the handle knob of which was a fossilized human head polished to a shine, and go out to work, selling magic beans door to door. He'd sent for the beans from an ad in the back of a magazine, and they were purported to grow into enormous stalks that reached the clouds. In the evenings, he'd play opera records—arias sung by the giantess Ybila, Diva of the Dog Spine—and the people in the cage would hear the melancholic strains of music wafting down the hallway from some other room in the house accompanied by titanic, mournful sobs.

The two men said everything they could think of to convince the woman the giant wasn't so bad—even that they thought of him as a kind of father figure. But the sneer never came off the woman's face. The days slipped by and they could feel themselves getting heavier. When they perspired, the sweat rolled from their pores, thick and amber like motor oil. They all had to take off their clothes because they had outgrown them. The giant often poked their stomachs and thighs with the long, sharp fingernail of his pinky. These jabs reminded the men that their two weeks were almost up.

On the night before the giant was prepared to eat them for breakfast, the two men cornered the woman against the bars of the cage and threatened her. "The only way we're all going to live is if you agree to marry the giant," the man with the white hair told her. The tall man wrapped his long fingers around her throat. "If you don't agree, I'll kill you right now," he said. The woman spit in the tall man's face, and he started to choke her. The man with the white hair punched her flabby stomach. Finally, they dropped her to the floor of the cage. "Yes or no?" they asked, one at a time. She nodded.

The giant came in wearing a bib that morning. "Well, well," he said in a thundering voice, "am I to have a meal or a marriage?"

The two men looked over at the woman. She smiled at them.

"Will you be my wife?" the giant asked, retrieving a monocle from his vest pocket. As she stepped forward, he eyed her up and down.

She stood just to the side of the cage door and said, "I'd rather marry a slug."

The monocle fell out of the giant's eye.

The men started for the woman. The giant gave a shrill cry of anguish and then smashed his hand through the cage door, grabbing the two just before they reached the woman. He ate the right leg of the man with white hair; blood raining down to sizzle and pop on the coals beneath the rotisserie. The screams were like the screams of dying mice in the enormous kitchen. When the woman saw the giant eat the head off the tall man, she jumped out of the hole in the cage and fell onto the slab of cow that was turning on the spit. As it spun, she raced across its slick surface, her feet burning with each step, and then leaped clear of the coals below, landing on the cobblestone floor.

The giant, still munching, tried to stomp her, but even with all her new weight she was too quick for him. He started after her as she made for the huge door of the kitchen. Not too far down the hallway lined with boars' heads, he scooped her up in his bloody hand. He did not eat her, though; he put her in his pocket and left his house.

Down the lane he went until he came to a cottage. He knocked on the door and another giant answered.

"Come in," said the second giant, whose head was that of a parrot and whose fingers were flexible as if made of rubber.

The first giant took the woman out of his pocket and held her at eye level. "Do you want her?" he asked. "I'm stuffed."

After thinking for a moment the second giant said, "Let's juice her." They took her into the parrot-head giant's kitchen, where he made his potions and medicines, and turned the juicer on. The first giant dangled her over the opening, the stainless steel blade whirring below, and said, "Goodbye. I think I could have loved you."

At the last instant, the woman said, "I'll marry whichever one of you can beat the other in a fight."

The giants looked at each other and nodded. They placed her in a glass box on the coffee table, latched the lid, and went to fetch their weapons. An hour later, in a clearing in the forest, the glass box holding the woman rested upon a tree stump in full view of the battleground. The parrot-head giant held a chrome steel pole with a pointed tip that glinted in the sun. Sea-green feathers at the back of his neck ruffled, his orange bird eyes twitched up and down, his black tongue played with the lower tip of his beak. The other giant held a club with spikes he had somehow made into a torch.

A leaf fell from a nearby tree and that was the sign to begin. They locked in combat, steel jabbing knee joints and fire raging across a feathered skull. Mighty squawks and groans filled the clearing. Strips of flesh, spurts of blood, singed feathers, and blue down as soft as a dream of water flew from them, littering the forest floor. The fight ended when the parrot-head giant drove his beak into the heart of the other giant and killed him. By that time, though, the parrot-head was irreparably charred. He staggered backward, gave one insignificant squawk, and fell dead.

The woman remained trapped in the glass box, growing thin while watching the flies as big as pigs come to feast on the remains of the giants. Birds of prey swooped down to tear off hunks of flesh from the corpses. A crow came along one day and, after eating the giants' eyes, snatched the glass box in its talons and flew off. The bird flew higher and higher, past the blue sky and into the night above, singing a birdsong that rattled the glass of the box. Out past Mars and Jupiter, it flew with ease. The woman in the box marveled at the stars and the sight of other worlds.

Then a sun exploded and the shock waves engulfed the bird and the woman in oblivion. When she woke, the woman found herself in a kitchen on her knees.

"What happened?" her husband asked as he leaned over to help her up.

"Nothing," she said, "nothing."

"You've got to go to the doctor," he said, helping her into a chair.

"Tomorrow," she promised. She finished making dinner, and the family sat down to eat. She discovered that she had made chicken and stuffing and corn.

When dinner was finished and the coffee was served, she turned to her husband and said, "What's my name?" He was about to reply, but then he looked off into the distance as if he had forgotten the question. She, herself, could not remember his.

"What's my name?" she asked each of the children, but each of them shrugged and shook their heads. Only then did she notice how unfamiliar the floral wallpaper was and that there were two cats instead of the usual one. What little she remembered was scattered and incoherent, but it was a near certainty she had not yet been married. She laughed to cover her fear. Her husband and the children laughed too.

As soon as she could, she cleared the dishes and announced that she was taking the garbage out. With the sagging plastic bag in her hand, she walked past her family watching television in the living room and said, "Be right in." As soon as she got outside and closed the door behind her, she dropped the bag and ran.

Before the night was over, she managed to find an unlocked car in which someone had left their keys. She fled town and headed out on the interstate. When she finally came to a stop, it was only because the ocean lapped the sand in front of the car. She got out and wandered up the beach.

Later that day, she found a small, deserted shack of a house on a dune overlooking the ocean. It had a fireplace and chimney, two warped glass windows that faced the surf, and comfortable furniture fashioned from the bones of whales, the cartilage of a giant manta ray. There was a parlor, a bedroom, and a kitchen. The absence of a bathroom was made up for by a roofless, wooden outhouse at the base of the dune, hidden amidst brambles and tall sea grass. She wasted no time but on that first day began to put the small house in order. Creating a broom from a stick of driftwood and sea grass, she proceeded to thoroughly sweep the place free of spider webs and sand.

Mounted on the wall in the bedroom were an old fishing rig with thick, string line, a reel that used no bale, and a heavy, treble-hooked lure made to appear like a silver baitfish moving through the water. In the late afternoon, she took this pole down to the shore and cast out the line toward the setting sun. Twice the string snarled, and twice she patiently unraveled it. She cast and reeled in, cast and reeled in, and not until night had descended and the moon had begun to rise did she feel a tug at the end of the line. That sudden resistance told her she would survive.

Her first fish, with human eyes, thick lips, and a top fin like a lady's fan, glinted in the moonlight as she reeled it onto the sand. It wheezed horribly, drowning in the atmosphere, and rolled its eyes up to look into hers. She could feel it silently pleading with her to spare its life. Although it pained her to watch the fish die, there was nothing else she could do as her hunger had made her weak and desperate. She took her catch home, and then scoured the dunes for driftwood. The sticks of wood she formed into a teepee, and then filled the pyramid inside with balled-up pages from a yellowed newspaper she'd discovered earlier while cleaning the house. In her jeans, she'd been carrying a cigarette lighter that she put to use, sparking a fire to life. It burned bright orange in the night, embers drifting high up into the darkness.

The fish tasted of saffron and renewed her strength. That night, in the whalebone bed, she wondered where she had come upon the cigarette lighter and if it was a link to her true past. When she fell asleep, she dreamed of the fish. It lay next to her in the bed and with its wheezing, dying voice, told her that when the giant had kidnapped her, she had been running away.

"From what?" she asked.

"From the little people," said the fish. It grew wings then and lifted into the air to fly in circles above her head.

She woke suddenly to find a bat flying in the same circles above her. Rolling off the bed, she crawled to where she had left the homemade broom. Once it was in her grip, she felt some courage. She swiped the air frantically, chasing the bat into the parlor. While continuing to swing the broom with one hand, she managed to open the front door and the intruder flew past her into the night. She did not go back to bed but stepped outside onto the dune. The breeze moved through the grass and the ocean lapped the shore in the moonlight. She contemplated her dream and briefly recalled an apartment in a city, a burning candle, an aria on the stereo, a broken wine bottle, the hands of a clock, a suitcase. Then crumbs of moments, the inconsequential debris of separate days, followed in a trail through her memory only to end in the gullet of a giant.

Many useful and marvelous things washed up after storms, and she walked the beach each morning to collect this bounty. Candles; kegs of grog; the horned, triple-socket skull of some unknown beast; a mirror from China whose stamped tin backing held the image of a dragon; mangoes; clothes made of vines from jungle towns half a world away; and a brown bottle, smelling of medicine, sealed with wax, ferrying one ringed finger and a message that read *HELP!* She slipped the ruby ring on her own finger and buried the rest. Once she found a knife that never dulled, once a leather-bound book wrapped in oilcloth titled *The Grammar of Constellations*. She read through its soggy pages at night by the glow of a candle while the creepers sang in the dunes.

Throughout the remainder of the summer and into the early autumn, she swam every day in the ocean. Her health slowly returned through a combination of this vigorous exercise and her simple diet of fish, clams, and berries from the nearby woods. Time, itself, withered, came apart at the seams, and was carried away on the tide. In the perfect calm of long afternoons, she sat at the water's edge and let her imagination blossom, following incredible story lines suggested by the items she found while beachcombing. For the most part, she went without clothing, and her skin bronzed. Her hair grew long and wild. The muscles of her arms and legs took on sleek definition. Whereas earlier, she had kept the dragon mirror facedown on the windowsill of her bedroom, by the time the geese flew south in formation, she had mounted the mirror on the wall in order to see herself each morning. Not knowing her name, she told her reflection her name would be *Anna*.

In mid-autumn, just before the ocean became far too cold for swimming, she woke one morning and looked out to sea. There, on a sandbar that had formed overnight, only a hundred yards from shore, lay what remained of a large wooden sailing ship. Without a second thought, she dove into a wave and swam out to it. As she drew closer, she could see that it had an enormous hole in its side. The hulking craft listed, its tall, cracked mast angled against the horizon. By the time she reached the sandbar, the tide had receded and the majority of the hull was visible above the waterline. She entered the craft through its gaping wound.

Save for the wide beam of daylight that entered, focused like a spotlight, it was dark inside the wooden giant. The boards creaked with every wavelet that rolled beneath it, and crabs scurried here and there over the sodden goods of the hold. Coming upon a passageway that led above, she leaned to her side and scrabbled up a set of steps to reach a middle deck. There she found the galley and rows of bunks for the missing sailors. Just beyond the sailors' quarters she discovered what appeared to be the captain's cabin. A globe, a compass, charts, piles of books lay scattered about as if a miniature typhoon had been loosed in the small compartment.

She looked around for things that might be useful back at her home. In her search, she came upon the captain's log. She opened it in the middle and began to read by the light that slipped in from a small hole in the deck above. The first thing she learned was the name of the ship, the *Lonreat*, which hailed from a place called Neerly. She flipped then to the last entry and read:

> *I have sent the men off on the life boats, for the ship is rapidly taking water through a hole suffered by way of the dragon-headed cannons of the pirate junk,* Jade Bloom. *They engaged us in battle as we sailed southward on our return trip from trading in Giant Land. The only thing that saved us from certain death was a sudden storm that distracted our pursuers' intentions from that of battle to merely*

*saving their own lives. Perhaps we were cursed by our un-
usual cargo, the great crystal ball containing the severed
head of Mar-el-mar, or perhaps because normal men were
never really meant to engage in commerce with giants. From
the sound of the winds up on deck, it is a good bet I will
never get a chance to figure it out.*

*My only hope is that some of my men will survive the
storm. I go now to strap myself to the wheel. There may be a
chance that I can beach the* Lonreat *somewhere. I have given
myself a reminder to thank God if I should survive this
calamity and return to Neerly. I would mark the time here,
but unfortunately I lost my watch in our fray with the pirates.*

Anna skipped back through the pages. In the middle of the log,
she read an account of the captain and his crew, when in Giant
Land, being entertained by the diva Ybila. They had to climb all
day up the side of a mountain, to a high ridge known as the Dog
Spine, and there in an amphitheater hewn from solid rock, under
the stars, the graceful behemoth sang an aria titled "What Is My
Name?" The captain attests that her voice had a sweetly melancholic affect upon his men, and they were plunged into a state not
dissimilar to that of the reveler upon opium. *I thought back through
my life—the journeys, the people, the places, the joy and sorrow—
and discovered a vast ocean inside of me,* he wrote.

Up on the main deck, beneath the tattered shreds of sails flapping in the breeze, she came upon the skeletal remains of the
captain. He was lashed to the ship's wheel by a leather belt, still
standing upright in a pose that suggested he was scanning the horizon. She thought it a shame that he did not know that he had
finally found a place to beach the ship. He wore a jacket with
golden designs stitched above the pockets, a hat, and tall boots.
Tied around his left index finger was a length of royal blue thread,
no doubt the reminder to thank the Almighty. Anna, beset by the
tragic end of the good captain, fled the ship by diving headlong into
the rising tide. The next morning, the *Lonreat* had vanished.

In winter, the night skies were clear, and she read their grammar. The icy prose told her she was only dreaming that she was
asleep and dreaming, and that really she was awake in a dream of
reality made actual by the ocean, and the stars, and the wind in the
dunes. She didn't really understand but felt in her heart it was true.
Then, one night, a star fell, trailing a fiery veil, and slipped into the
ocean with a distinct fizzle. A wisp of smoke curled up around the
milky moon. This radically changed the grammar of constellations
and made the old rules false, initiating a wicked freeze.

The ocean turned to ice, and wrapped in all her garments, those made of vine, the brocaded paisley shawl, obviously from the closet of a long dead queen, the Sherpa's cap, and sealskin boots, she ventured out among the crystal waves beneath a perfectly blue sky. Up and over, up and over, she went, exploring. Three hundred yards from shore, she found a wooden crate, the top missing. Lying in it was a human figure made of wax—an elegant woman, naked, with a wig of chestnut horsehair and delicate tattooed eyebrows, lashes, and pubic hair.

Over a period of days, while the water remained solid, she pushed that crate to shore. She stood the wax woman outside her house, afraid the figure would melt in the heat from her fireplace. She called her new companion *The Lady of Fashion* and visited with her daily. From her collection of sea treasures, she dressed the woman in a violet shift and put dried flowers in her hair, a corncob pipe in her mouth, and adorned her with a pendant of rarest malachite. At first the two merely gossiped, but before long, The Lady of Fashion revealed her story.

"I was made by a giant dollmaker to stand in the parlor of a giant child's dollhouse at the front window, staring out at my two wax children while they sat, one at either end of a seesaw. Maxwell was ever in the ascent, his arms thrown out wide, a smile on his face, while Cloe dropped, every second, toward the ground. I understood I had a husband, but I never saw him. His voice would come up from the basement where he was working on some infernal project. And you know, weeks went by and I stared out that window. What was my choice?

"Then, one night, in her play, the mischievous giant child picked me up and laid me on the bed in the master bedroom. A few moments later, she laid my husband down on top of me. She turned off the lights and left us there, perhaps in hopes of us making love and eventually siring another wax child. I only saw my husband briefly before the room went dark. He was a handsome man with a beard and long, black hair. 'I'm sorry to be crushing you,' he said.

" 'Do you feel any excitement?' I asked.

" 'No,' he said, 'I'm made of wax. But I have been devising a plan for your escape.'

" 'How is it you can move and make noise in the basement, but I can not stir even so much as a finger?' I asked.

" 'That noise you hear is coming out of my head. Through very hard concentration I have created a machine made of thoughts that will cast an aura of desirability around you that no giant can ignore,' he said.

" 'What about our children?' I asked.

" 'My dear, can't you tell they are not real? They are merely dolls, no more than stylized balls of earwax.'

" 'Why are you doing this?' I asked.

" 'Enough,' he said. 'I must think.'

"His mind sent up a racket then, a pounding, as if the headboard was rhythmically slamming the wall, with grunts and groans and protracted sighs. It must have been a marvelous invention. Eventually I fell asleep, and somewhere through the night, perhaps in my dreams, perhaps not, I felt something warm and inconsequential move between my legs.

"Two days later, a parrot-head giant came to the giant girl's house, traveling door-to-door, selling heart medicine in brown bottles. The girl's father went to fetch his money pouch, leaving the salesman alone in the room where the dollhouse stood. By then I had been placed back in the parlor by the front window. Upon seeing me looking out, the parrot-head giant opened the front door and stuck his rubbery fingers into my home. He grabbed me, and hid me in his pants pocket just before the girl's father returned.

"Parrot Head left town immediately and traveled to another place where there was an open-air market. He sold me for five gold coins to a bearded giant who was a magician. This magician, Mar-el-mar, took me down the street to an open place and set me in the middle of a chessboard atop a table. I was barely as big as the other chess pieces. In a loud voice, he called all those in the market place to come and witness a miracle. When the rabble had assembled, he pushed back the sleeves of his dark robe and cast a spell beginning with the word *Wendatamu* . . . Instantly, I came to life.

"The crowd of giants gasped, and the noise was deafening to me. I put my hands to my ears. Life, life, life was a strange, beautiful experience, being able to move, to breathe. My wax became flesh, and I heard myself scream, but just as suddenly as that sweet condition came to me, it was taken away. The Giant King's personal guard pushed through the masses and seized the magician. Right on the spot, they forced him to kneel in the street. The captain of the guard announced that the magician was guilty of practicing the dark arts. Mar-el-mar spat on the cobblestones and said, 'May the king's wife flee his kingdom and lose herself in the world.' They chopped his head off, and the life went out of me.

"I was whisked off the chessboard and given to an old woman, who was ordered to throw me into the furnace at the blacksmith's shop. This old woman went to the shop as she had been instructed, stood before the flames, but found she could not destroy me. Instead, she took me home and dressed me in the fine clothes from a doll she had bought long ago for a daughter, her only pregnancy, who had died soon after birth. She put me in a small box, and then at midnight, went to the stream that runs along the southern border of that town. She sang me a lullaby, and with tears in her eyes, set me adrift down the waterway that led to the ocean."

"But what became of the dress the old woman had put you in?"

"I've been sailing so long, it rotted away, turning to mere threads. Pieces of royal blue thread litter the oceans of the world."

In the early days of the following summer, during an unusual heat wave, The Lady of Fashion melted. Amidst soundless shrieks of agony and pleas to Mar-el-mar to spare her soul, she dripped away into an ugly puddle that eventually seeped into the sand. Nothing could be done to save her. The violet shift blew out to sea one bright and blustery afternoon. A beach rat stole the corncob pipe, and all that was left was the pendant of malachite lying on the sand to mark the presence of a missing confidant. Anna wept bitterly at the loss of her friend.

To the south lay the ocean. To the north, past a few hundred yards of sand and then a line of boulders, lay the woods. To the east, at some definite distance, but she was not sure how far, sat a rusted car, if it had not already been washed out to sea, and a path to the interstate. To the west, though, lay nothing but dunes, an immeasurable vista of rolling sand hills, some cresting in the far distance to magnificent heights. She decided, after the demise of her wax friend, that a journey might be just the thing to drive off her grief and loneliness.

She set out due west early one morning, carrying a knotted silk kerchief with enough dried fishes and berries to last an overnight stay. At first she did not take to the dunes, but made her way along the shore in order to save her strength, the better to climb in amongst the hills when she was farther from home. She found the act of walking, of simply moving, curative, and she covered a great distance before the sun began its descent. In the late afternoon, she turned toward the dunes and began to explore them.

Just before nightfall, she came to the base of a dune so tall, she could not see the top from where she stood. She realized then that the challenge its ascent presented is what she had been looking for. Before beginning, she sat down and had some dinner to rebuild her strength; as darkness came, she started up the slope. The stars were resilient that night in their beauty, and she felt as though she were climbing toward them. The wind was mercifully cool.

As she drew close to the top, she could feel beneath her that the sand was giving way to rock, and when she crested the peak the moon was visible, hanging low in the sky, having been blocked from her view all evening. In its pale light, she made out that she stood on the edge of a kind of ridge that snaked like a path to the east. She followed this path, and soon there was no sign of sand or sound of the ocean in the distance. Mountain ranges lay on either side.

As she traveled through this strange place, she heard from up ahead a noise not unlike a woman sobbing. The sound grew to near-deafening proportions. Then Anna came to an obstruction in the middle of her path: a giant boulder with a strange growth—some kind of long stringy moss, like hair, covering the top of it. The mournful vibration seemed to originate from within this huge formation. She stepped forward and placed her hand upon it, and when she did, she realized it was not a rock at all.

Stepping quickly backward, she saw two cracks form in the mass and open wide. She soon recognized they were eyes. What she had mistaken for a boulder was in actuality the head of a giant. Anna froze with fear, remembering her imprisonment in the birdcage. The giant, a female, looked up and saw her standing upon the path. The sobbing ceased abruptly.

"Hello," said the giant, pulling herself up to rest on her elbows. She wiped the tears from her eyes.

"I'm sorry to have awakened you," said Anna, hoping she would not be eaten.

A simple conversation ensued, and Anna soon learned she had nothing to fear, for this was the giant Ybila, and the path she had been traveling was the famed Dog Spine.

"Why are you unhappy?" asked Anna. "I have heard you are a great singer."

"True," said the giant. "But I want desperately to escape this prison."

"You can't leave?"

"My husband, the magician Mar-el-mar, is a jealous man and has put a spell on me so that I cannot descend from this remote ridge. If anyone wants to see me perform, they must travel up the impossibly steep cliffs. He says he does not want me mingling freely with other giants because he does not trust me, but I know the truth."

"What's that?" asked Anna.

"The art of my song is more perfect than that of his magic. He's jealous, all right."

"Isn't there anything you can do?"

Here, Ybila gathered herself up into a sitting position, her legs crossed in front of her. She leaned low over Anna and whispered, "I have a plan. A traveling salesman found his way here one day when Mar-el-mar was down in the world creating mischief. This giant was selling magic beans that when planted, sprout stalks that reach into the clouds where the giant giants live. Of course, my husband left me no money, but I used something else to pay for them. There is a type of royal blue thread found here and there floating willy-nilly atop the oceans of the world. It is highly prized, for it is said to give good luck in any enterprise. I had been given three very long strands of it by the human pirate captain of the junk, *Jade Bloom*. He was so entranced by my voice when he traveled here to listen that he made a gift of them in admiration. These I traded to the salesman. At first he was reluctant to take them, but then he said he had considered a foray into the world of men, and each of the three strands of blue thread might stand for one each of the items he wished to acquire there. The deal was made."

"Have you planted the beans?"

"Yes, but they take years to germinate. Then overnight they will shoot up suddenly into the clouds. All in a night. Mar-el-mar has blocked me from descending, but I, as is only right considering my voice, will ascend."

"I've heard a recording of you," said Anna.

"So then you know."

Anna nodded.

Ybila took a deep breath and sang her signature song, "What Is My Name?" Anna lay back on the ground, staring at the stars, and listened. The power of the giant's voice, the power of the meaning of the lyrics moved around Anna like a strong breeze. Before the first stanza was finished, she was floating above the ground on a cushion of air. She flew back along the Dog Spine to the crest of the enormous dune, and then descended like a feather. As the last phrase ended, she was set gently down at the base, asleep, the ocean sounding in the distance.

On her journey back along the shore to her home the next day, she wondered if her meeting with Ybila had been real or merely a dream brought on by the exhaustion of attempting to climb the huge sand hill, for she had brief flashes of memory in which she would climb a few feet and then slide back to the base due to the drastic attitude of the slope. Her memory of the giant singer's sorrow was much more real, though, and she found she could easily banish any doubts of the journey by merely humming the tune she had heard.

In the evening of the day on which Anna accidentally knocked the mirror off the wall and cracked it, she met herself picking berries in the woods. A miasmatic phantom of exactly *her* met her beside the blackberry bramble. She bowed to herself as a tentative greeting, and she bowed back. The phantom did not speak, but could understand her words. She invited herself back to the shack, where she made a splendid dinner of eel in blackberry sauce. She and herself drank from the keg of grog. They wound up the music box and waltzed to its plinking crystal tune of "The Last Time I Saw Paris" as the tiny dancer at the contraption's center tirelessly pirouetted. When the creepers ceased their chorus, the two retired to the single bed. The next morning, well before sunrise, when even high summer is cool, the phantom departed, traveling a path that was the light of the moon, out across the ocean and back to her apartment in the city.

Years more passed in the small house by the ocean. No need to tell of her startling revelations concerning the metaphorical nature of humans in relation to the citizens of Giant Land or her study of the natural history of the dune rat, the sea gull, the feral dogs that came for scraps to her back door on autumn evenings. It is, of course, indecorous even to mention the petrified log, fallen among the willows, with one perfectly formed nub of a branch severed close to the trunk, that she rode now and then for self-gratification. The scarring caused by her nails against this old log while she moved in the throes of passion, over time, etched a face in the smooth, gray wood—a bearded visage—and eventually she came to realize that it belonged to the necromancer, Mar-el-mar.

From the moment that she recognized the giant magician, he was ever in her thoughts. His enormous black robe flapped like the wings of a bat as he flitted from one end of her mind to another. She could find no peace from him, and she knew he meant to put a spell on her. Every time she tried to conceive of a plan to rid herself of him, his presence was there, in that part of her mind where the plan was being shaped, and he'd step on the spark of an idea and put it out.

One night while sitting in her parlor, the magician's voice boomed from her fireplace.

"Anna," he said.

"Leave me alone," she told him.

"Anna, I want to bring you to life."

"Why?"

"I have journeyed so long in the hold of your imagination, my head encased in a crystal globe, I need to be free."

"And how will bringing me to life make this so?" she asked.

"It is impossible to explain, but a long, intricate series of events will follow your birth and after a century or two they lead to my being released."

"I *am* alive," she said.

"Tomorrow," said the voice, "you will find a small box in your beachcombing. It will be covered in mother-of-pearl. If you open it, you will find yourself back in your car on the interstate, heading home."

"This *is* my home," she said.

"Someone waits for you there," said Mar-el-mar. Then his voice went silent, and, soon after, she noticed him in her head, circling like a bat.

As the magician predicted, she found the box with the mother-of-pearl facade. She brought it home and laid it on the table in the parlor while all the time he whispered from inside her ear to open it. She was tempted, first in order to remember the past, and secondly to put his persistent presence to rest, but she managed to stay away from it. Days passed, and it became more and more difficult for her to resist the urge to open the box. She knew he was slowly gaining control over her and would eventually have his way.

Then, a week later, the drowned captain's pocket watch that hung by its chain from the mantle in her tiny parlor, suddenly began to tick, and she knew, not in her head where Mar-el-mar could smother the notion, but in her heart, that something remarkable might happen. In her fishing that morning, she had no luck. Cast after cast was reeled in with an empty hook. On her last attempt, she did not bring in a fish, but knotted about the end of the hook was a length of the royal blue thread. She did not think about it, but picked it off, rolled it into a little pill, and swallowed it.

As soon as the blue thread was inside her, Mar-el-mar realized what she had done, but it was too late, for the single shred of lucky blue material made its way to her imagination and bound him like a fly in a spider's web.

All her thoughts circled in a slow, gray twister behind her eyes as she set fire to the shack. With what energy she had left, she stumbled down to the ocean and waded out into the deep water. The waves rose over her and she drowned easily, without fear, like going to sleep. Her body sailed the currents of the Gulf Stream for years, her features more perfectly preserved than those of The Lady of

Fashion. Of course, at one point, she was swallowed whole by a whale, and traveled in its gut for decades before being released when the creature finally died within the radius of the Arctic Circle. There was a season on an iceberg, a weeklong beaching on a crab-infested atoll, the brief embrace of a kraken. And smooth sailing from pole to pole, tropic to sea to bay and back, while Mar-el-mar, eyes rolled upward, watched from his crystal prison at the bottom of the world.

She was discovered, floating off the southern shore of the Woven Islands, by pirates of the junk, *Jade Bloom*. They sold her for a small fortune in malachite to a giant who placed her in a glass box on a bed of dried violet petals. Since it was the most beautiful thing he owned, he would open the box at night and pray over it before turning in. He believed the odd curio brought him luck, and he told the other giants her name was *Mother Paradise*. In later years, when the crops of Giant Land failed in spring, as a kind of sacrifice and plea to her spirit, he cut off her ring finger, leaving the beautiful ruby intact, placed the jeweled digit in one of the small brown bottles that had held his heart medication, along with a note that read *HELP!*, sealed the top with wax, and set it adrift on the ocean.

Giant Land

Story Notes

Alex Irvine, author of the novels A Scattering of Jades *and* One King, One Soldier, *got the independent-press publishing bug a while back, and he and his friend Thom Davidsohn, an illustrator, decided to put out their own anthology—*The Journal of Pulse-Pounding Narratives. *He asked me to send him something for the first volume, and I said I would, but when the deadline drew near, I had nothing. He told me he would be extending the deadline and that I should still send him something. I couldn't come up with a full-fledged story, so instead I wrote him a one-page story that was all just one grammatically correct sentence, titled "Spicy Detective #3," in keeping with the pulpy concept of the book. The day after I sent him that story, I got an e-mail in which Alex told me that he and Thom liked it, and as they knew I really didn't have anything to do, I should write them a few more. So I did, writing one a day (for a total of four more) after my regular work and sending it off to him in an e-mail each night. They were all in the same format as the first, only after the second one I could no longer vouch for the correctness of the grammar. They each dealt with a different pulp genre—Horror, Westerns, Science Fiction, etc. The anthology, once published, looked great. Thom had done these beautiful black-and-white illustrations for it. If you happen to come by a copy of it, check out Leslie What's "Grease and Sex at the King of Chicken," one of the funniest stories I've read. In fact there's a bunch of really fine fiction in it. The first installment of JPPN sold out and Alex and Thom decided to do a second one. They asked me for another story, and this time I felt I really had to come up with a story, because although some people dug the one-page, one-sentence stories, I'd seen some feedback on them and they had a unique effect of really pissing a lot of readers off. So I wrote a story and sent it to Alex, and then waited for* *volume two to come out—and waited, and waited, and waited. I think it's been like four fucking years since then. I hear that JPPN #2 is really coming out next month (from this writing), and if it does, I'm going to be disappointed, because its inability to materialize was such a great opportunity to bust Irvine's stones whenever I'd see him.*

The story of mine he's been sitting on like a hen all of these years, "Giant Land," had been one that I started writing about fifteen years ago. Over that period, I'd take it out every now and then and fiddle around with it. I remember how I came by it originally. I was in one of those slumps where I just smoke butts and stare at the blank screen. So one night I decided to write anything that came into my head, and the beginnings of the story slowly crawled out onto the screen. It's interesting that one aspect of the story is about the passage of time, that it took so long to write, and that it took so long to be published after it was sold. Things move slowly in Giant Land, but when they actually happen, watch out. Unlike his sizeable fiction output, as a publisher, Irvine works slowly, like the San Andreas Fault. I have faith the anthology will eventually appear and predict it will be great.

Coffins on the River

BARNEY AND I ARE GETTING LONG IN THE TOOTH. We've got bad knees, bad backs, bad eyes, and bad breath. We've got wives and kids and mortgages and car loans, and if that isn't enough to elicit your sympathy, we're both artists of a sort.

Barney's a painter, self-taught over decades. He turns out some very fine landscapes of his local area in deep South Jersey along the Delaware River, where the neighbors still eat muskrat and late June brings so many green flies that yawning becomes a repast, itself. He makes most of his income on scenes of meadows and giant oaks, white heron skimming along the estuaries in violet twilight, but his heart is really in his more expressionistic work—for instance, his series, *Coffins on the River*.

The theme plays itself out in a hundred canvases that show super heroes laid to rest in pine boxes. The viewer sees them from above as they glide in the flow—dark, turbulent waters churning to either side, occasionally a fish breaking the surface in an arc, a bit of the bank, a beer bottle on its way to the ocean. The coffins are missing their lids, and the fallen heroes are sometimes wrapped in colorful capes like winding sheets, or donned in spandex uniforms displaying chest emblems of, say, an hourglass, a vibrator, a thimble . . .

They are no super heroes you might know, but ones solely from the planets of his imagination, with powers never tested as they were created to lie in state. He has a little notebook with their names—Qua Num, The Ineffable, Biscuit Boy, Six Figures—a brief list of their powers, and how they met their respective ends. One carries a little doll by the neck, one, a ray gun, one, a cell phone, and all of their faces are like beautiful landscapes of frozen anguish or melted wonder.

Most people didn't grok *Coffins*, but nothing could stop him from making more of them. When he couldn't afford canvas, he used the sides of refrigerator boxes, pieces of discarded plywood, half a ping-pong table, panes of glass. At times, he was jazzed on them, at times he was depressed by them, and when he had done the last of them he told me, "They are their own worst enemies."

Whereas Barney might measure his life in brush strokes, I had pecked mine away at a keyboard, writing fiction of a speculative nature. My most recent novel, which you might have seen last year, was called *Deluge*, wherein the Earth is struck by a cosmic gamma ray from a relatively nearby exploding star, and pieces of reality are changed through a partial disturbance of the inherent nature of matter.

A great deluge sweeps the Earth, and a particular hundred-year-old apartment building made of wood cracks off its foundation in the onslaught of catastrophic flooding and is swept away containing its inhabitants. They sail the newly made world in the bobbing structure, searching for dry land and other survivors. Perno Shell, a previously quiet, bookish man, becomes the captain of the odd vessel and takes upon himself the task of bringing all of his neighbors to safety. The seas teem with mutated monsters, barges of blind pirates returned from the dead, sentient islands, as the unlikely adventurers search for the secret of how, through the manipulation of Time, to remake the world in its previous image.

It tanked like a lead doughnut. For all my hard work and sterling reviews, only two hundred people bought copies, and I got notice from my agent and publisher that I was on thin ice. That same day, at the bookstore, I found a tall stack of *Deluge* on the three-dollar bargain table—a Babel that reached to the bottom of my chin. For a moment, I rested my head atop it while standing upright.

Rough times for true artists, but Barney and I, we had a little ace in the hole. As old and cranky and screwed up as we were, we still puffed the weed from time to time whenever we needed to get the back legs of that creative beast twitching again. We were old potheads, warhorses from way back, who had thoroughly traversed the highways and byways of the world of weed. We were as familiar with the filthy, light headache engendered by a bolus toke of Coney Island Green as we were with the subtle, slowly dawning revelations of Thai Stick, the suped up crap chronic of the latter years of the twentieth century, the illusive but hallucinatory magic of high altitude, Northern California Red Hair. We'd smoked it out of bongs, pipes, cored apples, beer cans, power hitters, skins, and one-toke smokeless spy jobs.

Now, save your lectures about bad health and moral turpitude. Save your religion for the faint of heart and your jurisprudence for hardened criminals. You'll get no argument from us that a steady diet of rope is going to brutally eat your brain and turn your soul to mist. We know guys who are zombified from decades of waking and baking—the blank stare, the sighs, the drool. We've been through it, gone in one end of that joint, come out the other as nothing but smoke, and then had to reconstitute the corporeality of our lives.

On the other hand, when you're a true artist, there's nothing that will goose the muse like a strategic hit or two. All it takes sometimes is half a bone to crack the alabaster vault, and then the treasure comes spilling out—handfuls of vision, truckloads of inspiration. Do I wish it didn't have to be that way? Sure. I want to be wealthy and good looking too, but when the reservoir has gone dry, you'll do anything to get back in Athena's good graces. Why do you think so many artists cash in early, taking the gas pipe or swinging from the end of a rope?

Anyway, once every couple of months I'd drive south to Barney's home and visit with him in the studio out back, past the magnolia that hides the outhouse and just before that wall of cattails throughout which runs a swampy maze of a path that eventually leads to the estuary. We sit out there at night, in the glow of a storm lantern, amidst the thick, hair-raising scent of turpentine and oil paint, have a few beers, smoke a number, and bullshit for a while. We've known each other since college days, so there's always a lot to talk over— old times, how brilliant and ball-busting our kids are, how fed up our wives are with us, who's in the hospital, and who's in the ground. Not until we'd smoke up would we talk about the work, the glimmers of notions. Then the conversation would increase in speed and intensity and the ideas would fly like bats at sundown, like phone calls from our creditors.

We worked that pot jump-start for years, throughout our thirties and well into our forties, and it always served its purpose. Then, last November, after Barney had capped the paint on *Coffins on the River* and was searching around unsuccessfully for a new direction, and I had to come up with a blockbuster to follow *Deluge* and save my ass from the midlist chopping block, we met and puffed the weed. We were both empty as dried gourds and were hoping to bust things open and get back to work as quickly as possible, but when we left the studio that night, we were the same blank slates as when we had entered. We lit up, we smoked, and then we just sat there with nothing to say. My head was filled with fog, and Barney said, "Christ, if I strain any harder for an idea, I'm likely to crap myself."

So there it was. I went home and stewed for another week, smoking butts and staring at an empty computer screen. Then I called Barney. The phone was busy, because as it turns out, he was calling me. When we finally connected, we decided not to wait another month, but this time to get the good stuff and give it another go. Back I drove to South Jersey, over an hour trip. When I arrived, we hung out in his kitchen for a while, talking to his wife and little girl, but with the first lull in the conversation, we excused ourselves and repaired to the studio.

We couldn't light up right away, because we had to wait for Stick, our connection. He was also a painter, a young guy, incredibly talented *and* prolific. He did these brightly colored portraits— the hues of the flesh the most outlandish shades of violet and green and yellow, awe inspiring, two-hair brush, minute detail, and three-dimensional to boot. At his art shows, he laid out a dozen pairs of these spectacles, and when you put them on and turned to the work, those leering party heads looked like they were floating in midair with all the weight and mass of holiday hams. The kid had more talent than both of us ever had, and when we'd mention being stuck or burnt out, he'd laugh at us and call us old men.

His contempt was mitigated, though, by the fact that Barney and I knew a lot of stuff and didn't mind talking about it. If anything, over the years, we had become consummate gasbags. We had read widely and had eclectic tastes. Like my wife often said, "You've read all of Jules Verne, but you can't fix the fucking sink." And it was true. But Stick liked the conversation, so sometimes he hung out with us and just listened.

In addition to this kid being a great painter, he was also a can-do kind of guy. He could fix the sink, score the best weed in three states, work on a car, and play a mean bass. Somebody stole the stereo system out of his truck. He went to the local police, but when he could see they didn't care and told him to forget it, he bought a handgun and hunted the guy down. By canvassing local bars, buying a few drinks for seedy characters, he got a line on who the culprit might be. He traced the guy to an abandoned factory out in Shell Pile, found his stereo components and the thief, made a citizen's arrest, and turned the guy over to the police.

Out in the studio, Barney moved a couple of *Coffins on the River* so we could get to our chairs. I set the beer down between us and lit a cigarette. There was no heat in the studio and the autumn wind came in through a hole in the window, keeping the room cool, and whining as it squeezed through the jagged opening. From outside we could hear the fallen leaves rolling across the field next to his house. We sat there surrounded by dead heroes and he told me that: his cat had cat AIDS, a bar in town had become a meeting place for the Klan, his porch roof was in danger of collapsing, a young girl who went to his daughter's school had been abducted, his wife needed expensive dental work, a guy down the street had lit his own house on fire, he hadn't sold a painting in weeks. I let him vent, knowing that when the work wasn't flowing, the world in general was a uniquely frightening place.

Stick popped his shaved head in the door just when I'd had about enough of Barney's list of grievances. As always, the kid had the weed. Barney handed over his half of the cash and I did the same. A minute didn't pass before my old friend was rolling a fat number. He licked it, sealed it, and then held that blunt, white mummy up for inspection. I made like the Pope and shot a two-fingered sign of the cross at it. Stick found a chair and I handed him a beer while Barney fired up.

Barney had a weak right eye, and whenever he smoked, that eye would close and he'd squint on one side like Popeye. He tapped the ashes onto his jeans and rubbed them in a circle, exhaled, took another deep one, and then passed it on. The weed made the rounds, we drank, and I told Stick his portraits reminded me of the portrait of beef that Soutine had painted.

"Who's Soutine?" he asked.

"French painter, originally from Lithuania, early twentieth century, Paris. He did this painting, I guess it would be a still life, of a side of beef. He went out to the stockyard, bought a side of beef, and hung it up in his apartment."

"I like the sound of that," said Stick.

Barney took another hit and jumped in, "Soutine had a friend who worked for the department of health, and the guy would come around to his place every few days and inject the meat with something, probably formaldehyde, to keep it from rotting. It took him weeks to paint that beef."

"Must've stunk like hell by the time he was done," I said.

"I saw that painting somewhere," said Barney, "and all I remember is translucent pink and blue."

Stick put his beer down and took a pad and pen from the inside pocket of his leather jacket. "I gotta give that a try," he said, writing.

"Sure," said Barney, "you don't need a whole side of beef. Just get yourself like a London broil or something and string it up with fishing line."

"I was thinking along the lines of poultry. Maybe a twenty-pound butterball," said Stick.

"Absolutely," I said.

"In 3-D," said Stick.

"Why the fuck not?" I said.

"Make it a series," said Barney. *"Meat on the River."*

By the time the night had drawn to a close, Stick had three pages of ideas, and Barney and I were sitting there holding our own, still uninspired.

"What's next, trepanning?" said Barney.

"I had a couple of ideas that crawled out of the muck and fainted from embarrassment," I said.

"Well," said Stick, "you guys are dicking around with this pot. You need something more cosmic. You need to get in touch with your totem spirits and so forth."

"What are you talking?" asked Barney. "Meth, ecstasy, acid?"

"Last time I did LSD," I said, "about twenty years ago, an ambulance pulled up outside of my apartment, Saint Francis of Assisi got out, knocked on the front door, and handed me a slip of paper. On it was written the word *OVERDOSE.*"

"Yeah," said Barney, "we've got kids, we can't be tripping."

"No, no, no," said Stick, shaking his head. "Have you ever heard of ayahuasca? I'm telling you, one session with this stuff and you'll be good to go for a couple of years."

"Tell me more," said Barney.

"You see the quality and output I have?" he asked. "Pot's okay for watching television with the sound off and the stereo on or talking to you guys, but if you want to get in touch with the cosmic energy, you gotta have the Amazon jungle juice."

"Dangerous?" I asked.

"Don't worry, I'll watch out for you guys."

"What are the side effects?" asked Barney.

"A little dizziness, maybe some nausea, diarrhea."

"Sounds like a normal day," said Barney.

We asked for more details, but Stick said he had to be going. He jotted down the titles of a couple of books on a piece of notepad paper and then copied them again. He handed each of us a list and said, "Read these books, especially the first one, and then let me know if you want to take a shot at it. I swear, you'll see a story in every fallen leaf. Images'll tap your back and give you a phone number."

The next morning at home, sitting at the computer was like a restaurant with bad service. I looked out the window and watched those last few autumn leaves fall. Stick's promise came back to me: *a story in every fallen leaf.* Life was no longer whispering its secrets to me, and I was turning my back on it. My wife wanted to visit some friends, but I couldn't possibly get up the energy to be social. My sons wanted me to throw the football, take them to a movie, but I dared not stray from the office in case some trifle flitted across the desert of my imagination. I was a prisoner in that bleak November.

I drove to the local bookstore in search of the books on the scrap of notepad paper, still in my pocket from the night before. What were the chances Barnes & Noble would be carrying Stick's greatest hits of screwball drug writing? To my amazement they had one of the two volumes. The book he pointed to as being the most important, *The Cosmic Serpent,* by one Jeremy Narby, I was able to purchase. The second was by a fellow named Terrence McKenna.

When I got home, I made a pot of coffee, and then taking a cup, sat in my corner of the living room couch with *The Cosmic Serpent.* Just from the cover, it looked like some kind of New Age dither— *Cosmic, dude.* Nothing ventured, nothing gained, though, so I cracked the back and started reading. From the very first page, I was into it. My concentration had been like a leaf on the wind for the past few months, but even when the kids came in, played Eminem at top volume and wrestled with the dog, I didn't look up.

Narby's book tells about his experiences in the Peruvian Amazon region of Quirishari, in the Pichis Valley, among the Ashaninca people. While doing field work for his dissertation on the distribution of plant species—an attempt to stave off corporate developers and their desire to clear cut and "manage" the treasures of the jungle—he met local shamans, *ayahuasqueros* as they are called, who had an incredible grasp of the biochemistry of the local plant life and how it could be used in creating effective medicines. Narby was astonished at the knowledge these adepts had garnered about the abundant and diverse species of plants indigenous to the region.

When Narby asked one how the Ashaninca had learned so much from the jungle, the shaman answered that the knowledge was revealed from the plants themselves. In other words, Nature itself had told them. He dismissed this at first, thinking it was mere mythology, but the ayahuasqueros insisted that they were not speaking metaphorically. They offered to show him, but he would have to ingest ayahuasca.

In taking the drug, his hallucinations showed him images of entwined snakes and other odd creatures and designs that he later realized were very reminiscent of the figures found in biochemistry. One image that often repeated was the double helix of DNA—the substance responsible for all life on Earth. It came to him later that perhaps the drug was able to unlock the information stored in DNA.

Usually I am fascinated with ideas like this because they make interesting fodder for my fictions, but I didn't fall off the turnip truck yesterday and have developed a healthy skepticism about outlandish claims. Narby's argument for the Ashaninca shamans learning cures directly from the forest spirit convinced me, though, when he detailed the biochemical properties of ayahuasca itself. The drug is formed from two different plants, one a vine, the other a bush. Only one carries a hallucinogenic substance, a chemical that is also secreted under certain circumstances by the brain. It has no effect when ingested because existing chemicals in the stomach neutralize it. The other plant contains no hallucinogen but merely an enzyme that blocks the chemical in the stomach from rendering the hallucinogen ineffective. The odds that someone would be able to stumble upon this particular chemical reaction, out of 80,000 possible species of plants, is nearly impossible, not to mention all the hundreds of other intricate chemical combinations and cures the shamans were privy to. In short, ayahuasca put you in touch with, essentially, the *mind* of life.

"Crazy shit," said Barney when I spoke to him on the phone the next day. He'd read *The Cosmic Serpent* as well.

"Are we going to tap that DNA?" I asked.

"I'm going for it," he said. "After I finished reading the book the other day, I was heading out to the studio to sit there like a wooden Indian for an hour or so, and what did I see over by the outhouse but a snake. This long, multicolored job, winding through the leaves. What's the chances of seeing a snake in November?"

"It's your Lady of Fatima," I told him.

He'd already set up a date with Stick to take the ayahuasca. "Stick said eat a lot of bananas to keep your serotonin level up and no heavy stuff like meat or sweets for a couple days before. No sex for the same amount of time."

"Sounds doable," I said.

"You're a damn shaman," said Barney.

A week later, we were in Stick's truck, sitting three across in the cab. We headed out toward Money Island, a spit of land that juts into the Delaware at the farthest southern point on the west side of Jersey. Sometimes it's a peninsula and sometimes an island, but there's a little bridge that keeps it connected to the mainland. All the houses there are on stilts.

"No Ugly American stuff," said Stick. "This guy's a real ayahuas-quero."

"We're PC," said Barney.

"But what's he doing in Jersey?" I asked.

"He's on the run," said Stick.

"From?"

"He did some rabble-rousing against a couple of the companies raping the jungle down there."

We pulled up in front of a weathered gray shack on legs just as the sun was going down. The place had a boarded window and was listing forward slightly. It was at the end of a dirt road, all by itself. Behind it was a wall of reeds, and behind that the river. The temperature had dropped and it was really cold, but not enough to subdue the smell of low tide.

Stick led the way up the rickety steps and knocked on the door. As we waited for the shaman to answer, I started to have misgivings about this enterprise. I thought of my wife, Lynn, and my kids and got the urge to bolt back to the car. Barney, who was behind me on the steps, leaned in and whispered, "Did you really eat the bananas?" Just then the door opened.

The next thing I knew, we were inside and Stick was introduc-ing us in Spanish to this little brown fellow, Rosario. He had a lot of wild black hair and a big smile—perfectly white teeth. I put out my hand and he shook it, and although he had a small frame I could feel real power in his grip. He was dressed in a blue-and-red-striped dress shirt with the sleeves cut off and a pair of green polyester bell-bottoms, with sandals on his feet.

Barney shook hands with Rosario, and he and I stood there smil-ing and nodding, bowing as if we were meeting the emperor of Japan. We moved away from the front door to a living room with doctor's waiting-room furniture, a lot of mod vinyl. Barney and I took the couch, Stick sat in a chair, and Rosario fell, playfully, into a big, pink beanbag thing on the floor. He cocked his head to the side, a look of seriousness set in, and he started talking, making gestures with his hands.

Stick wasn't exactly Ricardo Montalban, but he translated as best he could. Still, he was able to relay that Rosario was welcoming us, that he was pleased to meet two artists, a painter and a writer, from the U.S. We did some more nodding and smiling and thanked him. The détente and pleasantries continued for a while, and then he told us that the *maninkari*, the spirits, had told him we would be coming. He said he had been instructed to administer the ayahuasca to us.

I asked him why, and when Stick translated, Rosario laughed and responded, "We'll see," in perfect English. When I looked over at him, he was lighting what looked like a big fat joint. It and the lighter seemed to have materialized out of thin air. He took a hit and launched into a monologue in Spanish.

Stick said, "This is real tobacco, not the poison of American cigarettes. Jungle tobacco. It will draw the spirits close to us, so that when we take the ayahuasca, they'll be present. Spirits feast on tobacco. Once they've gathered, the drug will focus your senses so that you might see and talk with them."

The jungle cigarette made the rounds, and it was strong. Barney, who didn't smoke cigarettes coughed like an old man. I wasn't unhappy when it was finally stubbed out in an ashtray on the table next to Stick's chair. The shaman then rose, and asking our friend to accompany him, left the room.

"If a cigarette smoked cigarettes, *that's* the cigarette it would smoke," said Barney.

"I'm on the verge of puking," I whispered.

"Are the spirits around us now?" he said, glancing briefly over his shoulder.

"You didn't eat the bananas."

"Fuck the bananas," he said. "I ate McDonald's only about two hours ago."

"I'm ready to bag this whole thing," I said.

I heard the floorboards creak then and knew Rosario and Stick were returning. The shaman was carrying a two-liter Pepsi bottle half-filled with a reddish brown liquid, and in his other hand what looked like a dried out sweet potato with holes in it. Stick carried three gas station giveaway glasses with scenes from *Star Wars* on them. He had promised that he wouldn't take the drug so he could keep an eye on us. Barney was specifically afraid of getting up on the roof and jumping off, trying to fly. He had mentioned it about a dozen times in the truck on the way over.

Rosario carefully poured juice into each of the glasses. He lifted his off the table and brought it up near his mouth. "May the force be with you," he said.

I held my breath and chugged the ayahuasca. It was horrible. Before I could even reach over and put the glass on the table, I could hear my stomach saying, *Wrong.*

Barney gagged once and then managed to get the rest down. Rosario drank his like it was chocolate milk. We didn't have time to say anything stupid, because Rosario started singing. His song sounded like gibberish, but his lone voice and the honesty with which he sang was immediately fascinating to me. I sat back, closed my eyes, and followed the permutations of the tune.

After a short time I became aware of a rush of images presenting themselves behind my eyes, like a slide show on fast forward: my vision of the character, Perno Shell, from *Deluge*, standing on the roof of the floating apartment building, staring through a spyglass at the horizon; my older son, shooting baskets; the computer in my empty office; a small, dilapidated ranch house, the color pink of Rosario's beanbag chair, nestled like a cottage out of *Hansel and Gretel* at the edge of a forest; Soutine's side of beef; my father teaching me to drive; my dog, Shadow, laying in a sunspot on the living room floor; my wife, fixing the kitchen sink.

Rosario's song turned into musical notes, and I opened my eyes to see how he was accomplishing this. He was blowing into one end of that crusty sweet potato and fingering the holes as if it was a recorder. Tracks of bright colors shot across my field of vision, and then a golden rain fell out of the ceiling. The song he was playing somehow turned into the flute solo from Eric Burden's "Spill the Wine."

"I know that one," I said, and laughed. Then I asked, "Where's the bathroom?" I knew I was going to puke. It's not that I felt particularly bad. In fact, I was buzzing throughout my body, but I just knew I had to puke.

Rosario said, "Follow the butterfly," and opened his hand to release a phosphorescent specimen as big as a small bird. The creature languidly flapped its wings, heading down the hallway to our left. I followed it. As I passed Stick, I saw that his face had taken on the characteristics of one of his paintings, super detailed with a complexion of violet and yellow.

I found the bathroom and puked; no big deal—the easiest puke I ever did. When I stood up, though, I got a rush, and the distant notes of Rosario's music started to sound like birdcalls. I stepped out of the bathroom into what had been the hallway only to discover that I was now in the jungle. I found this amusing instead of frightening. It was dark green (even the light) and extremely warm, trees everywhere and resplendent undergrowth of ferns and vines. Above, in the canopy, birds called out and monkeys screeched.

I started walking, heading in the direction I thought the living room was in. Before going too far, I came upon a tattered object hanging by a string from the branch of a small tree. Oddly enough, the tree was a dogwood, like the one I have in my backyard. The object was a kind of talisman I remembered having read about: a god's-eye. It is made of woven yarn and sticks, often having concentric color patterns in the form of rural hex signs, meant to ward off evil. I thought of taking this one down and carrying it off, but something told me not to touch it.

I realized I was on a path, and that path came to a turn that led into a small clearing where the jungle floor had been swept clean. There was a desk and chair and a lab table with test tubes, beakers, and a microscope on it. In the blink of an eye, there suddenly appeared, standing next to the desk, a luminous being with the head of a crow and whose arms were writhing snakes. It had a woman's body that wore a simple black dress, white sneakers, and a lab coat.

"You are the spirit of the forest," I said. I could feel myself start to sweat, her sudden appearance worrying me, as if she could see through to my empty center and might kill me for it.

The beak of the glistening crow head opened and a smooth, quiet voice said, "Do you know why you are here?"

"I took the ayahuasca," I said.

"But why are you here?" it said.

"For a story," I said.

"Well," said the creature, "I have a cure for you." She walked over and removed a beaker from the lab table. I could see that the glass cylinder held a jumble of words. Not words on paper, but just the words, as if type in black ink had been lifted off the paper of a book.

"Why don't you come and take the medicine?" she asked.

"I'm afraid," I said.

"Of course," she said. She let loose a deafening bird screech, and with that sound her features melted and reformed and she was a young woman with long brown hair and beautiful brown eyes. "Come now," she said.

I approached her and she handed me the beaker. I put it to my lips and poured the words into my mouth, chewing them and swallowing until the beaker was empty. They were brittle but sharp and tasted bitter.

When I was finished, I said, "And this will help me to write?"

"No," she said, and laughed. "These are your instructions."

"Instructions for what?" I asked as I handed her the beaker.

"To help you see in the dark," she said.

"Why did I think this experience would help me write?" I asked.

"Because your eyes are closed," she said, and her eyes grew wide. She dropped the beaker on the ground where it shattered. "He's coming," she said. With this, she evaporated into mist, her clothes dropping to the ground.

Off in the distance, I heard something moving through the jungle. When it roared, I started running. I ran and ran for what seemed like an hour. The path disappeared and I scrabbled frantically through the undergrowth. When I was out of breath, sweating profusely, my heart pounding, I stopped and slumped down against a fallen log. I coughed, cleared my eyes, and tried to listen for the approach of my pursuer. That's when I saw it, off to my right, the dogwood with the god's-eye hanging from its bare, lowest branch. I had gone in a complete circle.

Someone elbowed me in the ribs. I looked up and found I was in the cab of Stick's truck. Rosario was at the window. He put his hand in through the open window, past Stick, and I shook it. Barney leaned over and also shook his hand. We thanked him and then Stick drove off. All traces of the nausea had passed and I still felt a little high. I had some coffee at Barney's to wake up and then drove home. There was a full moon. I left the window open for a while to get some fresh air. Passing the fields and forests, I thought I heard them murmuring.

After the night out on Money, Barney and I had decided not to talk about the ayahuasca experience for a while. We didn't last a week, though. I called him a few days later on Friday afternoon.

"It was a coffin on the river for me," he said. "Two really little guys, imperious sons of bitches, with heads like blue jays sat perched at either end. I watched the clouds passing overhead as one of them told me, 'The knowledge that is about to be revealed to you is reserved for the dead or dying.' How do you think that made me feel?"

"Did you get sick?" I asked.

"The McDonald's wasn't a winning strategy."

"What was the knowledge?" I asked.

"We wound up on some island and I sat on a stone bench, really uncomfortable. Across from me was a big fat snake on a concrete throne, partially coiled and sitting upright, wearing a crown. It lectured me for a half-hour and then said I could go. I woke up out in the back of the house by the reeds."

"What'd the snake tell you?"

"I couldn't understand what the hell it was saying. It was actually talking English, but it hissed every word. I made out one or two, but . . ."

"Since then," I said, "every time I go near the plants Lynn brought in from the yard for the winter, I hear a vague whispering sound, and I get this recurring image."

He started laughing.

"No shit," I said. "I swear."

"There's a field," he said. "About a hundred yards in is the edge of a forest."

"A house," I said.

"Ranch style, pink," he said. "It's right at the tree line and two huge oaks kind of arch above it."

"Yeah," I said.

"Kind of disappointing after all that rigmarole with the ayahuasca."

"I haven't written a damn word. And I can't for the life of me figure out why I ever thought tapping into my DNA was going to help that."

"Well, I'm going to paint that pink house. I figure, I see it enough, I might as well paint it. You should write a story called 'The Pink House.' "

"Who do you think lives there?"

"Richard Burton and Liz Taylor."

I got as far as, *The Taylors lived at the edge of the forest in a pink house*, and then turned the computer off. I left my office with no desire to return. In the next two days, I walked both in the morning and at night, long wanderings with Shadow. As I went along, the pine trees put thoughts in my head that I heard as words. They told me to shave and lose weight. They ridiculed my attire. I paid the bills. I helped my younger son memorize the state capitals. I made a meatloaf. I sat with Lynn on the couch; we drank coffee and talked. When no one was home, I played the Ink Spots on the stereo, "The Trees Don't Need To Know," as I stood by the front window where the plants were gathered and daydreamed that place across the field. I had achieved a certain peace with my blankness.

Thanksgiving came and went, and I was surprised I enjoyed it so much. The weather turned bitter cold and it snowed lightly one night at the end of the month. Life was but a dream, all domestic harmony, the promise of Christmas, soft music, and fires in the fireplace. The hours came and went and I thought nothing of them. Then, one night I was in the kitchen, cooking dinner, and the phone rang.

"I found the pink house," said Barney.

"Bull," I said.

"I was sitting in the studio today, and I decided to get up and go out. So I hopped in the car and just started driving around, not really thinking about anything. I let myself get lost on a road out by the State Forest. The road was empty, the sun was shining, I was easing along. Then I saw the field out of the corner of my eye. I turned and there was the house, right at the edge of the tree line."

"Pink?" I asked.

"Pinker than the pink I remembered. You've got to come down and check it out."

"What for?"

"If it's the same one, I'll go up and knock on the door."

"Who do you think's in there?"

"Man, I hope it's not that snake." He proceeded to give me directions and told me to meet him there the next day at noon.

When people who don't know Jersey think of it, they usually envision the refineries in Elisabeth or the casinos in Atlantic City, maybe beleaguered Camden, but if you go far enough south, you get a clear sense as to why it is called the Garden State. Cumberland County is like something out of the Midwest—forests and swamps and acres and acres of farmland. There are long stretches of plenty of nothing in certain areas. The place that Barney led me to was one of them.

The day was clear and cold. He was sitting in his car, pulled over to the side of the road, at the edge of a wide field that had been cut out of the surrounding forest. The minute I laid eyes on the house, I knew it was the one. He got out of his car and stood staring toward the tree line. I got out.

"That's it," he said, smiling, pointing toward the house.

"Too strange," I said.

There was no question we were going to go to the door, so I put my trepidation aside and followed him across the field. A dirt driveway, leading in from the road, ended about fifteen yards from the house, but there was no car in sight. As we approached the structure, I could see it more clearly, no bigger than an oversized trailer, and because of its dilapidated appearance—missing roof shingles, peeling paint, crumbling concrete steps leading to a chipped front door—I said, "There might not be anybody living here now."

"Maybe," said Barney. The place was silent like a possum playing dead, though; like a snake coiled. I knew he could feel it too. Wind moved through the trees that arched above it and their barren branches clicked together.

"It's a tidy little ship," I whispered as he took the three steps to the door.

He knocked loud five times, took a precautionary step back, and then we waited.

Nothing. Just the sound of the wind in the nearby forest. I looked off to the side, in amidst the shadowed trees at the ground covered with oak leaves, the pines swaying. Barney knocked again. We waited. Then he turned his head to the side and said, "I thought I heard something."

"It's just the wind," I said. "The place is empty."

"Come on," he said, and jumped down off the steps. I followed him around the right side of the house. Just off the corner there was an oil tank sitting flush against the wall, like a small, galvanized submarine in port, and beyond that, a window. Barney stepped up to the glass and, cupping his hands around his eyes, peered inside.

"See anything?" I asked, and stepped up next to him.

"No," he said, "it's just a kid's room . . ."

It happened so suddenly, we both jumped back and Barney gave a short yelp. A face had popped up suddenly from beneath the inside sill—a young girl, with large, dark eyes and long hair, no more than six or seven years old. She stared at us, unmoving.

"We're busted," I said. "Let's get out of here."

"No," he said, stepping closer to the face. He leaned toward the window and squinted his bad eye to see better. Turning to me, he said, "That's the kid who got snatched."

"What are you talking about?"

"She's the one who was abducted from her yard."

We looked back at the girl and she had her hands on the glass. Her lips moved. "Help me," she said, and we could very faintly hear her.

I felt the fear start to rise in me.

"We've got to get her out of there," said Barney, who was visibly shaken.

"Are you absolutely certain it's her?"

He started moving around to the back of the house. "Yeah," he said. "She's in Alice's class at school. I know her."

When I caught up to him he was on the back steps, fidgeting with the doorknob, which was obviously locked.

"We've got to do this fast," I said. I took my sweatshirt off and wrapped it around my left hand. "What if whoever kidnapped her is in the house?"

Barney shook his head. "They would have answered the front door, right?"

"Not necessarily," I said, and punched in the pane. Glass shattered onto the kitchen floor. Reaching my arm carefully through the hole I'd made, I undid a deadbolt and chain lock. Seconds later, I had the door open and we were inside. The kitchen was dim with no light but that coming in from the outside where the woods cast the back of the house in shadow. Stained and peeling pink wallpaper with a design of cookie cutters and sinister gingerbread men made the small room absolutely claustrophobic. It stunk like old garbage. There were unwashed plates in the sink, pizza boxes on the table, and what looked like week-old creamed corn in a pot on the stove. I tried to ignore the god's-eye made from yarn and sticks hanging from a nail, beneath a clock with a different type of bird at each hour.

"What's the girl's name?" I asked him as we made our way down a short, dark hallway to the door of the room. There was a deadbolt with a key lock that fit through a hole in the center of the bolt, so whoever had taken her could be assured she wasn't going anywhere.

"Kara, something like that," he said. "Karen or . . . no, Carly."

I stood thinking what to do. I shook my sweatshirt out and put it back on.

"Any second, I'm expecting some *Deliverance* motherfucker to jump out of the woodwork and brain me with a hammer," whispered Barney.

"Tell her we're gonna kick it in," I said.

"Carly, this is Alice's father. You know Alice from your class? We're here to take you home, but we have to kick this door in, so stand back. Don't be afraid. A little noise and then we'll have you out."

"Okay," said a small voice from the other side of the door.

We put our backs against the opposite wall and counted to three in unison. On the first kick, I hurt my knee. On the second, we heard some wood crack. Five kicks later and the frame and molding of the jamb splintered free. The door swung back, and there was the girl, standing by the window, facing us.

Barney entered the room and approached her very calmly. He got down on his haunches in front of her and said, "Do you want us to take you home to your mom and dad?"

"Take me home," she said, putting her arms around his shoulders. She started to cry.

"It's gonna be okay, babe," I said.

"Everything's good now," said Barney, patting her shoulder.

She let go of him and moved back, drying her eyes.

"Ready to go?" he asked her.

She reached up to take his hand, and as their fingers touched, I heard, from out in front, the sound of a car door slamming shut.

She looked up at me, her eyes wide with terror. "He's coming," she said.

Barney lifted her and flung her over his shoulder. I gave him just a second to get by me, and then we were running—across the broken glass of the kitchen, out the back door. Neither of us bothered with the porch steps. We hit the ground and made for the path that led into the woods.

Adrenalin might be more amazing than ayahuasca. It carried my load at top speed about two hundred yards in beneath the trees on the first burst. Gray trunks, brown leaves, leafless bushes whipped by, and the intermittent light cutting through the tangle of bare branches above was dizzying. We finally ducked in behind a huge old tree just off the path. My beloved Marlboro ultra-lights had a tight grip on my lungs, and I was heaving like a hooked tuna. My Achilles tendons were ready to snap and both knees hurt. Barney, who was in somewhat better shape, gasped less but had to put the girl down and arch his back until it made a sound like knuckles popping. We were too scared to talk, but waited, listening.

The girl pulled on my shirt and I looked down at her. "He's got a gun," she whispered.

An insane bellow rose up from the head of the path. "Marta," cried the kidnapper. "Marta."

"Who's Marta?" I asked.

"That's what he calls me," she said.

Barney leaned out around the side of the tree. There came the report of a pistol from very close by followed by a voice. "Come back, please!" he yelled.

If we didn't start running again, I would have pissed my pants right there I was so scared. Barney had the girl by the hand, and we were dashing off the path through fallen leaves, over logs and sticks, around bushes. Stumbling in ruts, branches slapping our faces, we lurched frantically forward. I heard two more gunshots and expected any minute to feel a slug dig into my back.

We stopped again after a good ten minutes of flight, in behind a blind of tangled sticker bushes. Kneeling down, I tried to control my breathing so as not to give us away. Barney and the girl crouched beside me. Only inches from where my hands leaned against the ground was a broken branch, three feet long and the width of a baseball bat. I grabbed hold of it, more to keep myself anchored to reality than anything else.

"Here he comes," whispered Barney.

I looked up through the bush and saw him approaching about sixty yards away, walking slowly, looking side to side. Every so often he'd stop for a moment or two, turn, and then continue directly for us. I tracked him as he passed behind trees, and even at that distance, I could see he was a big guy. He wore a red plaid hunting jacket and a black wool cap. What struck me most was that his face was too large, overly prominent cheekbones and a shelf of a forehead.

"When he gets close enough, I'm going to rush him with the stick and see if I can catch him off guard," I said. "Don't start running until I hit him. Then take off, stay low, and zigzag."

"No, we've gotta keep going" said Barney. "He'll blow your friggin' head off."

"I have a better chance of staying alive against that guy. If I run five more steps, I'm gonna drop over."

"Okay," he said, shaking his head and looking doubtful.

The girl patted my back. I turned, smiled, and put my finger to my lips. She did the same.

I got quietly to my feet, making sure to stay hunched down beneath the top of the blind. Grasping the stick tightly with both hands, I lifted it back over my shoulder.

"Break his fucking skull," whispered Barney, and then we could say no more because the kidnapper was right in front of us, less than ten yards away. That big, ugly face was twisted with a look of anguish, and I noticed tears in his eyes. He stepped closer. "*Marta!*" he screamed. When he turned to look behind him, I bolted out from behind the bushes with nothing on my mind but swinging for the fence. As I moved, I heard Barney and the girl take off. I could smell the cigarettes and whiskey on the guy and brought the stick around. I had his head directly in my sights when I slipped on the leaves and went down like a 280-pound sack of shit at his feet. I lost my wind and the stick fell out of my hands.

I laid there, eyes closed, working to get my breath back, waiting for the gun to go off. Seconds passed, and then a minute, then two, and there was nothing, just the sound of the wind in the trees. When I finally got up enough courage to open my eyes, there was Barney and the girl looking down at me.

"Where's the guy?" said Barney.

"His name is Gerry," said the girl.

I staggered to my feet and looked around in a daze. "I took a fall on the leaves. I thought I was a dead man," I said.

"I didn't hear a gun shot, so we came back."

"Let's get out of here," I said. "If he didn't shoot me by now, he's not going to . . . I hope."

We saw no trace of Gerry on the way back to the house, but we were jumpy as hell, turning with every falling twig, always ready to bolt. Barney asked Carly what more she knew about him, so we could tell the police. She told us he drove a black van and also provided part of the license plate number. "The policeman in school told us to remember the numbers," she said.

The instant our cars came into view up by the road, we took off toward them. There was no sign of the black van. Barney and the girl ran and I hobbled as best I could. He opened the back door of his car and she climbed in on the seat.

"Put the belt on," said Barney.

She did as she was told and then said to us, "I'm tired," and lay down on the seat, closed her eyes. My heart went out to the poor kid; she was brave as hell.

He closed the door. "Follow me," he said. "I'm going to head into town to the police station."

I agreed, got into my car, and we drove off. Finally at rest behind the wheel, I began to feel every ache and pain from our adventure in the woods. The sky had, at some point, grown over-cast. It seemed later than it should have been. I didn't think the whole ordeal at the pink house could have taken more than an hour and a half at the most, but from the look of things it seemed night was now only an hour or so away.

The fact that we had rescued the girl had begun to sink in, and I felt good about it. With all my bruises, my creaking knees, instead of feeling my age, I felt like I was sixteen again and had just finished high school football practice. Then, on Bascomb Road, heading east toward town, I saw Barney turn into the lot of a closed farm market/gas station and park next to a pay phone. I pulled in behind him.

I thought he was going to get out, but he stayed seated in the car. I got out of mine and walked up next to his window.

He rolled the window down but didn't turn to look at me.

"What's the deal?" I said.

"Look in the back seat," he said.

I stepped back and peered in the window. She was gone. I opened the door and leaned down to touch the seat where she had been.

Barney got out of the car as I slammed the back door. He dropped some money into the pay phone and put through an anonymous call to the police. While I stood there listening as he told them what we thought we knew about the girl's abduction, snow started to fall. By the time he hung up it was really coming down.

I lit up and he bummed a cigarette off me. "We've been played," he said.

"What'd the cop say?" I asked.

"He warned me of the penalty of interfering in a police investigation. 'Get a life, buddy,' he said just before he hung up on me."

Three days later, the news reported that, due to the efforts of law enforcement and a nationwide Amber alert, Gerry Gilfoil had been arrested and the girl he had abducted had been rescued. The black van, the plate number, all of it was on the money. The cops caught up with them in Ohio. The girl, Carly, was fine. He hadn't hurt her. He said he was taking her to Disneyland. The reason he'd grabbed her was because his wife had left him and taken their daughter. She was about the same age as Carly and he missed her terribly. It seems he had grown despondent and depressed of late, uncommunicative, and his wife couldn't take it anymore.

Along with the story, there was a photo of the girl being reunited with her family, and beneath that a photo of poor Gerry, his eyes as empty as Carly's were luminous. I carried that image of her abductor around in my mind for weeks, and every morning, in the bathroom mirror, I'd compare my own to it and contemplate his loss. Sometime soon after that story ran, the kitchen sink busted again, and I can't readily describe what a pleasure it actually was to fix it.

The next time I saw Barney was about two months later, the night before New Year's Eve. We sat out in the frozen studio, dressed in coats and gloves, sipping from a bottle of Four Roses. Because of the bitter cold in recent weeks, the paint on some of the *Coffins on the River* series had cracked and fallen off onto the floor in big, bright chips.

"That's a shame," I said, eyeing Biscuit Boy's leprosy.

"What are we gonna do?" he said.

"I know what you mean," I told him. "I found out the other day that my publisher doesn't want to take a chance on another *Deluge*. They're dropping me." I took a taste from the bottle and passed it to him.

"Jeez," was all he could muster. He shook his head and then drank until he grimaced.

I hadn't mentioned our adventure at the pink house since we had parted in the snow that day, but there were a lot of times I had almost called him. "So," I said, "what did you make of that rescue?"

He reached down and lifted a large paint chip off the floor that held Qua Num's chest emblem: a beautifully rendered alarm clock. Spinning it slowly in his hands, he studied it while he spoke. "Life and Art," he said, "are the same thing; one illusion standing in for the other and vice versa. Even if no one is watching, the only happiness is to try to do your best." He dropped the chip and it broke in two.

"Maybe something's always watching," I said.

"Maybe not," he said. Then he pulled a fat joint out of his coat pocket, lit up, took a drag, and passed it over. "Hold those hits," he said, and I did, my head soon growing light. In the silence that followed the last toke, I heard the boards of the studio creak in the cold, and the wind coming in through the window was like the sound of water rushing by. I pictured that old, tired year, climbing into its coffin and pushing off into the flow, leaving the two of us behind to manage as best we could.

Coffins on the River

Story Notes

The central idea of this story was inspired by an amazing book I read by Jeremy Narby called The Cosmic Serpent: DNA and the Origins of Knowledge. *Since its premise is explained in the story, I won't bother to reiterate it here. Whether Narby's concept is close to truth or mere folly, I really don't care. This kind of imaginative speculative science is* The Breakfast of Champions *for writers like me.*

The character of Barney in the story is based on my painter friend (see the afterword for "A Man of Light") who actually created a series of pictures whose theme was coffins on the river. In the coffins were famous dead people, and they were moving along downstream as seen from above. He also did another series of paintings of super heroes of his own invention, basically as I describe them in the story, and so, in my narrative, I switched the super heroes with the famous dead people in the coffins.

Some people who read this story thought of Barney and the narrator as losers, but I don't think they are. In dedicating one's life to an art, there are myriad pitfalls and the possibility of never having your work recognized by the public. Still, there are millions of people who valiantly pursue their dreams long after others have forsaken theirs. To all those who think of art only in terms of success and remuneration, I suppose the two characters in this story would appear losers, but for anyone who keeps their creative dream alive in the face of grave consequences and a hostile populace of zombie-like naysayers, I see them as heroic. Our heroes in this story have traveled deeper and deeper inside themselves to chase that dream as the years have flowed on. Sometimes, in doing this, one can lose contact with the outside world and not realize that it is there that the answers to their questions sometimes lie (in both senses of the word).

I think some readers were put off by this story because it dealt with the use of drugs. Drugs have, from ancient times, starting with the Rig Veda, *been an integral part of fantastic literature—the elixir, the potion, soma, etc. They have always been agents of transcendence. Besides, they exist in the real world. To include drugs in a story does not mean that the writer advocates their use or is promoting them as a viable answer to life's dilemmas, but when they are part of life, they should be expected to appear in fiction sometimes, just as murder is included in the Bible. Remember, there's a reason we call it* fiction.

I took this story to the Sycamore Hill Writers' Conference and received good advice on key elements from some of the other writers in attendance. The story was published by Deb Layne and Jay Lake of Wheatland Press in the third installment of their incredible anthology series, Polyphony.

Summer Afternoon

ENRY JAMES ONCE SAID THAT THE TWO MOST beautiful words in the English language were *Summer Afternoon*, and after he spoke those words they hit the atmosphere and shattered. Pieces of them flew this way and that. Some of each went into the ears of his listener, who heard them and nodded as if in agreement, even though she thought all along they should be *Autumn Night*.

The shards that did not serve a purpose for James and the young Miss Pentrith flew on and later joined up as they left Earth's atmosphere. In space they became a tiny ball of green fizz drawn into the far blackness by the electromagnetic pulse of a quasar.

They made the cosmic pinball rounds at light speed—planets, suns, nebulae—rapping lightly against the door of Heaven, bouncing from moon to star, piercing molten cores and lodging momentarily between the ears of Sufra, Queen of the Harvang. In an ocean of gamma ray, a single seed of meaning germinated and grew into a thought that later had a memory of itself rolling off the spiral tongues of galaxies. Time came and went. On a summer afternoon those words returned to Earth, looking for Henry James.

They looked for a good long time, flitting here and there, miasmatic and ineffable, but they did not think to look under the ground. Finally, in South Jersey, on a screened-in porch, they overheard brief mention of their creator and gathered themselves up in the corner of the ceiling to learn what they could.

Beneath them, sitting on a wicker rocker, was a forty-year-old man holding a phone to his ear. He wore a shirt with no sleeves, gym shorts, and white socks. There was much of him, and he had a beard and glasses.

He wasn't speaking to Henry James on the phone as Summer Afternoon suspected. As a matter of fact, he wasn't talking to anyone. He was making believe he was talking to Henry James. He was a writer and for months he had been unable to write. Summer Afternoon didn't know he had sat every night for the past three months, smoking cigarettes, staring at a blank computer screen. He strained to pass greatness, but each night, the result—a mere handful of malodorous clichés. So he thought that while the kids were at school and his wife was at work, he would make believe calling Henry James for some advice.

The first thing James told him was to soak his feet in ice water twice daily.

"Whatever you say, Henry," said the writer.

Next, the old master told him to refrain from cursing.

"That's a toughie," said the writer, "I say 'fuck' every other word."

Henry didn't like to hear that and said it was a disgrace.

"What else?" said the writer.

"Moon bathing."

"Moon bathing?" he asked.

Then Henry started laughing and the writer laughed too. But Henry kept on laughing at his own joke way too hard.

"What a putz," said the writer as he slammed down the receiver. He wondered what Thomas Mann was up to.

The spirit of the words swooped down and filtered into the cigarette burning in the ashtray. The writer decided he didn't have time to climb *The Magic Mountain* and knew Mann's advice would be to clip his toenails or something equally innocuous. A better bet, he thought, would be to just dial at random and see who he got. He dialed and while the phone rang, he picked up his cigarette and took a drag. Finally a woman answered.

"Are you a writer?" he asked.

"Yes," she said, "my name is Dara Melsh. I wrote one novel called *Autumn Night*."

"Can you give me a little?" he asked.

"A planet always in autumn—falling leaves, all day twilight, pumpkins, and endless meadows of yellow brown-grass as tall as a four-story building. The captain and his son fly over the grass in a balloon ship in the early evening and see herds of white behemoths lumbering through the wind-tossed sea. When night falls and the stars come out, the boy beds down with a sleeping bag on the deck next to where the captain stands, gracefully moving the wheel. Above the sound of the captain's soft whistling, the boy hears the wind blowing through the grass and falls asleep to dream of summer afternoon."

"In the dream, is there a girl?" asked the writer.

"Two," said Dara.

"A greenhouse?" he asked.

"You guessed it," she said.

"A new strain of lily whose perfume draws a strange creature from the nearby forest at night?" he asked.

"Orchids," she whispered, "orchids with petals of human flesh."

"I see," said the writer.

"Why does the girl have to die in the last part?" he asked. "I mean, I know she spurns a monster of wisdom and all, but after they unveil the secret passageway to Queen Sufra's kingdom in the grass, shouldn't that have been it?"

"Don't forget the sullen countenance of the captain when he ceases whistling at the end of chapter three," she said.

"True."

"It's in paperback this summer," she said.

"I'll pick it up," he said. "Later."

He hung up and thought, "Fuck." He lit another cigarette and stared out through the screen at the summer afternoon. The sunlight fell through the leaves like bright rain. Dragonflies hovered over the koi pond and finches were at the feeder. Something insubstantial moved away from him. It passed through the screen like a breeze and headed out across the backyard. It walked in long, billowing strides, a halfhearted notion of a ghost.

"Come back," he called, and his words shot out to drill and splinter the well-traveled words of Henry James.

All that summer, whenever he was in the backyard, he heard a small voice say, "Summer Afternoon," and he'd look over his shoulder. The phrase was heard through August and even into the autumn when one night his wife, who was out in the backyard staring up through beams of the full moon at a balloon passing overhead, heard it too and wondered what it meant.

In winter when the snow fell so heavily that Route 70 was closed, both the writer and his wife stayed home. It was while they were sitting on the couch in the living room drinking coffee that she finally admitted having heard it.

"Do me a favor," he said.

"What?" she asked.

"When you're done with your coffee and you're ready to get up, how would you love to lean out the back door and swipe me up a bucket of snow?"

"Yeah, right," she said.

But she brought it to him, a big bucket of snow. He kicked off his slippers and plunged his bare feet into it.

"What are you doing?" she asked.

"Waiting," he said.

He stuck his feet in snow twice that day and twice the next. On the following day he had a thought. Three days later, while walking past the lake through melting snow, he had a memory of tall grass blowing in the wind of a summer afternoon.

Summer Afternoon

Story Notes

Back in the days when I used to drink in bars, I'd meet my friend Frank at this place near work and we'd have a few. Frank was a consummate storyteller in the Irish tradition, which, at times, made him a dangerous person to drink with. I could begin the evening with the idea that I'd have one or two and then head home, but when Frank was inspired, he could tell a story so long and involved, so rich with detail and looped with digressions, that the next thing I knew, Virgil, the bartender, was signaling last call and Frank would say, pulling his wallet from his pocket, "Okay, one more for the ditch."

On one of these nights, Frank told me a story that encompassed the entirety of his tour of duty in Vietnam. The next day, due to its deletion by a splitting headache, I remembered precious little of the story, but one small crumb of the aggregate stayed with me—a story about a guard tower in Saigon. This particular incident didn't happen to Frank personally, but rather to his brother, who was also stationed there. Frank was a master of digression in his story-telling, as I said, and I remembered we detoured out of the main story as he filled me in on his and his comrades' prevalent use of pot during the war. He told me you could buy marijuana cigarettes by the pack in Saigon. They even had a brand name—Park Lanes.

Anyway, one night his brother had pulled guard detail in the tower, but beforehand he'd met up with Frank for some drinking and a stroll down Park Lane. By the time he got to the base of the tower, he was burnt crisper than a cinder. The tower was just a tall, concrete cylinder with a metal shack at the top. Guard duty consisted of watching for mortar fire coming in from the area surrounding the city. If any action was spotted, details were radioed into headquarters along with the coordinates of its origin. To get to the trapdoor, the entrance to the shack, at the top of the tower, he had to climb straight up a ladder with 200 rungs inside that concrete cylinder.

By the time Frank's brother got to the base of the tower, he was already a few minutes late, and he knew the soldier who was up there was waiting to be relieved. He shouldered his M-16, and started up the ladder. Climbing that ladder was scary enough when straight, but climbing it fucked up was downright frightening. Huffing, puffing, hand over hand, trying not to let his boots slip off the rungs, he ascended. Halfway to the top, he had to stop and hold on for a few seconds until the whirling in his head subsided.

Eventually, he calmed himself and started climbing again, but now he was sweating. The sweat from his hands made the metal rungs slippery. A little less than three-quarters of the way to the top, his left foot slipped off the rung and then his right foot followed. The weight of his body pulled him down, and he managed to grab tightly to a rung with only his right hand. In the midst of this mishap, the shoulder strap of the M-16 slipped off, and the gun fell away.

Frank's brother had said that his mind became instantly clear, and in a single heartbeat he thought three things. The first thing he thought was that he never kept the rifle's safety lock on. The second thought was that if the gun actually managed to fall straight down, without flipping or turning, but perfectly straight down, and the butt end hit the floor below, the rifle could go off. And the third thing he thought was, Move your ass. He did, scrabbling like a monkey up the last few rungs. Reaching the top wrung just as the report of automatic gunfire exploded inside the tower below him, its roar and echo deafening, he pushed up the trapdoor and rolled onto the floor of the lookout shack.

The soldier who was on guard duty atop the tower heard the gunfire and thought they were under attack. Not knowing where the assault was coming from, he radioed headquarters and called in an air strike all along the perimeter of the city. Jets appeared out of the night and copious ordinance was dropped willy-nilly. Frank's brother had said it was like the Fourth of July.

This war saga, which went on for hours and included the incident of the tower, began with Frank taking his first sip of beer that evening and saying to me, apropos of nothing,

"I read once where Henry James said, 'The two most beautiful words in the English language are Summer Afternoon.'"

Chris Rowe, the editor of Say . . . *magazine (and author of the marvelous science fiction story* "The Voluntary State" *and chapbook* Bittersweet Creek and Other Stories), *asked me to contribute a story to the first issue. His enticement was one of the best lines I've ever heard from an editor: "Send me something. I can't promise I'll publish it, but I can promise you won't be paid." How could I turn down an offer like that? I sent him* "Summer Afternoon."

The Weight of Words

BACK IN THE AUTUMN OF '57, WHEN I WAS NO more than thirty, I went out almost every night of the week. I wasn't so much seeking a good time as I was trying to escape a bad one. My wife of five years had recently left me for a better looking, wealthier, more active man, and although she had carried on an affair behind my back for some time and, upon leaving, had told me what a drab milksop I was, I still loved her. Spending my evenings quietly reading had always been a great pleasure of mine, but after our separation the thought of sitting still, alone, with nothing but a page of text and my own seeping emotions was intolerable. So I invariably put on my coat and hat, left my apartment, and trudged downtown to the movie theatre where I sat in the dark, carrying on my own subdued affair with whichever Hepburn had something playing at the Ritz. When it was Monroe or Bacall, or some other less symbolically virtuous star featured on the marquee, I might instead go for a late supper at the diner or over to the community center to hear a lecture. The lecture series was, to be kind, not remarkable, but there were bright lights, usually a few other lonely souls taking notes or dozing, and a constant string of verbiage from the speaker that ran interference on my memories and silent recriminations. Along with this, I learned a few things about the Russian Revolution, How to Care for Rose Bushes, the Poetry of

John Keats. It was at one of these talks that I first came in contact with Albert Secmatte, billed as *A Chemist of Printed Language.*

What with the drab title of his lecture, *The Weight of Words,* I expected little from Secmatte, only that he would speak unceasingly for an hour or two, fixing and preserving me in a twilight state just this side of slumber. Before beginning, he stood at the podium (behind him a white screen, to his side an overhead projector), smiling and nodding for no apparent reason; a short, thin man with a slicked-back wave of dark hair. His slightly baggy black suit might have made him appear a junior undertaker, but this effect was mitigated by his empty grin and thick-lensed, square-framed glasses, which cancelled any other speculation but that he was, to some minor degree, insane. The other dozen members of the audience yawned and rubbed their eyes, preparing to receive his wisdom with looks of already weakening determination. Secmatte's monotonous voice was as incantatory as a metronome, but also high and light, almost childish. His speech was about words and it began with all of the promise of one of those high school grammar lectures that insured the poisoning of any youthful fascination with language.

I woke from my initial stupor twenty minutes into the proceedings when the old man sitting three seats down from me got up to leave, and I had to step out into the aisle to let him pass. Upon reclaiming my seat and trying again to achieve that dull bliss I had come for, I happened to register a few phrases of Secmatte's talk and, for some reason, it caught my interest.

"Printed words," he said, "are like the chemical elements of the periodic table. They interact with each other, affect each other through a sort of *gravitational force* on a particulate level in the test tube of the sentence. The proximity of one to another might result in either the appropriation of, or combination of, basic particles of connotation and grammatical presence, so to speak, forming a compound of meaning and being, heretofore unknown before the process was initiated by the writer."

This statement was both perplexing and intriguing. I sat forward and listened more intently. From what I could gather, Secmatte was claiming that printed words had, according to their length, their phonemic components, and syllabic structure, fixed values that could be somehow mathematically ciphered. The resultant numeric symbols of their representative qualities could then be viewed in relation to the proximity of their location, one to another, in the context of the sentence, and a well-trained researcher could then deduce the effectiveness or power of their presence. My understanding of what he was driving at led me to change my initial determination as to the degree of his madness. I shook my head, for here was a full-fledged lunatic. It was all too wonderfully crackpot for me to ignore and return to my trance.

I looked around at the audience while he droned on and saw expressions of confusion, boredom, and even anger. No one was buying his bill of goods for a moment. I'm sure the same questions I presently entertained were going through their minds as well. How exactly does one weigh a word? What is the unit of measurement that is applied to calculate the degree of influence of a certain sylla-ble? These questions were beginning to be voiced in the form of grumblings and whispered profanities.

The speaker gave no indication that he was the least bit aware of his audience's impending mutiny. He continued smiling and nodding as he proceeded with his outlandish claims. Just as a woman, a retired PhD in literature, in the front row, a regular at the lectures, raised her hand, Secmatte turned his back on us and strode over to the light switch on the wall to his left. A moment later the lecture room was plunged into darkness. There came out of the artificial night the sound of someone snoring, and then, *click*, a light came on just to the left of the podium, illuminating the fright-eningly dull face of Secmatte, reflecting off his glasses, and casting his shadow at large upon the screen behind him.

"Observe," he said, and stepped out of the beacon of light to fetch a sheet from a pile of papers he had left on the podium. As my eyes adjusted, I could make out that he was placing a transparency on the projector. There appeared on the screen behind him a flypa-per-yellow page, mended with tape and written upon with a neat script in black ink.

"Here is the pertinent formula," he said, and took a pen from his jacket pocket with which to point out the printed message on the transparency. He read it slowly, and I wish now that I had written it down or memorized it. To the best of my recollection it read some-thing like—

> *Typeface + Meaning* x *Syllabic Structure – Length +*
> *Consonantal Profluence* / *Verbal Timidity* x *Phonemic*
> *Saturation = The Weight of a Word, or The Value*

"Bullshit," someone in the audience said, and as if that epithet was a magical utterance that broke the spell of the Chemist of the Printed Word, three quarters of the audience, which was not large to begin with, got up and filed out. If the esteemed speaker had looked more physically imposing, I might have left, myself, timid as I was, but the only threat of danger was to common sense, which had never been a great ally of mine. The only ones left, besides me, were the sleeper in the back row, a kerchiefed woman saying her rosary to my far right, and a fellow in a business suit in the first row.

"And how did you come upon this discovery?" said the gentleman sitting close to Secmatte.

"Oh," said the speaker, as if surprised that there was anyone out there in the dark. "Years of inquiry. Yes, many years of trial and error."

"What type of inquiry?" asked the man.

"That is top secret," said Secmatte, nodding. Then he whipped the transparency off the projector and took it to the podium. He paged through his stack of papers and soon returned to the machine with another transparency. This he laid carefully on the viewing platform. The new sheet held at its middle a single sentence in typeface of about fifteen words. As I cannot recall for certain the ingredients of the aforementioned formula, the words of this sentence are even less clear to me now. I am positive that one of the early words in the line, but not the first or second, was "scarlet." I believe that this color was used to describe a young man's ascot.

Secmatte stepped into the light of the projector again so that his features were set aglow by the beam. "I know what you are thinking," he said, his voice taking a turn toward the defensive. "Well, ladies and gentleman, now we will see . . ."

The sleeper snorted, coughed, and snored twice during the speaker's pause.

"Notice what happens to the sentence when I place this small bit of paper over the word 'the' that appears as the eleventh word in the sequence." He leaned over the projector, and I watched on the screen as his shadow fingers fit a tiny scrap of paper onto the relevant article. When the deed was done, he stepped back and said, "Now read the sentence."

I read it once and then twice. To my amazement, not only the word "the" was missing where he had obscured it, but the word "scarlet" was now also missing. I don't mean that it was blocked out, I mean that it had vanished and the other words which had stood around it had closed ranks as if it had never been there to begin with.

"A trick," I said, unable to help myself.

"Not so, sir," said Secmatte. He stepped up and with only the tip of the pen, flipped away the paper covering "the." In that same instant, the word "scarlet" appeared like a ghost, out of thin air. One moment it did not exist, and the next it stood in bold typeface.

The gentleman in the front row clapped his hands. I sat staring with my mouth open, and then it opened wider when, with the pen tip, he maneuvered the scrap back onto "the" thus vanishing the word "scarlet" again.

"You see, I have analyzed the characteristics of each word in this sentence, and when the article 'the' is obscured, the lack of its value in the construction of the line creates a phenomenon I call *sublimation*, which is basically a masking of the existence of the word 'scarlet.' That descriptive word of color is still very much present, but the reader is unable to see it because of the effect initiated by a reconfiguration of the inherent structure of the sentence and the corresponding values of its words in relation to each other. The reader instead registers the word 'scarlet' subconsciously."

I laughed out loud, unable to believe what I was seeing. "Subconsciously?" I said.

"The effect is easily corroborated," he said, and went to the podium with the transparency containing the line about the young man's ascot only to return with another clear sheet. He laid that sheet on the projector and pointed to the typeface line at its center. This one I remember very well. It read: *The boy passionately kissed the toy.*

"In this sentence you now have before you," said Secmatte, "there is a sublimated word that exists in print as surely as do all of the others, but because of my choice of typeface and its size and the configuration of phonemic and syllabic elements, it has been made a phantom. Still, its meaning, the intent of the word, will come through to you on a subconscious level. Read the sentence and ponder it for a moment."

I read the sentence and tried to picture the scene. On its surface, the content suggested an image of innocent joy, but each time I read the words, I felt a tremor of revulsion, some dark overtone to the message.

"What is missing?" said the man in the front row.

"The answer will surface into your consciousness in a little while," said Secmatte. "When it does, you will be assured of the validity of my work." He then turned off the projector. "Thank you all for coming," he said into the darkness. A few seconds later, the lights came on.

I rubbed my eyes at the sudden glare and when I looked up, I saw Secmatte gathering together his papers and slipping them into a briefcase.

"Very interesting," said the man in the front row.

"Thank you," said Secmatte without looking up from the task of latching his case. He then walked over to the gentleman and handed him what appeared to be a business card. As the speaker made his way down the aisle, he also stopped at the row I was in and offered me one of the cards.

I rose and stepped over to take it from him. "Thanks," I said. "Very engaging." He nodded and smiled and continued to do so as he walked the remaining length of the room and left through the doors at the back. Putting the card in the pocket of my coat, I looked around and noticed that both the woman with the rosary and the sleeper had already left.

"Mr. Secmatte seems somewhat touched in the head," I said to the gentleman, who was now passing me on his way out.

He smiled and said, "Perhaps. Have a good evening."

I returned his salutation and then followed him out of the room.

On my way home, I remembered the last sentence Secmatte had displayed on the projector, the one about the boy kissing the toy. I again felt ill at ease about it, and then, suddenly, I caught something out of the corner of my mind's eye, wriggling through my thoughts. Like the sound of a voice in a memory or the sound of the door slamming shut in a dream about my wife, I distinctly heard, in my mind, a hissing noise. Then I saw it: a snake. The boy was passionately kissing a toy snake. The revelation stopped me in my tracks.

II

Having been a book lover since early childhood, I had always thought my job as head librarian at the local Jameson City branch the perfect occupation for me. I was a proficient administrator and used my position, surreptitiously, as a bully pulpit, to integrate a new worldview into our quiet town. When ordering new books, I set my mind to procuring the works of black writers, women writers, the beats, and the existentialists. Once I had met Secmatte, though, the job became even more interesting. When I wasn't stewing about the absence of Corrine, or imagining what she must be doing with the suave Mr. Walthus, I contemplated the nature of Secmatte's lecture. Walking through the stacks, I now could almost hear the ambient buzz of phonemic interactions transpiring within the closed covers of the shelved books. Upon opening a volume and holding it up close to my weak eyes, I thought I felt a certain fizz against my face, like the bursting bubbles of a Coca-Cola, the result of residue thrown off by the textual chemistry. Secmatte had fundamentally changed the way in which I thought about printed language.

Perhaps it was a week after I had seen his talk and demonstration that I was staring out the large window directly across from the circulation desk. It was midafternoon and the library was virtually empty. The autumn sun shown down brightly as I watched the traffic pass by outside on the quiet main street of town.

I was remembering a night soon after we were married when Corrine and I were lying in bed, in the dark. She used to say to me, "Tell me a wonderful thing, Cal." What she meant was that I should regale her with some interesting tidbit of knowledge from my extensive reading.

"There is a flower," I told her, "that grows only on Christmas Island in the Indian Ocean, called by the natives of that paradisiacal atoll, the Warulatnee. The large pink blossom it puts forth holds a preservative chemical that keeps it intact long after the stem has begun to rot internally. From the decomposition, a gas builds up in the stem, and eventually is violently released at the top, sending the blossom into flight. As it rapidly ascends, sometimes to a height of twenty feet, the petals fold back to make it more streamlined, but once it reaches the apex of its launch, the wind takes it and the large, soft petals open like the wings of a bird. It can travel for miles in this manner on the currents of ocean air. Warulatnee means 'the sunset bird' and the blossom is given as a token of love."

When I was finished, she kissed me and told me I was beautiful. Fool that I was, I thought she loved me for my intelligence and my open mind. Instead, I should have held her more firmly than my beliefs—a miasma of weightless words I could not get my arms around.

Memories like this one, when they surfaced, each killed me a little inside. And it was at that precise moment that I saw, outside the library window, Mr. Walthus's aquamarine convertible pull up at the stop light at the corner. Corrine was there beside him, sitting almost in his lap, with her arm around his wide shoulders. Before the light changed, he gunned the engine, most likely to make sure I would notice, and as they took off down the street, I saw my wife throw her head back and laugh with an expression of pleasure that no word could describe. It was maddening, frustrating, and altogether juvenile. I felt something in my midsection crumple like a sheet of old paper.

Later that same day, while wandering through the stacks again, having escaped into thoughts of Secmatte's printed language system, I happened to pass, at eye level, a copy of *The Letters of Abelard and Heloise*. At the sight of it, a wonderful thought, like the pink Warulatnee, took flight in my imagination powered by effluvia from the decomposition of my heart. Before I reached the coat closet, I had fully formulated my devious plan. I reached into the pocket of my overcoat and retrieved the card Secmatte had given me the night of his lecture.

That afternoon I called him from my office in the library.

"Secmatte," he said in his high-pitched voice, sounding like a child just awakened from an afternoon nap.

I explained who I was and how I knew him and then I mentioned that I wanted to speak to him at more length concerning his theory.

"Tonight," he said, and gave me his address. "Eight o'clock."

I thanked him and told him how interested I was in his work.

"Yes," was all he said before hanging up, and I pictured him nodding and smiling without volition.

Secmatte lived in a very large, one-story building situated behind the lumberyard and next to the train tracks on the edge of town. The place had once held the offices of an oil company—an unadorned concrete bunker of a dwelling. There were dark curtains on the front windows, where, when I was a boy, there had been displayed advertisements for Maxwell Oil. I approached the nondescript front door and knocked. A moment later, it opened to reveal Secmatte dressed exactly as he had been the night of his lecture.

"Enter," he said, without greeting, as if I were either a regular visitor or a workman come to do repairs.

I followed him inside to what obviously had once been a business office. In that modestly sized room, still painted the sink-cleanser green of industrial walls, there was an old couch, two chairs, stuffing spilling out of the bottom of one, and a small coffee table. Next to Secmatte's chair was a lamp that cast a halfhearted glow upon the scene. The floor had no rug but was bare concrete like the walls.

My host sat down, hands gripping the chair arms, and leaned forward.

"Yes?" he said.

I sat down in the chair across the table from him. "Calvin Fesh," I said, and leaned forward with my hand extended, expecting to shake.

Secmatte nodded, smiled, said, "A pleasure," but did not clasp hands with me.

I withdrew my arm and leaned back.

He sat quietly, staring at the tabletop, more with an air of mere existence than actually waiting for me to speak.

"I was impressed with your demonstration at the community

center," I said. "I have been an avid reader my entire life and . . ."

"You work at the library," he said.

"How . . . ?"

"I've seen you there. I come in from time to time to find an example of a certain style of type or to search for the works of certain writers. For instance, Tolstoy in a cheap translation, in Helvetica, especially the long stories, is peculiarly rich in phonemic chaos and the weights of his less insistent verbs, those with a preponderance of vowels, create a certain fluidity in the location of power in the sentence. It has something to do with the translation from Russian into English. Or Conrad, when he uses a gerund, watch out." He uncharacteristically burst into laughter and slapped his knee. Just as suddenly, he went slack and resumed nodding.

I feigned enjoyment and proceeded. "Well, to be honest, Mr. Secmatte, I have come with a business proposition for you. I want you to use your remarkable sublimation procedure to help me."

"Explain," he said, and turned his gaze upon the empty couch to his right.

"Well," I said, "this is somewhat embarrassing. My wife left me recently for another man. I want her back, but she will not see me or speak to me. I want to write to her, but if I begin by professing my love to her openly, she will crumple up the letters and throw them out without finishing them. Do you follow me?"

He sat silently, staring. Eventually he adjusted his glasses and said, "Go on."

"I want to send her a series of letters about interesting things I find in my reading. She enjoys learning about these things. I was hoping that I could persuade you to insert sublimated messages of love into these letters, so that upon reading them, they might secretly rekindle her feelings for me. For payment of course."

"Love," said Secmatte. Then he said it three more times, very slowly and in a deeper tone than was his normal child voice. "A difficult word to be sure," he said. "It's slippery and its value has a tendency to shift slightly when in relation to words with multiple syllables set in a Copenhagen or one of the less script-influenced types."

"Can you do it?" I asked.

For the first time he looked directly at me.

"Of course," he said.

I reached into my pocket and brought out a sheet of paper holding my first missive concerning the Column of Memnon, the singing stone. "Insert some invisible words relaying my affection into this," I said.

"I will make it a haunted house of love," he said.

"And what will you charge?"

"That is where you can assist me, Mr. Fesh," he said. "I do not need your money. It seems you are not the only one with thoughts of putting my sublimation technique to work. The other gentleman who was at the lecture on the twelfth has given me more work than I can readily do. He has also paid me very handsomely. He has made me wealthy overnight. Mr. Mulligan has hired me to create ads for his companies that utilize sublimation."

"That was Mulligan?" I said.

Secmatte nodded.

"He's one of the wealthiest men in the state. He donated that community center to Jameson," I said.

"I need someone to read proof copies for me," said Secmatte. "When I get finished doctoring the texts they give me, playing with the values and reconstructing, sometimes I will forget to replace a comma or make plural a verb. Even the Chemist of Printed Language needs a laboratory assistant. If you will volunteer your time two nights a week, I will create your sublimated letters one a week for you. How is that?"

It seemed like an inordinate amount of work for one letter per week, but I so believed that my plan would work and I so wanted Corrine back. Besides, I had nothing to do in the evenings and it would be a break from my routine of wandering the town at night. I agreed. He told me to return on Thursday night at seven o'clock to begin.

"Splendid," he said in a tone devoid of emotion, and then rose. He ushered me quickly to the front door and opened it, standing aside to ensure I got the message that it was time to go.

"My letter is on your coffee table," I turned to say on my way out, but the door had already closed.

III

My evenings at Secmatte's were interesting if only for the fact that he was such an enigma. I had never met anyone before with such a flat affect at times, so wrapped up in his own insular world. Still, there were moments when I perceived glimmers of personality, trace clues to the fact that he was aware of my presence and that he might even enjoy my company on some level. I had learned that when he was smiling and nodding, his mind was busy ciphering the elements of a text. No doubt these actions constituted a defense mechanism, one probably adopted early on in his life to keep others at bay. What better disguise could there be than one of affability and complete contentment? An irascible sort is constantly being confronted, interrogated as to the reason for his pique. Secmatte was agreeing with you before he met you—anything to be left to himself.

The work was easy enough. I have, from my earliest years in school, been fairly good with grammar, and the requirements of proofreading came as second nature to me. I was given my own office at the back of the building. It was situated at the end of a long, dimly lit hallway, the walls of which were lined with shelves holding various sets of typefaces both ancient and modern. These were Secmatte's building blocks, the toys with which he worked his magic upon paper. They were meticulously arranged and labeled, and there were hundreds of them. Some of the blocks holding individual letters were as large as a paperback book and some no bigger than the nail on my pinky finger.

My office was stark, to say the least—a desk, a chair, and a standing lamp no doubt procured at a yard sale. Waiting for me on the desk upon my arrival would be a short stack of flyers, each a proof copy of a different batch, I was to read through and look for errors. I was to circle the errors or write a description of them in the margin with a green pen. The ink had to be green for some reason I never did establish. When I discovered a problem, which was exceedingly rare, I was to bring the proof in question to Secmatte, who was invariably in the printing room. Since typeface played such an important part in the production of the sublimation effect, and those not in the know would never see the words meant to be sublimated, he set his own type and printed the flyers himself on an old electric press with a drum that caught up the pages and rolled them over the ink-coated print. Even toiling away at this messy task, he wore his black suit, white shirt, and tie. The copy that Mulligan was supplying seemed the most innocuous drivel. Secmatte called them ads, I suppose, because he knew that after he had his way with them they would be secretly persuasive in some manner, but to the naked eye of the uninitiated, like myself, they appeared simple messages of whimsical advice to anyone who might read them:

Free Fun
Fun doesn't have to be expensive!
For a good time on a clear day, take the family on an outing
to an open space, like a field or meadow. Bring blankets to

sit on. Then look up at the slow parade of clouds passing overhead. Their white cotton majesty is a high-altitude museum of wonders. Study their forms carefully, and soon you will be seeing faces, running horses, a witch on her broom, a schooner under full sail. Share what you see with each other. It won't be long before the conversation and laughter will begin.

This was the first one I worked on, and all the time I carefully perused it, I wondered what banal product of his mercantile web Mulligan was secretly pushing on its unwitting readers. From that very first night at my strange new task, I paid close attention to any odd urges I might have and often took an inventory at the end of each week of my purchases to see if I had acquired something that was not indicative of my usual habits. I did, at this time, take up the habit of smoking cigarettes, but I put that off to my frustration and anguish over the loss of Corrine.

These flyers began appearing in town a week after I started going to Secmatte's on a regular basis. I saw them stapled to telephone poles, tacked to bulletin boards at the laundromat, in neat stacks at the ends of the checkout counters at the grocery store. A man even brought one into the library and asked if I would allow him to hang it on our board. I didn't want to, knowing it was a wolf in sheep's clothing, but I did. One of the library's regular patrons remarked upon it, shaking his head. "It seems a lot of trouble for something so obvious," he said. "But, you know, when I was over in Weston on business, I saw them there too."

Good to his word, at the end of our session on Thursday nights, Secmatte appeared at the open door to my office, holding a sheet of paper in his hand. Printed on it, in a beautiful old typescript with bold and ornate capitals and curving l's and i's, was that week's letter to Corrine.

"Your note, Mr. Fesh," he'd say, and walk over and place it on the corner of my desk.

"Thank you," I would say, expecting and then hoping that he might return the thanks, but he never did. He would merely nod, say "Yes," and then leave.

Those single sheets of paper holding my message of wonder for my wife appeared normal enough, but when I'd lift them off the desktop, they'd feel weighted as if by as much as an invisible paperclip. While carrying them home, their energy was undeniable. My memories of Corrine would come back to me so vividly it was like I held her hand in mine instead of paper. Of course, I would send them off with the first post in the morning, but every Thursday night I would lay them in the bed next to me and dream that they whispered their secret vows of love while I slept.

The night I happened to discover on the back of the cigarette pack that my brand, Butter Lake Regulars, was made by a subsidiary of Mulligan, Inc., I saw another side of Secmatte. There were two doors in my office. One opened onto the hallway lined with the shelves of type, and the other across the room from my desk led to a large room of enormous proportions without lights. It was always very cold in there, and I surmised it must have been the garage where the oil trucks had once been housed. If I needed to use the bathroom, I would have to open that other door and cross through the dark, chilly expanse to a doorway on its far side. Secmatte's place—I would no longer call it a home—was always somewhat eerie, but that stroll through the darkness to the small square of light in the distance was downright scary. The light I moved toward was the entrance to the bathroom.

The bathroom itself was dingy. The fixtures must have been there from the time of the original occupants. The toilet was a bowl of rust and the sink was cracked and chipped. One bare bulb hung overhead. To say the bathroom was stark was a kindness, and when necessity called upon me to use it, I often thought what it would be like to be in prison.

On the night I refer to, I took the long walk to the bathroom. I settled down on the splintered wooden seat, lit a Butter Lake Regular, and in my uneasy reverie began to consider Mulligan's program of surreptitious propaganda. In the middle of my business, I chanced to look down and there, next to me on the floor, was the largest snake I had ever seen. I gasped but did not scream, fearful of inciting the creature to strike. Its mouth was open wide, showing two huge, curving fangs, and its yellow and black mottled body was coiled beneath it like a garden hose in storage. I sat as perfectly still as I could, taking the most minute breaths. Each bead of sweat that swelled upon my forehead and then trickled slowly down my face, I feared would be enough to draw an attack. Finally, I could stand the tension no longer and, with a great effort, tried to leap to safety. I forgot about my pants around my ankles, which tripped me up, and I sprawled across the bathroom floor. A few minutes later, I realized the serpent was made of rubber.

"What is this supposed to be?" I asked him as he stood filling the press with ink.

Secmatte turned around and saw me standing with the snake in my hand, both its head and tail touching the floor. He smiled, but it wasn't his usual, mindless grin.

"Legion," he said, put down the can of ink, and came over to take the thing from me.

"It scared me to death," I said.

"It's rubber," he said, and draped it over his shoulders. He lifted the head and looked into the snake's eyes. "Thank you, I've been looking for him. I did not know where he had gotten off to."

I was so angry I wanted a scene, an argument. I wanted Albert Secmatte to react. "You're a grown man and you own a rubber snake?" I said with as much vehemence as I could.

"Yes," he said as if I had asked him if the sky was blue. Without another word, he went back to his work.

I sighed, shook my head, and returned to my office.

Later that evening, he brought me my letter for Corrine, this one concerning the music of humpback whales. I wanted to show him I was still put out, but the sight of the letter set me at ease. He also had another piece of paper with him.

"Mr. Fesh, I wanted to show you something I have been working on," he said.

Taking the other sheet of paper from him, I brought it up to my eyes so that I could read its one typeset sentence. "What?" I asked.

"Keep looking at it for a minute or two," he said.

The sentence was rather long, I remember, and the structure of it, though grammatically correct, was awkward. My eyes scanned back and forth over it continually. Its content had something to do with a polar bear fishing in frozen waters. I remember that it began with a prepositional phrase and inserted in the middle was a parenthetic phrase describing the lush beauty of the bear's fur. The writing did not flow properly; it was stilted in some way. Unable to stare any longer, I blinked. In the instant of that blink, the word "flame" appeared out of context in the very center of the sentence. It wasn't as if the other words were shoved aside to make room. No, the sentence appeared stable, only there was a new word in it. I blinked again and it was gone. I blinked again and it reappeared. On and off with each fleeting movement of my eyelids.

I smiled and looked up at Secmatte.

"Yes," he said. "But I am some way off from perfecting it."

"This is remarkable," I said. "What's the effect you're trying for?"

"Do you know the neon sign in town at the bakery? *Hot Pies* — in that beautiful color of flamingos?"

"I know it," I said.

"Well . . ." he said, and waved his right hand in a circular motion as if expecting me to finish a thought.

The words came to me before the thoughts did: "It blinks," I said.

"Precisely," said Secmatte, smoothing back his hair wave. "Can you imagine a piece of text containing a word that blinks on and off like that sign? I know theoretically it is possible, but as of now I am only able to produce a line that changes each time the person blinks or looks away. It is excruciatingly difficult to achieve just the right balance of instability and stability to make the word in question fluctuate between sublimation and its being evident to the naked eye. I need a higher state of instability, one where the word is, for all intents and purposes, sublimated, but at the same time there needs to be some pulsating value in the sentence that draws it back into the visible, releases it, and draws it back at a more rapid rate. I'm guessing my answer lies in some combination of typeface and vowel/consonant bifurcation in the adjectives. As you can see, the sentence as it now stands is really not right, its syntax tortured beyond measure for the meager effect it displays."

I was speechless. Looking back at the paper, I blinked repeatedly, watching the "flame" come and go. When I turned my attention back to Secmatte, he was gone.

I was halfway home that night before I allowed myself to enjoy the fact that I was carrying another loaded missive for Corrine. Up until that point my mind was whirling with blinking words and coiled rubber snakes. I vaguely sensed a desire to entertain the question as to whether it was ethical for me to be sending these notes to her, but I had mastered my own chemistry of sublimation and used it with impunity. Later, asleep, I dreamed of making love to her, and the rubber snake came back to me in the most absurd and horrifying manner.

IV

Mulligan's flyers were myriad, but although the subject of each was different—the importance of oiling a squeaky hinge on a screen door, having someone help you when you use a ladder, stopping to smell the flowers along the way, telling your children once a day that they are good—there was a fundamental sameness in their mundanity. Perhaps this could account for their popularity. Nothing is more comforting to people than to have their certainties trumpeted back to them in bold, clear typeface. Also they were free, and that is a price that few can pass up no matter what it is attended to, save Death. I know from my library patrons that the citizens of Jameson were collecting them. Some punched holes in them and made little encyclopedias of the banal. They were just the type of safe, retroactive diversions one could focus on to ignore the chaos of a cultural revolution that was beginning to burgeon.

Coinciding with the popularity of the flyers, I began to perceive a change in the town's buying habits. It was first noticeable to me at the grocery store where certain products could not be kept in stock due to so powerful a demand. On closer inspection, it became evident that all of these desirable goods had been produced by the ubiquitous Mulligan, Inc. There was something undeniably irresistible about the sublimated suggestions hiding in the flyers. It was as if people perceived them as whispered advice from their own minds, and their attraction to a specific product was believed to be a subjective, idiosyncratic brainstorm. Once the products began to become scarce, others, who had not read the flyers, bought them also out of a sense of not wanting to miss out on an item obviously endorsed by their brethren. Even knowing this, I could not stay my hand from reaching for Blue Hurricane laundry detergent, Flavor Pops cereal, Hasty bacon, etc. The detergent turned out not to have the magical cleaning abilities it promised, the Flavor Pops were devoid of flavor, like eating crunchy kernels of dust, and Hasty described the speed with which I swallowed those strips of meatless lard. Still, I forbore the ghostly stains and simply added more sugar to the cereal, unable to purchase anything else.

Even though I knew what Secmatte and Mulligan were up to was profoundly wrong, I vacillated as to whether I should continue to play my small role in the scam. I was torn between the greater good and my own self-serving desire to win back Corrine. This became a real dilemma for me, and I would stay up late at night considering my options, smoking Butter Lake Regulars, and pacing the floor. Then one night in order to escape the weight of my predicament, I decided to take in a movie. *Funny Face*, directed by Stanley Donen, with Audrey Hepburn and Fred Astaire, was playing at the Ritz, and it was advertised as just the kind of innocent fluff I required to soothe my conscience.

I arrived early at the Ritz on a Wednesday night, bought a bag of buttered popcorn, my usual, and went into the theatre to take my seat. I was sitting there, staring up at the blank screen, wishing my mind could emulate it, when in walked a handsome couple, arm in arm. Corrine and Walthus passed right by me without looking. I know they saw me sitting there by myself. A gentleman alone in a theatre was not a typical sight in those days, and I'm sure I drew some small attention from anyone who passed, yet they chose not to recognize me. I immediately contemplated leaving, but then the lights went out and the film came on and there was Audrey, my date for the night.

My emotions seesawed back and forth between embarrassment at seeing my stolen wife with her lover and my desire to spend time with the innocent and affectionate Jo Stockton, Hepburn's bookish character, amidst the backdrop of an idealized Paris. When my dream date's face was not on the screen, I peered forward three rows to where Corrine and Walthus sat. Tears formed in my eyes at one point, both for the trumped up difficulties of the lovers in the film and for my own. Then, at the crucial moment, when Stockton professes her love for Dick Avery, the photographer, I noticed Corrine turn her head and stare back at me. Of course it was dark, but there was still enough light thrown off from the screen so that our gazes met. I detected a mutual spark. My hand left the bag of popcorn and reached out to her. This motion prompted her to turn back around.

I did not stay for the remainder of the film. But on my way home, I could not stop smiling. If there had been any question as to whether I would continue with Secmatte, that one look from my wife decided it. "My letters are speaking to her," I said aloud, and I felt so light I could have danced up a wall as I had once seen Astaire do in *Royal Wedding*.

The next evening, upon my arrival at Secmatte's, he met me at the door to inform me that he would not need my services that day. He had several gentlemen coming over to talk business with him. He handed me my letter for Corrine—a little piece about a pair of Siamese twins joined at the center of the head who, though each possessed a brain, and an outer eye, shared a single eye at the crux of their connection. The missive had been set in type and carried the perceived weight of his invisible words. I thanked him and he nodded and smiled. As I turned to go, he said, "Mr. Fesh, eh, Calvin, I very much like when you come to help." He looked away from me, not his usual wandering disinterest, but rather in a bashful manner that led me to believe he was being genuine.

"Why, thank you, Albert," I said, using his first name for the first time. "I think our letters are beginning to get through to my wife."

He gave a fleeting look of discomfort and then smiled and nodded.

As I turned to leave, a shiny limousine pulled up and out stepped three gentlemen, well-dressed in expensive suits. One I recognized immediately as Mulligan. I did not want him to identify me from the night at the community center, especially after I had questioned Secmatte's sanity, so I moved quickly away down the street. In fleeing, I did not get a good look at the other men, but I heard Mulligan introduce one as Thomas VanGeist. VanGeist, I knew, was a candidate for the state senatorial race that year. I looked back over my shoulder to see if I could place him, but they were all filing into the bunker by then.

When I visited Secmatte the next week, he looked exhausted. He did not chat with me for too long, but said that he had done a good deal of business and his work had increased exponentially. I felt badly for him. His suit was rumpled, his tie askew, and his hair, which was normally combed perfectly back in a wave, hung in strands as if that wave had finally hit the beach. Legion, the rubber snake, was draped around his neck like some kind of exotic necklace or a talisman to ward off evil.

"I can come an extra night if it will help you," I said. "You know, until you are done with the additional work."

He shook his head, "No, Fesh, I can't. This is top-secret work. Top secret."

Secmatte loved that phrase and used it often. If I asked a lot of questions about the sublimation technique in a certain flyer we were working on, he would supply brief, clipped answers in a tone of certainty that seemed to assume he was dispensing common knowledge. I understood little of anything he said, but my interrogation would reach a certain point and he would say, "Top secret," and that would end it.

I wondered what it was that drove him to such lengths. He told me he was making scads of money, "a treasure trove," as he put it, but he never seemed to spend any of it. This all would have remained an insoluble mystery had I not had a visitor to the library Wednesday afternoon of the following week.

Rachel Secmatte seemed to appear before me like one of her brother's sublimated words suddenly freed to sight by a reaction of textual chemistry. I had glanced down at a copy of the local newspaper to read more about the thoroughly disturbing account of an assault on a black man by a group of white youths over in Weston, and when I looked up she was there, standing before the circulation desk.

I was startled as much by her stunning looks as her sudden presence. "Can I help you?" I asked. She was blonde and built like one of those actresses whose figures inspired fear in me; a reaction I conveniently put off to their wayward morals.

"Mr. Fesh?" she said.

I nodded and felt myself blushing.

She introduced herself and held her hand out to me. I took it into my damp palm for a second.

"You are Albert's friend?" she said, nodding.

"I work with him," I told her. "I assist him in his work."

"Do you have a few minutes to speak to me? I am concerned about him and need to know what he is doing," she said.

I was about to tell her simply that he was fine, but then my confusion broke and I realized this was my chance to know something more about the ineffable Secmatte. "Certainly," I told her. Looking around the library and seeing it empty, I waved for her to come behind the circulation desk. She followed me into my office.

Before sitting down in the chair opposite me, she removed her coat to reveal a beige sweater with a plunging neckline, the sight of which gave me that sensation of falling I often experienced just prior to sleep.

"Albert is doing well," I told her. "Do you need his address?"

"I know where he is," she said.

"His phone number?"

"I spoke to him last night. That is when he told me about you. But he will only speak to me over the phone. He will not see me."

"Why is that?" I asked.

"If you have a few minutes, I can tell you everything," she said.

"Please," I said. "With Albert, there should be quite a lot to tell."

"Well, you must know by now that he is different," she said.

"An understatement."

"He has always been different. Do you know he did not speak a single word until he was three years old?"

"I find that hard to believe. He has a facility, a genius for language—"

"A curse," she said, interrupting. "That is how our father, the reverend, described it. Our parents were strict religious fundamentalists, and where there was zero latitude given to creative interpretations of the Bible, there was even less available in respect to personal conduct. Albert is four years younger than me. He was a curious little fellow with a, now how do I put this, a dispassionate overwhelming drive to understand the way things worked . . . if that makes sense."

"A dispassionate drive?" I asked.

"He had a need to understand things at their most fundamental level, but there was no emotion behind it, sort of like a mechanical desire. Perhaps the same kind of urge that makes geese migrate. Well, to get at these answers he required, he would do anything necessary. This very often went against my father's commandments. He was particularly curious about printed words in books. When he was very young, I would read him a story. He would not get caught up in the characters or the plot, but he wanted to know how the letters in the book created the images they suggested to his mind. One particular book he had me read again and again was about a bear. When I would finish, he would page frantically through the book, turn it upside down, shake it, hold it very close to his eyes. Then, when he was a little older, say five, he started dissecting the books, tearing them apart. Of course, the Bible was a book of great importance in our family, and when Albert was found one day with a pair of scissors, cutting out the tiny words, my father, who took this as an affront to his God, was incensed. Albert was made to sit in a dark closet for the entire afternoon. He quietly took his punishment, but it did not stop his investigations.

"He didn't understand my father's reaction to him, and he would search the house from top to bottom in order to find the hidden scissors. Then he would be back at it, carefully cutting out certain words. He drew on a piece of cardboard with green crayon a symmetrical chart with strange markings at the tops and sides of the columns, and would arrange the cutout words into groups. Sometimes he would take a word and try to weigh it on the kitchen scale my mother had for her recipes. He could spend hours repeating a phrase, a single word, or even a syllable. All during this time, he would be caught and relegated to the closet. Then he started burning the tiny scraps of cutout words and trying to inhale their smoke. When my mother caught him with the matches, it was decided that he was possessed by a demon and needed to be exorcised. It was after the exorcism, throughout which Albert merely stared placidly, that I first saw him nod and smile. If the ritual had done anything for him, it had given him the insight that he was different, unacceptable, and needed to disguise his truth."

"He has a rubber snake," I told her.

She laughed and said, "Yes, Legion. It was used in the pageants our church would put on. There was a scene we reenacted from the book of Genesis: Adam and Eve in the garden. That snake, I don't know where my father got it, would be draped in a tree and whoever played Eve, fully clothed of course, would walk over to the tree and lift the snake's mouth to her ear. Albert was fascinated with that snake before he could talk. And when he did speak, his first word was its name, Legion. He secretly kept the snake in his room and would only put it back in the storage box when he knew the pageant was approaching. When our parents became aware of his attachment to it, they tried many times to hide it, and when that didn't work, to throw it out, but somehow Albert always managed to retrieve it."

"It sounds as if he had a troubled youth," I said.

"He never had any friends, was always an outcast. The other children in our town taunted him constantly. It never seemed to bother him. His experiments with words, his investigations, were the only thing on his mind. I tried to protect him as much as I could. And when he was confused by life or frightened of something, which was rare, he would come into my room and get into the bed beside me."

"But you say he will not see you now," I said.

"True," she said, and nodded. "As a child I was rather curious myself. My main interest was in boys, and it was not dispassionate. Once when we were somewhat older and our parents were away for the day, a boy I liked came to the house. Let it suffice to say that Albert came to my room in the middle of the day and discovered me in a compromising position with this fellow." She sighed, folded her arms, and shook her head.

"This affected your relationship with him?" I asked, trying to swallow the knot in my throat.

"He would not look at me from that time on. He would speak to me, but if I was in the same room as him, he would avert his glance or cover his eyes. This has not changed through the years. Now I communicate with him only by phone."

"Well, Miss Secmatte, I can tell you he is doing well. A little tired right now because of all the work he has taken on. He is making an enormous amount of money, and is pushing himself somewhat."

"I can assure you, Mr. Fesh, money means nothing to Albert. He is more than likely taking all of these jobs you mention because they offer challenges to him. They require he test out his theories in ways he would not have come up with on his own."

I contemplated telling Rachel the reason why I had offered to help Albert but then thought better of it. The possibility of apprising her of the nature of our work for Mulligan was totally out of the question. The phrase "Top Secret" ran through my mind. She leaned over and reached into the purse at her feet, retrieving a small box, approximately seven inches by four.

"Can I trust you to give this to him?" she asked. "It was something he had once given me as a gift, but now he said he needs it back."

"Certainly," I said, and took the box from her.

She rose and put on her coat. "Thank you, Mr. Fesh," she said.

"Why did you tell me all of this?" I asked as she made for the door.

Rachel stopped before exiting. "I have cared about Albert my entire life without ever knowing if he understands that I do. Some time ago I stopped caring if he knows that I care. Now, like him, I continue simply because I must."

V

Being the ethically minded gentleman that I was, I decided to wait at least until I got home from work before opening the box. It was raining profusely as I made my way along the street. By then my curiosity had run wild, and I expected to find all manner of oddness inside. The weight of the little package was not excessive but there was some heft to it. One of my more whimsical thoughts was that perhaps it contained a single word, the word with the greatest weight, a compound confabulated by Secmatte and unknown to all others.

Upon arriving at my apartment, I set about making a cup of tea, allowing the excitement to build a little more before removing the cover of the box. Then, sitting at my table, overlooking the rain-washed street, the tea sending its steam into the air, I lifted the lid. It was not a word, or a note, or a photograph. It was none of the things I expected; what lay before me on a bed of cotton was a pair of eyeglasses. Before lifting them out of the box, I could see that they were unusual, for the lenses were small and circular, a rich yellow color, and too flimsy to be made of glass. The frames were thick, crudely twisted wire.

I picked them up from their white nest to inspect them more closely. The lenses appeared to be fashioned from thin sheets of yellow cellophane, and the frames were delicate and bent easily. Of course, I fitted them onto my head, curving the pliable arms around the backs of my ears. The day went dark yellow as I turned my gaze out the window. With the exception of changing the color of things, there was no optical adjustment, no trickery. Then I sat there for some time, watching the rain come down as I contemplated my own insular existence, my sublimations and dishonesties.

Somewhere amidst those musings the phone rang, and I answered it.

"Calvin?" said a female voice. It was Corrine.

"Yes," I said. I felt as if I was in a dream, listening to myself from a great distance.

"Calvin, I've been thinking of you. Your letters have made me think of you."

"And what have you thought?" I asked.

She began crying. "I would come back to you if you will just show once in a while that you care for me. I want to come back."

"Corrine," I said. "I care for you, but you don't really want me. You think you do, but it's an illusion. It's a trick in the letters. You will be happier without me." One part of me could not believe what I was saying, but another part was emerging that wanted to recognize the truth.

There was a period of silence, and then the receiver went dead. I pictured in my mind, Corrine, exiting a phone booth and walking away down the street in the rain. She was right, I had been too wrapped up in myself and rarely showed her that I cared. Oh yes, there were my fatuous transmissions of wonder, my little verbal essays of politics and philosophy and never love, but the real purpose of those was to prove my intellectual superiority. It came to me softly, like a bubble bursting, that I had been responsible for my own loneliness. I removed the yellow glasses and folded them back into their box.

The next evening, I went to Secmatte's as usual, but this time with the determination to tell him I was through with the sublimation business. When I knocked at the door, he did not answer. It was open, though, as it often was, so I entered and called out his name. There was no reply. I searched all of the rooms for him, including my office, but he was nowhere to be found. Returning to the printing room, I looked around and saw laid out on one of the counters the new flyers Albert had done for VanGeist. They were political in nature, announcing his candidacy for the state senate in large, bold headlines. Below the headline, on each of the different types, was a different paragraph-long message of the usual good-guy blather from the candidate. At the bottom of these writings was his name and beneath that a reminder to vote on Election Day.

"Top Secret," I said, and was about to return to my office when a thought surfaced. Looking once over my shoulder to make sure Secmatte was not there, I reached into my pocket and took out the box containing the glasses. I carefully laid it down on the counter, opened it, and took them out. Once the arms were fitted over my ears and the lenses positioned upon my nose, I turned my attention back to the flyers for VanGeist.

My hunch paid off, even though I wished that it hadn't. The cellophane lenses somehow cancelled the sublimation effect, and I saw what no one was meant to. Inserted into the paragraphs of trite self-boostering were some other, very pointed messages. If one assembled the secret words in one set of the flyers, they disparaged VanGeist's opponent, a fellow by the name of Benttel, as being a communist, a child molester, a thief. The other set's hidden theme was racial epithets, directed mostly at blacks and disclosing VanGeist's true feelings about the Civil Rights Act being promulgated by Eisenhower, which would soon come up for a vote in the legislature. My mind raced back to that article in the paper about the assault in Weston, and I could not help but wonder.

I backed away from the counter, truly aghast at what I had been party to. This was far worse than unobtrusively coaxing people to eat Hasty bacon—or was it? When I turned away from the flyers, I saw on the edge of another table that week's note for Corrine printed up and drying. Turning my gaze upon it, I discovered that there were no sublimated words in it at all. It was exactly as I had composed it, only set in type and printed. I was paralyzed, and would most likely not have moved for an hour had not Secmatte entered the printing room then.

"Is Rachel here?" he asked, seeing the glasses on me.

"Rachel is not here," I said.

"I asked her to bring them so that you could see," he said.

"Secmatte," I said, my anger building. "Do you have any idea what you are doing here?"

"At this moment?" he asked.

"No," I shouted, "with these flyers?"

"Printing them," he said.

"You're spreading hatred, Albert, ignorance and hatred," I said. He shook his head and I noticed his hands begin to tremble.

"You're spreading fear."

"I'm not," he said. "I'm printing flyers."

"The words," I said, "the words. Do you have any idea what in God's name you are doing?"

"It's only words," he said. "A job to do. Rachel told me I needed a job to make money."

"This is wrong," I told him. "This is very wrong."

He was going to speak but didn't. Instead he stared down at the floor.

"These words mean things," I said.

"They have definitions," he murmured.

"These flyers will hurt people out there in the world," I said. "There is a world of people out there, Albert."

He nodded and smiled and then turned and left the room.

I tore up as many of the flyers as I could get my hands on, throwing them in the air so that the pieces fell like snow. The words that were sublimated to the naked eye now were all I could see. I finally took the glasses off and laid them back in their box. After searching the building for a half-hour for Secmatte, I realized where he must be. When I was yelling at him he had the look of a crestfallen child, and I knew he must have gone to serve out his punishment in the closet. I went to my office and opened the door that led to the bathroom. That distant bulb had been extinguished and the great, cold expanse was completely dark.

"Albert?" I called from the door. I thought I could hear him breathing.

"Yes," he answered, but I could not see him.

"Did you really not know it was wrong?" I asked.

"I can fix it," he said.

"No more work for Mulligan and VanGeist," I told him.

"I can fix it with one word," he said.

"Just burn the flyers and have nothing more to do with them."

"It will be fine," he said.

"And what about my letters? Did you *ever* add any secret words to them?"

"No."

"That was our deal," I said.

"But I don't know anything about Love," he said. "I needed you so that you could see what I could do. I thought you believed it was good."

There was nothing more I could say. I closed the door and left him there in the dark.

VI

In the months that followed I often contemplated, at times with anguish, at times delight, that my own words, wrought with true emotion, had reached Corrine and caused her to change her mind. Nothing came of it, though. I heard from a mutual friend that she had left town without Walthus to pursue a life in the city in which she had been born. We were never officially divorced, and I never saw her again.

There were also two other interesting developments. The first came soon after Secmatte fell out of sight. I read in the newspaper that VanGeist, just prior to the election, dropped dead one morning in his office, and in the same week, Mulligan developed some strange disease that caused him to go blind. Here was a baffling synchronicity that stretched the possibility of coincidence to its very limit.

The other surprising event was a post card from Secmatte a year after his disappearance from Jameson. In it he asked that I contact Rachel and tell her he was well. He told me that he and Legion had taken up a new pursuit, something else concerning language. "My calculations were remiss," he wrote, "for there is something in words, some unnameable spirit born of an author's intent that defies measurement. I was previously unaware of it, but this phenomenon is what I now work to understand."

I searched the local phone book and those of the surrounding area to locate Rachel Secmatte. When I finally found her living over in Weston, I called and we chatted for some time. We made an appointment to have dinner so that I could share with her the post card from her brother. That dinner went well, and in the course of it, she informed me that she had gone to the old oil company building to find Albert when she hadn't heard from him. She had found it abandoned, but he had left behind his notebooks and the cellophane glasses.

In the years that have followed, I have seen quite a bit of Rachel Secmatte. My experience with her brother, with dabbling and being snared in that web of deceit, made me an honest man. That honesty banished my fear of women in that I was no longer working so hard to hide myself. It brought home to me that old saw that actions speak louder than words. In '62 we moved in together and have lived side by side ever since. One day in the mid-sixties, at the height of that new era of humanism I had so longed for, I came upon the box of Albert's notebooks and the glasses in our basement and set about trying to decipher his system in an attempt to free people from the constraints of language. That was nearly forty years ago, and in the passage of time I have learned much, not the least of which was the folly of my initial mission. I did discover that there is a single word, I will not divulge it, that, when sublimated, used in conjunction with a person's name and printed in a perfectly calculated sentence in the right typeface, can cause the individual mentioned, if he should view the text that contains it, to suffer severe physical side effects, even death.

I prefer to concentrate on the positive possibilities of the sublimation technique. For this reason, I have hidden in the text of the preceding tale a selection of words that, even without your having been able to consciously register them, will leave you with a beautiful image. Don't try to force yourself to know it; that will make it shy. In a half-hour to forty-five minutes, it will present itself to you. When it does, you can thank Albert Secmatte, undoubtedly an old man like myself now, out there somewhere in the world, still searching for a spark of light in a dark closet, his only companion whispering in his ear the wonderful burden of words.

The Weight of Words

Story Notes

I'd had the basic idea for this story for years. When I was a kid in school, I always had trouble with math, especially algebra. I think my final grade in algebra was a 30. I never understood why x equaled y, and from that point on it was a rapid descent into failure and plenty of time in summer school. I liked to read and write stories even back then, so when I'd look at the equations in the math book, instead of grasping the concepts taught, I used to see the equations as stories: the numbers were the characters, the functions of division, multiplication, etc. were the twists and turns of the plot. Of course, I'd get carried away by these tales, and then the teacher would call me to the blackboard and I'd have no idea what was going on. I'd pick up the chalk and just start writing down numbers and signs and stuff until she got fed up with my ignorance and told me to sit back down. That idea of numbers as characters and equations as stories stayed with me, and then one day when I was older I wondered if I could reverse the process and turn stories into equations. This idea eventually metamorphosed into the basic idea for "The Weight of Words." Still, how to write the piece always seemed a conundrum. I couldn't get my mind around it. The idea lay fallow until I noticed Michael Swanwick's "The Periodic Table of SF" stories on SCIFICTION, and although they weren't the same thing, in fact they were the reverse in a way, this brought the story idea back to me again. Then one day I was giving an exam in my Early American Lit class, just sitting there, drawing sketches of the students while they wrote their essays, and bam, why or how, I don't know, but the story presented itself to me with amazing clarity; the approach to the story lost all its difficulty and seemed very straightforward. I quickly wrote down notes for it, something I don't usually do, but in this case it seemed like a dream whose memory would vanish if I didn't get it down right away.

The story was published in the third installment of the anthology series Leviathan, *edited by Jeff VanderMeer and Forrest Aguirre. Both the story and the book were nominated for the World Fantasy Award in 2003, and* Leviathan Three *actually won (in a tie) for best anthology.*

The Trentino Kid

WHEN I WAS SIX, MY FATHER TOOK ME TO FIRE
Island and taught me how to swim. That day he put me on
his back and swam out past the buoy. My fingers dug into his shoulders as he dove, and somehow I just knew when to hold my breath.
I remember being immersed in the cold, murky darkness and that
down there the sound of the ocean seemed to be inside of me, as if
I were a shell the water had put to its ear. Later, on the beach
beneath the striped umbrella, the breeze blowing, we ate peanut-
butter-and-jelly sandwiches, grains of sand sparking off my teeth.
Then he explained how to foil the undertow, how to slip like a por-
poise beneath giant breakers, how to body surf. We practiced all
afternoon. As the sun was going down, we stood in the backwash of
the receding tide, and he held my hand in his big, callused mitt,
like a rock with fingers. Looking out at the horizon where the waves
were being born, he summed up the day's lesson by saying, "There
are really only two things you need to know about the water. The
first is you always have to respect it. The second, you must never
panic, but always try to be sure of yourself."

Years later, after my father left us, after I barely graduated high
school, smoked and drank my way out of my first semester at college, and bought a boat and took to clamming for a living, I still
remembered his two rules. Whatever degree of respect for the water
I was still wanting, by the time I finished my first year working the

Great South Bay, the brine had shrunk it, the sun had charred it, and the wind had blown it away, or so I thought. Granted, the bay was not the ocean, for it was usually more serene, its changes less obviously dramatic. There wasn't the constant crash of waves near the shore, or the powerful undulation of swells farther out, but the bay did have its perils. Its serenity could lull you, rock you gently in your boat on a sunny day, like a baby in a cradle, and then, with the afternoon wind, a storm could build in minutes, a dark, lowering sky quietly gathering behind your back while you were busy working.

When the bay was angry enough, it could make waves to rival the ocean's and they wouldn't always come in a line toward shore but from as many directions as one could conceive. The smooth twenty-minute ride out from the docks to the flats could, in the midst of a storm, become an hour-long struggle back. When you worked alone, as I did, there was more of a danger of being swamped. With only one set of hands, you couldn't steer into the swells to keep from rolling over and pump the rising bilge at the same time. Even if you weren't shipping that much water and were able to cut into the choppy waves, an old wooden flat-bottom could literally be slapped apart by the repeated impact of the prow dropping off each peak and hitting the water with a thud.

At that point in my life, it was the second of my father's two rules that was giving me trouble. In general, and very often in a specific sense, I had no idea what I was doing. School had been a failure, and once I'd let it slip through my grasp, I realized how important it could have been to me moving forward in my life. Now I was stuck and could feel the tide of years subtly beginning to rise around me. The job of clamming was hard work: getting up early, pulling on a rake for eight to ten hours a day. There was thought involved but it didn't require imagination, and if anything, imagination was my strong suit. Being tied to the bay was a lonely life, save for the hour or so at the docks in the late afternoon when I would drink the free beer the buyers supplied and bullshit with the other clammers. It was a remarkable way to mark time, to be busy without accomplishing anything. The wind and sun, the salt water, the hard work aged a body rapidly, and when I would look at the old men who clammed, I was too young to sense the wisdom their years on the water had bestowed upon them and saw only what I did not want to become.

This was back in the early seventies, when the bay still held a bounty of clams, a few years before the big companies came in and dredged it barren. There was money to be made. I remember certain weekends when a count bag, five hundred littleneck clams, went for two hundred dollars. I didn't know many people my age who were making two to three hundred dollars a day.

I had a little apartment on the second floor of an old stucco building that looked like a wing of the Alamo. There was a guy living above me, whom I never saw, and beneath me an ancient woman whose haggard face, half-obscured by a lace curtain, peered from the window when I'd leave at daybreak. At night, she would intone the rosary, and the sound of her words would rise through the heating duct in my floor. Her prayers found their way into my monotonous dreams of culling seed clams and counting neck. I drove a three-door Buick Special with a light rust patina that I had bought for fifty dollars. A big night out was getting plastered at The Copper Kettle, trying to pick up girls.

In my first summer working the bay, I did very well for a beginner, and even socked a little money away toward some hypothetical return to college. In my spare time, in the evenings and those days when the weather was bad, I read novels—science fiction and mysteries—and dreamed of one day writing them. Since I had no television, I would amuse myself by writing stories in those black-and-white-marbled notebooks I had despised the sight of back in high school. In the summer, when the apartment got too close, I'd wander the streets at night through the cricket heat, breathing the scents of honeysuckle and wisteria, and dream up plots for my rickety fictions.

That winter the bay froze over. I'd never seen anything like it. The ice was so thick you could drive a car on it. The old-timers said it was a sign that the following summer would be a windfall of a harvest but that such a thing, when it happened, which was rare, was always accompanied by deaths. I first heard the prediction in January, standing on the ice one day when some of us had trudged out a few hundred yards and cut holes with a chain saw through which to clam. Walking on the water that day in the frigid cold, a light snow sweeping along the smooth surface and rising in tiny twisters, was like a scene out of a fairy tale.

"Why deaths?" I asked wrinkle-faced John Hunter as he unscrewed a bottle of schnapps and tipped it into his mouth.

He wiped his stubbled chin with a gloved hand and smiled, three teeth missing. "Because it can't be any other way," he said, and laughed.

I nodded, remembering the time when I was new and I had, without securing it, thrown my anchor over the side into the deep water beneath the bridge. The engine was still going and my boat was moving, but I dove over the side, reaching for the end of the line. I managed to grab it, but when I came up, there I was in forty feet of water, my boat gone, holding onto a twenty-pound anchor. The next thing I saw was old Hunter, leaning over me from the side of his boat, reaching out that wiry arm of his. His hand was like a clamp; his bicep like coiled cable. He hauled me in and took me back to my drifting boat, the engine of which had sputtered out by then.

"I should've let you drown," he said, looking pissed off. "You're wasting my time."

"Thanks," I told him as I climbed sheepishly back into my boat.

"I only saved you because I had to," he told me.

"Why'd you have to?" I asked.

"That's the rule of the bay. You have to help anyone in trouble, as long as you've got the wherewithal to."

Since then he had shown me how to seed a bed, where some of the choice spots were, how to avoid the conservation guys who were hot to give tickets for just about anything. I was skeptical about what connection a frozen bay had to do with deaths in the summer, but by then I had learned to just nod.

Spring came but my old boat, an eighteen-foot, flat-bottom wooden job I'd bought for a hundred and fifty bucks and fiber-glassed myself, was in bad shape. After putting it back in the water, I found I had to bail the thing out with a garbage can every morning before I could leave the dock. Sheets of fiberglass from my less-than-expert job were sloughing off like peeling skin from a sun-burn. I got Pat Ryan, another clammer, to go out with me one day, and we beached the leaky tub on a spit of sand off Gardner's Park. Once we landed, he helped me flip it, and I shoved some new occum, a cottony material that expands when wet, into the seams and recaulked it.

"That's a half-assed job for sure," Pat told me, his warning vaguely reminding me of my father.

"It'll last for a while," I said, and waved off his concern.

Just like the old-timers predicted, the clams were plentiful that spring. There were days I would only have to put in four or five hours, and I could head back to the dock with a count and a half. It was a season to make you wonder if clamming might not be a worthy life's work. Then, at the end of May, the other part of their prediction came to pass. This kid, Jimmy Trentino, who was five years younger than me (I remembered shooting baskets with him a few times at the courts in the park when I was still in high school), walked in off the shore with a scratch rake and an inner tube and a basket, dreaming of easy money. A storm came up, the bay got crazy very fast, and either weighed down by the rake or having gotten his foot stuck in a sinkhole, he drowned.

The day it happened, I had gotten to the dock late and seen the clouds moving in and the water getting choppy. John Hunter had told me that when the wind kicked up and the bay changed from green to the color of iron, I should get off it as quickly as I could. The only thing more dangerous was standing out there holding an eight-foot metal clam rake during a lightning storm. I got back in my car and drove to The Copper Kettle. Pat Ryan came in at dinnertime and told everyone about the Trentino kid. They dredged for a few days afterward, but the body was never found. That wasn't so unusual, given what an immense, fickle giant the bay was with its myriad currents, some near the surface, some way down deep. As Earl, the bartender, put it, "He could be halfway to France or he might wind up on the beach in Brightwaters tomorrow."

A week later I was sitting on an overturned basket, drinking a beer at the dock after having just sold my haul. A couple of guys were gathered around and Downsy, a good clammer, but kind of a high-strung, childish blowhard, was telling about this woman who had shown up at his boat one morning and begged him to take her out so she could release her husband's ashes.

"She was packing the fucking urn like it was a loaf of bread," he said, "holding it under her arm. She was around thirty but she was hot."

As Downsy droned on toward the inevitable bullshit ending of all of his stories, how he eventually boffed some woman over on Grass Island or in his boat, I noticed an old Pontiac pull up at the dock. A slightly bent, little old bald man got out of it. As he shuffled past the buyers' trucks and in our direction, I realized who it was. The Trentino kid's father was the shoemaker in town and he had a shop next to the train tracks for as long as I could remember. I don't think I ever rode my bike past it when I was a kid that I didn't see him in the window, leaning over his work, a couple of tacks sticking out of his mouth.

"Hey," I said, and when the guys looked at me I nodded in the old man's direction.

"Jeez," somebody whispered. Pat Ryan put out his cigarette and Downsy shut his mouth. As Mr. Trentino drew close to us, we all got up. He stood before us with his head down, his glasses at the end of his nose. When he spoke, his English was cut with an Italian accent.

"Fellas," he said.

We each mumbled or whispered how sorry we were about his son.

"Okay," he said, and I could see tears in his eyes. Then he looked up and spoke to us about the weather and the Mets and asked us how business was. We made small talk with him for a few minutes, asked him if he wanted a beer. He waved his hands in front of him and smiled, shaking his head.

"Fellas," he said, looking down again. "Please, remember my boy."

We knew what he was asking, and we all said, almost like a chorus, "We will." He turned around then, walked back to his car, and drove away.

We were a superstitious bunch. I think it had to do with the fact that we spent our days bobbing on the surface of a vast mystery. So much of what our livelihood depended on was hidden from view. It wasn't so great a leap of imagination to think that life also had its unseen, unfathomable depths. The bay was teeming with folklore and legend—man-eating sharks slipping through the inlet to roam the bay, a sea turtle known as Moola that was supposedly as big as a Cadillac, islands that vanished and then reappeared, sunken treasure, a rogue current that could take you by the foot and drag you through underground channels to leave your body bobbing in Lake Ronkonkoma on the North Shore of Long Island. I had, in fact, seen some very big sea turtles and walked on an island that had been born overnight. By mid-June, the Trentino kid's body had, through our psyches and the promise made to his old man, been swept into this realm of legend.

Almost daily I heard reports from other guys who had seen the body floating just below the surface only twenty yards or so from where they were clamming. They'd weigh anchor and start their engines, but by the time they maneuvered their boats to where they had seen it, it would be gone. Every time it was spotted, some mishap would follow—a lost rake head, a cracked transom, the twin-hole vampire bite from an eel. We soon understood the kid to be cursed. One night, after Pat Ryan finished relating his own run-in with the errant corpse, Downsy, who was well drunk by then, swore that when he was passing the center of the bridge two days earlier, he'd seen the pale, decomposing figure of the kid swim under his boat.

"Get the fuck outa here," somebody said to him and we laughed.

He didn't laugh. "It was doing the goddamn breast stroke, I swear," he said. "It was swimming like you swim in good dreams, like flying underwater."

"Did you end up boffing it on Grass Island?" somebody asked.

Downsy was dead serious, though, and to prove it, he took a swing at the joker, inciting a brawl that resulted in Earl banning him from the Kettle for a week.

I asked John Hunter the next day, as our boats bobbed side by side off the eastern edge of Grass Island, if it was possible the kid's body could still be around.

"Sure," he said, "anything's possible, except maybe you raking more neck than me in a day. My guess is that you wouldn't want to find it at this point—all bloated and half-eaten by eels and bottom feeders. Forget the eyes, the ears, the lips, the belly meat. The hair will still be there, though, and nothing's gonna eat the teeth."

"Could it be cursed?" I asked him.

He laughed. "You have to understand something," he said. "If I was talking to you on dry land, I'd think you were nuts, but this is the bay. The ocean, the bay, the waters of the world are God's imagination. I've known wilder things than that to be true out here."

The image of what was left of the kid when John Hunter finished his forensic menu haunted me. At night, while I was trying to read, it floated there in my thoughts, obscuring whatever story I was in the middle of. Then the words of the rosary threaded their way up from downstairs to weave an invisible web around it, fixing it fast, so that the current of forgetting couldn't whisk it away. One hot midnight at the end of June, I couldn't take thinking about it anymore, so I slipped on my sneakers and went out walking. I headed away from The Copper Kettle, to the quiet side of town. I'd been burnt badly by the sun that day and the breeze against my skin made me shiver. For an hour or more I wandered aimlessly until I finally took a seat on a park bench next to the basketball court.

I realized it was not chance that had brought me to that spot. They say that when you drown, your life passes before your eyes in quick cuts like television commercials. I wondered if in that blur of events, the kid had noticed me passing him the ball, getting the older guys to let him play in a game, showing him how to shoot from the foul line. What before had been a vague memory, now came back to me in vivid detail. I concentrated hard on my recollection of him in life, and this image slowly replaced the one of him drowned and ravaged by the bay.

He was a skinny kid, not too tall, not too short, with brown silky hair in a bowl cut. When I knew him, he was about ten or eleven, but he had long arms, good for blocking passes and stealing the ball. He was quick, and unafraid of the older guys who were much bigger than him. What I saw most clearly were his eyes, big round ones, the color green of bottle glass tumbled smooth by the surf, that showed his disappointment at missing a shot or the thrill of playing in a game with high-school-aged guys. He was quiet and polite, not a show-off by any means, and I could tell he was really listening when I taught him how to put backspin on the ball. Finding him in my thoughts was not so very hard. What was nearly impossible was conceiving of him lifeless—no more, a blank spot in the world. I thought about all the things he would miss out on, all the things I had done between his age and mine. Later that night, after I had made my way home and gone to sleep, I dreamt I was on the basketball court with him. He was shooting foul shots, and I stepped up close and leaned over. "Remember, you must never panic," I said.

Come July, the bottom fell out of the market and prices paid for counts went way down due to the abundance of that summer's harvest. Not even John Hunter could predict the market, and although we'd all made a killing in May and June, we were now going to have to pay for it for the rest of the season. We'd all gone a little crazy with our money at the bar, not thinking ahead to the winter and those days it would be impossible to work.

I started staying out on the water longer, only getting back to the dock when the sun was nothing more than a red smudge on the horizon. Some of the buyers would be gone by then, but a couple of them stayed around and waited for us all to get in. I also started playing it a little fast and loose with the weather, going out on days that were blustery and the water choppy. In May and June I'd have written those days off and gone back to bed or read a book, but I wanted to hold on to what I had saved through the flush, early part of the season.

One afternoon in late July, while over in the flats due south of Babylon, I had stumbled upon a vein of neck, a bed like you wouldn't believe. I was bringing up loaded rake heads every fifteen minutes or so. After two straight hours of scratching away, the clams were still abundant. Around three o'clock, in the midst of my labor, I felt the wind rise, but paid it no mind since it invariably came on in the late afternoon. Only when I had to stop to rest my arms and catch my breath an hour later did I notice that the boat was really rocking. By my best estimation, I'd taken enough for two count bags of little-neck and a bag of top-neck. While I rested, I decided to cull some of my take and get rid of the useless seed clams and the chowders. That's when I happened to look over my shoulder and notice that the sun was gone and the water had grown very choppy.

I stood up quickly and turned to look back across the bay only to see whitecaps forming on the swells and that the color of the water was darkening toward that iron gray. In the distance, I could see clam boats heading back in toward the docks.

"Shit," I said, not wanting to leave the treasure trove that still lay beneath me, but just then a wave came along and smacked the side of the boat, sending me onto my ass between the seat slats and into the bilge. That was all the warning I needed. I brought in my rake, telescoped the handle down, and stowed the head. When I looked up this time, things had gotten a lot worse. The swells had already doubled in size, and the wind had become audible in its ferocity. By the time I dragged in the anchor, the boat was lurching wildly. The jostling I took made it hard for me to maneuver. I had to be careful not to get knocked overboard.

"Come on, baby," I said after pumping the engine. I pulled on the cord only once and it fired up and started running. I swung the handle to turn the boat around in order to head back across the bay to the dock. Off to my left, I noticed a decked-over boat with a small, red cabin, and knew it was Downsy. He was heading in the wrong direction. I followed his path with my sight and for the first time laid eyes on a guy who was scratch-raking about a hundred yards to my left. He was in up to his chest and although he could stand, the walk back to the shallows by the bridge was a good four hundred yards. He'd never make it. Without thinking, I turned in that direction to see if I could help.

As I chugged up close, I saw Downsy move quickly back into his cabin from where he had been leaning over the clammer on the side of the boat. His engine roared, and he turned the boat around and left the guy standing there in the water. His boat almost hit the front of mine as he took off. I called to him, but he never looked back. I pulled my boat up alongside the guy in the water and was about to yell, "How about a lift?" when I saw why Downsy had split.

Bobbing in that iron-gray water, trying to keep his head above the swells, was the Trentino kid. He wasn't the decomposed horror show that John Hunter had described, but his skin was mottled a very pale white and bruise green. Around the lower portion of his throat he had that drowned man's blue necklace. His hair was plastered to his head by the water, and those big green eyes peered up at me, his gaze literally digging into mine. That look said, "Help me," as clearly as if he had spoken the words. He was shivering like mad, and he held his arms up, hands open, like a baby wanting to be carried.

I sat there in the wildly rocking boat, staring in disbelief, my

heart racing. What good it was going to do me against the dead, I
didn't know, but I drew my knife, a ten-inch serrated blade, and just
held it out in front of me. My other hand was on the throttle of the
engine, keeping it at an idle. I wanted to open the engine up all
the way and escape as fast as possible, but I was paralyzed somewhere between pity and fear. Then a big wave came, swamping the
kid and slamming the side of my boat. The whole craft almost
rolled over, and the peak of the curl slapped me in the face with
ice-cold water.

The dead kid came up spluttering, silently coughing water out
of his mouth and nose. His eyes were brimming with terror.

"What the hell are you?" I yelled.

His arms, his fingers, reached for me more urgently.

"Deaths . . ." the old-timers had said, as in the *plural*, and this
thought wriggled through my frantic mind like an eel, followed by
my realization that what Downsy had been fleeing was the "curse."
I took another wave in the side and the boat tipped perilously, the
water drenching me. Clams scattered across the deck as the baskets
slid, and my cull box flew over the side. I felt, in my confusion and
fright, a brief stab of regret at losing it. I looked back to the kid and
could see that he seemed anchored in place, his foot no doubt in a
sinkhole. Another minute and he would be out of sight beneath the
surface. I dropped my knife and almost thrust my hand out to grab
his, but the thought of taking Death into my boat stopped me in
midreach. I thought I'd be released from my paralysis once the gray
water covered his eyes.

I had to leave or I'd be swamped and sunk just lolling there in
the swells. "No way," I said aloud, with every intention of opening
the throttle, but just then the kid made one wild lunge, and the tips
of the green-tinged fingers of his left hand landed on the side of
the boat. I remembered John Hunter telling me it was the rule of
the bay to help when you could. The boat got slammed, and I saw
the kid's hand begin to slip off the gunwale. I couldn't let him die
again, so I reached out. It was like grabbing a handful of snow,
freezing cold and soft, and a chill shot up through my arm to my
head and formed a vision of the moment of his true death. I felt his
panic, heard his underwater cry for his father, the words coming
through a torrent of bubbles that also released his life. Then I came
to and was on my feet, using my season-and-a-half of rake-pulling
muscle to drag that kid, dead or alive, up out of the bay. His body
landed in my boat with a soggy thud, and as it did, I was thrown off
balance and nearly took a dive over the side.

He was curled up like a fetus and unnaturally light when I lifted him into a sitting position on the plank bench at the center of the boat. A wave of revulsion passed through me as I touched his slick, spongy flesh. He'd come out of the water wearing nothing, and I had no clothes handy to protect him against the wind. He faced back at me where I sat near the throttle of the engine. There was a good four inches of water sloshing around in the bottom. I quickly lifted the baskets of clams and chucked them all over the side. I had to lighten the load and get the boat to ride higher through the storm. Then I sat down with those big green eyes staring into me, and opened the throttle all the way.

Lightning streaked through the sky, sizzling down and then exploding over our heads. The waves were massive, and now the storm scared me more than the living corpse. I headed toward the dock, aiming to over shoot it since I knew the wind would drive us eastward. If I was lucky, I could get to a cove I knew of on the southern tip of Gardner's Park. I had briefly thought of heading out toward Grass Island and beaching there, but in a storm like the one raging around us, there was no telling if the island would be there tomorrow.

I never tried harder at anything in my life than preventing myself from wondering how this dead kid was sitting in front of me, shivering cold. The only thought that squeaked through my defenses was, Is this a miracle? Then those defenses busted open, and I considered the fact that I might already be dead myself and we were sailing through hell, or to it. I steadied myself as best I could by concentrating on cutting into the swells. The boat was taking a brutal pounding, but we were making headway.

"We're going to make it," I said to Jimmy, and he didn't smile, but he looked less frightened. That subtle sign helped me stay my own confusion, and I just started talking to him, saying anything that came to mind. By the time we reached the bridge and were passing under it, I realized I had been laying out my life story, and he was seeing it flash before his eyes. I did not want to die that afternoon with nothing to show but scenes of the bay and my hometown. What I wished I could have shared with him were my dreams for the future. Then I noticed a vague spark in his gaze, a subtle recognition of some possibility. That's when the full brunt of the storm hit—gale-force winds, lashing rain, hail the size of dice —and I heard above the shriek of the wind a distinct cracking sound when the prow slammed down off a huge roller. The boat was breaking up.

With every impact against the water came that cracking noise, and each time it sounded, I noticed the kid's skin begin to tear. A dark brown sludge seeped from these wounds. Tears formed in his big eyes, became his eyes, and then dripped in viscous streams down his face, leaving the sockets empty. The lightning cracked above and his chest split open down to his navel. He opened his mouth and a hermit crab scurried out across his blue lips and chin to his neck. I no longer could think to steer, no longer felt the cold, couldn't utter a sound. The sky was nearly dark as night. The boat fell off a wave into its trough, like we were slamming into a moving truck, and then the wood came apart with a groan. I felt the water rising up around my ankles and calves. Then the transom split off the back of the boat as if it had been made of cardboard, and the engine dropped away out of my grasp, its noise silenced. One more streak of lightning walked the sky, and I saw before me the remains of the kid as John Hunter had described them. The next thing I knew, I was in the water, flailing to stay afloat amidst the storm.

I was a strong swimmer, but by this point I was completely exhausted. The waves came from everywhere, one after the other, and I had no idea where I was headed or how close I had managed to get to shore. I would be knocked under by a wave and then bob back up, and then down I'd go again. A huge wave, like a cold, dark wing, swept over me, and I thought it might be Death. It drove me below the surface where I tumbled and spun so violently that when I again tried to struggle toward the sky, I instead found the sandy bottom. Then something moved beneath me, and I wasn't sure if I was dreaming, but I remembered my father riding me on his back through the ocean. I reached out and grabbed onto a pair of shoulders. In my desperation my fingers dug through the flesh and latched onto skeleton. We were flying, skimming along the surface, and I could breathe again. It was all so crazy, my mind broke down in the confusion and I must have passed out.

When next I was fully aware, I was stumbling through knee-deep water in the shallows off Gardner's Park. I made the beach and collapsed on the sand. An hour passed, maybe more, but when I awoke, the storm had abated and a steady rain was falling. I made my way, tired and weak, through the park to Sunrise Highway. There, I managed to hitch a ride back to the docks and my waiting car. It was late when I finally returned to the Alamo. I slipped off my wet clothes and got into bed. Curling up on my side, I quickly drifted off to sleep, the words of the old crone's rosary washing over me, submerging me.

The next day I called the police and reported the loss of my boat, so that those at the dock who found my slip empty wouldn't think I had drowned. Later on, when I was driving over to my mother's house, I heard on the radio that the storm had claimed a life. Downsy's boat was missing at the dock. Ironically enough, they found his body that morning washed up on the shore of Grass Island.

A few days later, some startling debris was discovered on the beach at the south end of Gardner's Park, close to where I had come ashore. Two hikers came across pieces of my boat, identified by the plank that held its serial numbers, and a little farther up the beach, the remains of Jimmy Trentino.

I went to two funerals in one day—one for a kid who never got a chance to grow up, and one for a guy who didn't want to. Later that evening, sitting in a shadowed booth at the back of The Copper Kettle, John Hunter remarked how a coffin is like a boat for the dead.

I wanted to tell him everything that happened the day of the storm, but, in the end, felt he wouldn't approve. He had sternly warned me once against blabbing—even when drunk—about a bed I might be seeding for the coming season. "A good man knows when to keep a secret," he had said. Instead, I merely told him, "I'm not coming back to the bay."

He laughed. "Did you think you had to tell me?" he said. "I've seen you reading those books in your boat on your lunch break. I've seen you wandering around town late at night. You don't need a boat to get where it's deep."

I got up then and went to the bar to order another round. When I came back to the booth, he was gone.

I moved on with my life, went back to school, devoted more time to writing my stories, and through the changes that came, I tried to always be sure of myself. In those inevitable dark moments, though, when I thought I was about to panic, I'd remember John Hunter, his hand reaching down to pull me from the water. I always wished that I might see him again, but I never did, because it could-n't be any other way.

The Trentino Kid

Story Notes

"The Trentino Kid" came right out of my clamming years. I'd come near to flunking out of high school and when I made my first foray into higher education, Suffolk Community College, I did flunk out. I remember, somewhere around the end of that first semester at Suffolk, I found my Psych textbook under about 150 empty beer cans in the back seat of my three-door Buick Special and realized the gig was up. Then I began on a series of crap jobs from loading trucks to cleaning toilets to working in metal shops. Eventually, I saved up enough money to buy a clam boat and took to working the Great South Bay off the southern coast of Long Island. This was hard work, but for a time there, when I was eighteen to twenty, it was the greatest job ever—I made my own hours, the pay was good, and I was outside all the time. Something about that work matured me to an extent, and I finally realized there were other things I wanted to do with my life. The story of the Trentino kid is true: This kid, younger than me, who we'd let play basketball with us older guys, did drown while clamming, having walked in off the shore with a basket in an inner tube and a scratch rake. When his old man showed up at the dock and asked us not to forget his son—that was one of the saddest things I've ever witnessed. The death of that boy haunted me all summer and through the fallow months of the winter, and might have been one of the main reasons for my getting it together to go back to school. This was the fastest story I ever wrote. Three days. It appeared in Ellen Datlow's ghost story anthology, The Dark, *which won the 2004 International Horror Guild Award.*

"Jeffrey Ford's *The Fantasy Writer's Assistant and Other Stories* is the finest single author short story collection I've read in a decade. But everyone says that, so I'm not telling you something you couldn't hear somewhere else."
— Lou Anders, Senior Editor, *Argosy*

The Fantasy Writer's Assistant and Other Stories

With an introduction by Michael Swanwick

Jeffrey Ford's
First Short Fiction Collection
From Golden Gryphon Press
ISBN 1-930846-10-X
Cloth, 247pp, $23.95
www.goldengryphon.com

"In World Fantasy Award-winner Ford's enchanting first story collection, proof abounds that a fresh perspective or inventive approach can give the most familiar themes fresh life and startling clarity. . . . A lion's share of the stories explore the theme of artistic creation from invigoratingly original angles. Sure to be one of the keynote collections of the year, this book will be welcomed by fans of literate, witty modern fantasy." —*Publishers Weekly* Starred Review

"I don't know if Speculative Fiction is large enough to contain Jeffrey Ford for very long. But while it does, we have this book."
— Richard Bowes, author of
From the Files of the Time Rangers

Winner of the 2003 World Fantasy Award
For Best Single-Author Collection of the Year!

Three thousand copies of this book have been printed by the Maple-Vail Book Manufacturing Group, Binghamton, NY, for Golden Gryphon Press, Urbana, IL. The typeset is Electra with Apollo Semibold display, printed on 55# Sebago. Typesetting by The Composing Room, Inc., Kimberly, WI.